SMALL TIME CRIME

Mercy Watts Mysteries Book Ten

A.W. HARTOIN

Small Time Crime

Mercy Watts Mysteries Book 10

Copyright © A.W. Hartoin, 2019

www.awhartoin.com

ALSO BY A.W. HARTOIN

For my beloved daughter, Maddie, who, like most girls, is stronger than she knows or can even imagine.

CHAPTER ONE

P eople say every cloud has a silver lining. They insist upon it. They'll tell you that even if you're up to the hip in bullshit. Really? Every cloud? I ask because I'm waiting. My life has been pretty cloudy lately and I haven't seen any silver. Not a hint or glimmer of the good stuff. Instead, I got a bolt of lightning, right in the butt. Because if you're going to kick someone, you may as well do it when they're down.

I got fired. Of course, Shawna didn't call it firing because she's nice. Shawna is very nice, but I was still fired, even though she called it "letting go". What does that really mean? She's returning me to the wild so I can forage with the other unemployed nurses?

If so, I'll be all alone, because there are no other unemployed nurses. It's a field with more jobs than people to fill them and you can have your pick, unless you happen to be radically incompetent, one of those killer nurses you see on the news, or me, Mercy Watts. I'm the exception that proves the rule.

It was a real low point, employment wise. I'd already called my old temp agency and they said, "You've got to be kidding," and their biggest requirement seemed to be a warm body. Nobody was going to hire me, that much was clear, not with the current situation or, should

I say, situations. If you hired me, you'd have to expect the worst was coming and you wouldn't be wrong.

I closed my locker for the last time and leaned on the cold metal, blowing my nose and feeling so low I wanted to sink down and sob on the floor. No one would care. I was alone. Me and my sad little bag of crap would have to skulk out the back like a big, fat loser. The last thing I wanted to do was see patients. Plus, the cops were out there. They'd laughed the first few times, but they were past laughing now.

I peeked out into the hall and found it empty, which was rare, so I took off and dashed for the back exit.

"Where the hell are you going?" yelled Steve, the practice receptionist, as my hand hit the back door's metal bar.

For a second, I considered hoofing it out and not looking back, but I couldn't do it. Steve was a big sweetheart and it was hardly his fault, so I pushed the door open and let the chilly November wind rush in, drying my cheeks and providing a little clarity.

"I'm leaving," I said, eyes closed, not looking back.

"You can't leave," he said. "We've got a full waiting room. You've been requested."

"I know and yet...I'm leaving."

"Are you okay?"

"Nope."

Steve walked up and put a hand on my shoulder. "Oh, my God. Is it your mom? Is she okay?"

"She's fine. On vacation, actually."

"Then what happened?"

I took a breath and told him. "Shawna fired me." I have to admit it was pretty nice to see his mouth drop open.

"But...but...she can't fire you. Why would you get fired?" Steve asked.

"Have you seen the parking lot? "I asked.

Steve gulped a couple of times. Of course, he had. Everyone had. Just over a month ago, Beth Babcock rammed her enormous truck into the Columbia Clinic in a fit of rage over her unpaid bill. Then she tried to set fire to it and, in a moment of supreme stupidity, I tackled her and we rolled into a ditch, which would've been fine, but I ended up all over the news, not to mention YouTube, looking like I'd been in a wet tee shirt contest. That kind of thing really brings out the weirdos. Nutters drove in from all over to ram the clinic, in hopes I'd tackle them, too.

Currently, there was a guy, who claimed to be named "Heaven", chained to the porch, having stolen a tractor that was able to get over the barriers the practice had put in, and hit the front steps. For once, there wasn't much damage. He'd hit the steps going five miles an hour. He didn't steal wisely. It was a very old tractor.

But Heaven chained himself to a post, armed with fake grenades, bug spray, and a lighter. He said he wouldn't unchain himself until I kissed him all over.

Not going to happen. The standoff had been going on for forty-five minutes with Heaven keeping the cops at bay with his improvised bug spray flame thrower.

"He's just a nut," said Steve. "He needs treatment."

I shrugged. "The latest in a long line of nuts who need treatment."

"It's not your fault crazy guys want to, ya know, get close to you."

"The insurance doesn't see it that way. They're threatening to cancel the practice's policy and the provider policies if we don't get this under control."

"Oh."

"Yeah."

"Well, shit. What about us?" Steve asked, a set of frown lines forming on his incredibly tanned forehead.

"What about you? I'm the one with bills, a bad rep, and no job."

"You are very popular with the patients. They are not going to like you getting fired, even with everything else."

The "everything else" hung in the air like the stank from a broken septic tank. Steve shifted from foot to foot and avoided my eyes. "I'll talk to Shawna and the docs. There has to be something we can do."

"Good luck with that," I said. "It's been nice knowing you."

Steve hugged me. "We didn't get to have a going away party."

"It would be a get out and good riddance party."

"It wouldn't." He hugged me again. "We all love you."

"So do all the sex-crazed maniacs," I said. "And off I go."

"It'll calm down. You'll be back." Steve tried to sound cheerful, but it didn't come out all that well.

I stepped outside and a gardener yelled, "Hey, Smelly, where ya going?"

Steve winced and I said, "That's my life. Wanna trade?"

"Dude, you couldn't pay me enough to look like you."

This coming from a guy who did a drag routine every other weekend. I kill with drag queens. But my situation was so bad, I had it on good authority that even the Marilyn Monroe impersonators had to change up their acts, lest they be confused for me. There was a little odd satisfaction that, for the first time, Marilyn was taking it on the chin for looking like me, instead of the other way around.

The gardener yelled again. That time calling me "odious" and bursting into laughter. That word didn't mean what he thought it meant, but that didn't make me feel any better about it. The sooner I got home to hide out with a half-gallon of ice cream the better.

I rounded the corner and headed into the parking lot, keeping my head down and hoping for the best. I didn't get it.

The cops had cleared the area directly in front of the practice, except for the squad cars and the fire trucks. I was in clear view and Heaven spotted me straight away.

"Mercy! Mercy! I love you!"

I didn't look and wished my coat had a hood. I really could've used a hood right about then.

"Don't do it!" yelled Carrie, a local cop, who never called me anything but my name, which is more than I could say for her boss and the firefighters. "Oh man!"

The men started laughing and yelling, "Hey, Smelly! Get a load of this."

"Get a blanket, you assholes!" yelled Carrie.

"Smelly'll get it."

Then I heard a little kid say, "Why is Mercy smelly?"

That was rock bottom and I have to say there's some stiff competition for the honor. I think the parent said I wasn't actually smelly, but it didn't matter. Once the internet says you smell, you flipping smell. I wished that tractor had hit me. Maybe I should stick around. It was only a matter of time before another one showed up.

"Mercy!" yelled Carrie and I looked up on instinct. That did not work out for me. Heaven had stripped and was pouring something out of a plastic grenade all over his head.

"I'll do it! Come over here or I'll do it," he yelled, his skinny, pale body shaking violently in the cold.

Jordan, another cop and Carrie's boss said, "It's not gas, Heaven. For God's sake, pull up your pants."

"I want Mercy!"

A woman ran up to me, shielding her son's eyes, "This is ridiculous. Talk to him, Mercy. He needs help."

"I can't," I said. "Shawna fired me. I'm supposed to leave the premises immediately."

"You cannot be serious. Logan needs his shots."

Logan looked up, his blue eyes huge. "No shots."

"Other people can give shots," I said.

"I want Mercy," wailed Logan.

"Can they?" asked his mother. "Can they? I don't think so. Where is Shawna or Dr. What's-his-face?"

"Inside."

"I'll be right back," she said, marching past Heaven, who'd opened another grenade while holding a lighter to his face.

I will not be here.

I went for my car, my mother's car to be accurate, since my truck was still in the shop after being demolished by another kid that needed professional help.

"It's lemonade, Heaven," yelled Jordan. "You can't light lemonade."

"I can light roach spray. What do you think of this, Pig?"

There was the sound of streaming flames and a firefighter yelled, "Get Smelly over here!"

I ran for it.

"Mercy!" yelled Carrie. "Wait! You gotta help us with this guy!"

"Let's spray him!" yelled someone.

"We can't spray him. He'll get frostbite."

"Shoot him!"

"Get a hostage negotiator. This is getting old."

"There's no hostage."

"I'm a hostage. It's thirteen degrees out here. My butt's numb."

I got to the new Mercedes Dad bought Mom after she said she didn't want it and very nearly got the door open before Carrie hit the door full tilt, ramming it closed. She bent over gasping, "Why did you make me run? I hate running."

"I'm leaving. Get out of the way," I said.

"You can't leave. This guy...this guy, you gotta talk to him. Throw him a bone so we can break out the bolt cutters and get the hell outta here."

"Just spray him and do it," I said, tugging on the door handle.

"How's that going to play on the news? We spray a mentally ill guy with water and give him hypothermia."

"He's already wet with lemonade."

"He needs help."

"He needs a professional."

"You're a professional."

"I just got fired."

I was rewarded with a blank look.

"I don't work here anymore thanks to the flipping media and Heaven and all the other Heavens out there."

"You can still talk to him. You're still a nurse."

"Look. I just cleared out my locker and spent the last fifteen minutes crying, so I think I'm gonna pass."

Carrie pushed me away from the car and I flinched. She'd touched my casted arm and I was sensitive about it. Another young man, Porter Weeks, gave me a spiral fracture after he found out his father's secrets. Secrets and publicity were two things that never worked out for me.

"Oh, crap. I'm sorry, but please, Mercy, he really needs your help."

"It will just encourage this stuff." I pointed at a news van pulling up, satellite dish perched on top and ready to roll. "You know it will. I have to draw the line somewhere."

"Well, draw it somewhere else," said Carrie. "I know your life sucks right now, but his life is worse."

I looked over at the now sobbing Heaven. "This is so unfair."

"I know."

"I hate you."

"Don't blame you."

"I am not kissing him at all or anywhere," I said.

"Understood."

"Fine."

"Great. Let's go see what he'll settle for." Carrie turned me around and steered me toward Heaven. Jordan ran over to the news crew, ordering them off private property, but they were rolling and more vans were pulling up. No matter what happened this was not going to work out for me. Period. No chance at all of it working out.

We stopped ten feet away, well out of roach spray range. Now that we were closer, I realized Heaven was a lot younger than I originally thought. College-age. Twenty. Maybe less. That made it worse, for some reason, and I felt so sad it was like a big hand was pushing me down into the dirt.

"Hey there," I said.

He continued to cry.

"Heaven!"

He looked up and focused. Sort of. He was on something. His eyes were bloodshot and, even from there, I could tell his pupils weren't reacting right. "Mercy?"

"Yeah, it's me. Want to talk?"

"Really?"

"Sure. But I need you to put your clothes back on," I said.

"Why?" he asked, although the reason was painfully obvious.

I took a breath and kept my eyes up. You know how it is when you don't want to look at something? Your eyes just absolutely insist on going there.

"There are kids in the clinic. You don't want them to see...your stuff, do you?"

"Kids?"

With perfect timing, Logan's mom came out, still shielding his little eyes, and said, "Shawna says you can give Logan his shots. She'll put you in as being let go after."

Well, isn't it just my lucky day.

"Alright. Give me a minute. Kind of in the middle of something," I said.

She glanced over and clenched her jaw. "You're a good person, Mercy. And I want you to know that we all know that you don't smell."

"Could you put that on Twitter? I'm getting roasted."

"Yeah, I know. You were on *The Daily Show* last night," she said.

"I saw that," said one of the firemen.

"Friggin' hilarious," said another.

Don't start crying again. Don't do it. Crap. You're doing it. For the love of God, stop.

"People suck," said Logan's mom to the firefighters and they had the decency to look away.

"Yes, they do," said Carrie. "Can you go inside, ma'am? This will be resolved in a minute."

Will it? That sounds optimistic.

Carrie gave me a tissue and Heaven pulled up his pants. That was something anyway.

"Now the shirt," I said.

"No shirt," he said. "Why are people calling you Smelly?"

"It's a long story."

"I'm not going anywhere."

Swell.

"If I tell you, will you please toss me the roach spray and let us cut those chains?" I asked.

He thought about it and it took more consideration than I would've thought. Maybe the teeth chattering was inhibiting what little thought he could muster.

"Okay. I'll do it. For you. Nobody else."

So I told him, a mentally ill, half-frozen kid, why people were calling me smelly, even though I didn't think it would help and might possibly push him farther over the edge.

"I've got this uncle—"

"Is he drunk?" asked Heaven.

"Not usually. But that is a part of this story."

"Okay. Go ahead."

My Uncle Morty, hacker, gamer extraordinaire and best-selling author, had done what no one ever expected. He fell head over heels in love with Nikki, a Greek lady, who, for reasons no one could ascertain, fell in love with him, too. Then he did the one thing she couldn't stand. He lied to her about helping me with the Porter Weeks case. He didn't have to lie, but he did, and she found out. Nikki dumped him like toxic waste and skipped town. She went to Greece and would not respond to anything or anyone.

Uncle Morty blamed me. My case, my fault. I had to help get her back. He insisted and bought tickets for us to go to Greece and I was going to talk the love of his life into forgiving him, presumably by taking the blame. Whatever. It was a free trip to Greece and I had some snooping that I wanted to do on a little side interest of mine. So I packed my bags and took an Uber to the airport. That's when it went south. Like all the way south. Antarctica south.

Uncle Morty was there, waiting at the check-in counter and looking like no human I've ever seen, outside of a body in the morgue. He was drunk, crusted with food, and had body odor that could drop a deer at ten yards. He belched and farted up a storm while he argued with the airline rep. I stood there in shock. I hadn't seen him in a few days and I had no idea it had gotten so bad.

That was a time when I would've liked to have called my parents, but my mom was recovering from a stroke and the attack that caused it. My father was recovering from being a lousy husband and father, so they were out, and I was on my own.

I thought we'd have to turn around and go home, but somehow Uncle Morty talked his way onto the plane. He pulled out the celebrity card, *my* so-called celebrity card. That's how we became the Mercy Watts party, despite the fact that Uncle Morty paid for the tickets and was the lead passenger. I think he also bribed people. If he did, it must've been a whole lot of people. Did I mention there was gagging?

On the upside, I've never gotten through security so fast. The line cleared. People were ducking under the stringers and voluntarily going to the back of the line to avoid us. I was apologizing to everyone in sight, which elicited anger from Uncle Morty and more belching.

Someone must've called ahead because our seats smelled strongly of Febreze and I thought maybe we could get away with it. The plane took off. We weren't in the air fifteen minutes before Uncle Morty was asleep and began to snore like a gorilla with a deviated septum, only slightly less hairy and with worse table manners. I stuffed tissues up my nose and in my ears, as did everyone else. It didn't help. Kids were crying. The flight attendants' eyes were watering. I think I heard the lady in front of us retching.

Then we banked hard and the captain announced that we were returning to Lambert due to a situation in the cabin. Since all the regular gates were full, we went to a gate where you had to use one of those old-fashioned ramps. I couldn't get off that plane quick enough. It took three flight attendants and the co-pilot to get Uncle Morty out of his seat and down the aisle. I hustled off the plane first. I was so glad to get away from the cheers and clapping. I thought I couldn't get more embarrassed. I was wrong.

When the pilot radioed the tower, he named me, specifically. The man said, "We have a party with unusual odor. Flight is unsustainable. Party of Mercy Watts will have to be removed."

Then I stepped out on that ramp. Alone. There were cellphones everywhere, catching me doing what was deemed a smelly perp walk down the steps. Did I still have tissues up my nose? Yes, I did. The lead on the local news, which was quickly picked up by the national news, said, "Mercy Watts can't stand her own smell."

Yeah, Uncle Morty got off the plane. Yeah, he was photographed. Yeah, he looked like a rotting wildebeest, but did he make the news? No. That was me. If it gets worse than that, I'd like to know how.

"So that's why people call you smelly?" said Heaven.

"That's why," I said.

"Where's your uncle?"

"I don't know and I don't care. He can bite me."

Heaven looked at the firefighters. "You guys suck."

The guys fidgeted and looked at their boots.

"How about throwing me that spray can?" I asked.

Heaven tossed me the can and Carrie cut his chains. Together we got him into dry scrubs and gave him hot tea in the waiting room after the clinic declined to press charges. It wasn't as easy as it sounds. Heaven was pretty wasted and kept trying to kiss me. While I was giving Logan his shots, we found out that Heaven was really named Thomas Wright III and had been diagnosed with schizophrenia, which he tried to self-medicate with a wicked combo of pot, whiskey, and LSD. Why he thought that would help remains a mystery.

"Mercy?" Thomas Wright III looked at me as I picked up my sad, little bag of crap to once again try to slip out the back unnoticed.

"Yeah?"

"I see things."

"What kind of things?" asked Carrie.

Thomas kept looking around me. I got the odd feeling that there were bees swarming around me. I just couldn't see them.

"People," said Thomas. "I can smell them, too. They smell good, like candy."

"Weird," I said.

Carrie chuckled. "Dude, that's Mercy. She smells like candy. It's her lotion."

Thomas frowned. "I see people. Right now. Around Mercy. They're in the pictures."

A chill went up my back. "What pictures?"

"You have people around you."

The entire waiting room stood up and stepped back.

"This is freaking me out." Steve got on the phone and started talking to someone about needing a bed ASAP.

"I'm sure you see a lot of things," I said.

"People," said Thomas. "You have the most people. I wanted to tell you."

"Is that why you came here?" I asked.

"They love you."

"Well, that's good."

"Not all of them. Some want to hurt you."

Swell.

"Thomas, we're going to send you to a hospital so you can get the right kind of medicine. Okay?" I asked.

"But then I won't see the people," he said.

"That's probably a good thing."

"I don't think so. I like seeing what other people can't."

"Really?"

"Yeah." Thomas slumped down. The tranquilizer Shawna gave him finally took effect. "She's nice."

"Who?" I asked.

"The one touching your hair."

The waiting patients took another step back, but I noticed they couldn't look away.

"Who's touching Mercy's hair?" asked Carrie.

Jordan helped me get my coat over my cast and said, "Don't encourage him."

Thomas's head lolled to the side. "She's got red hair all piled up and an old-fashioned dress with an apron."

Jordan turned me toward the door. "That's enough."

"She loves you. She wants you to know her." With that, Thomas Wright III went to sleep.

Jordan opened the door for me and hustled me out. "Now get in your car and forget this ever happened."

"You make it sound like that's a real option," I said.

"It is, if you want it to be."

"I want a lot of things." I walked down the steps with chills still running up and down my spine. A red-haired woman. That was plausible.

"Anything I can help you with?" asked Jordan.

I turned around. "You could stop calling me smelly."

Jordan flushed to the roots of his hair. "Done. I'm sorry about that."

"Good. I'm glad."

I went for Mom's car and I made it. I got in, closed the door, and turned on the ignition. I put the gear shift in drive and a woman ran up to pound on my window.

"Son of a bitch," I muttered.

"Mercy! I need to be seen. It's an emergency."

I rolled down my window. "What is it, Mrs. Lundberg?"

"It's an emergency."

"Go to the ER."

She wrinkled her nose. "That takes forever. It's so inconvenient."

"Emergencies usually are."

"Can you get me in? Steve says they're booked, but I have to be seen."

I did my best not to sigh dramatically. I may have failed. Mrs. Lundberg always thought she had whatever was on the evening news. I kept expecting her to show up claiming that she got a shark bite in the Black River that would turn out to be a couple of chigger bites.

"I can't get you in. They really are booked."

Mrs. Lundberg started wringing her hands. "But this is serious. Can you take a look?"

"Shawna fired me. I don't even work here anymore."

She was already taking off her coat and didn't hear. "This won't take long. I know Shawna will see me if you confirm my diagnosis."

"Have you been looking on WebMD again?"

"I did. That site is so useful. I don't understand why you don't like it," said Mrs. Lundberg.

"I know you don't. What's the diagnosis?" I asked.

She straightened up and put on her suffering-with-a-terrible-disease face. "I have Lyme Disease."

Breathe, Mercy, breathe.

"Well that's...something. Why do you think you have Lyme Disease?"

"I had a headache. I'm so tired all the time and I have a rash."

"This just happened?"

"Yes."

"It's almost Thanksgiving."

She nodded vigorously. "I know. To have this happen right before the holidays. Can you believe it?"

No.

"People don't tend to get a tick in November," I said.

"I've always been unlucky."

Are people calling you smelly? I don't think so.

"Okay. Where's your tick?"

"It's gone," she said with an odd amount of pride. But removing a tick wasn't exactly rocket surgery as my dad would say.

"When did you remove it?" I asked.

"I didn't."

"Then what happened to it?"

She shrugged. "Must've fallen off. But I have the spot, like on WebMD." She rolled up her sleeve and thrust her arm at me. "See, it's warm to the touch and everything. What am I going to do? Lyme Disease is fatal. Fatal."

"It's rarely fatal. Very rarely fatal."

"But I'm very unlucky," she said, a tear rolling down her cheek.

"You don't have Lyme Disease, Mrs. Lundberg," I said. "Can I leave now? 'Cause Ben and Jerry are calling my name."

"What's this then?" She pointed at the reddish lump on her forearm. "It's got the bullseye."

"That is an ingrown hair," I said. "No big deal."

Her face went blank. "An ingrown hair?"

"Yes. That's it. You will live to peruse WebMD another day." I put the car back in gear.

"But wait." She thrust her arm in front of my face and I fought the urge to bite it. "It's hot and tender."

"It's infected," I said.

She drew back in horror. "Infected?"

That's when my bad angel poked me in the brain. "That's right, Mrs. Lundberg. You have an infection. In your skin."

"What do I...what is...an infection?"

"Yes and, on second thought, you should go into the clinic and demand to be seen. Right now. This instant."

"You think so?"

"I do. You might need antibiotics," I said with a sly smile.

Fire me, will you? Let's see how you like this.

"Antibiotics?"

Antibiotics are music to a hypochondriac's ears. Mrs. Lundberg once asked for antibiotics for menstrual cramps. Because that'll help.

"You never know." Then I said the magic words that would undoubtedly send the entire clinic into a tizzy. "Better safe than sorry."

"You are absolutely right." Mrs. Lundberg ran for the clinic, shoving people out the way and throwing the door open so hard she nearly took it off its hinges.

Some people might say this wasn't very nice to Mrs. Lundberg, but they'd be wrong. Yes, I got her all worked up over nothing, but, honestly, getting worked up over nothing was her favorite thing. I gave her a parting gift with a side of revenge for me. Nobody got hurt and I needed less ice cream.

If Thomas was less schizophrenic and more psychic, there might really be a red-haired woman hanging about in my car. If so, she was probably quite disappointed. I was good with it.

CHAPTER TWO

An hour and a shopping binge later, I pushed the self-park buttons on Mom's dash and allowed myself to be the tiniest bit disloyal to my sweet truck going through agonies of reconstruction over at Egon's Cherry Pit, so-called because when a vehicle comes out of there, it's cherry.

I have to admit having self-park, power steering, power brakes, and a banging stereo were pretty nice. Don't tell my truck.

While Mom's car parked I pulled my sad bag of crap and my happy bags of crap onto my lap. I bought it all. Ice cream (four kinds), butterscotch chips, potato chips, disgusting pre-made onion dip, Reese's Peanut Butter Cups, Hershey's chocolate syrup, a frozen pizza—the kind my mother said ought to come with a warning label—and a bag of carrots to ward off the guilt. I wasn't planning on eating the carrots, but I felt more virtuous knowing they were there, just in case I went insane and wanted fiber.

The car helpfully beeped to tell me we were parked and I looked around to see if anyone was watching from the construction at the apartment building behind me. It looked clear, so I jumped out and ran for the door. I did not make it. I got called "smelly" and a new unpleasantry "rank slut". I keyed myself in, amidst raucous laughter. This had to wear off. It'd been over a week.

Maybe there were rules I wasn't aware of. I'd never been bullied in school. Whitmore Academy didn't tolerate that kind of behavior, thankfully. If it had, I'd have been in some trouble, a cop's daughter who developed a lot and early among the flat-chested elites. It would've been bad. Now I had a small sense of what that kind of harassment was like and I didn't care for it. Time for sticks and stones. I wanted to break some friggin' bones.

"Mercy?"

I turned around to find my neighbor hobbling down the stairs with his recycling. "Mr. Cervantes, what are you doing?"

"Was someone yelling at you?" he asked.

"No. It's fine." I dropped my bags and grabbed his. "I told you I'd take this stuff out."

"You've got a broken arm."

"You've got a broken toe."

He smiled. "It was my own fault."

"Same here."

"Now that is just not true. You help people. I kicked my coffee table."

"Porter Weeks doesn't think I was helping him and since his family is a total mess since I showed up, I can't blame him," I said.

"I blame his father. A grown man should have more self-control," he said.

"Self-control is in short supply these days." I went for the door and Mr. Cervantes called out, "Don't go out there."

I went out there and was rewarded with a shout about how I should be a no-fly zone. Clever, coming from a guy with an infected nose ring. I closed the door on a discussion about how much they'd have to be paid to "do" me. A lot, I gathered.

"Why did you go out there?" asked Mr. Cervantes.

"Recycling has to be done, even if there are douchebag construction workers watching," I said.

"I don't want you going through that."

"That makes two of us." I picked up my bags and he eyed them suspiciously.

"Are you celebrating?" he asked.

Let's go with yes.

"Sure. Why not? I, the smelly slut, have gotten through another day."

"Don't call yourself that, Mercy. I don't like it and I have half a mind to go out there and tell those worthless—"

"Alright. Alright. I won't say it anymore." I went slowly up the stairs with Mr. Cervantes, hoping my ice cream didn't melt beyond that perfect point of gooeyness and wondering how long that stupid construction was going to go on.

"I think your phone's buzzing," said Mr. Cervantes.

"Yeah, it does that."

"Aren't you going to answer it? I'll take your bags."

"Not a chance. There's no one I want to talk to."

Mr. Cervantes didn't look too happy about that, but I offered an ice cream party and movie watching, his pick, and he cheered right up. He hadn't been getting out much with the toe and his daughters-in-law kept bringing him healthy food to aid in his recovery. He was too sweet to say, "Bring me a cheeseburger or leave me the hell alone," but I could tell he was thinking it.

We made it up to our floor and he gave me a pat. "Old movie or new?"

"Let's go with old," I said.

"Have you ever seen *Schindler's List?*"

Noooo!

"I have, but I can see it again," I said.

He chuckled. "I was joking. Nobody ever knows when I'm joking."

"It's because you're so sweet." I kissed his cheek and went for my door.

"I can bring enchiladas."

"Sounds good."

"They're meatless."

"Are they punishing you for something?" I asked.

He considered it. "Maybe they are trying to kill me with sad food."

"I don't think that's a thing."

"Wait until you taste the enchiladas." Mr. Cervantes hobbled inside and I set down my bags to fumble through my purse. Before I could dig my keys out, my door whipped open.

"What took you so long?" Uncle Morty stood there, fatter than ever and wearing an Adidas track suit that he bought in the 80s.

I just stood there, struck dumb by my own impossible life. I could go in and listen to he-who-made-my-life-a-living-hell or go back to the car through the gauntlet of living hell. It was a tough choice I have to say.

"What in the holy fuck are you waiting for?" Uncle Morty bellowed.

"A better option."

"What?"

Melting ice cream won and I went in, fearing the worst and, for once, not getting it. My apartment was as I left it, moderately clean with my cat, Skanky, curled up on the new fluffy donut bed I bought him. I had been thinking about getting a nanny cam to see if he actually moved at all during the day. Now I thought I needed one as an early warning system. At least I could check my apartment and see who was lying in wait. There was no use in changing the locks. Family always gets in.

Uncle Morty followed me into my tiny kitchen and eyed me as I unloaded my cache of hip-widening food. "I saw what happened on Twitter."

"Of course, you did." I almost got out a bowl, but Uncle Morty was there and he wanted something, so I took a whole half-gallon of Rocky Road and a serving spoon into the living room. Then I went back for *New York Super Fudge Chunk*. I had a feeling I was going to need it.

He plopped down in my chair, making it groan in a threatening way. "You did good."

The serving spoon stopped halfway to my mouth. "Say what?"

"I ain't saying it again."

"Heaven forbid. Dare I ask how I did good?"

"You know. We don't need to grind it into the dirt," he grumbled.

"We're nowhere near the dirt."

"I'm gonna reward you," he said.

The spoon finished its trip and I closed my eyes. "Whateber," I muttered through fudge and creamy marshmallow.

"Focus, Mercy."

"Nope. Eating. I deserve it."

"You do. That's what I'm saying."

I laid down, put the carton on my neck and started spooning.

"Stop doin' that you're gonna get sick," said Uncle Morty.

"I'll chance it."

He pointed a finger at me and said, "I don't want you sick for tomorrow."

I shouldn't have said it, but it just popped out, "What's tomorrow?"

"We're going to Greece," he said, happily.

I snorted and peeled the top off the Ben & Jerry's.

"I get it, but I'm better. I been showering regular and wearing that prescription deodorant Carolina got me. I'm all set."

"I'm not."

"You said you wouldn't try again because you had to work, but you got fired today. Time to hit the God damn road."

I sat up so fast the ice cream splatted on the sofa and I didn't even care. "Are you crazy? Have you hit your head? I'm not going to Greece with you. I wouldn't go to a gas station with you. Do you have any comprehension of what your actions have done to me? I get harassed daily. I can't answer my phone. I can't go to the store without the bag boy sniffing and yelling, 'Yep, it's pretty bad.' And yes, I got fired. This is not fab news. My job was good. I was good. People liked me. Patients requested me. Now I don't even have that!"

"You didn't get fired 'cause of the airport. That was those stalkers. Not my fault," said Uncle Morty.

"Not your fault? Not your fault?"

"Right. It ain't my fault."

"Get out."

"No."

"Get out."

"No."

"I'm not going to Greece. As far as I'm concerned, Nikki is well rid of you."

Uncle Morty drew back and his cheeks flushed to the point of being purple. "You don't mean it. You're just pissed 'cause you got fired, which ain't my fault. And they shouldn't have fired you."

"You wanted them to fire me so you could get me to Greece. Don't lie," I hissed.

If I didn't know better, I would've thought he was a little embarrassed. I didn't really believe he could do embarrassed, especially after the airport incident, which he shrugged off completely.

"They shouldn't have fired you. You did good today," he said.

"There has been nothing good about today."

"You talked that kid down. That's good." Uncle Morty heaved himself out of the chair and picked up my ice cream containers, carrying them into the kitchen.

"Hey, I was eating that," I said.

"Use a friggin' bowl. What are you, some kinda animal?"

"You should talk. I've seen you eat."

He brandished the serving spoon at me. "You wanna use me as your role model?"

"Not remotely."

"You're getting a bowl."

I got a generous bowl, including all four kinds and a normal spoon. I shoveled the mixture in my face and said through mouthfuls, "You can leave now."

"I got tickets for tomorrow. Air Canada. Different airline. We're all good," he said, settling down and kicking his scruffy Adidas up onto my coffee table.

"I'm not doing it. You had your chance and you blew it, while screwing me over royally."

He steepled his fingers. "That's why you're going."

"You're crazy."

"And right. You need to get outta Dodge until people get over it. Three weeks oughta do it."

"I can't go to Greece for three weeks. I have to get a job. I need money," I said. "I'd miss Thanksgiving."

"That's no problem."

"It really is. All of it is. I'm the nurse that gets clinics rammed by schizophrenics and the neighborhood nuts."

"Do what you're supposed to do and work for your dad. Tommy'll be thrilled," said Uncle Morty. "He could use some good news."

I combined all four flavors into a questionable blob and ate it without answering. Uncle Morty wasn't wrong. My dad was a high-profile private detective, who wasn't so high-profile anymore. He used to work with the FBI a lot, but, in an effort to protect the agency, they did their best to keep him from my mother after her attack. I uncovered the reason and that led them to a serial killer graveyard in Kansas. The FBI didn't look good and I wasn't exactly quiet about what they did to my parents, particularly my mother. My dad had a kind of breakdown after her attack and they used that as an excuse to cut him loose and they weren't quiet about the reason, citing instability.

"I'm a nurse, not a private investigator," I said.

"The hell you're not. You might as well get paid for it. Tommy'll give you the big bucks. He makes bank."

"Not right now. Their caseload is down two-thirds."

"Shit."

"Yeah." I considered licking my bowl but thought about baking the crappy pizza instead. I hadn't had my required amount of grease yet.

"He'll get the FBI back. That'll raise his profile back to normal," said Uncle Morty.

I'd gone into the kitchen but turned right back around. "Dad's not normal. He's on vacation with Mom at Cairngorms Castle. He's getting pedicures. And Claire says he only checks in three times a day."

"What do you want from the man?" he asked. "He's being with your mom."

"It wasn't her idea. She wanted to go with Grandma and he horned his way in. Mom wants him working and not pestering her. Instead, he bought her an 80,000-dollar car they can't afford and is living in her back pocket."

Uncle Morty scratched his five o'clock shadow and I could see the wheels turning, whether it was about Dad or getting me to Greece, I couldn't tell. I put my yuck pizza in the oven and set the timer.

"So I would like to invite you to leave and not come back," I said.

"You can fix that crap when you get back from Greece."

I should've known.

"I can't fix it. I tried."

"Then there's nothing to stop you from fixing my life. Carolina will like it. She likes Nikki. I was happy with Nikki."

"She didn't like it when someone thought she was me and called her 'Stinky bitch' at Target last week," I said. "She's only just starting to go out again."

"Oh, shit. Not Carolina." He put his head in his hands and then yanked out his phone.

"Do not call Mom." I tried to get the phone away from him and failed.

"I ain't calling her." He swatted at me and said, "Go check that pizza. It stinks worse than I did."

I didn't give up. Giving up is not my thing. We spun around in a circle in the living room until my boyfriend, Chuck, came in. "What in the hell are you doing?"

"Trying to get his phone," I said.

"How about you answer your own phone," said Chuck. "People are trying to get ahold of you."

"I'm against that." I lunged for Uncle Morty, missed, and he bull-dozed his way past me to lock himself in the bathroom. "I ain't calling your mother!" he yelled.

"You better not!"

"Pack your bags, sister! We take off at noon tomorrow!"

"I'm not going!"

"Bullshit!"

Chuck came up behind me and thrust a bunch of printouts in my face. "I have an hour. Let's look through these and make a decision."

"Let's do it tomorrow," I said.

"You'll be flying to Greece!" yelled Uncle Morty.

"No, I won't!"

Chuck got in front of me, bending over me with blue eyes intense. "You can't go to Greece. We have to find an apartment and move."

Oh, my God!

"We can talk about that later," I said.

"After Greece!" yelled Uncle Morty.

Chuck got me away from the bathroom and tried to put me on the sofa until he spotted Skanky licking up the ice cream I spilled.

"What happened there?" he asked.

"Don't worry about it." I tried to get past him, but he wasn't having it and there was a look in his eye that said this was happening one way or another.

Chuck and I had decided to move in together after the Porter Weeks case and I instantly regretted the decision, not because I didn't want to live with him. I did. I really did. I just didn't know it was going to be a thing. I didn't want to move. I loved my apartment. It was close to my parents, by that I meant my mother, and my godmothers, who were elderly and were starting to worry me a little. I tried to tell Chuck that, but he didn't seem to absorb the information and kept showing me apartments.

"Did you look at any of the listings I sent you?" he asked.

No.

"I scanned them. It was a busy day."

"Okay." He sat me at the breakfast bar. "Here's this one in Chester-field. I like the terrace. You can grow tomatoes."

Tomatoes. Me?

"It's...nice, but that's not walking distance," I said.

"Walking distance to what?"

"Here. I don't want—"

"Look at this kitchen. All that storage." Chuck grinned at me. His excitement should've been infectious, but all I could think about was my mom. What if she fell? What if something happened? She still wasn't comfortable being alone in the house. After Dad had gone back to work, such as it was, she'd call me and I'd walk over. I could tell she was afraid there in that house where it happened. During the day, someone was usually there, Claire, Aunt Tenne, Manny, somebody and it was okay. But in the evening, when they were gone, it wasn't. She tried to hold out and not call, but she did or I'd walk over, just to check in. It was nice. I liked it. She needed it.

"Chuck, I don't think that terrace is enough—"

"Space? I was thinking the same thing," he said. "I'm glad we're on the same page."

Same page. We're not in the same book.

"This has been a really long day and I don't want to do this right now," I said.

He got stiff and, it might've been my imagination, but I think his face got more angular, his shoulders wider. Veins were definitely popping out on his neck. "You don't want to move in together?"

"It's not that."

More veins. Plus, one on his forehead.

"I do want to move in together. You can move in here."

"Here? We can't live together here. What about my stuff?" he asked.

"Your stuff came from your mother's third husband that you hated," I said. "I think we can safely ditch that ten-year-old futon and the bed."

"Fourth husband."

"Whatever. Please let's do this tomorrow."

Uncle Morty yelled from the bathroom, "You won't have to talk about it tomorrow. You'll be on a plane."

"Shut up!" I yelled and then kissed Chuck. "Tomorrow."

"These properties are going fast and what's wrong with my bed?" he asked.

"It's so worn out it's like sleeping in a hot dog bun."

"I like it."

"You're the only one," I said.

"Pick likes it," Chuck said, like he had some kind of trump card.

"The poodle doesn't get a vote."

In response, he slapped down another listing. "Speaking of Pick, this is a house out in Manchester. We can get a yard. Pick would love a yard."

I think Uncle Morty was laughing in the bathroom. I was not laughing. And I wasn't laughing through the next five listings either. One was all the way over in Millstadt, for crying out loud.

"Hold on," said Chuck, when he paused to take a breath and answer his phone.

I jolted up to get away, but his long arm shot out and nabbed me. "She's right here. I don't know why she won't answer." He gave me his phone. "Fats wants to talk to you."

There was more laughter in the bathroom. That door must be made of papier-mâché. I held up my hands and backed away, shaking my head. The last thing I needed was Fats Licata crawling up my butt about one more thing that was not, I repeat, *not* my problem.

"Come on," said Chuck. "This cannot be a problem."

Sure it can. I have so many problems, I've lost count.

I shook my head and mouthed, "Not here."

"She knows you're here." He frowned. "Somehow."

"Answer the phone, Mercy!" Fats bellowed and let me say that when Fats Licata bellows, you do it, no matter what it is.

I took the phone. "Hi."

"What is your malfunction?" asked Fats.

"I don't know anymore. I've had a craptastic day. Can we get to the point pronto?"

"Sorry you got fired."

"How did you know?" I asked.

"I know a guy, who knows a guy. Plus, it was on the news."

I slapped my forehead and blindly went for the freezer. "It was on the news? Me getting fired is newsworthy now?"

"No, you talking some psychic kid into giving up, so the cops don't shoot him is. Channel Five broke into *Days of our Lives*. You were Breaking News," said Fats.

I got the Ben & Jerry's. No bowl. "It's a new low."

"You've been lower. I've seen it. Let's get cracking. When are you going to talk to Tiny?"

Tiny was my distant cousin from New Orleans. He worked for my dad and had become, almost instantly, the love of Fats' life.

"Never. This is not my job," I said. "I can't make Tiny do anything. I can barely make myself do things."

There was renewed laughter from the bathroom.

"Shut up! And get out of my bathroom!" I yelled at the door.

More laughter.

"Who's in the bathroom?" asked Fats.

"Uncle Morty. He wants me to go to Greece."

"I thought you weren't speaking to him."

"I'm trying not to. Believe me," I said.

"So about Tiny," Fats started in. Chuck booted up my laptop and started making a spread sheet apartment pro/con list and Uncle Morty came out of the bathroom. He did not leave. He crossed his arms and leaned on the wall, waiting, like the know-it-all bastard he is.

"Did you ever think that maybe you shouldn't do this?" I honestly don't know where that came from. Desperation, but more likely insanity.

There was silence on the phone and I went all in, like I tend to do, 'cause I am crazy. "You're a modern woman. You don't need a man."

Chuck frowned. Epically. It was an epic frown.

Uncle Morty smiled and I knew it was bad.

"Fats?" I asked.

Nothing.

I'm scared.

"I'm just saying you're independent." *Large. Terrifying.*

"And pregnant," she said.

"You can take care of things." *Assuming you don't crush the baby accidentally, like a beer can.* "Lots of people don't get married."

Chuck's face kind of collapsed in on itself, he was frowning so hard, and Uncle Morty had to clamp a hand over his mouth to keep in the laughter.

"You don't think Tiny will marry me?" asked Fats in a low, throaty voice.

I swear I peed a little. She made me incontinent.

"I'm...I'm sure he will. Once he knows—"

"I want him to ask me because he loves me, not because I'm pregnant. I'm coming over there," said Fats.

"Don't come over here!"

Uncle Morty ran back into the bathroom and slammed the door, his laughter rattling it on its hinges.

"I want your help," said Fats. "I love your cousin and I'm pregnant. I'm feeling a little..."

Please don't say irrational.

"Irrational."

Dammit!

"It's fine. Really it's fine. I'll think of something to inspire Tiny."

Fats took a deep breath. It sounded like a fireplace bellows. "You should tell him that getting married is nice. It's the thing to do when you are in love."

"I'm going to try something else. The last time I mentioned marriage, he—"

"What? What did he say?" Fats' voice got tuba deep.

"Nothing. Nothing. Forget I mentioned it."

"Tell me."

I'm going to pee again.

"It was innocent. He just said that you haven't known each other that long and there was no hurry. He thought Chuck and I would be getting married first."

"Do that," she said.

"What?"

"Tell him you are marrying Chuck and then maybe he'll get excited and want to marry."

The hormones had to be out of control. I might have to call her ob/gyn. "I don't think men work like that," I said.

"Who says they don't?" she asked.

"Um...men."

"I say we try it," said Fats.

"I'm not going to pretend to marry Chuck," I said.

Chuck smiled at me. "We could just get married."

Oh, my God.

"Do your spreadsheet," I said to him.

"I'm running out of time here," said Fats.

"You're like, what, eight weeks?"

"What's your point?"

I sat down and put my head on my breakfast bar. "I don't know."

"You'll think of something?" Fats asked.

"I will think of something. Can I get back to my ice cream?"

"Ice cream. I haven't had ice cream since I don't know when," said Fats. "I am starving."

"I think we may have hit the root of the problem," I said. "Go eat something."

"I'm on a low-carb, zero processed sugar diet, you know that."

"Eat ice cream, I beg you."

"The baby wants vegetables and tofu."

Then the baby is crazy.

"You should talk to your doc about your diet. It's extreme, considering...ya know," I said.

"You think so?"

"I do."

She talked about the "baby's" preference for lean meats and carrots, until I begged off with a claim of nausea from too much ice cream. Like that happens. There's no such thing.

Chuck saved his spreadsheet and closed my laptop. "Okay. I've got to go. Somebody stabbed a couple of tourists." He checked his phone. "At the Arch."

"Seriously?" I asked.

"Looks like it. We will continue this discussion tonight," he said.

"You'll be working."

He thought about it. "You're probably right. Tomorrow night. It's a lock. We will pick an apartment and put down a deposit."

That is not happening.

"Whatever," I said.

He scowled.

"I love you very much." I wound his scarf around his neck and only thought about throttling him a tiny bit. "Now catch that attempted murderer."

"Will do." Chuck laid a kiss on me that totally made me forget about throttling him and made me start thinking about other things.

"Maybe you should stay," I purred.

"Morty's standing behind you."

"Never mind."

His phone buzzed again. He checked it and held it up for me to see. It was the FBI. "What is going on? They have been calling me about you."

"I don't know," I said.

"You're not answering your phone."

"Correct."

Chuck kissed me again. Just a short one. Mildly impressive. "You have to talk to them."

"They screwed over my family and they're still doing it. They are dead to me."

"Tommy won't like it."

"Dad doesn't need to be the FBI's go-to guy anymore. He can do something else."

"Oh, yeah? His rep isn't in the toilet or anything," said Chuck.

"That's not my fault."

"I know, but you have to answer them. It could be interesting."

"Last time I dealt with the FBI, Kent Blankenship bit me on the face," I said. "Forget it."

"Okay, okay. But remember they are the FBI. If they want to talk to you, they're gonna talk to you."

I sighed and gave him a little finger wave. Chuck hurried out the door.

"Greece sounds more tempting, don't it?" asked Uncle Morty with a huge smirk.

"Not remotely."

Chuck jolted back in the door. "Don't forget. Tomorrow night. Apartment. Maybe a house. We could buy a house."

"We're not buying a house."

"We could. We'll talk about it tomorrow."

"Holy crap. Go to work," I said.

He started to duck out but came right back. "Fats texted. Something about timelines."

No. No. No.

"I don't know what she's talking about," I said, pushing his noggin out the door.

"Here it is. She wants to discuss her deadline."

"Swell."

"Fats has a deadline? Is she a reporter now?" asked Chuck.

"She's not a reporter. She's just driving me crazy for free," I said.

"Now you've got me interested. We can talk about it tomorrow.

Call Fats. She wants to meet." His phone buzzed again. "And call the
FBI. They're driving me nuts."

I shoved him out and closed the door, leaning back against it and
facing a super smug Uncle Morty. "How many things is that?"

"I don't know."

"You're going to Greece."

Think of something. Think of something.

He grinned at me. "You got nothing."

"I could," I said.

"But ya don't and you're going to Greece."

I sighed, too tired to fight it any longer. "Yeah."

"Tomorrow."

"Fine."

"Eight o'clock show time. Don't be late."

"Don't be smelly," I said.

Uncle Morty held out his hand and I shook it. I was too tired not
to. "Don't worry about the money. I put some in your account to cover
you for a while."

"Really?" I could've cried.

"I'll take it out of your inheritance."

"I'm not getting squat."

"You might get squat. A whole lot of squat, if you help me win
Nikki back over."

"Okay. I'll do what I can."

He smiled at me. "I know you will and I'll make it worth your
while. I took a good hard look at your accounts. You need a cash injec-
tion. It's a sad state of affairs."

"Thanks."

Uncle Morty left and Skanky looked up from my well-licked sofa,
yawning with ice cream on his whiskers.

"I guess I'm going to Greece," I said.

And then my cat threw up. It was not a good sign.

CHAPTER THREE

Our Uber driver parked in the departures lane at Lambert and popped his trunk. I got out and stared for a second at all the space. "Where's your luggage?"

Uncle Morty yanked out his computer bag and a carry-on and eyed my large roller bag. "This is it. Where do you think we're going? Antarctica? You got a parka in there?"

I hauled out my bag and I'm not going to lie, I might've popped out a hernia. "We're going for three weeks. This is three weeks' worth of clothes."

"Greece has washers."

"I'm not using 'em. This is a vacation," I said, hooking my carry-on over my shoulder.

"Well, I ain't carrying that shit," said Uncle Morty. "You pack it, you deal with it."

I rolled my eyes. "I never thought you'd deal with my bag, but you might want to tone it down after we find Nikki."

He stopped his grumpy march to the airport door and turned around. "Huh?"

"Men typically offer to help to be polite. Nikki likes polite."

"Gimme that." Uncle Morty came back and whipped my roller bag away from me.

I waved to the Uber driver and he rolled down the passenger window. "Good luck!"

"Thanks."

"You smell great by the way!"

"Tell your friends," I said, laughing.

He gave me a thumbs-up and drove off, leaving me to follow Uncle Morty into the airport. I slapped on a floppy hat and sunglasses and put my head down.

Nobody noticed me and I've never been so grateful, but it didn't last. Uncle Morty was standing at a kiosk, passport in hand, which should've been easy, but it was us, so it wasn't. There were two gate agents with him and two more on the way. Our reservation must've been flagged. I pictured a skunk emoticon next to our names and I couldn't blame them.

"Mr. Van der Hoof, we just need to make sure there's no issue with your flight today," said the lead gate agent.

"There ain't no issue," said Uncle Morty. "Does it seem like there's an issue?"

"No, but on your last flight, there was—"

"That wasn't you. What the fuck do you care?"

"There's no need for that kind of language, Mr. Van der Hoof," she said, looking dangerously like she might call security. Attention was the last thing we needed.

I rushed up and said, "Good morning. What's the problem?"

"Oh," said the gate agent with visible relief. "It's you. Thank goodness."

And then she did it. She sniffed me.

"That's the issue!" bellowed Uncle Morty. "Don't be smelling my niece. That's just freaking rude."

Another agent ran over and got in between them. "I'm sorry, sir. We've been instructed to make sure—"

"Now you're sure!"

I grabbed Uncle Morty's arm. "They're sure. They're sure." I glared at the agent. "Are you sure?"

"Yes, ma'am," he said. "I didn't want to have to do this."

"Me, either," said the original agent. "But after the last time…"

"I get it," I said, turning and giving Uncle Morty the stink eye. "Don't you have something to say to these nice people who are going to let us get on a plane to go see Nikki?"

"Get outta my way," he said. "I got a plane to catch."

"That's not it," I said.

"Gimme an upgrade."

I groaned. "For God's sake, apologize for losing your temper and it wouldn't hurt to tell them who actually stunk last time."

"Why would I do that?" he asked, genuinely puzzled. "They're causing the problem."

"*You* caused the original problem."

"Huh?" the female gate agent asked.

"Tell them," I said.

Uncle Morty got shifty eyed. "It depends on your point of view. We could've flown to Greece. People being snowflakes and fancy ass pain in my—"

"It's not a POV problem. Tell them."

He grumbled and groused.

"Do it."

"I don't want to."

"Do you want me to get on that plane?" I asked.

Uncle Morty said through gritted teeth, "I'm sorry for yelling and cursing and being an ass."

"Thank you, sir," said the male gate agent.

"And?" I said.

"Do I have to?" Uncle Morty asked.

I glared and he said, "It was me that stunk last time, not Mercy. She smelled like roses. I smelled like dumpster fire. It was me."

The gate agents gaped at us.

"You?" said the female. "But we were told and it was on the news…"

"The news was friggin' wrong," said Uncle Morty. "Imagine that."

The male was doubtful. "That was widely reported and the pictures were very persuasive."

Uncle Morty pointed at me. "Look at her and look at me. Who do you think made babies cry and a lady barf up her burrito?"

"I see your point," he said. "May I ask what was going on?"

"No." Uncle Morty pushed past him and practically punched the big red start button on the check-in kiosk.

I pulled the agents aside and whispered, "There was a breakup. He was in a bad way."

"Oh," they said in unison. "Good luck."

"I hope I won't need it," I said with a smile.

I did need it. I needed it bad. As soon as Uncle Morty put my passport in the scanner, the screen went red and security ran up, encircling us.

"What the holy hell?" asked Uncle Morty. "If this is about the stink, I apologized. What do you want from me?"

One of the guards spoke into his walkie and then looked at me. "Miss Carolina Watts?"

"Er...yeah," I said.

"Take off the hat and glasses."

I sighed and did as I was told. People were looking and they definitely knew who I was and not because I was DBD's cover girl or that I solved a few murders or had a now infamous bikini shot taken in Honduras. It was because I supposedly smelled.

"It's her," said the guard. "Should I cuff her?"

"Cuff me?" I asked.

"Hell, no," said Uncle Morty.

"Not necessary," squawked the walkie. "Bring her in."

"What about her companion?"

"He's clear."

The guards took my suitcase, carry-on, and purse. Then they took me by the arms and pulled me away from Uncle Morty.

"Hey! What are you doing?" Uncle Morty yelled. "Let her alone. We're going to Greece."

"Feel free to check in, sir," said the guard. "Miss Watts isn't going anywhere."

"What's going on?" I asked. "What did I do?"

"You've been flagged."

"As what?"

"A terrorist."

That's right. I, Mercy Watts, was on the No Fly List, flagged as a flipping terrorist, and I got all that comes with it. Yanked into the bowels of Lambert Airport, I got searched, strip searched, and then searched again. I got x-rayed, body scanned, bomb sniffed, and they literally took apart my shoes. Those were my new Bob's and I'd just gotten them broken in.

There was a moment when I thought they might just cut my cast off to see what was inside. Hint: it's an arm. A supervisor put a halt to that when I said I would sue them, since I had a spiral fracture that was almost healed and that they ought to have known that, if they bothered to google me at all.

So instead, they decided to x-ray my arm three more times from different angles. I'm so gonna get bone cancer.

Then they searched my luggage and bomb sniffed it and scanned it and then repeated the process before taking every single thing I packed out and examining it. I'm pretty sure my thongs did not need three dudes to take a closer look. I half expected them to sniff them and I know I packed ten pairs. I counted. Homeland Security owes me four pairs of Victoria's Secret lacy thongs. I don't want to think about where my poor panties are spending their time now.

"Are we done?" I asked. "I can still make the flight."

"No," said nondescript Homeland Security guy.

I checked the clock. "Pretty sure I can."

"You aren't allowed to leave the country."

"What in the world is going on? I'm not a terrorist. You know who I am. It's crazy."

"You're on the list."

"Take me off."

"I can't," he said.

"Why not?"

"I didn't put you on. It's not up to me."

I took a thong out of his hands and put it in my suitcase. "Who did then?"

"I'm not at liberty to say."

"Then what am I supposed to do?" I asked.

"You don't have to do anything."

"Hello. I have to get off the No Fly List."

"Good luck with that," he said. "You're free to go."

I started repacking my suitcase. "What do I do?"

"You can submit a form to the Department of Homeland Security. The Traveler Redress Inquiry Program."

"A form?"

"Yes," he said.

"Then they'll tell me why I'm on the list?" I asked.

"Maybe."

"What do you mean 'maybe'? How can they not tell me?"

"They don't have to."

"Why not?"

"Because they don't." With that, he turned around and left me with a sunglass-wearing guard, who absolutely refused to speak, period.

I threw away my Bob's, put on a pair of beach sandals, and had the exit pointed at. I went out into a maze of halls, passing other hapless travelers with various issues and managed to get pointed at multiple times. There was some video taken and plenty of pictures. I figured I was on YouTube at that very moment, now known as a smelly terrorist, but that didn't compare to having to face Uncle Morty. If he got on the plane without me, it would be a miracle and miracles were in short supply.

I got turned around a number of times and it took an extra five minutes to get back out into the regular airport and to my dismay Uncle Morty was waiting, red-faced, sweating, and livid.

"Hurry the fuck up!" he bellowed. "We can still make it through security."

"We can't."

"Why not?"

"I'm still on the No Fly List," I said.

"Why? What'd you do?" he asked.

"Nothing. I don't know what's going on."

Uncle Morty began muttering obscenities and walking in a circle, flailing his arms and sweating more and more.

"You'll have to go without me," I said. "Apparently, all I can do is fill out a form."

"A form? What fucking form?"

"I don't know. Some form."

He pointed at me. "You!"

"Yeah?"

"Stay here."

"No problem. The only place I can go is home," I said.

That made him redder and he marched off yelling for Homeland Security and I'd be lucky if they didn't arrest him for sheer belligerence.

I pushed my suitcase over to the wall and pulled out my phone. I'd have to tell my parents. Chuck. They couldn't hear it on the news. Gaskets would be blown and somehow that would be my fault.

Who to call first? Maybe Aunt Tenne. Sweetheart that she was, she might be willing to tell Mom and calm her down. Maybe Chuck. He was generally rational.

As I scanned through my contacts considering my options, there was a cough behind me. I ignored it. Somebody wanted a better shot. Not happy to oblige for your Instagram post, dude. Beat it. I've peoples' days to ruin.

More coughing and it was a particular kind of coughing. I can't say exactly how I knew who was behind me, but I did, on the third cough. There was no way to avoid it. I turned around and there, standing in the terminal, wearing black suits and exceedingly boring haircuts were two FBI agents, the rookies, Gordon and Gansa.

"Ah crap!"

They smiled, identical in their blandness, and Gansa gave me a finger wave. I flipped him off.

"Don't be like that," said Gordon. He was the taller of the duo by a half inch. I'd known them for months and I still had a hard time telling them apart, other than the height. Gansa was slightly blonder, but it wasn't super noticeable.

"I'll be however I want," I said.

"We're here to help you," said Gansa.

"Doubtful."

Gordon smiled. "We heard you had a little trouble getting on your plane."

"Oh, really?" I asked. "You heard it?"

"We did."

"Could it be that you put me on the No Fly List because you're totally douchebags?"

The rookies almost had expressions. I think they were surprised, but whether it was about being called douchebags or me figuring it out, I couldn't say.

"We want to talk to you," said Gordon.

"The feeling is not mutual."

"It's important."

"I'm sure you think it is." I grabbed my suitcase and started pushing it in the direction that Uncle Morty stomped off in.

They rushed after me, protesting.

"It is important," said Gansa.

"You want to hear what we have to say," said Gordon.

"That's where you're wrong." I broke into a jog. I don't know where I was going. Away was my only goal.

They came after me and Gordon hissed, "We can get you off the list."

"Piss off. I'm not that into going to Greece anyway."

"You won't fly anywhere ever," said Gansa.

That is a problem. Nope. Don't care.

I continued to wheel away and tried to use my phone with my bad hand.

"It's about Kansas," said Gordon.

"You mean the task force I got you on?" I asked. "No good deed goes unpunished."

"We have to talk to you."

"But I don't have to talk to you."

"We'll arrest you."

"Screw you," I said, heading for the women's bathroom. That might be safe.

Gansa grabbed my arm. "Trust me. You want to hear this."

"Trust me. I don't," I said.

"It's to do with your family," said Gansa.

I got in his face and he backed up, bumping into a mom and her stroller. Still a rookie. "You mean about how your bosses screwed my parents over and then cut ties with my dad? Bite me."

Gansa got a little less bland. "I'm not going to lie. That sucks. Not our idea."

"Really not," said Gordon. "We don't want to hurt your parents."

"But I'm fair game?" I asked.

"You're not."

"You put me on the No Fly List," I said. "What is wrong with you?"

The rookies got in front of me. "We couldn't get you to answer the phone. You're avoiding us," said Gordon.

"I wonder why?" I tried to dart past them and they grabbed me.

"We need your help," said Gansa.

"And this is how you get it?"

"We're desperate."

I rolled my eyes. "The FBI is desperate for *my* help. Give me a break."

Gordon and Gansa shuffled their feet and avoided eye contact.

"Wait a minute. Is this you two? Like just you two?"

"Well...there's a situation and our superiors—"

"Hey!" Uncle Morty yelled across the terminal and then he did what I didn't think he could do. He ran, coming at us like a bull in Pamplona. The rookies jumped out of the way and Uncle Morty chased Gansa around but being that Uncle Morty was about sixty pounds overweight, the rookie was never in any real danger of being caught.

Uncle Morty finally stopped and bent over, gasping, "They... put...you..."

"I know. I know," I said.

"On...the...list."

"I told you that I know."

Gordon hazarded coming close and said, "Mr. Van der Hoof, we only want Mercy to come with us and get some information."

Uncle Morty's hand shot out and he yanked Gordon down to his level by his innocuous striped tie. "You'll take her off the list?"

Gordon gagged out, "Yeah, sure."

Uncle Morty straightened up and put his hands on top of his head, revealing the tremendous sweat stains under his arms. "You bastards. You got some nerve."

"We couldn't get her any other way and this is important," said Gansa.

"So important they sent rookies?"

More shuffling of feet.

"Goddammit." Uncle Morty pointed at them. "I want her off the list."

They put their hands up.

"We just need a little help," said Gordon. "It's a case connected with the Kansas situation."

Uncle Morty eyed them. "What about your superiors?"

"You see, they don't think this is a case, but we think if we can just get a little more—"

Uncle Morty put up his hand. "Shut up. I don't give a fuck."

"But this is big. It could—"

"I don't care." He looked at me. "Go with them, Mercy."

"They screwed over my mother," I said. "Have you forgotten that?"

"Not these two dipsticks. Get off the list. I'm going to get a refund."

"This is ridiculous," I said. "They're blackmailing us."

Uncle Morty pulled me close. "Blackmail 'em back."

"What?"

He took my suitcase and carry-on. "I'll expect an update by the end of the day. Beat it, losers."

I'm pretty sure "losers" was referring to the rookies, but I was the loser that day. No doubt about that.

CHAPTER FOUR

Gordon and Gansa put me in the back of an unmarked car and got in another car. My driver, as chatty as Homeland Security, drove with his mouth in a thin line.

"Where are we going?" I asked.

"Federal building."

"Do you have any idea what's going on?"

"No."

Then I looked back and saw the rookies take a different ramp on the maze of highways outside Lambert.

"Hey! We took a wrong turn," I said.

"No."

No amount of questions or prodding—I did try poking him—got another word out of my driver. In the end, I had no idea if he was an agent or some kind of lackey roped into doing Gordon and Gansa's bidding.

When we arrived at the Federal building, my door was whipped open, and I got out into a swirl of snowflakes. A guard directed me inside to the fifth floor, where I waited for an hour and drank the most God awful coffee you've ever had in your life. Just when I was about to say screw it and leave—I wasn't under arrest—Gansa came in and gestured me through an unmarked door and through yet another set of hallways. There were so many hallways in that building I was beginning to wonder if there were any offices at all.

"Are you going to tell me what this is about or what?" I asked.

"You're going to tell me." He stopped and opened a door marked "Conference RM E5". "Here we go."

I walked in and to my astonishment there were two people inside, unsurprisingly Gordon and very surprisingly, my Great Aunt Miriam. Sister Miriam is my grandad's older sister and you'll excuse me for saying this, a kind of holy terror. She sat at the conference table, stiff as a grissini breadstick and just as skinny. She had her oversized black purse on her lap, the one she was known to put bricks in so she could whack unsuspecting pimps and drug dealers when she was doing the Lord's work, mainly helping runaways and teenaged prostitutes.

Aunt Miriam didn't glance at me or acknowledge my presence. She stared straight ahead. I'd call it a 1000-yard stare, but she was sharp-eyed and missed nothing.

"Sit down, Mercy." Gordon pulled out a chair next to Aunt Miriam. I sat down and whispered, "What's going on?"

She didn't respond, but she had a death grip on that purse. I shouldn't have sat so close.

Gansa sat down and said, "Now do you know why we're here?"

"Nope. Haven't a clue," I said.

"Really?"

I plunked my purse on the chair next to me and crossed my arms. "Really."

"I told you this was about Kansas." He gestured to Aunt Miriam. "And here she is."

"So what?"

The rookies exchanged a glance.

"We've interviewed Sister Miriam four times," said Gansa.

"About what?" I asked.

Another glance and Gordon got a briefcase off the floor. He opened it and pulled out an evidence bag. I glanced at Aunt Miriam. She didn't blink, but the line of her mouth got a tiny bit thinner. It took family to see it.

Gordon slid the bag over to me. "Do you recognize that?"

I glanced at the bag and shrugged. "It's a St. Brigid medal."

"But do you recognize it?"

The way he was looking at me said I was supposed to. So I picked up the bag and turned it over. The metal was crusted with dirt, but it was an ordinary medal as far as I could tell, other than it had initials engraved on the back, M.E.M.

"No," I said. "It's pretty common."

"What about the initials?" asked Gansa.

I wracked my brain and came up with nothing. "No. How about you just get to the point? Did you find that in Kansas?"

"We did."

"Whose is it?"

Gordon pulled a slim file out of his briefcase and slapped it on the table. I wasn't impressed and Aunt Miriam didn't seem to notice at all. Wherever she was, it was far from there.

"Nobody you know has a medal like that one?" asked Gansa.

Then I got it. My brain must've been fried by the terrible coffee. "Well, yeah, Aunt Miriam has one. I'm sure lots of people have them."

"Do you?"

"Um...yeah, I think so," I said. "What are you getting at?"

Gordon put the briefcase on the floor and steepled his fingers. "It's hard for us to believe that Sister Miriam hasn't told you about this."

"Believe it," I said. "I don't know why I'm here and I'm caring less by the second. Are you going to take me off that stupid list or what?"

"If you get her to talk to us," said Gansa.

I pivoted in my chair. "Aunt Miriam, talk to them so they'll take me off the No Fly List."

Aunt Miriam turned her head toward me in a way that I half expected it to go all the way around like an owl or that chick in *The Exorcist*. It chilled me to my core and made me nauseated at the same time. She didn't say anything. She just looked at me with her icy blue eyes and then looked forward into nothing again.

"I'm going with she's not going to talk to you ever about anything," I said. "Can I go because I don't want to be here anymore."

"She's your aunt," said Gordon.

"That's not a bonus prize in this situation."

"Does the name Sister Margaret Mullanphy mean anything to you?" asked Gansa.

"No."

"You've never heard that name before?"

I thought about it. I really did. "No. Who is it?"

Gordon got a picture out of the file and slid it over to me. I took a good look, but one glance was really enough. That was an old picture. Black and white. Sister Margaret, if that's who it was, appeared to be about twenty-five years old and wearing an old school habit. They gave those up after Vatican II, well before my time. Hell, it was before my parents' time.

"Nope. Who is she?"

He slid over another picture. This time a later one of a group of nuns without habits, wearing conservative twin sets, A-line skirts, and short veils. "Recognize anyone there?"

I barely looked. "It's still black and white. Why are you bothering me with this?"

"We can't get ahold of anyone else in your family," said Gordon. "Your parents and grandparents are on vacation. Your aunts, uncles, and cousins hang up on us."

"So you decided to pick on me," I said.

"We could've brought your cousins in, but let's face it, they don't have the relationship with Sister Miriam that you do."

"If by relationship, you mean she whacks me with her cane, then yeah, but I still have nothing for you."

"She didn't call you about this?"

I resisted the urge to scream. "No. No. And no." I pointed at Aunt Miriam. "She's not going to speak to you and I don't know what this is about, so we're leaving right now. Get up, Aunt Miriam. We're hitting the bricks."

Then the most remarkable thing happened. She did it. Aunt Miriam obeyed me. She stood up. I was so astonished that I didn't move and that gave the rookies a second to regroup.

"It's about murder, Mercy," said Gordon. "Sister Margaret was murdered."

Aunt Miriam swayed and I caught her, lowering her down into her seat. "It's fine. Don't listen," I said.

She didn't answer and went right back to staring.

"My aunt's upset," I said. "We need to leave."

"How can you tell?" asked Gansa.

"I can tell. So say what you want to say and leave us alone."

"This could take a while," said Gordon.

It could've taken a while, but it didn't. Sister Margaret Mullanphy was murdered in 1965. 1965, for crying out loud. She was found in the woods, strangled, and it was thought that a priest did it. Father Dominic Kelly threw himself off the Eades Bridge before he could be properly questioned and the case was closed.

"What in the world do you want me to do about it?" I asked.

"Your aunt was close friends with the deceased." Gordon pointed at the group picture and there was Aunt Miriam, right next to Sister Margaret.

"So what?" I asked. "The case is solved."

"It isn't," said Gansa. "Not really."

"You said the priest did it."

"That's what they thought," said Gordon. "But it wasn't proven."

"They must've had a reason for thinking he did it," I said.

Gansa leaned over the table. "They had a priest jumping off a bridge because the nun he apparently loved was dead so he must've killed her."

"Works for me."

"Aren't you supposed to be good at this?" asked Gordon.

"What do you want from me? I got you on the Kansas task force," I said.

"We want to reopen the case," said Gansa.

"Fine. Do that."

The rookies gritted their teeth.

"We can't. The higher-ups don't agree. They think it's a dead end," said Gordon.

I picked up the medal and examined it. "But you don't because this was found in Kansas?"

"Look at the initials," said Gansa. "It's Sister Margaret's medal. We need your aunt to confirm it."

I looked over at Aunt Miriam. Nothing. Not going to happen, although I couldn't imagine why. If it was her friend's medal, what was wrong with saying so?

"Okay. So what if it is?" I asked, although I already had a feeling. That feeling that something wasn't right. Aunt Miriam wore her St. Brigid medal constantly. You couldn't see it, but it was there under her clothes, next to her heart. It had her initials on it. I remembered seeing them there and I was pretty sure, if I went home and dug around, I'd find my own medal with my initials on it, done in the exact same way.

Gansa took the evidence bag from me and shook it in my face. "It wasn't found on her body. Her Mother Superior said she always wore it. Never took it off and it wasn't on her body."

"They thought Father Dominic took it?" I asked.

"They assumed he did." Gansa shook the bag again. "But he didn't. He couldn't have. It wasn't in his effects and, if he jumped off the bridge with it, it'd be at the bottom of the Mississippi river."

"You found it in Kansas in the serial killer graveyard," I said, feeling more sick by the second.

"The team did."

"Where was it?"

"Between two bodies."

Aunt Miriam stood up, walked around the table, and left the room. We just watched her go and it didn't occur to me to say anything or stop her. It was Aunt Miriam and she undoubtedly had a brick.

"So have you identified the bodies?" I asked.

"We have," said Gordon with satisfaction.

"And?"

"Shawn Gibson, nineteen, missing 1972 and Joan Gilbert, twelve, missing 2001."

I swallowed and tried not to picture those two victims, the state in which they were found, what happened, but I couldn't fight it. My mind went there. "Was it sandwiched in between?"

"Yes, it was," said Gansa.

"You think Sister Margaret was killed by one of your serial killers."

"Yes, we do."

Gansa reached for the doorknob and said, "Get her to identify the medal. That's all you have to do."

"That's all?" I asked. "Gee. No problem."

"Are you being sarcastic?"

"No. Not at all. Dealing with my aunt is a piece of cake."

His incredibly smooth forehead got one wrinkle. "I feel like you're messing with me."

"Ya think?"

Gordon stepped up. "You want to fly to Greece, get her to do it."

"How about *you* convince *your* guys that you're right? How about that?"

He clenched and unclenched his jaw. "This is just between us, but we just found another cache of bodies about fifty meters away from the first group. We're up to our eyeballs and the press is going to be brutal."

"You deserve it," I said.

They frowned, showing more personality than I thought they possessed.

"Not you personally."

"I'm glad you make the distinction. We're the good guys," said Gansa.

I wouldn't go that far.

"If you get me off the list, you can be the good guys."

"We wouldn't have hauled you in here, if we could get this done any other way," said Gordon.

"What about the Sister's family, friends?"

"Everyone that might've remembered is dead. Sister Miriam is who we've got. The bureau's stance is that the medal could belong to someone else, a man, for instance."

"As in it might belong to one of the killers?" I asked.

"Correct," said Gansa.

Hope lit up in my chest. "Maybe it did."

"They're running that line of inquiry into the ground and you better hope they aren't too attached to it."

I stepped back involuntarily. "Don't say it."

"It's going to happen."

"No."

"I won't do it," I said. "Send someone else."

"They tried," said Gordon. "Yesterday, as a matter of fact. Blanken-ship wouldn't come out of his cell."

I touched my lip. The scar, although faded, was still there and would always be there. I'd been forced to go to Hunt Hospital for the Criminally Insane to get information out of mass murderer Kent Blankenship, and I paid for it in spades. He gave me what I needed and it led the FBI to Kansas. I always knew it was only a matter of time before I was asked to go back in and talk to Blankenship. We had what they like to call a rapport, but it was more like ownership, as in Blankenship thought I belonged to him.

"I'm not going back to Hunt," I said.

"You will."

"Won't."

"If it's in the interest of your family or justice, you will," said Gordon.

"I don't like you two," I said.

Gansa opened the door. "We know, but that changes nothing. Talk to her."

I flounced out with my nose in the air. I wasn't talking to Aunt Miriam and I sure the hell wasn't talking to Blankenship. I had three seconds of superiority and then I ran straight into Aunt Miriam, who stood in the hall, hawk-eyed and disapproving.

"What are you doing?" she asked.

I just about turned around. The rookies were preferable. "I was leaving with style."

"You look proud of yourself."

"I was. Don't worry. I'm over it."

"Good. Let's go."

She has a cane. Where'd she get that?

"Um...I'm sure we're not going to the same place," I said.

Aunt Miriam got squinty. "Where are you going?"

Wherever you aren't.

"Well..."

She brandished the cane. "Speak up. I haven't got all day."

"Home, I guess," I said.

"Good, then you're not busy."

"I am busy. I've got to look for a job and—"

The cane came dangerously close to my shin and I jumped back.

"I need a ride," said Aunt Miriam.

Thank you. Thank you. Thank you.

"I didn't drive," I said, trying not to sound happy, but from the increasing squintiness, I failed.

"We can go together," she said, marching off down the hall.

"I'm going to walk. I need the air." I spun around, looking for an exit or an elevator. The rookies were gone, having slipped out when they saw a chance for escape.

"This way," she yelled.

"I'll just go somewhere that's not there."

"Carolina Watts!"

Dammit.

I jogged down the hall, almost losing a sandal, and caught up to her at the elevator. "I guess we can share an Uber."

"I'll order one," said Aunt Miriam.

"You'll order one?"

She gave me another core-chilling look as if her ordering an Uber was perfectly normal. It wasn't. She'd yet to master turning on her phone and that is not an exaggeration. We waited a good five minutes for the elevator, took it down ten flights, and left the building before she managed it.

"There," she said in triumph. "These things are poorly designed. I'm going to write a letter."

"A letter?" I asked.

"Yes, Mercy, a letter. That is how it's done. Civilized people write coherent letters of complaint."

"Maybe they did in 1985, but now they email or tweet."

"Don't be ridiculous."

"I'm not being ridicu— never mind. Please order the Uber."

Aunt Miriam went through her apps and, at one point, somehow ended up playing DJ Khaled at incredibly high volume. My feet were freezing and the flurries had turned into snow. There was an excellent chance that'd I'd have frostbite before she opened her app.

"This service is terrible," she said.

"You should write a letter."

She whacked me on the shins and while I danced around in pain, she opened the Uber app and claimed to have ordered a ride.

"Are you sure?" I asked.

"What do you mean?"

"Nothing."

"Why are you wearing those sandals? Have you no sense of the appropriate?"

Not usually. No.

"Homeland Security took the *appropriate* shoes I was wearing when you got me on the No Fly List," I said.

"I did no such thing," said Aunt Miriam. "I'm certain that you did something."

"I'm related to you and apparently we're close."

"There you go."

I turned to her and stepped out of cane reach. "Is it Sister Margaret's medal?"

Her mouth went into a thin line.

"If it is, it is. If it isn't, it isn't. Just say so and we're both off the hook."

"There is no hook."

"I'm on the No Fly List. That's a pretty big hook. What's my mom going to say?"

"Carolina will understand," she said.

"No, she won't and neither will my dad or Grandad or anyone," I said. "What is wrong with telling the truth?"

She looked at me and I quaked. "I have nothing to say and the matter is closed."

"Except it's not. She was your friend. Don't you want to help her?"

"The time to help her was then."

"It's not your fault. You didn't do it."

Aunt Miriam's mouth twitched and her eyes got moist. "I will not besmirch her memory by letting this all be slobbered over in the press. She was a dignified person. She will remain dignified."

"Wouldn't it be dignified to catch her murderer, if they were wrong about the priest?" I asked.

"It was fifty years ago. The person is long dead."

"You're not."

"You don't know what you're talking about," she said.

"I do. You *know* I do. If those dufus rookies are right and I have a feeling they are, that person got away with murdering a nun."

Aunt Miriam sighed and her rigid shoulders relaxed, just a bit. "It's over, Mercy. I don't want to think about it ever again. Can you understand that?"

I didn't know what to say. Of course, I understood. I didn't want to see Richard Costilla's face, the teenager I killed in New Orleans, ever again. I didn't want to remember how Mom looked when I found her stroked out after her attack. But those things were in my mind and pushing them away didn't make them go away. It just didn't.

"Good. It's agreed then," announced Aunt Miriam. "Here's our ride."

A super long, old Q45 pulled up and the driver leaned over to look at us. He didn't have the moderately friendly look of most drivers. If I had to name that look, I'd say it was dread.

"Do you know him?" I asked.

"Naturally," said Aunt Miriam. "Get in."

I got in and the driver looked somewhat relieved that I got in the front seat instead of Aunt Miriam. I didn't blame him.

"Hello, William," said Aunt Miriam.

"Good morning, Sister Miriam," said William. "How are you today?"

Somebody had been trained in Sister Miriam politeness.

"I'm very well. Thank you," she said.

He pulled out into traffic so slowly we got blasted with twenty-eight horns and I counted at least three fingers. William was gripping the wheel like he was afraid it would escape. "I will have you to the hospital in a reasonable amount of time."

"I see your skills have improved," said Aunt Miriam.

"Yes, ma'am."

"Excellent."

I shifted in my seat and looked back. "So what are we—"

"Shush," she said. "William is driving."

I turned back around, so William could concentrate on being at a red light, and tried to figure out what to do. I could call Chuck. He was working on Kansas, at least where it pertained to Missouri. I doubted he had enough pull to get me off the list, but there was also Morley and Harwood, formerly known as Hatchett Nose and Toupee back when I hated them. They were higher up the food chain in the FBI than the rookies. Maybe they could do it. But there was a better than average chance that they'd want something in exchange, like a trip out to Hunt. I didn't want to go to Greece that bad.

William pulled up at SLU's main building and breathed a sigh of relief. "Here you go, Sister Miriam. Have a nice day."

"Very well done, William," said Aunt Miriam. "I will be ordering you later."

"Yes, ma'am."

She got out and I said, "Okay. I need to go a few more blocks, close to Hawthorne Avenue."

Aunt Miriam rapped her cane on my window.

"I don't think so," said William.

"No, really. I'm not going into the hospital."

"The cane says you are. I don't argue with the cane."

I rolled down my window. "What's up? Is this the wrong hospital?"

"No," she said.

"What are you waiting for?"

She heaved an exasperated sigh and said, "Oh, fine. I give up, you can come with me."

"Er...no, really I'm good."

"That's debatable. Get out of the car, Mercy. You may accompany me on this one occasion."

"What occasion is it?" I asked.

She gave me the stink eye and it was my turn to heave an exasperated sigh. "I guess you're right, William."

"I'm starting to know her pretty well," he said, "and I'm a little afraid for you."

"Me, too," I said. "I suggest you go on break about three-thirty."

William grinned. "Thanks for the tip, but it's okay. She scares the crap out of me, but she tips well and gives me a good review every single ride."

"Really?"

"I know, right?"

"Well, good luck and God bless."

He gave me a thumbs-up and I got out to follow Aunt Miriam into the hospital. She could really move when she wanted to and I practically had to jog to keep up. I thought we'd be going to the volunteer section where she bullied people into doing the right thing on a daily basis, but instead, we ended up in the doctor's building on the third floor going into Dr. Amed Harrison's office, an obstetrician and gynecologist.

Aunt Miriam marched up to the reception desk and barked, "We're late."

The poor receptionist jumped a foot and hastily said, "It's fine. It's fine. He's free. He had a cancelation." The poor woman ran to get some paperwork, but Aunt Miriam held up hand. "We don't need that."

"Okay," said the receptionist. "Right this way."

I went to sit down in the waiting area, but Aunt Miriam pointed at me.

What was happening? Was I seeing a gyno? Had I had my own stroke and completely forgotten that I needed one?

"I really don't think—"

"Quiet," said Aunt Miriam and I followed her back to Dr. Harrison's office, a spartan affair with Danish design elements.

The doctor jumped up and showed us a pair of blond wood chairs in front of his desk, like we couldn't have found them on our own. He had also been trained.

"Sister Miriam, it's good to see you." Dr. Harrison smiled, but he didn't mean it.

"I'm sure it is," she said. "You have a living to make."

"Er...yes, I do and I see you've brought someone along today." He leaned over the desk and extended his hand. "Miss Watts, a pleasure."

I shook his hand that was disturbingly moist. "Thanks."

He squeezed my hand and said with his large dark eyes intense, "I'm a huge fan. I'm very happy to meet you."

That was more worrying than the brick in Aunt Miriam's bag. "Oh. Okay."

I sat down and so did the doctor. Aunt Miriam folded her hands on top of her purse and sat ramrod straight.

"So...may I ask what brings you along today, Miss Watts?" His eyes were pleading.

"I have no idea," I said.

"You're not here to help your aunt with her—"

Aunt Miriam coughed.

"Um...difficulty?"

"I didn't know she had a difficulty," I said.

"You're a nurse?"

"Yep."

Dr. Harrison sat back in his chair and frowned. "She hasn't told you?"

"Tell me what? Is something wrong?" I asked.

"I assume so," he said.

"You assume?"

"Yes."

"You don't know? You're the doctor."

Dr. Harrison kindly explained to me that this was Aunt Miriam's third visit to see him and she had yet to tell him what was wrong with her.

I turned to her and said, "Are you serious? Tell him."

"It's private," said Aunt Miriam.

"He's a doctor. *Your* doctor."

"I will."

"When? The next millennium?" I asked. "If you have an issue, let's have it."

Aunt Miriam wouldn't look at me and she sure wasn't looking at Dr. Harrison. "I told you I will. I have to get comfortable first."

"I hate to break it to you, but gynecologists' offices don't get more comfortable than this," I said. "And he's the number one gyno in the city. You're taking up his valuable time."

"He's well paid."

"Not enough to just sit there."

Dr. Harrison shifted in his chair nervously. "No, no. It's perfectly fine. Really. As long as it takes."

I stood up. "This is crazy. Just tell him."

Aunt Miriam stood up and said, "I will. Thursday at ten."

The doctor glanced at his calendar. "Yes. I will see you then, Sister Miriam."

"No," I said. "You will not see him then. You're seeing him now."

"It's fine, Miss Watts," said Dr. Harrison.

"No, it's not. Cancel that appointment. This is why I and all the normal people can't get appointments when we need them."

Aunt Miriam booked it out the door, calling over her shoulder, "Thursday."

"You have to cut her off," I said. "This is nutty, even for her."

"I can't," he said, resigned and not at all like you'd think the top gyno in St. Louis should look.

"Why not?"

"Have you ever heard of Dr. John Mills?"

"No."

"He was one of my partners. He's now living in Micronesia, foraging for fruit in the jungle."

"I don't follow."

Dr. Harrison explained and it pained him to do it. Five years ago, Aunt Miriam discovered Dr. Mills had the habit of soliciting teenaged prostitutes. Being who she was, Aunt Miriam wasn't content to warn him off or even just call the cops. She wrecked him. I'm not saying Dr. Mills didn't have it coming. He did. One of the girls was fourteen. But when my Aunt Miriam decides to come after you, you know you've been gone after. His wife was informed. The police and his partners, the hospital, the AMA, every professional organization he belonged to, not to mention his homeowners organization and the neighborhood watch. She told his accountant and stockbroker, for crying out loud. Somehow he didn't go to jail. There was a plea bargain with some ridiculous time served crap, but Dr. Mills completely freaked and when he got out of a cushy mental health facility, he fled the country to hunt bananas with orangutans.

"Wow," I said.

"Yeah."

I squinted at him. "You haven't been…"

"Or course not. I haven't done anything," said Dr. Harrison. "But Sister Miriam makes me think I did and just don't remember, so I'm taking no chances. Understand?"

"Alright, but I think it's crazy to waste your time," I said.

He came around the desk, peeked out the door, and said, "See if you can get her to talk to me. Something is definitely wrong. She's in pain. I can tell, but I can't do anything if I can't examine her."

"I'll try, but you know how she is."

"I do, but I'm very concerned."

I shook his hand that was happily less moist and went out to find Aunt Miriam in the waiting room.

"Well, I hope he can help you, Mercy," she said, loudly. "These things can get serious."

"What the—"

She whacked me with her cane until I left the office.

"Mercy, I'm going to my office. I will see you on Thursday at ten," said Aunt Miriam.

"No, you won't." I did an about-face and went for the stairs.

She came after me, waving her cane and hopping mad. I grabbed the cane, twisted it out of her hand, and brandished it myself. "I'm not going to another useless appointment."

Hands went to bony hips and faded ginger hair curled around her face, having escaped from her veil. "We will go to my office to discuss this."

"You go to the office," I said. "I'm going home to contemplate the error of my ways."

"Excellent. Then I will see you on Thursday."

"Not that error. It's not an error."

She got squinty. "What error then?"

"Getting up this morning and thinking something could possibly go right for me," I said.

"Don't exaggerate," she said. "You were always dramatic, even as a child."

"Oh, yeah? Because you refused to identify your friend's medal, I got strip-searched by Patricia and Eloise at the airport and they are not nearly as gentle as they sound. Strip-searched. Naked."

"Mercy, please," said Aunt Miriam. "This is a medical facility. People are ill."

"Yeah, me. I'm sick and tired and I want to go to Greece and have umbrella drinks for free." I whipped open the door to the stairs and tossed her cane down the hall. "Do not call me unless you want to help me."

"I need you to come to the doctor," she said.

"For what?"

"You're a nurse."

"I'm not a mind reader."

"I'm family."

"Great," I said. "If family is what you require, I'll call the family. How about my mother? She's almost got the drooling under control. Or my dad. No? You don't want to take my dad to the gyno. How about this? I'll call your brother. Grandad surely wants to sit in an office with Dr. Harrison and think about what all those speculums do."

"You wouldn't," she said, blushing more red than her hair.

"Before today? No. Absolutely not. After Patricia and Eloise? You bet." I went into the stairwell and ran down the stairs. I did not have on the right bra for that and it hurt, but I didn't care.

"Mercy! Mercy!" There was a pleading to Aunt Miriam's voice and Dr. Harrison said there was something wrong. She was old and family and old.

I stopped. "What?"

"Mrs. Haas called. You have to go take down your mother's Halloween decor. Tommy didn't do it."

I am so over family.

CHAPTER FIVE

F amily was not over me. I smelled the family stink from the hallway outside my apartment. It was oily, fatty, and heavy with despair. Uncle Morty was in there, cooking up kielbasa and sauerkraut. Why he had to do it in my apartment was anybody's guess. I couldn't face it. I really couldn't.

Luckily, I knew someone who could. I pulled out my phone and Mr. Cervantes stuck his head out in the hallway. "Mercy, I think Morty's in there. It really smells."

"I'm on it," I said, dialing.

"Why didn't you go to Greece?"

"You don't want to know."

He paused for a second and then said, "I believe you."

The phone was ringing and I waited while giving Mr. Cervantes a thumbs-up so he'd trust me and go back into his apartment where it smelled nice.

"Huh?" my friend and occasional sidekick, Aaron, answered.

"I need help. We didn't go to Greece and Morty is making that cheap kielbasa in my apartment. It's the kind where you can see the veins and comes with snout hairs."

No answer. Typical. Aaron was not a talker unless he was talking

about hotdogs or Star Trek. Sci-fi is big in my life and his, since he
owns a Star Trek-themed restaurant, Kronos, and just opened a Klin-
gon-themed bakery, Sto-Vo-Kor.

"Aaron?"

He hung up. Also, typical. I figured it would take the little guy
about fifteen minutes to get whatever cooking supplies he needed from
Kronos and hoof it over. I could either go in, absorb that smell, and
actually stink the way people thought I did, or I could go put away
Mom's Halloween stuff. Dad had promised he'd do it, since Mom
couldn't climb a ladder and was opposed to paying anyone to do it, like
everyone else on the block did. I knew very well I was going to have to
do it. I'd just been putting it off. If Mom came back from Cairngorms
Castle with a skeleton still up in time for Thanksgiving, she *would*
climb a ladder. That could not happen and Dad's new leaf wasn't
completely turned over, no matter what he said.

I borrowed a pair of running shoes from Mr. Cervantes so my feet
wouldn't freeze and went slowly down the stairs. No jogging. My chest
hurt bad enough already and I had to admit it felt nice outside. The
snow had stopped, leaving everything sparkly with a light frosting and
when I got to my parent's street, I realized how far behind we were.
All the mansions were done up with stalks of corn, professionally
carved Thanksgiving-themed pumpkins, and the occasional pilgrim
diorama. I particularly liked the McCallisters' where all the pumpkins
were Lenox porcelain and cream-colored, for some reason.

I grew up on the avenue, so you'd think I'd understand them, but I
didn't. My family didn't have china and I carved the pumpkins, badly.
Mom didn't believe in fancy pumpkins that the parents bought or
carved themselves, although that was the fashion, especially after
Pinterest started. Moms were all about the Pinterest and perfection.
My mother couldn't be bothered. She bought a pumpkin that was so
misshapen that she got it cheap and then handed me a dull steak knife.
I went to town, doing some seriously bad artwork that she invariably
loved. I think she didn't do as the others did because she was perfect
herself and didn't need to prove anything with a flipping pumpkin, not
that she said she was perfect. It was just one of those things. I never
met anyone who didn't love my mom. She was just her and that was

enough. Not something I inherited. I got the face and bod, none of the charm or elegance. What a rip-off.

When I stopped at our house, I have to say Mrs. Haas was right. Our house was bad. I'd done my usual stellar carving job on three pumpkins that were ugly to start. Now they were sunk in and rotting with some ooze running down the front steps. Our bedraggled skeleton that Mom got at a yard sale when I was five had lost a foot, both hands, and, most importantly, his head. Our house was a three-story Tudor, designed by Josiah Bled, so it came with a built-in creepiness, even more than the other mansions on the street. They all had a not-really-lived-in quality that lent credence to the ghost stories that went around and were now part of the history of St. Louis. Our house was supposed to have the ghost of Bernice Collins. She was Josiah Bled's mistress and she disappeared. It was generally thought that he killed her in the butler's pantry. It was abnormally cold, for no good reason, but I'd never seen her or any other ghost on Hawthorne Avenue.

I'd have to get out the ladder and climb up to cut the wires Dad used to hang that skeleton. There was no way I could undo the wires with my arm in a cast. I wasn't even sure I could carry the ladder, but I managed it, mostly by dragging it and cursing. My phone started going off with my mom's ringtone, "Survivor" from Destiny's Child.

I answered without thinking twice. There wasn't any mistake I wouldn't make that day. "Hi, Mom."

"Why'd they bring you in?" Dad whispered.

"Ah, crap."

"Quick. Tell me. I don't have much time."

I leaned against the tree and swatted the skeleton's remaining foot out of my face. "Very cloak and dagger, Dad. What's up?"

"It's cloak and your mother. She'll be back from her high tea any second. Why did those morons haul you into the Federal building?"

"Did Morty call you? Don't tell Mom. She'll get upset."

"I'm not telling her anything and that bastard didn't tell me. I know people."

"Who do you know?"

"Focus, Mercy. What did you do?" asked Dad.

"Nothing. Not a thing."

"Why are you on the No Fly List?"

I groaned and hauled the ladder upright. "'Cause they're pissed and they want me to do something that I'm not going to do."

"Do it," he hissed. "Do it now. Today. Yesterday, if possible."

"Are you smoking crack? You don't even know what it is."

"I know that business has gone down sixty-two and a quarter percent since they cut ties with me and announced that I'm an unreliable dipshit."

"They never called you a dipshit." I was smiling. I couldn't help it. Usually, it was me under fire. Totally Dad's turn.

"Can you not hear me? Sixty-two and a quarter percent downturn."

"That's a lot."

"You're goddamn right it is. Now do what they want, but make sure bringing me back on is part of the deal."

"Dad, I've got to get a skeleton out of a tree right now, so this will have to wait."

"What skeleton?" he asked. "Is that part of the case?"

"It's part of pissing me off. You didn't take down the Halloween decor like you promised."

"Nobody cares about that."

"Incorrect. You don't care. But Mom cares. I care. The avenue cares," I said.

"It's not important. Oh, shit. I think that's her," said Dad. "Get me back in. I need back in."

I started climbing the ladder. Such a bad idea. It was unstable at best, kinda like me. "They're total dirtbags, Dad. Look what they did to you and Mom."

"Mom understands," he said.

"She prays they get herpes. All of them. The whole FBI."

"Oh, good. It wasn't her," he said. "Okay. Do we have a deal?"

I got to the top of the ladder and eyed the wire. It was pretty far. I might have to get Chuck. "No."

"Mercy, it's for the family."

"It's for you."

"The business is a family business."

"Whatever."

"Mercy." Dad's voice turned sweet and pleading. "I need this and make no mistake, your mother does, too. What are we without the business?"

"A happy couple?"

"We are happy. I'm here on vacation, not drumming up business. I got a pedicure today. A pedicure!"

"Dad, as much as I enjoy saying no, I'm not just messing with you. I already tried to do what they wanted and it's a no-go." I told him about Sister Margaret and Aunt Miriam. I finished up with our delightful trip to the gyno. That alone almost made him choke on his tongue.

"Don't say anymore," he said.

"The doc wants to do an exam."

"Girl, if you don't shut up about that I'll—"

I laughed. "Come home and deal with it yourself? I dare you to try it. You horned your way into that vacation. You can't just ditch them when you find something better to do. That's the old you."

"Help them, Mercy," he said, pulling out the charming voice that was so rarely used with me. "It's the right thing and you know it."

"You want *me* to help the FBI. *That's* who you want to help?"

"Yes, and don't be difficult about it."

"Dad, if I ever do anything to help anyone ever again, rest assured it won't be for the FBI. Kent Blankenship bit my face because of those crapbags. I wouldn't help *them* to the toilet if they had amoebic dysentery."

"Mercy, as usual, you misunder—"

I hung up and flung my phone across the yard into a pile of leaves. So satisfying. You have to try it.

I turned my attention to the skeleton, holding onto the ladder with my bad hand, mostly fingertips, and reached out with the wire cutters.

Just another inch. Almost there. Shift a little. Lean. You won't have to ask Chuck to do it, like a wussy short person. You can do it.

"Mercy!"

I fell so fast I don't remember it happening. I remember lying on the ground, unable to breathe and mentally cursing my father. Myrtle and Millicent, my Bled Godmothers, bent over me, their gentle faces wreathed in fear.

"Are you alright, dear?" asked Millicent.

"Can you breathe?" asked Myrtle.

They asked a lot of questions. I didn't answer a single one, but it wasn't really necessary. They talked enough for the three of us and examined me for a blow to the head, which they were sure I had, otherwise why would I ever climb a ladder in my condition. In their world, a broken arm was a good reason to take to your bed for at least a month, not that they would do that. For little old ladies that looked as delicate as Murano glass, they were surprisingly tough.

Millicent got me upright by threatening to call 911 and then checked me for broken bones. New broken bones.

"She seems fine," said Myrtle.

"This isn't normal. Look at her eyes," said Millicent.

"What's wrong with my eyes?" I asked.

They threw up their hands and hugged me as I struggled to my feet. Apparently, I had circles under my eyes in addition to my presumed head injury. I tried to explain about Mrs. Haas, but they weren't having it.

"That is ludicrous, Mercy," said Myrtle. "You're already injured. How does your arm feel?"

Hurts like hell.

"Fine. The same."

Millicent picked leaves and twigs out of my hair and Myrtle tried to pull down the ladder until I put a stop to that. "I need that up."

"You certainly do not. We will have a service do it," said Millicent.

"You know how Mom feels about paying for things that we can do ourselves."

"We'll pay for it," said Myrtle.

"That still counts and it's not your problem."

They watched me, calculating their next move and straightening their tartan wool trousers and the short capes they wore over their silk blouses. They didn't match but they went together, like they had all their lives.

"We'll ask Chuck to do it," said Millicent with a decided air.

"It's not his problem," I said.

"That's what men are for," said Myrtle, pulling me away from the ladder.

"Lawn care?"

"Among other things. He'll want to help."

"I don't know about that." I dug my phone out of the pile and turned it off, ignoring the fifty thousand messages from Dad. "Chuck was an apartment kid. I don't think he speaks lawn care."

"He'll learn." Millicent eyed me putting my phone in my back pocket. "I assume that was Tommy."

"You assume right." I took them onto the front porch and settled them in the cushy chairs with lap blankets while I threw away the pumpkins and scrubbed off the ooze. They watched, sipping chamomile tea, but they weren't happy about it. The Girls often wanted to help us, especially Mom and even more especially after the stroke, but Mom wouldn't go for it. The Girls had given us our house for reasons I hadn't put my finger on yet and paid for my pricey education. Mom said that was more than enough. It wasn't enough for me. I wanted to know *why* they gave us what they gave us, but that information wasn't forthcoming, so I was determined to figure it out on my own.

"Do not go back up that ladder," warned Millicent. "I don't care what Tommy says. For a brilliant man, he hasn't an ounce of sense when it comes to you."

"Dad doesn't care about the skeleton or any of this stuff. He's just hassling me as usual," I said, pouring the hot soapy water down the stairs.

The Girls frowned in unison.

"It's not a big deal," I said. "He wants back on the FBI payroll and he thinks I can help him."

"Surely not?" said Myrtle aghast. "After how they treated your mother?"

"Yep. You know him, all about the business."

"I don't understand it," said Millicent. "He loves your mother so."

I shook my scrub brush off and stretched my back until it popped.

"He loves work, too, and the FBI has cachet that he can't get anywhere else."

Millicent swirled her tea and asked, "Why does he think you can help? You've been rather hostile to them."

"They want a favor. He thinks I should do it." I sat down at their feet like I did when I was little, looking up into their kind faces and feeling safe and warm no matter the temperature.

"Is it about that place in Kansas and that horrible man?" asked Myrtle.

I frowned. "What man?"

She touched her lip. "The one that bit you."

"Oh, him. No, nothing to do with Blankenship, but it is to do with Kansas," I said.

"About your mother's case then? Or one of your other cases?"

I laughed and put my head on Myrtle's warm knee. "No. Nothing to do with me at all."

"Then why are they coming to you?" asked Millicent.

I didn't want to answer. A murdered nun. No good could come from talking about that. "What are you guys doing out here anyway? You didn't just happen by."

"We saw you pass and wanted to talk to you about something," said Myrtle.

"What?" I asked.

"Don't let her change the subject," said Millicent. "Why are they coming to you?"

I yawned and closed my eyes as Myrtle stroked my hair. I might as well have been five. It was wonderful. "It's about Aunt Miriam. But it happened a million years ago. They want her to talk. She won't talk. You know how difficult she is."

The Girls were quiet and I started to get a feeling, a sinking, this-is-about-to-be-a-pain-in-your-ass kind of feeling, but I said nothing. I had enough pain. I was full up on pain.

"A case?" asked Millicent after a few minutes.

"Sort of. It's solved, so nothing dramatic," I said. "You should go home. I think the temperature is dropping and those capes aren't enough."

"Was it a murder case?" Myrtle stopped stroking my hair and she was gripping it so tight it almost hurt.

"Yes," I said, slowly.

"Sister Maggie?"

My stomach flipped and I looked up. Their faces were pale and their cups shook slightly. I gently took the cups and put them on the side table. Millicent looked away and Myrtle put her hand over her mouth.

"Is Sister Margaret Mullanphy Sister Maggie?" I asked.

Myrtle nodded.

"Did you know her?"

"Very well."

"I'm sorry. I didn't know that."

Millicent turned to look at me like she'd never looked at me in my whole life. Her eyes flashed and her soft, cultured voice was hard and accusing, "Tell us what happened."

My voice caught in my throat. "I...I..."

"It's not Mercy's fault, my dear," said Myrtle quickly.

Millicent softened. "Of course not. You're not to blame one bit, but tell us, dear, we need to know."

I don't want to.

"There's not a lot to tell," I said.

"Then it won't take long."

The Girls watched me intently and there was no escape. "Well, they found something to do with Sister Maggie and they wanted to talk to Aunt Miriam about it."

"What did they find?" asked Millicent, her voice strangled. It hurt to hear it.

"A medal."

Their hands pressed to their chests. "Her St. Brigid?"

"Yes, but it might not be hers," I said. "They're not sure."

They took each other's hands. "Why did they come to Miriam if they're not sure?"

I stood up. Millicent was shaky and getting paler by the second. Myrtle wasn't much better. "I'm taking you home. Do you think you can walk?"

Millicent shook her head. "Tell me. I want to know."

"I'll tell you at home, preferably in bed."

"You will?"

"I will. I promise."

Myrtle and I got Millicent out of her chair and down the stairs. We walked down Hawthorne Avenue supporting her as the wind picked up and blew leaves in our faces and a few icy snowflakes for good measure. I wasn't at all sure we would make it. I felt her age and something new. Sorrow. Deep unrelenting sorrow.

CHAPTER SIX

I got Millicent tucked up in bed, wearing her flannel nightgown
with a heating pad and a box of tissues. She was so shaken we
had to take her upstairs in the miniature elevator that their
mother, Florence, had installed during the war for a wounded cousin
who was recuperating with them. Millicent wasn't happy. She felt like
avoiding stairs was a slippery slope and, once you did that, you might
as well give it up, but we convinced her these were extraordinary
circumstances. She wasn't decrepit.

Joy, The Girls' housekeeper, settled Myrtle in the overstuffed wingback chair next to Millicent's bed and covered her in a quilt that my
grandmother made her.

"I'm fine. No need to fuss," she said, glancing at Millicent, who was
dabbing at her eyes with a shaky hand.

"I know," said Joy, "but it was cold out there. You have to be
careful."

"A brisk walk does a body good."

Joy pursed her lips.

"They weren't outside that long," I said.

"I know exactly how long they were outside."

"We're fine," said Millicent, before blowing her nose and having a tear slip down her pale cheek.

Joy shot a harsh look at me. "Come make some of your father's Hot Toddies."

"You know the—"

She raised a brow.

"How about I go make some hot toddies?"

"Good idea," said Joy.

"That would be lovely," said Myrtle and Millicent nodded.

Joy took me by the arm and practically dragged me out of the room, closing the bedroom door firmly behind us. "Stop upsetting them. What are you thinking?"

"I didn't see this coming," I said. "I'm not upsetting them on purpose."

"Millicent looks like she gave blood three times in two hours."

"Well, she didn't."

"That Dr. Bloom called and you didn't answer. Then they went tearing off down the street when that busybody Mrs. Haas told them you were up a tree at your parents' house. They were excited, but you brought them back needing heating pads and whiskey. They are old, Mercy. I know you don't see it. But they are. If they break a hip, it's game over."

"They're not going to break a hip. Their bone density is all good. I watch it."

Joy took a breath and marched me down the long curved staircase. She didn't let go of my arm, like there was a chance I'd go back and start shouting obscenities or something equally crazy.

"I know you keep a good eye on their health, but it's been a lot this last year. Carolina's stroke, Lester, and let's face it, you've gotten in trouble aplenty."

We walked into the massive kitchen and there was the chair that Lester died in, attacked by emissaries of The Klinefeld Group in yet another attempt to find out what Stella Bled Lawrence sent back from the war. It had been a very bad year and very hard to pinpoint what was the lowest point.

I went to over to the enormous stove and put on the kettle. "I don't go looking for trouble."

"I know, but still."

"Still what?"

"The Girls worry about you." Joy got out four mugs, the homeliest ones they had. I'd made them in middle school pottery class. I'm so bad at art it's embarrassing. "They love you like no one else."

I let that hang in the air to see if she would elaborate, but, of course, she didn't. That I was a favorite was well-known in and out of the Bled family. Why wasn't well-known. The Bleds became connected with my mother's family, the Boulards, in 1938 when Amelie and Paul Boulard did something to help The Girls' cousin, Stella Bled Lawrence. That secret was so well-kept The Girls didn't know it and they didn't know what The Klinefeld Group was after either.

But there was more to it. Isn't that always the way? Nothing's simple. The Bleds favored my father's family, too. That started when The Girls met my grandad, Ace Watts, after one of The Klinefeld Group's break-ins. He was a detective assigned to the case and from that moment on, they were oddly attached to us, going so far as to arrange a meeting between my parents. I guess they knew what they were doing, because here I am and, as far as I can tell, it's what they wanted. Me. A combo of Boulard and Watts. The only one.

"Joy?"

"Yes?"

"Am I a Bled?"

She carefully arranged the mugs so that the gnarly handles all faced the same way and said, "Yes, I think so."

"Did The Girls say something?" I asked.

"No. It's just a feeling about you, your father, and Ace."

"Not Mom's side then?"

"I don't think so. Lester always said all you Watts were family."

"Then he knew something?"

"He must've. He was with them long before me. I'd find the three of them curled up looking at the scrapbooks. The family tree. I heard your name, more than once. Something was going on," said Joy.

"Why don't they just tell us?"

"I'm sure they've got their reasons and they are sensible ladies. Don't force the issue."

"As if I could make them tell me." I rolled my eyes.

She laughed and got out a hefty bottle of good Irish whiskey and a jar of loose tea. "Now you tell me what's upset them."

"How about you tell me what Dr. Bloom wanted?"

"I can't, because I don't know." She measured the tea into the strainer and then faced me. "Tell me what happened. Millicent has had a blow and she's no snowflake."

I poured the boiling water into the tea pot and reluctantly told her about Aunt Miriam and Sister Maggie's medal. She listened without interrupting, but her face got more and more grave.

"Did you know about this?" I asked.

"I knew about her death, the murder, I mean," said Joy, rolling one of my mugs between her palms.

"How? They never mentioned her to me and the only pictures of nuns that I've seen are those cousins, Lidija and Paloma."

"My mother was housekeeper before me. She was a maid with the family when it happened," said Joy.

"I totally forgot that."

"My family has been with the Bleds for three generations."

I measured out a jigger of whiskey into each mug and started cutting up a lemon. "So you know everything."

"I wouldn't say that, but I know what my mother said about Sister Maggie. She told me to never ever bring it up. To say it's an open wound is an understatement."

"No kidding. I wish somebody had told me."

Joy shrugged. "It was so long ago. I didn't think it would be a problem. Do you really think it's Sister Maggie's medal?"

I nodded. "I do. Aunt Miriam would've said if it wasn't, and that would've been the end of it."

"I agree."

"Do you think The Girls can identify it?"

"For goodness sake, don't ask them to look at that. It was on her when she died, I don't think they can take it," said Joy in a rush.

"How do they know her? What's the deal?"

It's amazing how you can know someone your whole life and still be in the dark on the most important things. In my case, I do mean my whole life. The Girls attended my birth. My dad didn't cut the cord. They did. Dad was out on a case and Mom gave birth without him, but The Girls were there. They didn't miss a second of me, but I didn't know the story of them, not all of it, not even close.

The Girls were very attached to Margaret (Maggie) Mullanphy. There was some kind of family connection that Joy wasn't sure about, but she did know that they knew her from childhood. There were pictures of the three of them in the atriums, playing hide and seek and having tea parties. The connection was never lost, even though Maggie went to Catholic school while The Girls were educated at home. Maggie and Millicent were especially close. Best friends, Joy's mother had said and they did everything together, but Maggie wasn't the only one close to Millicent. Maggie had an older brother, Patrick. Joy went to the library and found a small scrapbook that I'd never seen before. It wasn't like the big ones, handmade with fine leather covers. The Girls had those scrapbooks. This one was small and handmade, but not by a professional. It had wood covers and the initial "P" carved into the front. Inside were pictures of Millicent and a handsome young man at dances, having ice cream, reading, doing all the things that kids do. There were ticket stubs pasted in the pages and flowers, carefully dried and preserved. The last picture was of Patrick sitting in the back garden of the mansion among the roses on a lounge with blankets up to his chin. Millicent knelt beside him with her face pressed against his hand. He was smiling but clearly very sick.

"So he died," I said.

"He did," said Joy. "Lymphoma, I think."

"Looks about twenty."

"Sounds right. I believe Millicent was seventeen. My mother said she was devastated. The family thought she might hurt herself. Maggie and Myrtle were the only people she could bear to be with. Florence didn't know what to do and in desperation, she sent The Girls and Maggie to Europe so they wouldn't have to be reminded every day. They were gone a year."

"It must've worked," I said.

"As well as anything does. They came back and The Girls married their husbands. Myrtle had Lawton and Maggie became a nun. But I don't think Millicent really got over it."

"How come?"

"He died on May fifteenth in your mother's bedroom. The Girls are never in the house on that day. Didn't you ever notice?"

I thought about it. Maybe. I wasn't sure. They traveled a lot, particularly when they were younger. "I guess so."

"It's not a guess, Mercy. It's a fact. They go to Europe or New York. Sometimes it's just out to Prie Dieu, but they are *never* in this house on that day. Lester usually went with them. He said Millicent would stay in bed and refuse to see anyone, but the next day she'd come out like nothing happened."

"I remember times when she'd stay in her room. Myrtle said she was sick or was tired. I didn't think anything of it."

"No reason you should," said Joy. "Please don't bring up Patrick and if you can stay off Maggie, that would be good."

"I don't think they're going to let it go." I finished the toddy with a dash of bitters and put the mugs on a tray.

Joy sighed. "I know. But her murder is all wrapped up with Patrick. My mother said they were incredibly close until the day she died and they went into mourning for a year."

"I can see that." I picked up the tray, but Joy put a hand on my arm.

"Mercy, they stopped going to church for that year."

I nearly dropped the tray. "Are you serious?"

"Dead serious."

"But they always go. They're hard core about it. When we traveled, no matter where we were, they had to attend mass. We'd drive hours, if we had to. I always tried to get out of it, but that wasn't happening."

"I know. My mother said they were angry about something to do with the church, but they didn't discuss it with her."

"They obviously got over it," I said.

"People do. When Lawton's father died, they needed their faith. The church came with it."

"I'll try to stay away from the subject."

"Please do. They're older than they seem and they've had so many sorrows. It won't help to remember them," said Joy.

I did my best. I really did, but some sorrows don't grow old like people do.

Millicent smiled at me when I came in with the tray. "I'm sorry, dear. Just a foolish old lady. I shouldn't have alarmed you."

"There's nothing foolish about it," I said, putting the tray on the foot of the bed. "Now what's this about Dr. Bloom calling?"

The Girls looked like they might object, but they let me lead them away from Sister Maggie's medal and I was seriously relieved.

"Oh, yes that," said Myrtle, blowing on her toddy. "He had some information and you won't answer your phone."

"Yeah, well, it's been a rough week." I sipped my toddy. I should've doubled up on whiskey.

"Surely people don't really think you smell," said Millicent.

"They surely do or, at least, they like thinking I do, which is basically the same thing," I said. "What did Dr. Bloom say?"

Myrtle pointed at Josiah's scrapbook on Millicent's dresser. "Can you get that, dear? Wait until you hear. It's very exciting."

I got Josiah's book, holding it tight to my chest before I laid it on Millicent's lap and cuddled up next to her. I'd always thought Stella's book was the key to everything, but a few weeks before I'd had a brainstorm. We'd been trying to figure out who our family lawyer, Big Steve's, mother was. Constanza Stern was brought back to the US from Switzerland by Aleksej Bled after she survived an Auschwitz satellite camp. We knew she had something to do with Stella and The Klinefeld Group. All we'd discovered so far was that Constanza Stern was an alias and that most likely she wasn't the real owner of the objects she sold in 1947, but the things she kept were a clue. Chuck found out that her locket and pin were from Prague and that was the first time Czechoslovakia had come up in relation to Constanza.

Big Steve had long given up on finding out about his mother, but he had a couple of pictures of her. Bad pictures. Constanza had a serious aversion to being photographed, that was the reason we thought she was probably a spy with Stella or maybe in the resistance. When I looked at those pictures, something sparked in me. It took a while to figure it out, but I knew I'd seen that face before.

Millicent opened Josiah's book and turned to the critical page and there she was. Constanza Stern in black and white, standing with Josiah Bled and Stella in front of an amazing staircase in an impressive mansion, possibly a palace. Josiah was wearing a uniform so it was definitely during the war and it was the only picture of Constanza where she was facing the camera. That picture revealed her in more ways than she could ever have imagined in the moment. She was young. We'd guessed that the picture was taken in 1942. She was supposed to be seventeen at the end of the war. That would've made her fourteen in the picture, but she appeared considerably younger than that. I'd have guessed eleven. She had no breasts to speak of, was exceedingly thin and bruised with deep, dark grooves under her intense, angry eyes and masses of thick, dark hair. She stood stiff in an ill-fitting dress that might've been part of a servant's uniform between the smiling Josiah, looking jaunty in his uniform and Stella, who, while thin and tired, was beaming, looking past the camera at someone off to the left.

Millicent and I couldn't stop gazing at her face. It was that kind of face, pretty, striking in its angles, but it was the eyes that drew you to her. Constanza had been places and they were bad.

"Do we know who she is?" I asked, still looking at those eyes.

"No," said Myrtle, smiling. "But we know where she is."

I looked up. "Really? Where?"

"Bickford House in England."

"Bickford," I said. "Never heard of it."

The Girls chuckled. "You certainly have."

"Um...what?"

"You've been." Myrtle picked up a manila folder and tossed it on the bed. "Take a look."

I opened the folder and it was creepy. I got a chill. I mean it, an actual chill. The photo inside was in color, but it was eerily similar to the Constanza photo. I was standing between Millicent and Myrtle, about four years old and mad as hell. My eyes were as angry as

Constanza's and The Girls were as happy as Josiah and Stella. Millicent was even looking off to the left.

"We were there," I said. "I can't believe it."

"I knew I recognized that staircase," said Millicent. "But I couldn't place it."

"Why were we there? Was it about some pieces from the Bled Collection? Stella's pieces?"

Stella had spent a good deal of energy smuggling property and people out of the Third Reich. The pieces she saved ended up with Florence, The Girls' mother, for safekeeping until the owners could come and claim them. Most didn't survive. The Girls had taken over the search for survivors and relatives after Florence passed away. It was a consuming passion and I had begun to suspect a duty that I would inherit.

"No," said Myrtle. "We were actually going through a local archive that included children from the *Kindertransports* and were invited to dinner by the earl when he heard we were there."

"It was an amazing house," said Millicent.

"House?" I asked.

They laughed.

"So did you find what you were looking for?"

"We did. Four children belonging to...oh, I can't remember the family name off the top of my head, but their property was returned," said Myrtle.

"Did the earl help you with that?" I asked.

"No, it was simply a dinner," said Millicent. "That happened a lot. We were often invited to dinner, fetes, even State occasions because of the brewery."

That was very true. I'd sat through dozens of dinners with boring aristocrats, bribed into goodness with the promise of chocolates and pony rides.

"But didn't he know that his family knew Josiah and Stella?" I asked.

"We don't know that they did. Perhaps they were there the same way we were. The name has always been a key to most gates."

My gaze went back to Constanza and then to Stella. "Do you think Stella had anything to do with the *Kindertransports?*"

The Girls' eyes widened.

"It's not mentioned in her book and I never heard anything to that effect," said Millicent. "Have you, Myrtle?"

"No, not a peep. What are you thinking, Mercy?"

"Constanza is certainly young enough to have been included in the rescue operation," I said.

"The earl's family were guarantors for the transports," said Millicent.

Myrtle shook her head. "No, I don't think so. 1942 is too late."

She explained that the *Kindertransports*, brainchild of Norbert Wollheim, took place from 1938 after the Kristallnacht until 1940. Children were allowed to emigrate to Britain as long as someone was willing to pay for their upkeep. They were supposed to go home after the war. No one imagined that most of the Jewish population would be wiped out and there would be no families to return to.

"We could be guessing the date wrong," I said.

"Perhaps, but Josiah's uniform indicates it's later. He wasn't stationed in England until '42."

"Oh," I said disappointed.

Millicent patted my hand. "You could be right and Constanza could've been on a transport."

"Dr. Bloom gave us a number for us to call, but we didn't want to call without you," said Myrtle.

Dr. Bloom was an Oxford historian, who, through his research on resistance fighters during WWII, accidentally pointed out my great grandparents, Agatha and Daniel, to The Klinefeld Group. Agatha and Daniel were murdered in a plane crash on their way to St. Louis because they knew or had something that The Klinefeld Group wanted.

"A number?" I asked.

"For an architectural historian, Dr. Wilfred Wallingford. He was the one who recognized the staircase. Dr. Bloom says he's lovely and would be happy to talk to us about Bickford House. The number's in the folder."

I took a slip of paper with an international number written on it. "Should we give Wilfred a ring?"

"Let's," said Myrtle and she gave me her phone.

I dialed and the most Scottish-sounding dude on the planet answered. I wasn't even sure he was speaking English for a second.

"Dr. Wallingford?" I asked.

There was a garble of something that didn't sound like a no.

"Um...this is Mercy Watts. I'm with Myrtle and Millicent Bled. Dr. Calvin Bloom said we could call you about Bickford House."

Dr. Wallingford's accent got a whole lot easier to understand once he realized he was talking to Americans. "Yes. Yes. Of course. I am happy to help you in any way I can."

"Thank you. Can I put you on speakerphone so everyone can hear you?"

"Certainly."

I put him on speakerphone and The Girls expressed their gratitude and amazement at his recognizing Bickford House. They explained that they'd been there and hadn't. He laughed and said that he didn't recognize it at first either. He had to dig through some archives on staircases before he found it. He'd never been to Bickford himself.

"What do you know about the family?" I asked.

"I'm not an expert, but then no one is. The family is notoriously private and it's a private house, not part of the National Trust and not open for tours."

"I seem to remember the family and the earl, in particular, as very friendly," said Millicent.

"Oh, they are. Great favorites among the local population, but they have no interest in being the object of lurid fascination."

"I can understand that," I said.

Dr. Wallingford chuckled. "I imagine you can."

"You've examined the picture?" asked Myrtle.

"I have and I understand you have an interest in the young girl," he said. "I can tell you that she isn't a member of the family or a servant. She *is* wearing a servant's dress. It's hard to recognize because she isn't wearing the apron."

"How do you know she isn't a servant?"

"First of all, she's posing with two Bleds, which would be highly unusual. And second, the dress doesn't fit correctly. There are a few pictures of the Bickford servants floating around on the internet. A group photo was taken every year since 1860 and copies were given to senior servants as a gift. The uniforms fit perfectly and I couldn't find this girl in any of the photos I viewed."

"Perhaps she was there only a little while," said Millicent.

"I very seriously doubt that. Bickford is unusual. Would you like me to explain?"

"Please do."

Dr. Wallingford did explain, like the university professor he was, quick, concise, and very enthusiastic. Bickford was a grand estate of an extremely wealthy family that married well and for love. They didn't fall victim to the financial crises in the 1880s or after the First World War like other great families. As a result, they paid their servants extremely well and were unusual in their permissiveness. At a time that other wealthy families required servants to devote their whole lives to their masters, the Bickfords' servants often married and had children. The estate had family apartments in the servants' quarters and houses out on the estate for servants' use, if they had several children. As a result, servants didn't leave to marry and their children tended to stay. There were servants at Bickford currently that could trace their lineage back to the building of Bickford. That was over four hundred years.

"You like them," I said.

"I do. I think few would find the family disagreeable. They're generous and charitable, but I'm sorry to say that girl is not one of them."

"What about the *Kindertransports*?" I asked.

"I wondered if you'd ask me about that," Dr. Wallingford said, happily. "The family was extremely generous with donations. I don't have the exact number of children they helped get out of Germany and the Reich, but I can find out. It would be several hundred, I'm sure."

The Girls exchanged a look, a look I'd seen before. They smelled a lead that might bring them to more families in the Stella Collection.

"Can you get those names for us?" asked Millicent. "Our search wasn't completely satisfying."

"I have a friend. She's an expert on the *Kindertransport* children. Her grandmother was one of them."

"We will be happy to pay for her time and yours, naturally," said Myrtle.

"That is unnecessary, but I appreciate the offer," he said. "Do you have any other questions?"

"I don't think so," said Millicent before taking a huge glug of toddy.

"I don't," said Myrtle.

"Then I will let you go. Please feel free to call me at any time."

"Hold on," I said.

"Yes?"

"Has Bickford House had any problems?"

The Girls smiled at me approvingly and I gave them a grin in return.

"Like what?" asked Dr. Wallingford

"Robberies?" I asked.

"Why in the world would you ask that? I thought this was research, family research."

"It is, but someone is trying to get information about Stella Bled Lawrence and we've been broken into."

He paused and then shuffled through some papers. "That's interesting. What happened?"

"The Bled Mansion has been broken into several times over the years. The last time, the chauffeur was murdered, and there have been attempts on my parents' house."

"I see, but I don't know how those incidents could be related to Bickford. Except for the picture, there appears to be no connection between the families. The Bickfords don't have any interest in brewing either socially or commercially."

"But have they been robbed or just broken into?" I asked.

"Well, yes. Bickford has been broken into a couple of times that I know of."

"When?"

"Years ago," he said. "That can't be related to the murder of your chauffeur."

Millicent spoke up. "I'm afraid it can, Dr. Wallingford. There's history that is difficult to explain."

"Does it have to do with the Jewish artwork in the Bled Collection?"

"It's related," said Myrtle. "When were the Bickford break-ins?"

"Bear with me, ladies," said Dr. Wallingford as he typed madly. "Oh, yes, here it is, but I don't believe this will help you."

"What is it?"

"In 1939, Bickford House's butler Mr. Smith reported a burglary in the library. This is too early, before the war was declared on Germany."

"What did they take?" asked Millicent, breathless with excitement.

"A few things. Nothing of real value. Books, a silver letter opener, a small statue." He paused for a moment. "Now this is odd. All the stolen items were recovered. They were found in a dustbin at a pub in the village."

The Girls and I shared knowing glances.

"Sounds like the stuff they took was just a cover for what they were really doing," I said.

"I would have to say so," he said. "And this will interest you."

"Yes?" asked Myrtle, leaning forward and splashing toddy on her lap.

"A young maid got clubbed with the statue. At least that's what's in the report."

I pictured Lester in his chair, dying for no reason. From the looks on The Girls' faces they did, too.

"Did she survive?" I asked.

"I assume so. It doesn't say she didn't. There's no mention of any arrest or suspects. I found a newspaper clipping. It doesn't mention murder, but it was printed the morning after. She may have died of her injuries later."

"Any other robberies?"

"Looks like 1947. Mr. Smith reported that he caught someone posing as a butcher's delivery boy in the library. He was searching the desk. Nothing was taken and the man got away. That's it. I don't see anything else."

"Thank you very much, Dr. Wallingford," said Millicent. "You've been quite helpful."

We said our goodbyes and promised to keep in touch. Like all good historians, Dr. Wallingford knew people and he was happy to make introductions to his counterparts in other countries. He was clearly curious about Bickford House and I could practically hear the wheels turning. Maybe we could get him in. His focus was Elizabethan architecture and not to be allowed in such a stunning example pained him. I'd do it, if I could, but there wasn't any reason to think that very private family would let me in, much less him. I doubted anyone remembered we were once invited and it's not like I could count on being invited because I was connected to The Girls.

After we hung up, Millicent got shaky again and started eyeing me. Myrtle said she ought to take a nap. She wasn't taking a nap. No way. Not going to happen.

As a delaying tactic, I asked to use her laptop. She nodded, growing paler. Joy came in and tried the nap thing, too. The idea barely got acknowledged.

I quickly opened the laptop and Joy asked with a warning in her voice, "What are you looking for?"

"Bickford House," I said and the ladies all relaxed.

"That estate in England?" asked Joy. "What for?"

"Stella was there with Josiah and Big Steve's mother."

"You don't say? That's interesting. I hear it's a fabulous house."

Myrtle sat up. "How do you know it? We've been there with Mercy when she was little and I barely remember the visit."

"I heard about it on my tour of great country estates last year," said Joy.

"But you didn't see it?" asked Millicent. "We just heard from Dr. Wallingford that it's not open for visitors."

"It's not. It was part of the tour of Hardwick House. They had a whole display to compare the buildings and the ladies who built them."

Millicent's laptop booted up and I typed in Bickford House. It was on Wikipedia, of course. There were a few other sites that named it as a fine example of Elizabethan architecture and listed as a Grade 1 stately home and historical site. I saw very little on the family. The current earl was the son of the earl Millicent and Myrtle liked so much. He was married and ran some sort of multinational company.

"Anything good?" asked Joy.

"Not really."

I searched back through the listed earls and they were as Dr. Wallingford described them, rich and private. "Here's the earl during the war. George. Married to Agatha. Four sons. He was an ambassador."

"That's political," said Millicent. "Perhaps that's how he knew Stella and Josiah. The family was very active in trying to change our emigration policies to let the Jews in. The earl said that when we were talking about the *Kindertransports*, I think."

I looked up grinning. "He resigned in November 1938."

"That can't be a coincidence," said Myrtle.

"I agree. You should investigate that thoroughly." Joy gathered our mugs and, since we were well off the subject of Sister Maggie, she said she was going to make us a snack and left.

I breathed a sigh of relief. I didn't need her beady eyes on me. "I'll tell Spidermonkey when he comes back from vacation. His wife wants him to concentrate on family for once and not get distracted by working."

Spidermonkey was a super hacker and Uncle Morty's number one rival in the world of internet snoops. So far, I'd been able to hide what I was doing from Morty, but it couldn't last. Neither he nor my dad knew Chuck and I were investigating The Klinefeld Group and by extension my dad's involvement with the Bleds, namely Josiah Bled's mysterious disappearance before I was born.

"He'll get everything there is to know," said Millicent. "Show me the house. It was winter when we were there and evening. I didn't get a good look."

Myrtle chuckled. "It was enormous. I remember that."

Bickford House was enormous, more like a palace or a Loire Valley chateau. Made of dark stone, Bickford had everything. Turrets, giant windows, gables, and a beautiful lake.

Millicent pointed at the steps. "We stood out there, taking in the view."

"You were so angry," said Myrtle.

"Me?" I asked. "Why?"

"The countess had taken us on a tour of the house and you were enamored of the turrets. Oh, did you kick up a fuss."

"About turrets? Weird."

Millicent put an arm around me. "Don't you remember at all? There was a nursery in one with a collection of toys and horses like you've never seen. We had to peel you off a large carousel horse to finish the tour."

Myrtle stood up and picked up the photo of us. "That's why you look so angry. We paid for taking you off that horse in spades. You were absolutely in love."

"I was a serious pain in the butt," I said.

"You were passionate and four." Millicent kissed my cheek.

I zoomed in on the house. "Which turret?"

The Girls went back and forth about right or left. Main staircase or another one. I stopped listening and zoomed in further, looking closely at the top of the house. A coincidence? Could be. No. No. It couldn't.

I gave Millicent her laptop and raced out of her bedroom and over to mine where Chuck and I had set up a kind of war room with all our investigation up on corkboards. I plucked a notecard off the corkboard with all the names and carried it back to The Girls.

"What is it?" asked Millicent.

I came over and pointed at the screen. "Check out that stonework."

Millicent and Myrtle peered at the screen.

"Initials," said Myrtle. "I remember that. The first countess built the house and put her initials on top so everyone would know whose house it was."

"CMB," I said.

"Yes," said Millicent. "She was named..."

"Cecily," said Myrtle in triumph.

"That's right, but why does that matter?"

I turned the card around. CMB was printed in bold letters. "We thought this was a person."

"It's a place," said The Girls in unison.

I got The Girls working on the CMB references in Stella's book and they were happy to do it. Chuck and I had noted that it was used, but we hadn't gotten as far as tracking it. Now it looked like Stella was at Bickford House repeatedly during the war. The question was why. What was the connection and how did Constanza Stern fit in?

Joy bustled around with delicate finger sandwiches of Parma ham and gruyere, insisting that The Girls eat and drink buckets of tea. She gave me a wink when I handed over a clipboard and said I had to go. Happily, The Girls didn't object and I slipped out easily.

Because I was all about making mistakes that day, I made another one. I stopped on the curve of the stairs to look at a photo of Stella, radiant on her wedding day. She was so young and unaware of what was coming and who she would become. Even if The Klinefeld Group disintegrated, I had to know what happened in November 1938 and why it kept going. We couldn't give them what they wanted.

"Mercy." Myrtle leaned over the stair rail and crooked a finger at me.

Son of a bitch.

"I have to go," I said, poised to sprint away.

"Just a moment."

I trudged back up, cursing my stupidity. The Girls could get out of beds and chairs. Out of sight was not out of mind. I knew that.

"Thank you for distracting Millicent," said Myrtle.

"You're welcome. Got to go."

She grabbed my arm. "Is this thing with Miriam...is it going to be a case?"

"I don't know," I said.

She looked at me and took my hands. I couldn't lie to her. My only hope was that she wouldn't ask any more questions. I kissed her cheek. "I really have to go."

"She was our oldest friend. We knew her...I don't remember not knowing her."

"Joy told me."

"Where did they find her St. Brigid?" she asked, so quietly I almost couldn't hear her.

"Myrtle, it might not be her medal," I said.

"What did Miriam say?"

"Nothing. That's why they came to me."

She put her hand to her mouth and went back to Millicent's room without another word.

I'm knocking it out of the park today.

CHAPTER SEVEN

I walked back to my apartment bone tired, but, on the upside, I only got called "Smelly skank" once. My record was five times in three minutes. I was going to beat that no question. When I got to my apartment building, I had a choice to make. Choices suck when it comes to me. They're all bad and they were that day, too. Coming down the street was a gardening service truck with three dudes stuffed into the cab. In my experience, lawn care guys have definite opinions on me, combined with excellent lungs and a complete lack of give-a-crap. There would be yelling. I could beat the record right then. Or I could dart into the alley and go around to the parking lot entrance where the construction guys were. My only hope was that they were still on lunch.

I decided to chance it and went into the alley. Wrong choice. So wrong I couldn't get any wronger. I don't think that's a word, but it should be, just for me.

"There you are." Agent Gordon leaned on the back door of my building, wearing standard issue sunglasses and a Bluetooth in his ear. "I got her. See if you can get the nun alone."

"Did you do Rock, Paper, Scissors?" I asked.

"Huh?"

"How did Gansa get Sister Miriam?"

He smiled and a tiny dimple formed on his cheek. It was almost charming, but I hated him, so no. "We cut cards."

"Good luck to him. She's not going to do it."

"You tried?"

"I did and it's not happening. I, on the other hand, have to go to a gyno appointment with her on Thursday. Thanks. You're awesome."

"Nuns go to the gynecologist?" he asked.

"They're women."

He frowned. I guess that was debatable in his opinion.

"Hey, Skanky whore!" yelled a voice from above. Hint: it was not God.

"What the?" Gordon whipped off his sunglasses and squinted up.

"Ignore it," I said. "And get out of my way."

"Why don't you come up here and smell me up?" yelled an additional voice.

A barrage of sexual innuendos—if you want to make it sound fancy, which it wasn't—and scent-related insults rained down on me. Gordon's mouth fell open and for the first time he wasn't bland. He was shocked.

"I guess they're not at lunch," I said. "I should've known."

"Is this...do they..."

"Yep. Every chance they get." I took a breath that I hoped would pass for dignity and attempted to push him out of the way.

"This is ridiculous."

"I know."

Gordon took me by the shoulders. "This can't go on."

"And yet, here we are."

"Stop touching my smelly slut, you bland motherfucker!"

"I'm going to take care of this," said Gordon. "You're with us and this is not happening."

I got teary-eyed. I swear to God, I did. I knew he couldn't do anything, but it was nice all the same.

Gordon put me inside and flashed his badge at the building, which only got him spit at and I think there was some urine involved. He knocked and I let him in the building, which I wouldn't normally do, but he was trying to help me, for once.

He used his scarf to wipe off his face and Bluetooth before taking out his phone. "Gansa, I need to pull the permits on the building behind Mercy's."

"Can you do that?" I asked.

"You're on the No Fly List, what do you think?"

"I think I'm starting to like you."

He gave Gansa the address and a rundown on what was happening. I gathered that Gansa was pissed. I showed Gordon to the front and he left without asking any more favors, which was likely to get him one. That's how I roll.

Before going all the way up to my floor, I took a good sniff. No lingering kielbasa. But there was something else. Something good. I jogged up and burst into my apartment, expecting to find Aaron, cooking up a storm and being weird. He was. That was the good news. The bad news was Uncle Morty was still there and by Uncle Morty, I mean all of him.

"What the heck is happening?" I said as Aaron put a mug of luscious hot chocolate in my hand.

"What'd ya mean?" Uncle Morty had blubbed onto my sofa and set up shop.

I waved my cast at him. "This. Why are you here with all these laptops?"

"I'm staying."

"For what?"

"To make sure you stay on friggin' task," he growled.

I sipped the hot chocolate. Ah, yes. That was what I needed. Chocolate, creme de menthe and plenty of whipped cream. Aaron bobbed up and down in front of me and I impulsively gave him a hug that he didn't acknowledge in the slightest.

"It's good. Exactly what I needed. You threw away that sausage, right?"

"Yeah, he did," bellowed Uncle Morty. "Perfectly good sausage."

"Perfectly gross."

"You know what he's making? Do you?"

I sniffed and felt my body relax. My new favorite. "Moussaka?"

"Yeah, he is." Morty wiped his eyes. "Like a knife in my gut. Nikki's moussaka. And I've been his dungeon master for twenty years. No loyalty."

"You hungry?" asked Aaron.

I didn't get the word "yes" out and he was running into the kitchen to finish up Nikki's moussaka and her sliced zucchini that had the thinnest batter on it that you've ever seen. I don't know why it was incredibly delicious. It's zucchini, not bacon.

I squished onto the sofa next to Uncle Morty and took a peek at one of his laptops. "Oh, my God. Nikki sent you a picture. That's a good sign. She looks fantastic."

Uncle Morty sorta collapsed down into himself and his lower lip poked out.

"What?" I looked closer. Nikki did look great. She was on the beach with her sister and a hot guy wearing cutoffs and an electric smile. Nikki managed to get a tan in November, wore zero makeup and looked better than ever.

"You see that?" he asked.

"I see it. It's a great picture."

"She's with that guy."

I laughed and he glared at me. "She's not with him. They're standing there. He's probably a waiter or a cousin."

"I've seen every cousin. Nikki has pictures. He's not a cousin."

"He's not her date. He's half her age, less than half her age."

"She's happy."

There was no good answer to that one.

"I gotta get over there. Now. Pronto," said Uncle Morty.

I looked him over. He didn't stink, but it was a low point. Nose hairs. Ear hairs. Hadn't shaved in three days. If Uncle Morty thought he could stop the Greek god by standing next to him, freaking forget it.

"Go," I said. "Nobody's stopping you."

He looked up, suddenly sharp-eyed. "You didn't fix it."

"You thought I got off the No Fly List today? Dude, come on." I stood up and kicked off Mr. Cervantes' shoes. "I'm taking a shower. I have got to wash off this day. Expect me back in an hour or two."

"Hell, no," yelled Uncle Morty and I froze. He wasn't typically a yeller. Bellowing, crabbing, and the occasional snarl were as far as he went.

"Are you saying I can't take a shower in my own house?" I asked as Aaron came out and stood beside me, spatula in hand. I know that doesn't sound like support, but the little guy was supporting me. He had a spatula and the will to use it.

Uncle Morty saw it, too. He took a breath and said, "No, I ain't. You can do what you want."

"Glad to hear it. And on that note." I turned to go for the bathroom, but Aaron grabbed my arm. He didn't say anything, naturally, or even look at me, but I knew he wanted me to listen. So I turned back around and looked at a once-again deflated Uncle Morty. "Let's hear it."

He grumbled.

"I'm not standing here all day, Aaron or no Aaron."

"You gotta get off that list."

"Yeah."

"Now. ASAP."

I crossed my arms. "You don't need me for Greece. Just go. Win her back. Sweep her off her feet."

He mumbled something that I could barely catch a word of. Something about being alone and overseas.

"I don't know what you're saying."

He flushed and balled up his hands. "I don't go alone."

"Er...what?"

"I don't fly alone. I ain't good at travel and overseas...I'm not good with people. Nikki won't talk to me. You got to go and get her to talk to me."

I glanced at Aaron, who was staring somewhere to the left of Uncle Morty's head. Not helpful. He probably heard though. "What do you think?"

"Feta ice cream," he said. "You like feta ice cream?"

"What the—no. We're talking about me going to Greece, not food."

"I'm making feta ice cream." Aaron almost looked at me. Actually, he did, if you counted my ear. "You like ice cream."

"Focus, Aaron. Greece."

The little weirdo dashed back into the kitchen and started rummaging around through cabinets.

"You can't make ice cream," I said. "I don't have an ice cream maker."

Then he came out of the kitchen and set a large silver rectangle on the breakfast bar.

"What the hell is that?"

"Ice cream maker."

Dammit, Chuck!

"Where was it?" I asked.

"Under the sink."

"I thought that was another coffee maker." That's a testimony to how many coffee makers I had. Five at last count. I'd completely given up on stopping my nutty boyfriend from buying stuff I didn't want.

"No." Aaron plugged the thing in and got a bunch of cheerful beeps in response.

"I hope that didn't come from a bloody crime scene," I said.

He shrugged. Not a good sign.

"You're not helping."

The little weirdo didn't care. There was bizarre ice cream to be made.

"Alrighty then." I turned back to Uncle Morty, who was waiting with patience. That alone was enough to give me pause. "What?"

"I want you to go. What do I gotta do?" he asked.

"For starters, say you *need* me to go."

"Don't make no difference."

"You're a writer. Words mean stuff. You *need* my help. That means it's not optional."

He gritted his teeth and muttered, "Yeah. I need you."

"Okay. Good," I said. "We've got a problem then, because those rookies want something from me that I can't give them."

Uncle Morty perked up and his hands went to his keyboard, ready for action. "We can beat those rookies at every fucking game there is."

"Maybe, but they want information. I can't get it."

"Bet I can."

"Nope."

He got smug, and, for good reason, Uncle Morty could get information. It was his thing, not just a side business. He did it for the challenge, to win against anyone that dared to imply he couldn't. It was disturbing how much info he could get. "What do we need?"

"You can't get this. It's not on the internet," I said.

"Every God damn thing is on the internet."

"Not this. It's somewhere else. Totally inaccessible and the defenses can't be breached by any known method."

"Where is it?" he asked.

"Aunt Miriam's brain."

His mouth dropped open. So satisfying.

I took my sweet time, boiling myself into lobster condition. There's nothing like a burning hot shower when you want to relax and avoid unpleasantness. Eventually you have to come out, but it's great while it lasts.

When I stepped out into the thick haze I'd created, I nearly squashed Skanky, who was barfing up an oddly blue hairball on the bathmat.

"What the crap!"

He continued his barfing and Uncle Morty banged on the door. "Are you done yet? Ya used up all the water in Michigan."

That's random.

"We're in Missouri."

"You know what I mean."

Not really.

"I'm done."

"Well, get your butt out here. We got work to do."

"Swell."

"Damn right."

I did not hurry. I buffed myself dry, did a full-body lotion, tweezed my eyebrows, and checked my rear for cellulite. No comment on the last one. Then I cleaned up Skanky's hairball, which made him angry. He attacked my hand multiple times. That meant he was planning on eating it. Gross. And bad for him, more than usual even. He'd eaten a blue crayon. Where in the world my indoor cat found a blue crayon will forever remain a mystery as would why he ate it.

"Come on, Skanky." I picked up my furball and took him into the bedroom, plopping him on the bed, where he gagged a few times before settling down to purr. "There's something seriously wrong with you."

Purr.

"You eat cat food. That's what you eat. Period. End of discussion."

He yawned and proceeded to clean his rear. Message not received.

"Are you done?" Uncle Morty pounded on my bedroom door.

"I told you I was," I said.

"You're still in there."

"I'm getting dressed."

"It's taking too long."

I pointed out that it famously took Nikki an hour to get dressed and that didn't include hair and makeup. Unfortunately, that didn't drive him away or make him reconsider his quest.

"God, I miss her," he said. "Put on some of them ugly yoga pants chicks dig and get out here."

I didn't do as I was told. I put on sweats, Chuck's from high school, the kind with cuffs at the bottom that made my butt look humongous. They were so comfortable in their ugliness. To top it off, I put on a Seaweed face mask from LUSH.

"Holy crap," said Uncle Morty. "I didn't want *you* to be ugly."

"Thanks, I guess." I settled into the sofa, displacing a laptop.

"Hey. I need that."

"You've got two other ones." I crisscrossed my legs and began filing my nails. "So did you hack your way into Aunt Miriam's brain?"

He sat down next to me and gulped down half a beer. Not a good sign.

"I take it you didn't," I said.

"This is crap."

"Agreed."

"You wanna hear what I got or not?" he asked.

I raised a shoulder. "Eh."

"You're a pain in my ass."

"And yet..."

Uncle Morty got down to business. He really did "need" me to go to Greece with him. There wasn't a single mention of money. That was a first, but I wasn't holding my breath. If there was a way to monetize my situation, he'd find it. What he *didn't* find was a whole lot of information. I got about the same amount from the rookies.

"That's it?" I asked, astonished.

"Yeah." He scratched at his five o'clock shadow so hard I thought he'd get bloody. "Something stinks and I don't mean maybe. Check out this article."

I read through an article on the murder in the Post-Dispatch written three days after Sister Maggie's body was discovered in the woods outside of St. Sebastian. If you weren't in the know, you might think her death was an accident. It was that light on details. No cause of death. No particulars at all. It did cover her and how wonderful she was, but even that was generalized. She was a registered nurse, worked at St. Vincent's, many good works with orphans and the mentally ill, etc. No mention of her family or friends. Buried at the bottom was a short statement that her death was under investigation, but I was willing to bet the average reader wasn't going to make it that far.

"There must be other articles," I said.

He brought up another one from a week after. It announced her funeral and which church officials and local dignitaries would be attending. Aunt Miriam wasn't mentioned. That didn't surprise me. But The Girls weren't mentioned either. Bled connections were big news. Any reporter would want to include that. *Beloved Bled family friend murdered* or *Intriguing mystery behind Bled family friend's murder.* That should've happened. Sensationalism didn't start with the twenty-four-hour news cycle.

"That's it? What about St. Seb?" I asked. "They must have a newspaper."

"Yeah. The Saint Sebastian Sentinel."

"So?"

"Nothing digital before thirty years ago."

"They have to have a record of the papers they put out."

"They do. Microfiche."

I'd heard the word, but I didn't really know what it was. Slides. God, I hoped not. "Microfiche? You can't access it from here?"

"Hell, no. You got to go down to the paper and look. Manually."

"Oh my God."

He chuckled and then grimaced. "It was the dark ages."

"So this is the only reporting? Two articles?"

"Pretty much."

"Who investigated it?" I asked.

"Not St. Louis. I'm guessing it stayed with St. Seb."

"And they've got no files you can access?"

Uncle Morty put his nose in the air. "I can access everything they got. They ain't got shit. This is fifty years ago."

I looked back through the Post-Dispatch articles in case I missed something, but I didn't. "No suspects?"

"Not that anyone mentions. I checked Jeff City and Kansas City, too. Everybody reported the same thing."

"Nothing?"

"Yeah."

St. Sebastian. Great. I could smell a road trip in my future and I was pretty sure they weren't fans. I'd discovered a kidnapped girl's body in the dry lake bed in that little town and while everyone said "good job" I made the locals look like they'd been on snooze patrol. It wasn't their fault. I found that girl through a bizarre set of circumstances that were best left unexamined.

"So St. Seb. Do they get a lot of murders?" I asked.

Uncle Morty began typing furiously. "No."

"How many in 1965?"

He typed for a minute more and then said, "There were about three hundred murders in the whole freaking state, so not a lot."

"What was their population?"

"Eight thousand. It's fourteen thousand now."

"Would they know how to investigate a murder?"

"In 1965, nobody did. You got fingerprints and eyewitnesses. Maybe blood, but you could only type it."

"And if you don't have that..."

"You ain't got squat. No DNA. No video surveillance. Credit cards. Bubkiss."

"Can you find how many murders they had?"

"Who friggin' cares? They had one. For a podunk town like them, that's a lot."

"I want to know if they had a clue. How many cops?"

He grumbled but went to work. "Five. A chief, two full-time deputies, and two part-time."

"That's pretty small," I said.

"Little farming town. Not much going on."

"Any other murders around that time?"

"One in '62, but it wasn't exactly a head scratcher," he said.

"What happened?"

"Farmer poisoned his wife and put her in the compost heap. After the family started asking questions, Chief William (Woody) Lucas went out and he confessed. Said she annoyed him."

"How do you know all that, if the papers are on microfiche?"

"Reported in the Post. Big write-up. I guess farmers who kill are big news." He brought up the article for me. They certainly weren't shy about the killer farmer. Grisly details galore, grieving family listed, even local reaction got reported. I got that farmers killing their wives wasn't exactly an every day thing, but a murdered nun...come on. That was huge and Maggie got no interest.

"Well, I officially don't know what to do," I said.

"Give them rookies what they want," said Uncle Morty.

"How? Aunt Miriam is not going to crack. She's never cracked in her life."

He gritted his teeth and grumbled, "You got to do something."

I did not want to go down to St. Seb on some wild goose chase. If two FBI agents couldn't crack it open, how was I supposed to do it?

"What are you expecting? Nobody gives a crap about a fifty-year-old *solved* case."

"Make 'em fucking care. Make 'em reopen it. That's what the rookies want."

"Am I talking to myself? I don't know how. I doubt there's any evidence left and those cops are probably dead."

"Probably."

"Well..."

Uncle Morty polished off his beer, belched, and said, "Figure it out. What else you got to do?"

Heal. Get yelled at. Eat weird ice cream.

"Since we're not going to Greece anytime soon, I've got to get a job," I said, although the prospect was depressing as hell. Going outside was depressing as hell.

"You got a job," he said, handing me his computer and heaving himself off the sofa.

"I do not and it's not looking good. I'm going to have to do telemarketing or something."

He stretched and I got a full view of a bulbous, hairy belly. One more thing I would never get out of my memory. Gag.

"I'll pay ya to do it," he said.

"Pay me to..."

"Get whatever the hell you gotta get to open this case and get off that No Fly List." He put on his ancient Members Only jacket and tried to zip it up. Not happening.

"By pay..."

"Tommy's rate. No discount. Get cracking."

I couldn't speak. Dad's rate. Holy crap.

"We got a deal?" asked Uncle Morty.

"I will figure it out."

"Good. Familiarize yourself with St. Seb then and now." He pointed at the laptop next to me. "I got a map in there and I marked some possibilities for the crime scene."

He went for the door and I said, "Are you leaving?"

"I'm going to the gym."

What now?

"Did you just—"

"Shut up," he said.

I tossed my nail file on the coffee table and picked up the laptop. "Did you really join a gym?"

"I might've."

This is serious. Paying and exercise.

"May I suggest that you hire a trainer?"

He put on a pair of gym shoes that were so old the leather was cracked. "I ain't paying some douchebag to tell me to run on a treadmill."

"First of all, do not run," I said.

"You think I look like shit," said Uncle Morty, somehow both defiant and sad at the same time.

"I did not say that. Please don't run. Walk. Walking is good."

"I got to lose weight."

"Running's a recipe for a heart attack."

Uncle Morty stopped as he reached for the doorknob and I got a bad, bad feeling. "What are you thinking?" I asked.

"She'd probably come back if I had a heart attack."

I tossed aside the laptop. "No. Nope. Nuh-uh. I won't do it."

"You need the money."

"I do, but you aren't giving yourself a heart attack."

"It's a solid plan," he said.

"It's a death wish. You could die. You probably would die."

He crossed his arms over his huge belly. "'Cause I'm fat, right?"

Duh?

"'Cause you're out of shape. Have you considered therapy?"

"Massage therapy?" he asked. "Does that help ya lose weight?"

"No, ya dingus. Actually therapy with a counselor," I said, rolling my eyes.

Uncle Morty was not down. He thought therapy was for wusses and said so several times.

"I'll be sure to tell Chuck that," I said.

"That's different. He saw disgusting shit with kids. I just got to lose weight."

"And not lie about stuff that you don't need to lie about."

"Whatever. Get out."

I picked up the laptop. "I live here."

He cursed up a storm and opened the door.

"Maybe clean your apartment and stop eating food that says you're trying to kill yourself through fat, sugar, and carbs," I said. As my mom would say, in for a dime, in for a dollar, although I've never really understood what it meant.

Uncle Morty flushed and sweat beads popped out on his forehead. "I ain't trying to kill myself. I like it. It's fucking fine."

"You're sweating right now. It's November and you've turned down my thermostat. It's like sixty-two degrees in here."

"Shut up."

"Seek professional help."

"Get me to Greece. All I need is Nikki."

I swept an arm up and down in his direction. "If I were you, I'd think about what she'd be coming back to. She's pretty awesome and you are...I don't know what."

"I'm fine," he said.

I frowned, not convinced.

"I am. Just get me to Greece. That ain't so much to ask."

I clicked on the map tab. Wow. There was a whole lot of woods around St. Seb. "As a matter of fact it is."

"Do it and you'll make bank," he said.

"Clean up your act or Greece won't do you any good."

Morty started out the door with a funny look on his face.

I pushed the laptop off my lap. "Are you thinking about having a heart attack again?"

"No."

"You are. Stop it. You could die."

He scratched his chin. "I'm thinking I won't die."

"Have you seen you? It's a wonder that you haven't had one already."

"Then it won't be hard." Uncle Morty slipped out before I could protest and I didn't have the wherewithal to chase him down. Besides, what could I do? Somehow force him to listen? Only my mom could do that.

Now that was an option. I could call Mom and get her after him. Then I pictured my mother down at Cairngorms Castle, creepy as hell, but also luxe to the max, getting pampered and Dad being like a regular guy. If I called, that would come to an abrupt stop. No. Uncle Morty was my problem.

"You ready?" asked Aaron.

"Bring it on," I said and he did, on a platter, literally. I ate myself into a food coma that lasted well into the next day and I didn't regret it.

CHAPTER EIGHT

The way I see it, you have two choices when you wake up at noon with moussaka in your hair and feta ice cream on your sweats. Go back to sleep or question your life choices. I went to sleep.

"Mercy." Somebody shook me. "Mercy."

I tried to opossum. If they thought I was dead, maybe they'd be scared and leave the carcass alone.

"Mercy, get up. Don't make me get the hose."

That's when I recognized the voice. Joy. What on Earth was she doing in my bedroom? I was so tired I didn't much care. I'd slept so long I'd skipped awake time and headed straight into my next night's sleep.

If I'd been more coherent I would've heard the warning in her voice and known her threat wasn't idle. As it was, she didn't get the hose, she got the pitcher and dumped it on my head.

I sat up squawking and she clapped a hand over my mouth.

"Quiet. You'll upset her."

I peeled her hand off my face and said as I wiped the water out of my eyes, "If you don't want me to yell, don't throw water on me."

"I've been trying to wake you for fifteen minutes. She's starting to get worried," said Joy.

"Who's she?"

"Myrtle, of course."

That woke me up quick and I focused on Joy's tense face. "What happened?"

"She wants to speak to you and you wouldn't answer the phone."

"I was sleeping."

She plucked at my sweats. "Dear Lord. What happened to you?"

"Aaron came over and Uncle Morty is considering inducing a heart attack to get his girlfriend to come back from Greece."

"I thought she dumped him."

"That's what you're focusing on?"

She dragged me out of bed and gave me the once-over. "Morty isn't my concern."

"Well, he's mine."

"Not right now. This is important. You know Myrtle wouldn't leave Millicent alone when she's fragile unless it was serious." She started tugging on my sweatshirt, trying to pull it over my head.

"Get off me." I slapped her hands. "You left Millicent alone?"

"No. Rocco is with her. By the way, both Tiny and Fats have been calling you, too. Something is going on with them. Rocco wants you to handle it."

"I bet."

Rocco was Fats' brother and currently enjoying the good life as The Girls' chauffeur. The two siblings were close in a *Fight Club* kind of way. But the one I was worried about was Tiny. If he wanted to break up with Fats, I might as well give up on life. Fats would kill me in a fit of hormonal rage.

"Put on something decent," said Joy.

"How decent?"

"Clean."

That I could handle. I scurried into the closet and closed the door on Joy. I found jeans and an oxford that wasn't too wrinkled, stuffed myself into them—I think I gained ten pounds overnight—and scrubbed the food off my face and hair with the sweats. Then I flung the door open and presented myself for inspection. "Good?"

Joy's upper lip twitched, but she said, "Better."

"I'll take it. Where is she?"

"In your so-called living room," said Joy.

"So-called?" I asked.

"It smells in there."

"That's Uncle Morty. He's having a time."

"He's not there."

Bonus!

I hurried out into my smelly living room and found Myrtle perched on the sofa, wearing her going-to-a-board-meeting suit and holding a cup of tea. "Mercy, dear, are you alright?"

"I'm fine. Aaron fed me a lot last night and I couldn't wake up," I said before firing up one of my many coffee makers. I had to push a button. Even that seemed hard in my condition. "What's up? Do you have a meeting?"

"With you," she said.

I grabbed the milk steamer and sniffed for badness. All good. "We have a meeting?"

"I wanted to meet with you," said Myrtle.

"You sound formal and you're dressed for church or the hospital board."

"I dress to suit the occasion."

"I'm the occasion?"

"Yes."

I looked down at my wrinkled, bloated self. Oh, well. That's life. I pressed the button on Chuck's fancy pants super automatic espresso maker and watched it turn out a cracking good latte. I tried to think of what could've happened while I was sleeping. I hadn't told Morty to steer clear of The Girls, in regard to Sister Maggie, but I didn't think I needed to. He referred to them as the "old bags" and was, frankly, petrified of them on a good day and they weren't his biggest fans either.

I sat down on a chair opposite Myrtle and hoped for the best. Nothing could've prepared me for what she said.

"I would like to hire you to identify Sister Maggie's murderer. I will pay you twenty-five thousand dollars to get conclusive proof of guilt and fifty if you secure a conviction." She picked up a slim manila folder off the sofa beside her and held it out to me. "I took the liberty of having Big Steve draw up a contract. I will pay you Tommy's going rate for your time as well. I realize the chances of success are slight, but I'm willing to try. What do you say?"

I didn't say anything. I looked at Joy. She just stood there like someone had eaten a live cockroach in front of her.

"Take the folder, Mercy," said Myrtle.

I took the folder. Twenty-five thousand dollars. Fifty for a conviction, plus Dad's fees. I'd totally underestimated how The Girls felt about a crime from their youth. Time heals all wounds is bullshit.

"It's all there," said Myrtle. "The offer is simple. You don't need to convince the police or the FBI or anyone else of the suspect's guilt, only us."

"I'm not going to take your money," I said.

She leaned forward. "Is it not enough? We do value your time and effort."

"It's more than generous, but you don't have to pay me. If you want me to do it, I'll do it."

Myrtle sat up primly. "You would be doing a job. We will pay you."

"You've already paid me, if you want to call it that. My education, all the travel. How many birthday parties did you host? I'll do it. No question. I just..."

"What?"

"Millicent was not happy yesterday. Just the mere mention of Sister Maggie's medal brought her to her knees. Now you want me to investigate? What's that going to do to her?"

"Nothing," said Myrtle. "If you don't find anything, she never has to know. We won't ever mention it again."

"You want me to lie?" I asked. That alone was astonishing. The Girls weren't big fans of lying.

"You can do it." She smiled at me with a twinkle in her eye. "I've seen you in action."

"I can, but I don't want to. It's Millicent."

She held out a hand and I went to her, sitting on the sofa beside her.

"I know, dear. But it's for her own good," she said.

"And what if I do find something out? What then?" I asked.

"Then I prepare her and you lay out the case."

"What makes you think that's a good idea? It's bound to be ugly."

"Because the truth is better than not knowing. We've imagined the most horrible things."

It'll be worse than that.

I set down the folder and picked up my coffee cup, looking at Joy for some kind of guidance. Wide-eyed, she shrugged. Not a whole lot of help. I took a big drink and said, "You do know that the case is closed. They had a suspect."

"Poppycock!"

Those were strong words coming from Myrtle. If she knew curse words existed, I'd seen no evidence of it.

"You don't think the priest did it?" I asked.

"Absolutely not. Ridiculous notion."

Joy sat down. "How do you know?"

"Because we knew him," said Myrtle. "Father Dominic Kelly was a lovely person. A gentle soul."

"Card-carrying psychos don't always come with warning labels. I should know," I said.

"I know." She squeezed my arm. "Look in the folder."

I opened the folder on my knees and flipped past the contract. Underneath were several pictures of a priest in the Bled Mansion, chatting with Myrtle in the library and at what looked like a charity function where he was standing with Sister Maggie. On his face was a look of radiant admiration. There was the same group picture of nuns with Aunt Miriam standing next to Sister Maggie and a group picture of priests with Father Dominic on the right, smiling broadly.

"Okay. He's handsome. She's pretty. They knew each other well. It doesn't change anything," I said. "The cops thought he killed her because he was in love with her." I pulled out the picture of the two of them together. "This certainly implies that they were right."

"He was in love with her," said Myrtle. "Head over heels."

Joy took the picture and frowned. "You're not making him sound innocent. How do you know he didn't do it? She said no and he got mad. That's common, isn't it, Mercy?"

"It is," I said. "Some men can't take a no."

"He didn't have to take a no," said Myrtle. "She was in love with him, too."

Joy gasped. "But their vows."

Myrtle chuckled. "Maggie and Dominic took their vows seriously, but they fell in love. It happens."

"Did you tell the police?" I asked.

"We did, but Dominic would not have killed her."

"Were they going to leave the church?" Joy could barely squeak that out.

Myrtle nodded. "I think so. Maggie was absolutely tormented by the idea, but she couldn't imagine living the rest of her life without him as a partner or as a lover."

She told us the whole story as she understood it. Father Dominic arrived in St. Louis three years before Maggie died. They worked closely together at the hospital on fundraising and updating the children's services program. The Girls recognized a connection between them right away. Dominic had lost a brother to an accident. Maggie had lost Patrick. He understood her pain and shared her concern for children and the mentally ill. About eight months before her death, Maggie confided her feelings to Millicent. Nothing physical had happened between them, but Maggie was teetering on the edge. She didn't want to leave the church and she felt it was her calling, but the feelings weren't waning, only growing stronger.

Maggie and The Girls discussed the options. Dominic offered to leave the parish, if that's what she wanted, but she couldn't bear the idea. About six months before she died, they did try to separate themselves with regards to work. Maggie left the hospital and began working in administration at the St. Vincent Orphan Asylum and Mental Hospital. They weren't in the same building, but the two institutions were under the same umbrella and shared funding.

Dominic stayed at the hospital running the volunteer services, but it didn't help. They missed each other terribly. Myrtle described it as "pining".

In the week before her death, Maggie came to lunch and looked very tired and stressed. She said she wasn't sleeping. The Girls asked how she was and she said everything was fine, but they thought she was holding something back. The day she died, she was supposed to meet Millicent about fundraising and donations for St. Vincent's, but she called that morning and left a message with a maid saying she had to cancel because she was going to have a meeting with Bishop Fowler and Dr. Desarno. Millicent called back to inquire what the meeting was about, but Maggie didn't answer. She and Myrtle thought that Maggie had reached a decision. She was leaving the church and she didn't tell them first, because she was afraid they'd try to talk her out of it.

Myrtle got tearful when she got to that part of the story. She said that they would've supported anything she wanted, but they did worry that she might regret leaving the church and Maggie knew that. The day she disappeared they waited for her to call and tell them, but she never did.

"Wait a minute," I said. "Disappeared?"

Myrtle wiped her eyes with an embroidered handkerchief. "Yes. She disappeared. Didn't the FBI tell you that?"

"No. They didn't tell me much."

"They aren't very good, are they?" Joy blew her nose for the fifth time. Maggie's story was hurting her more than Myrtle.

"This is a pretty old case and they haven't been cleared to work on it, so their hands are tied," I said.

"But yours aren't," said Myrtle with a wan smile.

"No, they aren't," I said. "So what happened? How long was she gone before they found the body?"

Myrtle almost couldn't make herself say it. The answer was eight days before Maggie's body was found. She described it as the worst time of her life—and there was some serious competition for that distinction—the waiting and wondering where Maggie was, if she was hurt or dead, and then the finding of her body. Awful, excruciating, she said. It was like

Patrick, Maggie's brother, was dying all over again, too. The memories they shared, the understanding, the loss, everything came back, especially for Millicent. She couldn't bear to hear the details, to think about Maggie's body lying out in the woods for eight, long days. All they did know was that she was murdered and that she didn't suffer. Uncle Josiah had been the one to tell them Maggie was dead and that was what he said.

"I knew he wasn't telling us the truth, but Millicent couldn't stand the truth," said Myrtle.

"So you didn't ask?" asked Joy.

"I didn't, but I knew however it happened, Dominic couldn't have done it," she said.

I went to the kitchen to put the kettle on for more tea and to make another coffee. Mostly, I had to think. So many questions.

"Did she go to the meeting?" I asked from the kitchen and Myrtle looked up startled.

"I'm sorry, dear. I was thinking. What did you ask me?"

"The meeting. Did Maggie go to that meeting with the Bishop and doctor?"

She shook her head. "No, she didn't."

"Do you know when the meeting was?"

"No. I don't think we ever knew."

I got my latte and brought a fresh pot of tea out into the living room.

"What are you thinking?" asked Joy.

"Timeline," I said. "When was the meeting with Millicent supposed to be?"

"Oh, dear," said Myrtle. "I don't know. So long ago."

I sipped my coffee and considered. I was lucky Myrtle remembered as much as she did and I couldn't ask Millicent. The bishop and doctor were definitely dead. Church records maybe. "Do you remember when she called?"

Myrtle smiled. "That I remember."

"Really? That's lucky."

"Not really. Millicent and I took Lawton for a walk every single morning, rain or shine. It's good for children to get out in the air. We always took you when you were with us. Maggie called while we were out."

"You were living at the mansion?" I asked.

"Yes, dear. We never left, even when we married."

Joy raised an eyebrow. "How did the husbands feel about that?"

"It was not negotiable," said Myrtle, "but they didn't mind. It was hardly a punishment."

"No kidding," I said. "So Maggie called, canceled her meeting with Millicent but didn't make it to the other meeting?"

"Right. Now that I think about it, Millicent was probably meeting Maggie in the morning. Yes, I think she probably was."

There was something in Myrtle's voice that caught my attention, nothing major, but there was something in there.

"Why do you think that?" I asked.

She looked away and I glanced at Joy. She caught it, too. "You have to tell her everything, Myrtle. Mercy needs all the information."

"Lawton was little at the time. He still napped." She smiled. "He was always a big napper. Still is."

"So Millicent would've had a meeting in the morning because of Lawton's nap schedule?" I asked, trying to keep the disbelief out of my voice. Lawton was Myrtle's son and, let's face it, that kid had a full-time nanny, not to mention a house chock full of servants.

"Yes." Myrtle glanced at me and then looked away.

She was lying. Myrtle didn't lie.

"You want me to investigate this?" I asked.

Then she looked at me, worried now. "Yes, dear, I think Millicent needs to know who did it and why."

"Then tell me why you think the meeting was in the morning."

"I told you," she said.

I blew on my lukewarm latte and waited.

"I did, my dear."

"That reason doesn't make sense. Just tell me. How bad can it be?"

Myrtle poured herself a fresh cup of tea to stall and then she said, "It's not bad. It's private."

"Nothing's private in a murder investigation," I said. "Nothing."

"This is. It's not my secret to tell and it has nothing to do with Maggie's death," said Myrtle. "I can swear to that."

"You're certain?" asked Joy.

She looked her in the eye and said, "Yes, absolutely."

"So the meeting with Millicent was most likely in the morning, which means the meeting with the bishop and doctor was, too."

The ladies nodded.

"Okay. So when did you walk? I remember it being early and cold," I said.

"We went after breakfast. Lawton was an early riser. He usually woke me by six o'clock so breakfast at seven, I think. Mrs. Perkins will have the time precisely."

"Mrs. Perkins?" asked Joy.

"Our housekeeper at the time. She was a bit of a dragon about schedules. She kept a household diary that kept track of everything, menus, expenses, even illnesses."

Joy laughed. "I'm so glad you don't want me to do that."

"Nobody asked her to do it," said Myrtle. "It's how she was trained."

"Do you have her diaries?" I asked.

"Probably. Somewhere in storage. We can check."

We figured out that The Girls were probably out walking by eight and the walks were around the neighborhood and took about an hour. So Maggie called between, say, a quarter to eight to maybe nine in the morning. The meeting with the bishop and doctor wouldn't have been later than eleven. I didn't need Myrtle to tell me that. The Girls didn't like meetings to start after eleven in case they ran long into lunch, which might cause an awkward situation. That meant Maggie disappeared between eight and eleven. A three hour window was pretty wide, but it could've been way smaller. She could've called right before The Girls got home just before nine or so, and the new meeting could've been at ten or earlier even.

"Did Maggie have a car?" I asked.

"No. She didn't drive," said Myrtle.

"Did Dominic?"

"I have no idea. He may have."

Joy clasped her hands together. "I get it. How did she get to St. Seb?"

"Exactly," I said. "Something happened that morning and it must've happened here in St. Louis."

"Uncle Josiah said she died in St. Sebastian," said Myrtle. "I remember that. He was quite specific."

"Maybe she did. Maybe she didn't. I want to know how she got there and why."

Myrtle thought about it. "She could've taken a bus. Maggie took buses everywhere or she walked. She was a great walker."

"But she called to cancel her meeting with Millicent, I don't think she would've stood up the bishop," said Joy with a touch of pride.

"You're right." Myrtle sat back and sipped her tea. "She was never rude. Something happened here."

"Do you think she was kidnapped?" asked Joy.

"I think if she was, the cops here screwed up royally," I said. "They should've investigated. Can you think of any reason why Maggie would go to St. Seb voluntarily?"

She couldn't think of any reason. She wasn't even sure if she'd heard of the town until Sister Maggie died there, but, of course, that didn't mean there wasn't a connection. I wondered if Aunt Miriam would be willing to tell me that. Probably not.

First things were first. I needed to find out what the timeline was, whether Father Dominic had a car or not, if there was an investigation into his death or not, did he leave a suicide note, cause of death for Maggie. At that point, I wasn't taking anything for granted.

"Joy told me that you and Millicent mourned for a long time after Maggie died," I said gently.

"Yes, we did." Her pretty face curved into remembered grief. "It was a terrible time. You know my husband died not long after."

"A year later?"

"A little over a year. Please don't ask me about that. Maggie is enough to think about."

"I won't. I just want to know why you and Millicent stopped going to church."

Myrtle jolted into sharp focus and looked at Joy. "Did your mother say that?"

Joy nodded.

Apparently, The Girls didn't stop going to church. They stopped going to the cathedral and started using the tiny chapel at Prie Dieu, the family's country house. They didn't tell the staff because they didn't want to talk about it. Lester knew, of course, but he wasn't a gossip. I questioned whether or not Lester's wife, Mary, knew, but Myrtle wasn't sure. They were extremely close to Lester, Mary less so, but she wouldn't be surprised. Lester adored Mary.

"I'm going to talk to her," I said.

"Mary?" asked Joy. "What for?"

"I'm thinking Lester talked to his wife. She might remember something. Did she know Maggie?"

"Yes." Myrtle frowned. "But I don't think they were close. I hope you'll be gentle with her. She's not doing well since Lester died."

"I didn't know that," I said. "I'll be careful, but I want to talk to her."

Joy and Myrtle didn't get it and it was just as well. I should've thought of it before. What did Joy's mother say? The Girls and Lester would be curled up looking at the Bled family tree and talking about me. Mary might know if I was a Bled for sure and how. That and Lester was a keen observer. He might've had his own theories about Maggie's death. He went everywhere with The Girls and was practically a fixture in the kitchen where they did their best chatting. He'd have known Father Dominic and a man wouldn't be blinded by a pretty face. If Lester didn't like that priest, I'd bet the farm that he told Mary.

"So why did you stop going to the cathedral?" I asked. "Was it because of Father Dominic being accused?"

"In part, but it started before that. Did you know that Maggie wasn't reported as missing for four days?"

I didn't and I didn't know that the bishop had said that Maggie probably ran off with a man and he couldn't be bothered with wanton women. Myrtle would never forget sitting in his office asking what was being done to find Maggie and being told nothing. The bishop thought she'd purposely left him waiting and he didn't have any more time for her. He implied to The Girls that a woman with a face like that could not give herself to God. It was the same old story. He judged her by her cover and her disappearance solidified his opinion. The Girls went over his head and together with Uncle Josiah they got Maggie listed as a missing person against the church's—really the bishop's—wishes. Myrtle didn't remember what the police found out. It was a blur of fear and sleepless nights. She did remember Father Dominic in a panic sitting in that office with them, begging for help and not getting it. Dominic organized a search party around the convent and had flyers printed out of his own pocket.

"Uncle Morty looked at the papers at the time. There was nothing in there about Maggie until she died. What's up with that?" I asked.

"The church wanted it hushed up. They didn't want anyone knowing that a nun was missing, that she'd run off, in their opinion. Dominic couldn't get it in the papers. He tried. He was frantic. Out of his mind he was so worried. Her family searched with him. The Mullanphys tried to get the newspapers interested, too, but they wouldn't go against the church. And then when she was dead..." Myrtle choked off and I took the cup from her hands.

"The church thought he did it," I said.

She nodded.

"Did that bishop do something about it then?" asked Joy. "My mother didn't say anything about any of this."

"He...he acted like Maggie's death was an accident and at the same time he accused Dominic of murdering her. He kept her from having the funeral she deserved. He forced the Mullanphys to agree to not having it at the cathedral, but instead at St. James the Greater in Dogtown. He said it was because it was her family parish, but it was really because he didn't want the publicity. He said such things had to be kept quiet, like it was Maggie's fault someone murdered her and it shamed her somehow."

I exchanged a glance with Joy. She was pale and I knew she was thinking what I was thinking. The bishop might've been an ass, but he had a reason. I had to get ahold of the autopsy report if it still existed.

Joy leaned forward and said softly, "Do you think that's why Father Dominic killed himself?"

Myrtle broke down and we let her cry it out as if that was possible. People say that. Cry it out. Like if you cry the sorrow leaves your body permanently. Let me tell you it doesn't. I cried myself into hysterics after my boyfriend David disappeared. My sorrow didn't go anywhere. Like The Girls, it's the not knowing what really happened that gets you.

Once her sobs quieted, she said, "The worst thing was…"

I braced myself. The worst thing? There was something else? No wonder Aunt Miriam didn't want to talk. I felt drained and I was born decades later.

"What was it, Myrtle?" asked Joy. "Mercy has to know."

"He…he barred Dominic from the funeral."

"Oh crap," I burst out. "Sorry, Myrtle. I didn't mean to say that out loud."

"I'm glad you understand," she said. "I think that broke him. He couldn't say goodbye. The accusations were one thing. But that…he couldn't stand it."

"The Mullanphys couldn't do anything about it?" asked Joy.

"We were all so upset. She was their last surviving child with Patrick gone. I don't know how they got through. I don't know how we did. Millicent wailed for hours when Uncle Josiah told us. We couldn't do anything for her. And then Dominic was dead. I didn't believe it at first. They never found his body. We thought they were wrong. They must be. He was a priest and he never said anything to us about doing something like that."

"He was distraught," said Joy.

"But suicide," whispered Myrtle. "Not to be buried in consecrated ground."

My mind was racing. First Maggie and now this.

"You don't think he killed himself," I said, my heart sinking. Two crimes. Fifty years ago. God help me.

"I honestly don't know," said Myrtle. "The police thought so. There was a witness."

"A witness? Someone saw him jump?"

"I don't remember. He was on the bridge, I think. I don't know. I'm so tired." Myrtle sank down, deflated by telling the story.

"Let me get you home," said Joy.

"Do you need—"

My apartment door burst open and Uncle Morty stomped in, bringing a wave of stench with him. "God damn shit that was horrible. Mercy! Are you the fuck up yet?"

"Hello, Morton," said Myrtle, eyeing him with an incredibly neutral expression, but I knew she was disapproving. She was normally friendly to everyone.

He spun around. "Oh, fuck, I mean...hello...Mrs. Bled. I, uh, went to the gym."

"I see that and I was just leaving."

"Um, Mercy, why didn't you tell me you had guests?" He meant why didn't I warn him.

"It wasn't planned," I said. "*Myrtle* was just telling me what she knows about Sister Maggie's death."

"Really?" he asked.

"Really," said Myrtle, breathing through her mouth. "Mercy will fill you in. Do not under any circumstances speak to my sister about this."

"No problem."

Joy helped her up and they were out the door in a flash. The second the catch clicked, he rounded on me. "That old bag gives me the creeps. Jesus, you got to warn me."

"I don't," I said. "There's nothing creepy about Myrtle or Millicent."

He poked me in the forehead. "That's where you're wrong. It's like they stepped out of a BBC production from four decades ago."

"They're not British."

"They seem British."

"Whatever, weirdo," I said, holding my nose. "Take a shower or better yet go home and take a shower."

"Hell, no. I'm keeping you on this. If I have to work-out, you have to get us on the plane."

"Oh, I'm getting us on a plane, don't worry about that," I said.

Uncle Morty wiped his tremendously sweaty brow with his sleeve, leaving a wide, wet streak. "Oh, yeah? What'd she say?"

"She asked me to find out who killed Sister Maggie."

"And?"

"That's it."

"Goddammit. I ask you and all I get is guff. That old bag asks you and it's assholes and elbows."

"Correct."

"I'm writing you out of the will again," he said.

"I was never in the will."

"I could change it."

"Don't bother," I said. "I'm good. Now I've got stuff to do."

"Like what? You got a plan?" he asked, like that was not at all possible.

I started involuntarily gagging. "Leave now. You might have to get that smell checked out. It's not normal."

"I had crab cakes."

"Before working out?"

He screwed up his mouth and thought for a moment. "That probably wasn't a great idea."

"Ya think?" I asked.

"I'm showering. What are you gonna do?"

"I need to figure out the timeline," I said. "Oh crap! I forgot."

I ran out and chased Myrtle and Joy down the stairs, catching them near the bottom. Myrtle agreed to get Millicent out of the house, so Joy and I could look for the housekeeper's diary.

I'm not gonna lie, I stayed on those stairs long after Myrtle and Joy left. A stairwell never smelled so good.

CHAPTER NINE

"So what am I doing?" asked Uncle Morty, freshly showered and feeling feisty. "Sitting here with my thumb up my ass."

"Thanks for the visual," I said. "But no, you will be hacking the church to find out what they knew and when they knew it."

He dropped onto my poor sofa and ran a dishcloth over his red face.

I snatched the dishcloth away and held it out at arm's length. "Gross. This is for dishes."

"I'm sweaty again."

"How is that possible?" I asked. "You just took a shower."

"It's hot in here."

It was not hot. It was sixty-seven degrees in my living room and sweat was beading up on his forehead. There was something wrong with him.

"I want you to go to the doctor," I said. "This isn't normal."

"I ain't never been normal," said Uncle Morty.

There was no arguing with that. "You're still getting checked out."

He eyed me for weaknesses and found none. "When you get off the list. Not before. Don't ask me."

"Fine." I tossed him the dishcloth. "Don't drip on my sofa."

"Whatever," he said. "There aren't gonna be any church records about Father What's-his-face."

"Dominic. Why not? The church's digitalized."

"The Vatican is digitized. All the manuscripts, incunabula, stuff like that. The parish stuff from that far back would still be paper. What do you want to find anyway?"

I told him about the church not reporting Maggie missing and the rest of it. Uncle Morty scowled and more sweat rolled down his face. He had issues with the church and organized religion, in general. I suspected that the word "organized" was the key.

"I'll take a peek, but the most I'll get is a list of priests in the parish at the time," he said.

"Oh, good," I said. "Get that."

"What for?"

Uncle Morty got a to-do list. I think he'd have been happier with the thumb thing. I needed to know if Father Dominic had a car, and, if so, what kind. If he didn't, I wanted to know if any of his fellow priests did. He could've borrowed a car. After that, I wanted any newspaper articles on his death. I doubted from what Myrtle said that there would be any, but you never know. After that, it was all about the families, Maggie's and Dominic's. Was anyone still alive that was around at the time? Was there anybody period?

"Alright. Fine. I'll get that crap. When are you going to St. Sebastian?" he asked as he began typing on two keyboards at once. It really was fascinating to watch.

"Tomorrow." I threw on a jacket and checked the time. Myrtle should have Millicent out of the house by then.

"Today. Hit it today, hard and fast."

"This isn't a surgical strike on an enemy stronghold," I said.

"That's what you think. Get out. I'm busy."

I got out of my own apartment and called Chuck on the way down the stairs. He was happy that I didn't go to Greece until he found out why and that Uncle Morty was now living with me. But for the moment, all he could focus on was apartments and a pile of new possibilities. My guy was thinking about laundry rooms and counter space. I think he was nesting, but that didn't seem like something hot cops did.

I promised to consider how big a washer we might need and got off the phone after he asked if I needed a potting room. What the heck is a potting room?

Outside the sun was already waning, but I pulled my poof ball hat down low and put on a pair of sunglasses. I looked stupid. But what can I say? I felt better. Anonymous.

By some miracle I got over to Hawthorne Avenue without getting harassed and dashed down the alley, letting myself into the stables/garage. If I'd have been thinking, I wouldn't have done that. But thinking isn't my strong suit so I didn't and I ran smack dab into Rocco Licata, sitting on the floor in front of a car that had never been there before. A ruby red 1935 Auburn Boattail Speedster.

I did an about face, but Rocco shot out a hand and grabbed my ankle. "Where do you think you're going?"

Away from you.

"I forgot something." I kicked my leg but didn't manage to shake him loose. "Let go."

"You forgot to avoid me."

Correct.

"I'm not avoiding you. I'm busy."

"I called you fifteen times."

"Stalker."

Rocco jumped to his feet so fast I wasn't able to make a break for it and grabbed my arm. "My sister's acting weird. Tiny's acting weird. Do something."

"You do something."

"Is that bastard breaking up with my sister?" Rocco got in my face and it was not pleasant. He wasn't the beast his sister was at a mere five ten, but he had the same look in his eye that Fats got when we were talking to a suspect. Violence was always an option.

"Not that I know of," I said quickly. "What's he doing?"

"Acting weird."

"That's not descriptive."

"He keeps asking me what's wrong with her. She keeps asking me what's wrong with him."

"Maybe nothing's wrong," I said.

"Something's wrong. People don't ask if something's wrong, if nothing's wrong. Got it?"

"I guess. I didn't know you liked Tiny that much." I tried to get his fingers off my bicep. It was not happening and I was losing the blood supply to my hand.

"He's fine, but I think he might be sleeping with Princess Porks-a-lot."

Was there any doubt?

"Er...maybe. Fats is a grown woman. She can decide."

"Damn straight, but she takes this shit seriously," said Rocco with a dangerous glint in his eye. "She's picky. There's only been a few guys."

I hope they're still alive.

I decided it was best not to point out that I happened to know that Fats wasn't all that picky. She slept with Lorenzo Fibonacci, who, while unbelievably hot, had his intelligence unfavorably compared to a meatball.

"I get it and the last time I saw Tiny he was still in love with Fats," I said.

"In love?"

"Yes."

"With my sister?"

I wasn't sure where this was going, but it probably wasn't good. "I have to go. I'm doing a thing for Myrtle, your boss. Can't be late."

His grip on my arm tightened and I squeaked.

"Tiny loves my sister?" asked Rocco. "You sure? Fats? Six foot five hundred. A thousand pounds of muscle."

"She's not that big, but yes. Mary Elizabeth Licata. Your sister."

Rocco let go my arm and slapped his thigh. "Holy shit! I never thought I'd see the day."

I backed away slowly toward the garden door. "So you're happy."

"Hell, yeah. My mom wants grandchildren and I am not made for that business. She's serious about him?" he asked.

"I think so." I got in front of the doorknob and turned it slowly.

"Hey! Where are you going?" Rocco came over and grabbed me. "What do you think about this car?"

"Er...nothing. Can I go? I've got stuff and things."

Rocco held a battered toothbrush aloft. "This is a 1935 Auburn—"

"Well, I know that."

"Why did you say you didn't know?" asked Rocco. The warning was back.

I grabbed the toothbrush and smacked him with it. "Because I've got stuff to do. What's with the toothbrush?"

"I'm cleaning the headlamps. A thing of beauty and a winning thing of beauty."

"Huh?"

"This is The Girls' grandmother's car. It's usually over at Prie Dieu. I got them to let me bring it over so I can clean it up."

I eyed him. "What for?"

"The Amelia Island Concours d'Elegance," he said proudly.

"A car show?"

"For charity. This baby could win. She is in original mint condition." He leaned in close, his minty breath hot on my cheek.

Oh, no. Not good.

"Good luck with that." I went for the door, but he slammed a palm against it. I had no hope. "What do you want, Rocco?"

Rocco bent over me, his liquid brown eyes boring into mine. Did I mention that Rocco, despite being named Rocco, is hot and smells fantastic. He had all of Fats' electric power without the 250 pounds of beef.

"I want you to fix my sister and Tiny. I don't like her talking to me about feelings. I don't have feelings. I'm against it." He moved in closer.

I rolled my eyes, but my stomach was churning. "And?"

"You like me."

Like? No. Want...

"Get off me, ya turd." I shoved him back. "I'll see what's up with Fats and Tiny. Happy?"

"Mildly. Now about the car," he said, moving in again.

"Look, Skinny McSwizzle Stick, if you want this car to go to that show, I suggest you ask The Girls."

"Don't call me that." Rocco turned red.

"That's what Fats calls you," I said sweetly.

"I can't believe she told you that."

"She also told me that you had some tummy trouble when you were ten at a sleepover."

"I will kill her."

"I'd totally pay to see you try."

Rocco picked up his phone and started yelling as I went out into the garden. Strike one against family unity. The scary thing was that if Tiny did marry Fats, Rocco Licata was part of the deal. My dad had yet to notice the Licatas in our midst. When he did, it wasn't going to be pretty. He always said we had to be above reproach, no questionable business dealings, connections, etc. The Licatas were neck deep in the Fibonacci crime family and I'd dipped my toes in, too. Not on purpose, but I dreaded that coming out.

"Mercy!" Joy called out from the back door. "Where have you been?"

I jogged up. "Rocco waylaid me."

"I thought so. He is absolutely fixated on that car. I caught him cleaning the dash with Q-tips the other day."

"He might be obsessive."

She grinned at me. "But he looks good doing it. I only wish we had a pool."

"Joy." I fluttered my hand over my chest.

"I'm just saying."

She and I giggled our way up to the attic, gossiping about the hotness of Rocco and a few others. She thought Chuck won hands down, although he lost points for the crazy presents thing and advised that I handle all finances if we got married. That was a must. I'd seen him buy Kobe beef treats for Pickpocket. If we're not eating Kobe beef, neither is the dog.

After about an hour of digging through the attic, we found Mrs. Perkins' household diaries. They were remarkable and not a little OCD. I got the feeling that she'd have kept a record of the family's

bowel movements, if she could've. The diaries were on a shelf, organized by year, twelve diaries to a year. Joy found the right year and
month and we hunched over it, holding a flashlight and trying not to
breathe too deeply. The books were turning to dust, which was kind of
a shame. It was a detailed account of a famous family, done without
sentiment or embellishment.

Myrtle called Mrs. Perkins' books diaries, but that made them
sound small. They weren't small. They were legal ledger sized and had
everything in them. They were Mrs. Perkins' smartphone.

"Here we go," said Joy. "December third. 1965." She chuckled. "She
got up at five in the morning every day. Nightmare."

I bent over the book. "She lived-in then?"

"In one of the apartments over the stable. Let's see the day's to-do
list. Cook made breakfast for service at seven, like Myrtle said. I'm
surprised she didn't count the grains of salt used."

"They probably did walk at eight until quarter to nine."

"Hold on. I bet that's here. She's a nut," said Joy.

Mrs. Perkins was meticulous. The breakfast menu was there and
included any dislikes by the family. Millicent was judged not to have
liked her sausage. There was a lunch menu and dinner. A cleaning
schedule. Staff schedule. Joy turned the page and found exactly what
we needed. The family activities schedule. The Girls did walk at eight
for exactly forty-six minutes and Lawton came back with a little cough.
He was immediately bundled off to the nursery by Nanny who gave
him a medicinal bath.

I pointed at a line that was originally printed in black ink, but then
crossed out in red.

Millicent 10 a.m. Meeting with Sister Maggie—St. Vincent affairs

The one thing that Mrs. Perkins didn't note was when the call came in
to cancel, but we didn't really need it. Sister Maggie had a small
window to disappear. At most, two hours, but probably less.

"So now we know the meeting with the bishop must've been at ten," said Joy. "Does it help?"

"Not yet," I said. "But it will. Someone got between Maggie and that meeting. I have to find out where she would've been that morning and where the meeting was."

"I know that," said Joy. "She'd have gone to the bishop with the doctor."

"Where though?"

"The offices are in Shrewsbury now. They probably were then."

"If she was at the asylum that morning and Dr. Desarno worked there..."

Joy grabbed my arm. "They would've gone together."

"Who was that doctor?" I asked.

She grinned at me. "It can't be that hard to find out."

I called Uncle Morty and gave him Dr. Desarno's name. As he predicted there wasn't anything online about Father Dominic. He did find out which rectory he would've lived at and the names of all the priests that lived there at the time. Four priests had cars registered to them and Uncle Morty was running down the cars to see if they still existed somewhere. I didn't think it was necessary, but you never know. A couple of years ago, Dad took a thirty-year-old cold case and found a likely suspect in the neighborhood loser that had been known solely for boosting cars. Twenty years later though, he'd been convicted of rape and attempted murder. Dad had Morty track down the car that the guy stole around the time of the murder. It was sitting in a barn slowing disintegrating, but, low and behold, the fabric in the trunk was intact and had the victim's blood on the underside. That guy's on death row now.

"What about the families?" I asked. "Are they still in St. Louis?"

Uncle Morty was typing so fast it sounded like one continual keystroke. "Hold on."

Joy and I went into the kitchen for coffee and I tore into a coffee cake that Millicent must've made. It had her combo of allspice and nutmeg in the streusel topping. Delicious.

"He ain't your guy," said Uncle Morty.

"Dominic?" I asked.

"The doc."

"How do you know?"

"Check your phone."

He continued to type and I found pictures of Dr. Desarno in my inbox.

"He's not that old," I said. "If he incapacitated her somehow with a blow to the head, he could've done it."

Uncle Morty snorted. "The dude is seventy-two going on ninety. He had prostate cancer and a heart condition."

"Dr. Desarno was probably the last per—"

"He died four days after Sister Maggie disappeared. That's how healthy he was. That guy did not kidnap a young, healthy nun and strangle her."

My mind raced around, trying to escape the feeling in my gut. Something wasn't right. Four days? Ah, crap.

"Mercy?" asked Uncle Morty.

"Yeah."

"Goddammit, girl."

"What?" I asked.

"You got a feeling about that geezer, don't you? Forget it. He had a heart attack."

The feeling got stronger. I couldn't ignore it. The Tommy Watts in me wouldn't allow that.

"Where?" I asked. "And how?"

He grumbled and started typing again.

Joy whispered, "What is it?"

"Dr. Desarno died four days after Maggie disappeared," I said. "Heart attack."

She shrugged. "You think he died from stress over murdering her? Do murderers do that?"

"Not as a general rule, but that's not what I'm thinking."

Uncle Morty came back. "It ain't nothing. Heart attack after a car accident. Like I said that guy was in no shape to be murdering anybody."

I didn't think the feeling that something wasn't right could get any stronger, but it did.

"Where did that happen?" I asked.

"I don't have a police report. It's 1965 for fuck's sake."

"What do you have?"

"Newspaper."

"Lay it on me."

The articles and Dr. Desarno's obituary laid it out pretty well. Dr. Desarno—man of impeccable reputation—got hit in his 1963 Buick Riviera in the parking lot of the asylum, which caused a severe coronary, killing him. The original article said that the good doctor was in stable health, despite his condition at the time of the accident. In other words, Dr. Desarno wasn't on death's doorstep. The article blamed the accident for his untimely death and the police were searching for the hit and run driver. The vehicle they were looking for was a green Dodge pickup truck, but it didn't say why.

"I take it they never found the truck," I said.

"No."

"You know what I'm getting at, right?"

He grumbled, "You're gettin' distracted. You just gotta get Maggie's case reopened. That's it. Focus, Mercy."

"Not anymore. The Girls need this solved. That's the goal."

Cursing spewed out of my phone and Joy took a step back, wrinkling her nose. "He's salty."

"He's something," I said, waiting for the avalanche to peter out.

"So what's next?" she asked.

"I'm going to call a lanky detective with a great butt and ask a little favor."

"Sidney Wick?"

We both burst out laughing. Sid was Chuck's partner. He was a great guy and excellent detective, but about as far as you could get from lanky. I didn't know about his butt and I didn't want to.

"What are you chicks laughing about?" snarled Uncle Morty. "This ain't funny. I've got to get to Greece before Nikki falls for that hairdo with abs."

I swallowed the last of my laughter. "Sorry, but I can't help it if this isn't simple."

"Just stay on Maggie."

"I will, if I can."

"Give me one good reason why you think this decrepit old doctor kicking it in a parking lot has anything to do with Maggie," said Uncle Morty.

"The church delayed reporting her missing."

"Yeah?"

"For four days."

"Shit."

"Yup."

"Could be a coincidence," he said.

I smiled. It was so much fun to bother him. "Could be."

"But it ain't."

"No."

"We gotta go get the accident report. That isn't online."

"That's okay," I said. "I know a guy that wants to show me houses."

"You don't play fair."

It was my turn to snort. "This coming from the guy camping out on my sofa."

"Point taken. What else you need?" Uncle Morty asked.

"Did you find any family?"

I was in luck, sort of. Dominic was an only child and his surviving relatives were third cousins living in Colorado. They probably didn't know his name, but Maggie's family was living in Dogtown, mere blocks from St. James the Greater where her funeral was.

"Who are they exactly?" I asked.

"We got a Patrick Mullanphy. He's the grandson of Maggie's uncle."

I made a face. "That's close and not close at the same time."

"Oh, it's close. The family built that house in 1935. Maggie was raised in it."

"Score!"

He chuckled and it was nice to hear. I'd hardly gotten a smile out of him since Nikki left.

"You got any more questions for me?" he asked.

It was one of those leading questions. All in the tone.

"I guess I do."

Uncle Morty went silent while continuing to type. I went through what we had. I'd missed something, but I had no clue what.

"What's going on?" asked Joy.

"I'm forgetting something. He wants me to guess what it is."

Joy looked at the clock and grabbed the phone from me. "Just tell her, you pain in the ass. We don't have time for this crap."

She gave me the phone and it took me a second to recover. Strong words from a prim housekeeper.

"You got that?" I asked Uncle Morty.

"I got it," he said. "You forgot about Dominic."

"I didn't forget him."

"The church did."

"Huh?"

"Google the poor bastard."

I asked Joy if I could use Millicent's iPad that lived on the counter for recipes and quickly googled Father Dominic Kelly. Zero hits. I tried every combo I could think of. Priest. Suicide. Catholic. First name only. Last name only.

"He doesn't exist," I said.

"Now try this one. Father Bernard Potter."

Potter didn't have lots of hits, but he had them.

"Who is he?"

"Another priest living at the rectory with Dominic. It's the same with everyone else at the time. They exist. He doesn't."

"What about newspapers?" I asked.

"We've got two mentions. The first one is him starting a medical outreach at a homeless shelter with a picture. Good looking guy. You'd never figure he'd jump off a bridge six months later."

"What's the second?"

"An article about him jumping off the Eades Bridge. Looks like it came in just under the print deadline about four hours after he jumped."

"No follow-up?"

"Nope."

"Does it mention a connection to Maggie?"

Uncle Morty read it out to me and it wasn't what I expected. The reporter didn't say suicide. He said, "fallen to his death". Three witnesses said they'd seen a man fall and a car belonging to Father Bernard Potter was found nearby. Father Bernard confirmed that Father Dominic borrowed the car to run an errand. He said that Father Dominic seemed fine and he didn't think that he was going to harm himself. It did say that Father Dominic was a close, personal friend of Sister Maggie, the recently murdered nun, and knew Dr. Desarno, victim of a hit and run.

The article sounded a whole lot like Uncle Morty's leading question. The reporter was suspicious and he wasn't trying to hide it.

"What was the errand?" I asked.

"Doesn't say. But listen to this. 'Another person was seen on the bridge by a fourth witness at the same time. Police are seeking to identify this unknown man. Any information, blah, blah, blah'."

"Oh, my God."

"It don't mean he was pushed," said Uncle Morty.

"It means that reporter thought he was and that's a good place to start."

The wind went out of his sails. "If our body count keeps going up, I'm never getting to Greece."

"We'll get there," I said. "We've just got a little more to do."

"A little? Three freaking murders and they are ice cold," he said.

"We'll just have to heat them up. Find out if any of those priests are still alive and take a peek at Bishop Fowler. See what his problem was."

"What're you gonna do?"

"Interviews."

I hung up and Joy asked, "What can I do?"

"Call Mary and see if I can come over for a chat."

Joy called Mary's daughter to see what kind of shape Mary was in and I called Chuck. He was in an autopsy, waiting for a slug to be dug out of some poor guy's brain, so he was bored and chatty. Less so when it became clear that I wanted a favor.

"You have got to be kidding?" he asked.

"How hard can it be?" I used my wheedling voice, good for getting candy bars in checkout lines and extra time on research papers.

"A hit and run in 1965? Who cares?"

"Your girlfriend. Uncle Morty, who's living on my couch until this job is done. The Girls. Joy."

"Alright. Alright," said Chuck. "I'm not giving you that report, just so you know."

I rolled my eyes at Joy and she rolled hers back, whispering, "Men."

"I don't need to see it. You'll see it. You're a really great detective. You'll know if it's hinky."

Chuck was preening. I could tell and it was adorable.

"What are you looking for?" he asked.

"Dr. Desarno was hit in a parking lot. I want to know how hard."

"Hard enough to kill him," said Chuck. "But...you say he was in stable condition."

I smiled. "Yes."

"Parking lots are generally minor fender benders. Maybe fifteen miles an hour, if it's big enough, but people slam on their brakes and the contact should be less. He was in a Buick Riviera?"

I grinned at Joy and gave her a thumbs-up. "He was. Those are big cars, aren't they?"

"They're boats and heavy. My third stepfather had one. It was a beast. You'd have to hit it with some speed to cause an occupant any real damage. Five or ten miles an hour? I doubt it, but he did have a heart condition. I have to see the report. Pictures will be helpful." Chuck went on. He was working it through like my dad did. Thinking out loud. He went through the connections. Doctor was a witness in Maggie's disappearance. An unknown suspect on the bridge at the time of Father Dominic's fall. Three witnesses to the fall didn't see the second person on the bridge. Why? Who saw the second person on the bridge?

"I like it," he said. "I think you're on to something."

"Excellent. I don't suppose you could take a peek at Father Dominic's file?"

"I got it on the list. So Morty doesn't think we looked at Sister Maggie's case, even though it logically originated here?"

"That's what he said."

Chuck was quiet for a moment and I knew that silence. He was a cop and that went to the bone. He didn't want to say that the department screwed the pooch on Maggie's disappearance and murder, but it didn't look good.

"I'll let you know," he said finally.

"Tonight at dinner," I said.

The worry turned happy. "Your place? I'll bring wine."

Wine. You sneaky bastard.

"No way. Not with Uncle Morty stinking up the place. Let's meet at Kronos at eight."

"This is why we need to move out of the city proper. No more uncle camping."

I ignored that volley and we said goodbye.

Joy rinsed out her cup and put it in the dishwasher. "Mary's having a good day. We can see her now."

"We?" I asked.

"I want to go. I've never investigated anything before."

"Won't Millicent expect you to be here when they get back?" I kept the hope out of my voice. I didn't relish a partner. I just wanted to interview and get the job done. No chatting. No nothing. Done.

"Oh. You're probably right." Joy was so crestfallen, I broke down and promised to give her an update as soon as I was done with Mary.

It worked and I escaped without a partner. It lasted exactly thirty-five seconds.

CHAPTER TEN

"You!" Fats Licata leaned against the Bled stable/garage, angrier than I'd ever seen her.

I turned to run back into the house, but she was on me before I got over the threshold, dragging me back and quietly closing the door. The woman had skills and they all worked against me. She got me under her arm like a troublesome two year old, sashayed back to the garage, whipped open the door, and tossed me inside.

I stumbled across the floor and bumped into the Auburn, causing Rocco to shriek, "My girl! Are you fuggered up, woman? Don't touch her."

Rocco took me by the shoulders and removed me from the vicinity of the Auburn, who, might I add, wasn't injured or even smudged. "Run," he whispered. "Save yourself."

"What the hell is going on?" I asked, backing up as Fats glared at me. Think angry cheetah in hot pink workout wear and Timberland chunky-heeled boots because she needed to be taller.

"I told her you weren't in Greece."

"And..."

He shrugged and held his toothbrush like a shiv.

"You didn't tell me you were going to Greece," Fats said in a low malevolent tone that made shivers go up and down my spine at break-neck speed.

"I didn't go to Greece, so we're all good," I said.

"Calpurnia knows you tried to go to Greece without telling me and then failed because you are on the No Fly List."

"Nice," said Rocco. "It doesn't take a lot to get on there, but still, I'm impressed."

"It's not impressive. It's a strong arm tactic by the FBI."

He tossed his toothbrush in a bucket and cracked his knuckles. "What are you into? A girl like you, I'm betting designer drugs. Probably not prostitution, but you never know, everybody's got a dark side."

"Shut up, idiot," barked Fats. "Mercy doesn't have a dark side. She's a human marshmallow Peep."

"I wouldn't go that far," I protested.

"Peep!"

I clammed up and Fats pointed at Rocco. "Get out."

"I work here. You're just erupting here."

Fats lowered her sunglasses. "Are you saying that I am the size of a volcano?"

Rocco paled and that took some doing. He was born with the perfect tan. I'd seen the pictures. "I'm saying you're angry and you should go see some fucking shrink and get over yourself."

I had to give it to him. He didn't pee. He said it like he could back it up, which he obviously couldn't without a weapon of mass destruction. Anything less and Fats would crush him like a saltine cracker.

Fats advanced on her brother and Rocco stood his ground, but I bet he wished he had his toothbrush back. It wasn't much, but it was something.

"You're lucky that my mother calls you son," she hissed.

"I'm her favorite child," he said.

"You had to repeat kindergarten," she said.

"You peed on Grandma's fur stole."

"I thought it was your cat."

I raised my hand and backed up toward the alley exit. "This sounds like a family thing. I'm going to go."

"Don't move," said Fats. "Rocco was just leaving."

"I'm not leaving."

God help me. These people are crazy.

"Can we just not do this right now?" I asked. "I've got to ask an old lady some questions and she's waiting on me."

"What old lady?" asked Rocco. "The Girls okay?"

"They're fine," I said. "It's another thing that I've got to go do."

"Rocco, leave," said Fats.

"No."

"Didn't you hear what I said?" She bent over him. Her forehead was almost touching the top of his head, but Rocco said, "Fuck you, ya big pink sasquatch."

"You are insane," I said.

"I said, '*Calpurnia* knows Mercy tried to go to Greece without telling me and then failed because she's on the No Fly List.'"

Rocco stepped back, held up his hands, and said, "I'm starving. Anybody want anything from Kronos? Raw meat, perhaps?"

"I'll have a metaphysical malt, double chocolate, and cheese fries, double bacon," said Fats.

"Got it," said Rocco. "Mercy...wait what? You want a malt and cheese fries?"

"Never mind." Fats grabbed him by the collar and waistband, literally lifting her brother off the floor and carrying him to the door.

"You don't eat fat," said Rocco. "You don't eat anything good. Did Tiny dump you?"

"Mercy," said Fats, "open the door."

Rocco waved his arms at me. "Don't open the door."

I opened the door. Sometimes you have to choose. I chose life.

Fats tossed Rocco outside in one smooth movement. He ran full tilt back at us, but she slammed the door in his face.

"Fats!" he yelled. "It's freezing out here."

"Go away!"

"Mom's going to hear about this!"

She banged on the door and I guess he went away.

"You and I are going to have a talk," said Fats.

I so wanted to go with Rocco. I ate fat. I loved fat. "What about? Greece? I'm allowed to go to Greece."

"Not anymore."

"That's temporary."

"We'll see." Fats paced in front of me. "I had to hear about this from Calpurnia. Do you know how this makes me look? Do you have any idea?"

I really didn't and it must've showed.

"You are my problem. I'm supposed to keep an eye on you."

"Since when?"

"Since Calpurnia decided to like you and you keep trying to get killed," said Fats.

"You knew about Greece the first time."

"Yeah."

"So?"

Fats yanked out her hairband and shook her light brown hair. It didn't help. She was just more lion than cheetah. "So I knew where you were and what was happening. I have to be in the know. If I'm not in the know, Calpurnia will know that I don't know and pretty soon I won't know anything. Understand?"

Not even a little bit.

"Sure. Why not?"

"We're friends. Friends tell each other when they're going to leave the country or investigate fifty-year-old murders," said Fats.

"You know about that?"

She took off her Wayfarers and gave me the *obviously* look. "Calpurnia has an interest."

"Oh, God."

"He will not help you with this."

"Why are you telling me this?" I asked. "I'd rather not know anything about Calpurnia."

"Because we're friends," she said. "You're going to be my maid of honor."

What now?

"Er...I didn't know that," I said.

"Obviously, I need a maid of honor and you are my only female friend."

If I was her only female friend, that wasn't a good sign. She was kinda foisted on me.

"How can that be? What about high school friends? Other body-builders?"

She shrugged and put on her sunglasses. "I scare other women. It's always been like that. I can't wear clothes off the rack and I can't make female friends. That's why Calpurnia keeps me with you. I don't scare you."

Not remotely true.

"I don't really see why you have to keep track of me, but okay."

"It's a family thing. Plus, you're useful. Take this nun thing, for instance," said Fats.

"What about it? Please say Calpurnia isn't related to Sister Maggie."

Calpurnia Fibonacci wasn't connected to Maggie or anyone related to the case. She was aware of the case before it came up on my radar. As a deeply religious Catholic—I know, it doesn't quite make sense being the head of criminal enterprise—she was concerned about what I was going to uncover about the church.

"She's worried I'm going to make the church look bad?" I asked.

"She's worried that the church covered up what really happened. They've had a continuous black eye for years. They don't need another one."

"Are you serious?" I asked. "If they did do something, I'm not going to cover it up again and let some murderer off."

Fats took me by the arm and steered me out the back door. "If you find out that someone other than the priest did it and they're still alive, believe me, they will not be getting off. It's just that nobody needs to know about it."

"I can't control that. The FBI knows."

"We don't expect you to control it. We'll handle it. You just do whatever you've got to do."

Fats put me in her truck, slammed the door, and locked it. Like I could escape. Puhlease.

She got in. "Alright. Where are we going?"

I gave her Mary's address and that's how I got Fats Licata helping me investigate three murders that I very much suspected the Catholic church did not want me to solve.

I begged Fats not to come in. I begged. I didn't want to explain why I had this giant, angry woman with me when I already had to explain why I wanted to talk about Sister Maggie's murder and the rest of it.

"Save your breath," said Fats as she trailed me to Mary's front door on a quiet suburban street out in Crestwood.

"You just said you scare women," I said.

"In this case, it's useful."

"No, it's not. Mary is a newly-minted widow and seriously old."

"Then this won't be hard. Good. You'll have time to talk to Tiny today. He's acting weird."

"Define weird."

"I don't know. Weird. Nervous."

Awesome. He's going to dump her.

"You make people nervous. It's what you do," I said.

Fats pulled open the storm door and said softly. "Not him. Everybody but him. Now knock."

I raised my hand, but I didn't get the chance. The door flew open and there was Mary. Tiny little Mary with her favorite blond wig on and a smile crinkling a face the color of a well-used paper bag. "Where have you been? I've been waiting here, doing nothing just waiting."

"Um...I...I'm sorry. I was delayed. I should've called."

"It's fine. I've just got bingo at seven, but I do like to get there early so Mabel West doesn't steal my seat." She looked over at Fats, slowly craning her neck up to the six eight Fats was in her boots. "Well, I'll be. You are one tall woman."

"Yes, ma'am," said Fats.

"You planning on having children?" asked Mary.

That took Fats back for a second. It occurred to me that people didn't tend to talk to Fats. She talked to them and they tried to get away. "Yes, ma'am."

"Is your man large?"

"He is."

"Those will be some big babies. My sister married a big man and those babies were a handful. Could not keep them in shoes. I swear I saw one grow an inch during church. He split his pants when he reached for a donut afterwards and I am not kidding. He was a linebacker for the Eagles, but he's a pastor now. He has some big kids, too. Oh, my lord. Why are you standing out there? It's cold. You're letting all the heat out."

We went into the blast furnace that was Mary's living room. It had to be at least eighty degrees in there and Fats started peeling off the layers. I only had one layer to peel, and I wished I could take off my shirt.

"Would you like some coffee?" asked Mary. "I made a fresh pot for you."

I'm going to melt from the inside.

"Yes, please," I said with a glance at Fats, who was looking like coming in was the biggest mistake of her life.

"I'd love some coffee," said Fats.

We sat down on Mary's plastic-covered couch while she got the coffee and Fats whispered, "Why?"

"Which part?" I asked.

"All of it."

"She's old. What can I say?"

Mary came in, put down a tray, and adjusted her hearing aid. "What was that?"

"Nothing," I said. "It's just that you seem to be doing well."

"They told you I'm wasting away, pining for my Lester?"

"Kinda."

She nodded and poured us mugs of steaming hot coffee and a bead of sweat rolled down my cheek. "I did that, but now I'm over it."

"Over it?"

"Wasting away. Mourning. Wailing. Didn't care for it." She sipped her coffee. "Lester wouldn't like it. I was his firecracker. He called me his Fourth of July girl. I've got life left in me and he'd want me to live it, not sit around like those other old widows, moaning about how they don't have anything to live for. Lester was my husband. I loved him with every fiber, but he wasn't my whole being. Those women act like they can't turn on a light switch without a man. I raised five children. None of them are in jail or stupid. I can do anything. How do you two know each other?"

"We're friends," said Fats a little more emphatically than she probably intended.

Mary eyed her and said, "I assumed that. How did you become friends? I've known Mercy every day of her life and I don't know you."

"I...uh..."

"Mary Elizabeth is my cousin Tiny's girlfriend," I said quickly.

She threw up her hands. "Tiny, of course. He's a good man and huge. You better start setting aside food money right now, Mary Elizabeth."

"Yes, ma'am."

"Now to what do I owe this visit?" asked Mary.

I explained the situation and drank my coffee, sweating so much my panties were damp.

"Oh, yes. Sweet Maggie. That was a tragedy and you know Father Dominic didn't kill that girl. Ridiculous to even suggest that." Mary leaned forward, conspiratorially. "I think he was murdered, too. Don't tell my daughter that. She'd have me hauled off to a home. I'm not going to a home."

"You know what, Mary," I said. "I think you might be right. Tell me everything you remember."

Mary remembered quite a lot and, as with everything, she had an opinion. She thought the church had let Maggie, Dominic, and The Girls down. This was unforgivable and I agreed. Lester told her everything that happened during those horrid days and would come home to report it all to his firecracker. When it became clear that Maggie was gone and no one was looking, Mary helped with the search headed by Dominic. She thought he did everything possible to find her. No one could've done more, but Bishop Fowler thwarted him at every turn. The man was actually mad that she'd missed their appointment and left him sitting there "like a fool" as if that was the important thing. Lester overheard the bishop chastising Dominic for pressing the case to report Sister Maggie as missing, calling her a fallen woman and saying that this would put the church in a bad light. Dominic didn't care about what light it cast. He wanted Maggie found.

The Girls were frantic as were Maggie's family and Dominic. Everyone who knew her was in a state, except the bishop. And after her body was found the panic turned to hysterical grief and anger. Mary was there at the mansion making sandwiches to feed the search team when Uncle Josiah came to tell them Maggie was dead. The bishop showed up shortly afterward and offered to pray with The Girls. They wouldn't get near him.

Mary said that she would never forget the look on the bishop's face. She described him as annoyed when Dominic and The Girls' husbands pressed for a widespread investigation, newspaper, and TV news coverage. And then he said, "The church must always be our priority. It is time to move on from this unpleasant affair lest it stain our most holy of missions."

Lester had to stop Uncle Josiah from punching the bishop. Dominic screamed at him that he didn't care that Maggie was dead and that God was watching and judging his callousness to one of his own. The bishop never changed expressions and the two priests that had come with him had to persuade him to leave, saying things like "this is not helping."

"What do you think that was about?" I asked.

Mary poured another cup of coffee. "Isn't it obvious? The church was the priority. Bishop Fowler wanted to protect the reputation of the church at all costs."

"Makes you wonder who else he protected," said Fats.

"I think we can all guess," said Mary. "But this situation with Maggie, Lester always wondered about it."

"Wondered what?" I asked.

"What he had against Maggie. He never lifted a finger to find her or showed any concern at all. I suppose I can understand not wanting the lurid details in the newspaper after she was found. Maggie was a nun, after all, but he didn't want the real criminal found. He wanted it to be Dominic, even though nobody believed that. The bishop just wanted it to go away."

"He didn't like her," said Fats. "You said he called her wanton."

"Yes, he did, among other things."

"It was personal," I said. "I wonder how well he actually knew Maggie."

"You should ask Father Bernard," said Mary. "He was one of the priests that got the bishop out of the mansion that day."

"He's still alive?" asked Fats.

Mary scowled. "Yes, young lady. We haven't all dropped dead."

"Sorry. I assumed he was older at the time."

"I seem to remember Father Bernard as younger." She looked at me. "About Miriam's age at the time."

How old was that? Aunt Miriam young was a foreign concept.

"Do you have any idea where he is?" I asked.

"He'd be old enough to retire, I think. Priests work longer than normal people, you know."

I didn't. I never thought about it. Growing up, all the priests seemed ancient.

"Where do priests retire?" asked Fats. "Florida?"

Mary chuckled. "They wish. If he retired here, he's probably down at the home by the Cardinal Rigali Center. The Girls raised money for it."

I remembered that. Regina Cleri. I'd been roped into serving at a fish fry and more than a couple pancake breakfasts to raise funds for some updates.

"We'll go there next." Fats stood up, leaving moisture on the plastic. I hated to think about the sweat pool under me.

"You should," said Mary. "Liven up his day. Tell him to fess up or I'll come visit."

"Does he know you?"

She got cagey. "I may have said some things that day."

"Oh, yeah?"

"And at the funeral."

"Really?"

A little smile came over her face. "They deserved to know how everyone felt. They didn't care for Maggie and had the nerve to officiate her funeral. I let that so-called man have it."

"How did Lester feel about that?" I asked. Lester was a mild-mannered man. I never had a harsh word from him, not even when I set fire to the garage.

"He wasn't happy. But I'm a grown woman. I don't ask permission."

"Mary," said Fats, "I think you're my hero."

"Good and when you have those babies, bring them around. I love the young ones."

"I will." Fats went for the door, but I stayed put.

Mary raised a penciled-on eyebrow. "Cat got your tongue, Mercy?"

"I wanted to ask you about something else," I said.

She gathered the coffee mugs and picked up her tray. "Go on. I haven't got all day."

"Did Lester ever talk to you about me?"

"God, yes. You were the most troublesome child. Always asking questions. Getting into things. You wanted him to read to you and let you drive when you were four. My goodness the stories. Do you remember when you dug out the root ball of one of those huge banana trees?"

"I did that?" I asked. "Why?"

"Who knows. Lester thought you wanted to find out what was in there. You couldn't just assume it was dirt like a normal child. You had to see for yourself."

"That explains a lot," said Fats.

"What happened?" I asked.

"It fell over. Took down three other trees with it. Huge mess. Lucky it didn't take out any of those glass walls. The Girls just said you were curious and set about cleaning it up."

"No punishment?" Fats was aghast. So was I.

"Probably no dessert or something like that. She set the garage on fire later on, so it didn't work."

"Why did they put up with me?" I asked to get us back on track.

"They love you," said Mary. "Simple as that."

"Do you know why?"

Mary watched me for a moment, weighing her options, and then carried the tray into her small but immaculate kitchen. I followed with Fats squeezing in behind me and we watched her tidy up.

"Mary?" I asked. "Am I a Bled?"

"Why don't you ask The Girls?"

"I have. They avoid the subject, but with everything that's happened and how we're all treated it seems like..."

"You're family? Yes, it does seem that way," said Mary.

"Did Lester tell you anything? Joy's mother said she saw them curled up with a family tree and were talking about me."

She wiped off the counter and wrung out her dishcloth. "That man did not tell me anything about that and don't think I didn't ask."

"Nothing?" asked Fats. "But you're so..."

"Persistent?" She laughed. "Yes, I am, but he wouldn't say a thing. My Lester was loyal. I think he gave his word and he stuck to it. Do you want my opinion?"

"I do," I said. "Very much."

"You're a Bled. I don't know how, but you are. Tommy is. Ace and Miriam are."

I thought about everything I'd heard about Grandad, my dad, but, also, Aunt Miriam. "I had the impression that The Girls found out about us when they met my grandad. There was a break-in at the mansion. He was assigned the case."

Mary nodded. "Sounds right."

"But Sister Maggie was very good friends with my Aunt Miriam. How come they didn't know about us back when Maggie died or even before? Aunt Miriam was here in St. Louis."

"Mercy, girl, the first time I ever remember laying eyes on Miriam was at Maggie's funeral."

"Really?" I asked. "She wasn't at the house when the bishop came or during the searching?"

"If she was, I didn't notice her," said Mary. "Try to remember. It was a crazy time. A lot of people were at the mansion that I didn't know. The whole Mullanphy family was there. All the charities that The Girls served on were there and quite a few nuns and priests."

"But you noticed her at the funeral," said Fats.

Mary sighed. "I did. Lester did. St. James was packed to the rafters. Everybody and their brother was there. The papers outright refused to cover Maggie's case or her funeral. She got the smallest obituary you've ever seen, but The Girls got the word out and Maggie was mourned."

"Then how in the world did you notice Aunt Miriam?" I asked.

Mary told me why and I got the saddest pang in my chest. All the nuns were together assembled up in front, together in grief, sisters. But one tiny little nun wasn't there with them. When the pallbearers carried Maggie's casket out to the hearse, Mary spotted her, standing half hidden behind one of the pillars by herself and sobbing silently. Mary noticed her again at the graveside service. Aunt Miriam stood off by herself and didn't speak to anyone and left the moment it was over, riding off on a battered bicycle in below freezing weather. Mary asked another nun who she was and the nun said that Sister Miriam was Sister Maggie's good friend and that Maggie was a mentor to her.

"Who was the nun?" asked Fats.

"You don't think I'll remember, do you?"

"Um..."

"Well, I do," said Mary. "It was Sister Frances. You could hardly forget her. She's over six foot and had the oddest habit of wearing ugly men's shoes."

"Sister Frances," I said. "Of course."

"What's with the shoes?" asked Fats.

"Her feet are huge," I said.

"I can relate."

Mary started shooing us toward the door. "I need to lie down for a while before bingo. It's a battle in there. If you have any more questions, ask them later. I'm old, if you haven't noticed."

We gathered up our coats and Fats' many layers and I gave Mary a hug. She was surprisingly cool to the touch. "Thank you."

"Are you going to find out who killed Maggie and Dominic?" she asked.

"I'm going to do my best."

"That's all anyone can ask." She opened the door for us and said as we walked out. "Maybe Father Dominic will get the memorial he deserved when you're done."

I turned around as a gust of wind chilled the sweat on my body and made me shiver. "He didn't have a memorial?"

"No," said Mary with a grimace. "He went into that river and was gone without a trace."

CHAPTER ELEVEN

We found Father Bernard right where Mary thought he'd be, at the retirement home, Regina Cleri, in Shrewsbury. He was snoozing after dinner, sitting in a small common room in a wheelchair, watching *Wheel of Fortune*. There were several other priests there. Most were awake and chipper and pleased to see us.

"Hello, girls," called out one. "Come to visit anyone in particular?"

"Yes, Father," said the attendant who brought us in. "They're here for Father Bernard."

The old men chuckled.

"Good luck with that," said one of the younger priests, who said his name was Father Jerome. "We had roast beef for supper. He'll snooze for another hour."

"Well, they can't wait an hour," said the attendant cheerfully and she patted Father Bernard's shoulder. He struggled to wake up. It took a few minutes and Fats was getting antsy with all the priests looking at her. I don't know what her problem was. She was Catholic and not scared of Aunt Miriam, which was unusual.

"What in the world," said Father Bernard. "I was having a nap."

"We know," said one of the priests. "You're always having a nap."

"I'm tired."

"We're all tired."

That sparked a little competition over who was the most tired. Bernard won, on account of all the napping, which he did pretty much anytime and anywhere, including mass.

The attendant rolled him out of the common room so we could talk in the hall and I sat down on a bench next to the door. Father Bernard had already gone back to sleep and I had to shake him awake. "Sorry to disturb you, Father Bernard."

He blinked at me, once again bleary-eyed. "Do I know you?"

"No. We've never met."

He squinted at me. "Am I dead?"

"Um...no. Why do you ask?"

"Because you're Marilyn Monroe and I think she's dead," said Father Bernard.

Fats put a hand on her hip. "I predict that this will not be helpful."

"You've got a big man with you, Marilyn. I don't think he likes me."

"That's a woman, Father," I said.

"No." He squinted up at Fats. "I don't think so."

Fats walked away in a huff and he reiterated, "That's a man, dear."

"It's not," I said. "You'll just have to take my word on it."

"Alright, Marilyn." He looked around. "So I'm dead. I have to say this isn't the improvement I was expecting."

I took his hand and patted it. "Father, you are not dead. My name is Mercy Watts and I'd like to ask you a few questions."

"I'd like to ask *you* a few questions. How's Joe? Do you see him? I think he loved you very much."

Oh, my God.

"I'm not Marilyn Monroe. I'm Mercy Watts and I want to ask you some questions about some people you knew in the sixties."

"The sixties? When you died?"

Breathe. He's old, not obnoxious.

I took his face in my hands. "Marilyn died. I'm alive. She had blue eyes. What color are my eyes?"

"I want to say blue."

"Try again."

Another priest walked out. "For crying out loud, you old codger. Her eyes are green and she's not Marilyn Monroe."

Father Bernard squinted at me again. "I don't know. That's a face you don't forget."

"I'll give you that," I said. "But I'm still not her."

He gave a little shrug. "If you say so."

The other priest sighed. "He's hopeless. I'm going to get an after-dinner drink. Would you two ladies care for something? Whiskey sour, perhaps?"

"I don't drink," said Fats.

"And you?" he asked.

"No, thanks."

"Suit yourself, but I think you're going to regret it." The priest walked away and I quickly got down to questioning the Father once he was out of earshot.

"Father Bernard." I tapped his knee, but he was looking at Fats again.

"Men can wear anything these days, but those boots don't look comfortable," he said.

Fats came over and squatted in front of him. "Look here, Father. I'm a woman and I want you to look in my eyes."

"You've got those glasses on."

A muscle twitched in her cheek and she whipped off the Wayfarers. "Better?"

"You are a woman. Well, does that just beat the band. You must've been corn fed."

A whole parade of muscles twitched in Fats' cheek. "Yes. I was corn fed. Listen to Mercy. She wants to ask you about that murdered nun you knew."

"Murdered nun?" His hands started trembling. "What happened? Who did that?"

I took his hand and pressed it between mine. "It was a long time ago. Sister Margaret Mullanphy."

"Who?"

"Sister Maggie, Father Dominic's friend."

He remembered and it took several minutes to get his emotions under control. When he could speak he wasn't happy with me at all. "Why would you come here and bring that up? He was my good friend. He died." Then he whispered, "He killed himself. Didn't you know that?"

"You think Dominic killed himself?" I asked.

"Well, yes. Everyone said so. The police said so." He wiped his eyes and Fats got him a tissue. "It was my fault. I never told anyone that, but it was."

"How was it your fault?"

"I let him take my car. He drove it to the bridge and he jumped off. If I didn't give him the car maybe he wouldn't have jumped." He blew his nose and needed a few more tissues.

Father Bernard had been carrying that guilt for over fifty years and it all came out in a torrent. After Dominic died his name was never spoken again. It was like he never existed. His things were packed and disappeared. He had a coin collection from his father. Bernard didn't know where that went.

"Why do you think Dominic killed himself?" I asked.

He straightened up and looked me in the eye. "It's not because he killed Maggie. If you think that, you can leave right now."

"I don't think that at all," I said. "I'm trying to clear his name and find out who did kill her."

Father Bernard didn't really know Maggie all that well and he didn't know who would've wanted to kill her. He didn't remember Dominic having any ideas either, only that he was upset. His memory was vague from the time, but I got the feeling there were things he didn't want to say. He didn't want to talk about the scene in the Bled Mansion and didn't seem to think the bishop had anything to do with Maggie not being reported missing.

"He liked Maggie," he said. "I remember that. They had a lot of meetings."

"Why was he meeting with Maggie?" I asked.

"Church business, I suppose."

I glanced up at Fats and she pursed her lips.

"How did he feel about Dominic?"

"Oh, I don't know," he said.

I tilted my chin down and batted my eyes. "Come on, Father. You can tell me."

The priest smiled. "You are the spitting image of her."

"Tell me what Bishop Fowler thought of Dominic," I said.

"He didn't care for him truth be told. He thought he was too handsome to be a priest. He called Dominic a smooth-talker. It got worse after Maggie disappeared."

"What happened?"

"Oh, I don't know. I'm tired." He looked away.

"Father, please," I said. "Tell me what happened after."

Father Bernard remembered Dominic going after the bishop over Maggie and the bishop having him barred from his office. Bishop said that Maggie had run off and Dominic said she hadn't. After she was found dead, the bishop said that Dominic and Maggie were inappropriate with each other and that couldn't get out. The bishop was having a lot of meetings at the time and was stressed and upset.

"He was stressed about Maggie?" I asked.

"No. It had nothing to do with that." Father Bernard clammed up tight. I couldn't get him to say another thing about the bishop.

"I just have a couple more questions," I said.

He pulled his hand away. "You want to make us look bad. You should see the good we do not the bad."

"I'm talking about Maggie's murder. What are you talking about?"

"Nothing. Wheel me back in."

I took his hand again. "I want to clear Dominic. Really I do. Just another few questions."

Father Bernard looked away. "I wish you were Marilyn. She'd be more polite."

That was an interesting view of Marilyn. I usually got drug-addled sexpot, not polite.

"Well, Marilyn couldn't clear Dominic. I can. Do you ever remember Dominic or Maggie talking about St. Sebastian?"

He focused back on me. "St. Seb? That's a lovely little parish."

"Did Maggie or Dominic go out there for any reason or talk about it?"

"I don't remember. I've only been there a couple of times. Why do you ask?"

"Maggie's body was found there."

"Yes. I remember. She went there and someone killed her."

"Do you know how she would've gotten there?" I asked. "Did she borrow your car?"

"Of course not. I wouldn't let a woman drive my car."

I could hear Fats gritting her teeth, but I said, "What about Dominic? You said he borrowed your car the night he died, did he borrow it a lot?"

"No. He rode his bicycle and took the buses. I only had a car because I was driving the bishop."

"Did the bishop drive?"

"He did, but he didn't like to. What's this all about?"

"Do you remember Dominic borrowing your car the day Maggie disappeared?"

Father Bernard looked down. "I'm tired. Take me back in."

"Please, did he borrow it?"

"I don't know. That was a lifetime ago."

Fats came in close. "Father, he was your friend. Could he have had your car that day?"

He put his head in his hands. "I don't know. I don't know."

"About nine o'clock in the morning on December third," I said.

He looked up, his eyes red-rimmed. "Morning?"

"Yes."

"No matter what they said," Father Bernard's voice shook. "I didn't think he killed her."

"Father, did he have your car?" asked Fats.

Father Bernard squeezed my hand. "It had to be the morning? You're sure? They told us they didn't know what time she'd gone."

"It was the morning after eight o'clock and before ten." I squeezed his hand. "I'm absolutely positive that's when Maggie was taken."

He smiled, his blue eyes running over. "He didn't have it then. He didn't. I couldn't let anyone borrow it during the day. It was for church business. If the bishop needed to go somewhere or a parishioner needed a ride, I had to have it."

"Why were you so upset when I asked you?" I asked.

"He borrowed it the night she disappeared. He said he was going to pick up the wreaths for the rectory, but he never picked up any wreaths." Tears rolled down his cheeks.

"You thought maybe..."

"No, I never thought that." His eyes said he did, that it was a possibility.

I stood up and thanked him. "You've helped a lot."

"Do you think you can do something?" he asked. "I let him down when I gave him that car. He asked and I gave him the keys."

"I'll do my best," I said.

"Good. Someone should. I don't think we did then, but I don't remember why."

I started to wheel him back in, but Fats said, "Hold it. What about everybody else's cars?"

Father Bernard chuckled softly. "We were priests. Not everyone had a car."

"But there were other cars registered," I said.

He reached up and I took his hand. "Don't you worry about that, Marilyn. Dom could only drive my car. That's why he waited so late to go to the river that last night. I was out late working with the ladies' choir."

"How come he could only drive your car?" asked Fats.

"Dominic was the son of a wealthy man, not a dirt poor farmer like me. He could only drive an automatic."

I leaned over and kissed him on his incredibly soft cheek. "Thank you. That's super helpful."

He patted my cheek. "I'm glad."

"Can I ask you one more thing?" I asked. "It might be painful."

"It's all painful, Marilyn. Go ahead."

"Why did Dominic say he needed the car? Where was he going?"

Father Bernard sighed. "I've thought about that so many times, but the truth is that I don't think I asked. I don't know why I didn't."

"Was he upset?"

"Not that I remember. When the police came and said they'd found my car by the bridge and a man had jumped, I was sure it couldn't have been Dom, but they said it was. He never came back so it must've been him."

I gave Father Bernard my dad's card, wheeled him in, and thanked him again before Fats and I left, walking down the hall slowly. I don't know about her, but my mind was racing. Was it Dominic that went into the river? Nobody found a body. Who was on the bridge? If he wasn't suicidal where was he going?

"Are you thinking what I'm thinking?" asked Fats.

"I never know what you're thinking," I said.

"The bishop had a thing for Sister Maggie."

"That wasn't what I was thinking, but you're right."

"But he didn't kill her," said Fats. "That would be too easy."

"The question is why didn't he want to save her and what was he so stressed about if it wasn't a missing nun."

We got outside and it was dark. Fats stretched and did a little jog in place. "I have got to get to the gym and work off some of this crap. Thinking about that Maggie has me down."

"When was the last time you went?" I asked.

"This morning."

"You're really slacking off." I got in and buckled up. "I can't remember going to the gym and that's how I like it."

"You're gonna regret that someday."

"I doubt it."

"Where to next?" asked Fats.

"Don't you have something else to do?" I asked.

She arched an eyebrow at me. "Like plan a wedding?"

"Never mind. Let's see if Maggie's family is in."

"Then we can talk wedding."

Swell.

CHAPTER TWELVE

Patrick Mullanphy was the third generation to live in the same house in Dogtown, an adorable little brick bungalow with stone trim and an arched front door. My mom always looked at those houses with envy. I know that sounds odd, because our house with its Tudor beaming and fancy fireplaces was the envy of many, but Mom said those houses were sweet and manageable, and, let's face it, there was only three of us on a good day and more often two. We didn't need Josiah Bled's six bedrooms and butler's pantry, however much we might love it. Plus, the heating bill was outrageous.

Fats pulled up in front and said, "Uncle Moe has one almost exactly like that on The Hill."

"I love these houses," I said. "They're so cute."

"Yeah, they're just not big enough," she said.

"Big enough for what?"

"Me and Tiny. You know it's probably under 1500 square feet. The bathrooms are tiny. I can't fit in Uncle Moe's shower. Tiny would have to squat to get his head wet."

"I never thought about that."

"You wouldn't." She got out and assumed a boxer's stance and began air punching.

"What are you doing?" I asked.

"Getting ready. This baby's got me all warm and fuzzy."

This is warm and fuzzy?

"The Mullanphys aren't suspects."

She did a couple of side-kicks and managed to get herself in a complete split position that a gymnast would envy. "Everyone is a suspect."

"This guy was born three years after Maggie was murdered and he's her third cousin or something."

Fats did a super-fast whip kick that ruffled my hair and conceded, "Alright, so he's in the clear, but we need what he knows."

"I'll give you that, but don't expect much." I skirted Fats as she did another kick and trotted up to the front door and checked my phone for the time. The house was lit up, but dinner should be over.

It took longer for someone to answer than I expected and I had time to get nervous. No matter how many times I talked to victim's families, I never got used to it. At least, Patrick was pretty far removed. I just hoped he wasn't completely removed.

A girl about eleven answered the door and didn't say a word. She saw Fats and that was the end of speaking.

"Hi," I said. "Is your father home? I'd like to speak to—"

"For God's sake, Marlee," called out a woman. "No solicitors."

Marlee started to close the door, but Fats slapped a hand against the wood and it bounced back.

"Mom!" Marlee yelled in panic.

"Pat!" yelled the woman.

"What?"

"The door!"

"What?"

They went back and forth with Marlee staring at us with embarrassment. "Those are my parents."

"We've all got them," I said. "And they're surprisingly similar."

Marlee didn't think so and I had to say there was a lot of yelling and not a whole lot of listening going on in that bungalow.

"For fuck's sake, Pat, get the door! I'm dying my hair!"

"I'm doing the quarterlies!"

"Are they dripping?"

Pat let out a stream of obscenities that got louder as he got closer. If it hadn't been for Fats, I might've turned tail and taken off. Angry is no way to start an interview, especially about a family murder. But I was in luck, also because of Fats. When Pat saw her, he stopped yelling and froze in the doorway.

"We're not selling anything," I said, quickly. "I'm Mercy Watts and this is Fats Licata. We'd like to ask you some questions."

"I know who you are," he said. "I just never expected you to show up at my door. I'm a huge fan."

"Well, thanks for that," I said. "Can we come in?"

"I didn't mean you." Pat rushed forward and reached past me. "I can't believe I'm finally meeting you."

Fats shook his hand and grinned at me. "You're not the only one with a fan base."

"Are you still competing?" Pat asked. "I haven't seen you on the circuit."

"I'm retired, but it's nice that you remember me." Fats smiled at that man in a way that I could see him melting. Unfortunately, so could his daughter, who was giving him what had to be a youthful version of her mother's stink eye.

"Can we come in?" I asked. "It's a bit nippy out here."

Pat focused. "Oh, my God. I'm sorry. Sorry so. In here. Come in here."

"Dad! What's wrong with you?"

"Nothing. Go play or something."

Marlee crossed her arms. Nope, not going to happen. "What do you want?" she asked.

I pulled out one of my dad's cards and gave it to her. Marlee was the nut I needed to crack. "We'd like to ask your father about a case we're working on."

She examined the card and frowned. "Your name isn't on here."

Fats laughed. "You don't miss a thing. That's her father, the famous detective. We're helping him out."

Patrick shooed Marlee away and led us into the living room with his daughter in pursuit. "Please sit down. I...do you..."

"Water would be great," I said.

"Marlee, water," he ordered, not looking at her but staring at Fats with glowing admiration. Not a good thing.

"How about you go with her, Fats?" I asked, giving her a look. I had to get her away from Pat or it was nowhere's-ville.

She grinned at me and then turned to Marlee, who had the stinkiest stink eye I'd ever seen. "I love these houses. My Uncle Moe has one just like it."

"Yeah?"

"He does. On The Hill." Fats steered her through an arched door. "Let's get that water."

Marlee wasn't so easily distracted. "Mom! There are hot girls here!" she yelled as they left the room.

Pat slapped his forehead. "I'm so sorry. Marlee's a...I don't know what."

"My grandad would call her a pistol," I said.

"That's accurate." Patrick saw me for the first time and I had the satisfaction of seeing his eyes widen.

Alright. Who's the famous one now.

"Aren't you the girl that stank up the airport?" He sniffed and, I swear to God, I almost got up and left, but a woman wearing a stained men's undershirt and plastic bag on her head rushed in. You know a woman's concerned about her man when she's willing to be seen like that. Pat had been a bad boy.

"Who the...oh, it's you," she said, relaxing and I waited for her to say that she wasn't worried about me since I stank, but she didn't. She sank into the cushy armchair opposite me and heaved a sigh of relief.

"Hi," I said. "I'm Mercy Watts and I'm investigating a case and I was wondering if I could ask you some questions."

"I know who you are. How could I not?"

I winced and she grinned at me. "I don't believe everything I read, unlike some people I know."

It was Pat's turn to wince and I enjoyed it, I have to say.

"That airport thing was my uncle. He was having a time and it got pinned on me," I said. "Do you have time for some questions? It won't take long."

Fats walked in and the wife took one look and said, "You bet it won't."

Pat turned multiple shades of red, ombré, if you will. Dark red on the neck to pale pink on his balding head.

Marlee looked back and forth between her parents, grabbed a Coke off the tray Fats was carrying, and plopped down on the floor next to her mother. "She's a bodybuilder and the other one is a nurse."

"I know," said her mother. "Believe me, I know."

Pat's ombré got a little darker. "I'm. I think we can answer some questions, can't we, Nancy?"

Fats set down the tray and held out her hand to Nancy. "I'm Fats Licata, former bodybuilder."

Nancy shook her hand and asked, "Are you sure you're former?"

"I shake it up every now and again, but I'm retired." Fats sat down in the chair next to her and it wasn't easy. She barely squeezed in.

"So what's this about?" asked Nancy. "We haven't seen any crimes. It's a pretty quiet neighborhood."

"It's not a recent crime," I said, "and it wasn't necessarily in St. Louis."

"Then I don't know how we can help you," said Pat, starting to turn a normal human shade of pink.

I glanced at Marlee. The girl might not know and I sure wasn't going to be the one to tell her about a family tragedy. "Can we talk in private? This may not be appropriate."

Marlee scowled. "No way. I'm not leaving."

Nancy pointed at the door. "Go to your room."

"No."

"Go."

"No."

"I'm your mother and I say go."

"No."

That went on for a good five minutes and I had the feeling that Marlee won her battles by attrition. I envied her. My mother did not get worn down. Maybe I didn't stick to it long enough because Nancy was already wavering and Pat was already over it. Kid one. Parents zip.

"Fats, you might be a mother someday," I interjected. "How would you handle this?"

She stood up so fast she was a blur and picked up Marlee with her arms pinned to her waist. I grabbed the Coke out of her hand before she dropped it and Fats held her straight out, stiff armed, like she weighed no more than a five pound bag of flour. "I'd take her to her room. May I?"

Nancy burst into laughter and nodded as her daughter protested about being an abused kid and calling children's services. Marlee's complaints faded away as Fats carried her upstairs.

"Wow," said Pat.

"Where has she been for the last eleven years?" Nancy shot a look at Pat. "Other than the garage wall."

Garage wall? Oh! At least I'm not the only one.

"She does security work," I said. "And helps me on occasion."

"Doing what? I thought you were a nurse and in that band."

"I'm just DBD's cover girl."

Pat leaned forward. "You sing. We saw you at that benefit. Not bad."

Thanks, I guess.

"Under duress, I sing. Nursing is my regular gig."

"And all those murders." Nancy wrinkled her nose. "How do you stand thinking about all that stuff?"

"I can't stand it, but ice cream helps."

She grinned and said, "Ask away before Marlee escapes."

"She will not escape," I said.

Pat leaned back and ran his fingers through his sparse hair. "That's what we thought too many times to count."

"Okay, then. First of all, let me say I'm sorry to bring this up and I wouldn't do it, if I didn't have to."

They came to attention and Nancy balled up the tee shirt in her fists. "Go ahead."

"It's about Sister Maggie's murder."

"Huh?" she asked. "The nun? Wasn't that like fifty years ago?"

Pat frowned. "It was before I was born. I never knew her."

"I realize that, but something's come up in her case and things have changed," I said.

"But they know who did it," said Nancy. "Right?"

I picked up a glass of water and took a sip. "It's less solved than you'd think."

Everyone got a glass and held them while I explained about the medal, leaving out Aunt Miriam's unwillingness to cooperate, and just saying that it couldn't be positively identified just then.

"So why don't they just reopen the case?" asked Pat.

"Not enough evidence. I'm doing a favor and trying to find more."

They went quiet. It was a lot to take in. I held nothing back, except Aunt Miriam's weirdness. I told them about the bishop's behavior, what Father Bernard said, all of it.

"Well," said Pat, after a minute or two, "I can tell you that my family never believed the priest did it."

"No?" I asked.

"No. Not at all. My dad said it was total bullshit." Pat got red again, but no ombré that time, pure tomato. "He left the church because of how it was handled. Everyone did. Dad never stepped foot in another church again."

"Because of the investigation? The church didn't have anything to do with that."

He scoffed. "Oh, yeah? You believe that? Dad said the church only cared about how they looked and wanted it to go away."

"Sounds like what I've heard, but your dad thought that they stopped the investigation?" I asked.

"I don't know about stopped, but they didn't help. That's for sure."

"Do you know any details?"

"Faith said she was strangled," said Nancy.

"Who's Faith?" I asked.

"My mother," said Pat. "I didn't know you two talked about it. Dad hated to talk about it. He always got pissed off."

"We only talked about it the one time," said Nancy. "Your dad, that last Christmas, you know how he was."

Pat went on to explain his father had a drinking problem and would only talk about his cousin's murder if he got wasted. He'd died five years ago. His last Christmas he got really drunk and started spewing anger and obscenities. When the kids got him to bed, Faith talked about the toll Maggie's death had taken on her husband. He and Maggie had been close, since she'd lost her own brother to cancer. Faith didn't say much, just that Maggie had been strangled and people thought the priest did it, but Joseph didn't.

"Did your mom believe it?" I asked.

"I never asked," said Pat. "Probably. Mom's all about authority. She doesn't question much. She mostly hated Dad getting upset. It's not like we could do anything. Cops said he did it, so he did it."

"But now maybe you can prove he didn't," said Nancy. "That medal's a pretty big deal for the case."

I nodded. "It is, but I don't know if it'll go anywhere."

"It's too late for my dad," said Pat, bitterly.

"But not your mom and everybody else."

He put his head in his hands. "I don't know anything and I don't think Mom does either. Not really. Dad just railed on about the church and he was drunk. He'd say all kinds of crazy shit."

"Anything about who he thought did it?" I asked. "Any names?"

Pat didn't remember any names. His father's accusations were general, not specific. But he did talk about Maggie's job at the asylum. He didn't like her going there, even though she worked mainly with children.

"Maybe that's something," said Nancy. "You'd have to be crazy to kill a nun."

"I agree and the St. Louis cops never took a look as far as I know," I said.

Fats appeared in the door and startled all three of us. "What about where she died?"

"Holy crap!" exclaimed Nancy. "How'd you do that?"

She grinned. "I have skills."

Pat sighed. "So Marlee will be down any second."

"Nope. I gave her twenty bucks to stay put."

Nancy shook her head. "We've tried bribery."

"Do you have the ability to take twenty bucks off her and no problem doing it?" asked Fats.

"Not so much."

"Then we're good. What about that town?"

Nancy shrugged. "I have no idea where it happened. Faith didn't mention that."

"St. Sebastian," said Pat.

"Where they have that big fair?"

"That's the one," I said. "So does your family go there or have a special connection?"

They shrugged and couldn't think of a reason why Maggie would go there. Joseph never said anything about it. Most of his rage was at the church. The actual murderer seemed to have slipped his mind for the most part, except that he got away with it, but that, in Joseph's opinion, was mainly the church's fault.

"Did your father say anything about Maggie's death at all? How it happened? Where? Who might've known something?" I asked.

Pat sighed. "Like I said, he was drunk and angry. I think he couldn't get over that the church somehow betrayed us. That's what he talked about. He really loved her. Sometimes he'd cry and talk about how he should've protected her. How he was her brother since her brother died. He was my namesake. Patrick. He died young."

"Who would've gotten Maggie's belongings?" I asked. "Even nuns have stuff. Books and whatnot."

"My grandparents, I guess."

Fats came in and sat down. "What did they say about it?"

"Nothing. I don't remember them ever saying her name. My mom warned me never to talk about Maggie to them after Dad was on a bender."

"Were they there when he was talking about it?" asked Fats.

"Usually, but they would just leave the room and everyone would try to shush my dad. My Aunt Linda would get mad at Dad and tell him off. It was a mess."

"Where's Linda?" I asked.

"Scottsdale, but don't ask her. She says it's ancient history. She won't help."

I tried to think of more questions, but he only knew what his drunken father said and that was the height of unreliable. It was inter-

esting that the family agreed with everyone else that knew Maggie and
Dominic. They didn't believe he did it and, like The Girls, were mad at
the church over it. It was one of those where there's smoke, there's fire
kind of things. I'd be very surprised if they were totally off base in how
they felt.

"So your mother's still around, right?" I asked.

"She's in Florida, but I don't think she knows any more than I do,"
said Pat.

"We can call her," said Nancy.

Pat groaned.

"It can't hurt."

"You'll do it then."

Nancy agreed and got her phone. Faith was quite elderly and,
although living on her own in a retirement village in Tampa, she wasn't
good about picking up the phone. It took four tries to get her and I
was reminded of Aunt Miriam. I'd say it was an old person thing, but
Grandad didn't do it and neither did The Girls. Maybe there was
commonality I was missing.

Nancy greeted her mother-in-law and pointed at the phone. Pat
shook his head and Nancy rolled her eyes.

"So, Mom," she said, "I wanted to ask you something about Sister
Maggie."

During the back and forth, Pat got up and went out to peer up the
staircase. He came back and said, "I'll be damned. She's still in there."

"You should see how quick she trained her dog," I said.

"Thirty minutes?"

"Five."

Fats smiled. "Give or take ten minutes. It's all in the tone."

"And the fact that you could crack Moe open like a peanut."

"Isn't Moe your uncle?" asked Pat.

I explained that Moe was named after Moe and for good reason.
That weird-looking dog with the moist bulging eyes did bear a striking
resemblance to Uncle Moe who was one of the oddest looking guys I'd
ever met. Even his short-cropped hair had a brindle pattern to it and
Fats assured me that it was natural because who would dye their hair to
look like that? I didn't know, but I'd seen some pretty questionable

fashion choices at three in the morning in the ER, including genital self-piercing and a guy who tried to dye his beard with wood stain. Nothing's off the table.

"Alright. Faith does have a clue, " said Nancy walking in and checking the clock. "Ah, crap. I've got to wash this out or I'll look like some trailer trash biker chick."

"Works for me," said Pat.

"Idiot."

He grinned as she dashed for the stairs and I chased her with Fats right behind me. "Wait. What does Faith know?"

"No details, but we've got the sister's stuff." Nancy dashed into the bathroom.

"Where?"

"Basement. She said you can have it. That box was a millstone around Joseph's neck." Nancy cranked the shower and slammed the door.

"I can't believe it," I said.

"Don't," said Fats. "It'll be full of bibles and veils."

"That *is* my luck."

A door opened and Marlee stuck her head out. The girl didn't say a word before Fats snapped her fingers and Marlee disappeared.

"You have got to teach me that," said Pat from the bottom of the stairs.

Fats trotted down, each stair complaining as she went. "That cannot be taught. Scaring people without being scary is a God-given talent."

"Hello," I said. "You are scary."

"No, I'm not. I'm direct."

Okay. I'll just let you live with that delusion.

I came down the stairs much slower. "Is it okay with you if we take the box?"

"Fine with me. I didn't know it was down there." He opened the door to the basement. "Have at it."

I should've known it couldn't be that easy. 'Cause it's never easy. The Mullanphy family had been in that house since 1935 and I'm pretty sure they never cleaned out the basement. Three generations of clutter were stacked up in crazy towers to the floor joists overhead, sometimes cardboard boxes were wedged in against ancient and frighteningly frayed wires and the whole thing smelled like mold and fresh dirt.

"Just like Uncle Moe's house," said Fats, ducking under Christmas lights hanging from hooks and a pair of dusty tennis rackets.

"A fire hazard?"

"Yes, it is. My dad thinks he's got some serious dough stashed down there."

Don't ask. You do not want to be an accessory after the fact.

I clamped my teeth together and, for once, I didn't ask the obvious question, but Fats answered it anyway.

"He robbed some banks in the eighties. He wasn't working for Calpurnia then so he didn't have to kick it up to her, so Dad says it has to be in that basement. He's not living high on the hog."

"I didn't hear that." I started looking in boxes and searching for labels.

"Too late," said Fats. "It was three banks in Arkansas and Dad thinks probably another couple in Iowa. He did spend some time in Minnesota in the seventies and according to Calpurnia there was plenty of dirty going on then."

"Shut up."

Fats gave out a throaty laugh.

"I could tell the rookies about your dear old Uncle Moe. They're looking for a leg up. He might do it."

"I'm really worried about you telling the Feds about Uncle Moe." She moved a stack of boxes that had to weigh over a hundred pounds without breaking a sweat.

"I could," I said, digging back between towers.

"No."

"Why not?"

"Because you'd have to tell the great, and now hanging by a thread, Tommy Watts how you know about Uncle Moe and worse, who I really am."

"He has to find out some time," I said.

"Nope. My grandmother will still tell you that Rocco was three months premature. She totally believes it."

"That's different."

"Tommy doesn't want to know. It'll make his life hard." Fats wormed her way past several towers of boxes by a combo of pushing and hip checking. I think the boxes feared her. "It is difficult to get a man to understand something when his salary depends on him not understanding it."

"Who said that?" I asked.

"Upton Sinclair."

"*The Jungle?*"

She grinned at me over the boxes. "It's about meat packing. I have an interest."

"I bet." I dug through some more boxes. "I think I'm seeing a pattern."

"In me? I would think so."

"Not you, although I can. This basement goes by decade. The deeper you go, the further back in time. Where are you?"

"Eighties. Somebody saved this thing." She held out a crimping iron.

"My mom has one of those," I said.

"I want to try it."

"Don't. It's bad."

We dug back through the eighties. I found a whole box of what could've been prom dresses. I hated to think there was a time when girls wore metallic gold dresses with a black lace overlay. I don't even want to talk about the big butt bows.

"Seventies!" announced Fats. "That's a whole lot of polyester. Didn't they throw anything away?"

"No, they didn't," said Nancy, arriving with a towel wrapped around her head. "There are three ratty old Christmas trees down here somewhere."

"We found them," said Fats. "I'm thinking about reporting your house as a health hazard."

"Fine with me. I called those junk guys once to have them clear it out and Pat nearly had a conniption. He thinks there's buried treasure down here or something."

I hope he's right.

"Hey, Fats," I said. "Can you see the label on that box way back there?"

She produced a mini Maglite and aimed the narrow beam at the box stuffed under a ton of sporting equipment, including a kayak, that was hanging from the ceiling. "Bingo. Nineteen sixty something."

We dug through seventies camping equipment and a collection of pool toys to find the sixties off in a back corner. It was slow going with my cast getting in the way.

"I can't get in there," said Fats.

"Convenient," I said. "It's like the nest of Aragog back there."

"Nice reference. Follow the spiders, Ron."

"But it's the Dark Forest."

"Get a move on. I've got a wedding to plan," said Fats.

"A wedding? Congratulations," said Nancy and I was completely forgotten.

I pulled some boxes labeled Candice's wedding out of the way and shivered. The closer I got to Maggie's belongings the more I didn't want to find them. I'm not going to claim it made any sense. I just had a bad feeling about it. Not the something's-not-right feeling. The this-is-going-to-be-bad-for-you feeling.

"Got it yet?" asked Fats.

"Almost. Nancy, do you have any bug spray? I don't think I'm alone back here."

"You're fine. We just bug bombed a month ago."

"I don't think it took."

I know you can't hear people rolling their eyes, but let's just give me the benefit of the doubt, and say I could, in that instance, because those eyes were a-rollin' like pinwheels.

"You want to come back here?" I asked.

"It's your case," said Fats.

"My case," I muttered. "It's not even a case."

"What was that?"

"Nothing. Toss me your Maglite."

Fats tossed it the way she does everything. Hard and fast.

"Son of a bitch!"

"You should've caught it," she said.

"I've got one useable hand." I rubbed the small knot on the side of my head and switched on the light. After digging for a few more minutes, I spotted a box with "Maggie" written in lovely script. It made me sad to see it back there tucked away for over fifty years all her stuff; things she cared about, shoved in beside boxes of paperbacks and unused school supplies.

"I found it," I said.

"Finally," said Fats. "Grab it and let's go."

I passed back the box and looked to see if there was another one. "Hold on." I squatted and reached back to pull from the back and my hands touched something. Not warm. Not fur, thankfully. But something and then I felt a kind of odd tingling that wasn't really a tingle.

"I think I feel something," I said.

"If it's the creeps then I'm with you," said Nancy. "I hate it down here."

"It's not—ow—son of a—shit!" I came spinning out of the depths of the basement, flapping my arms and screeching. For once, Fats didn't leap into action. The snippets I caught were of mouths dropped and astonishment.

"Help me!" I yelled. "They're biting me."

"What?" asked Nancy.

"I don't know."

"Spiders!"

That's right. I got overrun by spiders, hundreds of spiders. Face. Eyes. Arms. Legs. Other places. And what did Calpurnia Fibonacci's bad ass bodyguard do?

"I'm out!" Fats booked it up the stairs, hitting each tread so hard I thought the whole thing would come down on my head. Getting knocked out might not have been the worst thing at that point, but still, come on.

Nancy grabbed a hideous prom dress and smacked me with it. "Get your clothes off! They're in the clothes."

She didn't have to tell me twice. I screamed and stripped. Chuck dreamed of me stripping that fast, but that was spider-induced psychosis. I would've done anything to get those things off me. If someone said, "Shoot Nancy and those spiders will be off you," it'd have been bye-bye, Nancy. I was gone, totally and completely gone.

Down to my cast and the granny panties I'd decided to wear that day, I wildly screamed and smashed spiders. "Get them off! Get them off!"

"Water!" yelled Nancy.

She found a bucket, filled it with ice water, and threw it at me. Freddie Mercury couldn't have hit the note that came out of me. Every dog in the neighborhood started barking and Nancy's cat burst through their cat door and wasn't seen for three days. I think I damaged my own hearing. On the upside, it worked. Spiders don't like getting doused in ice water anymore than humans and they either died or ran back to the nether regions of that God-awful basement.

I stood there, shaking violently with a burning, raw throat and squashed spiders all over me.

"Jesus!"

Did I think about who said it or that I was basically naked and that my granny panties had several holes that I didn't mind because they were super comfy? No, I didn't. I turned around. Standing at the base of the stairs was Pat, carrying a fire extinguisher, Fats, carrying a can of roach spray, Marlee with her twenty dollar bill, and a boy about fourteen years old with eyes coming out of his head like Roger Rabbit.

"You have really big boobs," said Marlee.

That got everyone moving. Nancy threw a bridesmaid's dress at me and yelled, "Get him out of here, Pat!"

Pat dropped the extinguisher and forced his kids up the stairs. Marlee went willingly. The word "spiders" did it for her. Pat had to use a broom on the boy and I'm not sure that would've worked without the threat of losing Fortnite for the rest of his life.

I wrapped myself in an extraordinary confection of shiny purple with white fur trim. Somebody wore it in a wedding. No kidding. Nancy emailed me the picture later. Faith in 1973. It was worse in a group and included a fur muff that would've been handy for my frozen hands.

"I'm so sorry. I thought the water would help," said Nancy.

"Really?" asked Fats, still holding out the roach spray at arm's length.

"Shut up," I said through chattering teeth. "You were going to spray me with poison."

She lowered the can but didn't concede that poison wasn't a great idea. If it's worth doing, it's worth overdoing was her motto.

Nancy got me upstairs, past her lingering son, who got a stinging smack for looking, and I went into the shower to defrost until the water heater ran out way too quick with a bag over my already soggy cast. My clothes went into the washer, spiders and all, and I ended up dressed in some of Fats spare gym clothes because Nancy, a fifty-year-old mother of three, didn't have anything big enough to fit over my butt.

"That's it," I said, sitting at their kitchen table hunched over a cup of Tension Tamer.

"You're not giving up on Maggie, are you?" asked Pat. "Please don't say that."

"I'm giving up on ice cream. It hates me and my butt."

Nancy towel-dried my hair and said, "You're not fat. You're curvy. Curvy's in. Look at Kim Kardashian. Now that is a big butt."

She thought she was helping, but knowing my butt wasn't quite as big as Kim Kardashian's wasn't going to do it.

"My leggings are too big for you," said Fats, still clutching her can o'poison.

"Only because you've got bigger thighs than The Rock."

She stuck out a leg. "You think so? I've been working on it."

"Is that a good thing?" asked Nancy. Her eyes said no.

"Ya, it is," said Pat, earning him a smile from Fats, but Nancy gave him the stink eye and he slunk back down to the basement with Fats' spray to carry up the box.

"We should go," said Fats. "We'll be late."

"If you think I'm going out to dinner," I said, "you're out of your mind."

"We have to. Tiny's meeting us at Kronos in fifteen minutes."

"Tiny can meet me in the dumpster out back. 'Cause that's where I'm going to throw myself."

"It's not that bad," said Fats.

I stood up and spread out my arms. Nancy recoiled, but Fats gave me a look and shrugged. "You've looked worse."

I have, but I'm not admitting it.

"You're out of your mind. Look at me." I had on the stuff she threw in her bag for emergencies. What emergencies would require pink and purple tiger-striped leggings and a neon green hoodie with "Ain't No Bitch" printed on it was a mystery. And don't let me forget, underneath I had on one of Nancy's old nursing bras because it was the only thing I could stuff my "really big boobs" in. No, I didn't have panties. They were optional. A bra was not.

"Nobody will care. It's Kronos and you have to talk to Tiny."

"I'm covered in spider bites and Calamine lotion. I'm pink polka-dotted."

"Sorry we didn't have the clear stuff," said Nancy. "We never use it."

"Don't worry about it," I said. "We invade your house. Bring up an ancient murder and wreck your basement and give your son an eyeful. It's me that needs to apologize."

Nancy smiled. "Never mind that. Pat agreed to clear out the basement. He hates spiders. I owe you."

"If you say so."

"I do," she said. "I think your phone's been buzzing."

I sighed and reluctantly took a peek. Uncle Morty. Awesome. I ignored him but couldn't ignore Nancy and Fats taking a closer look at my arm.

"It has to come off," said Fats.

"You're going to cut off her arm?" asked Marlee. "Ew."

"Her cast, stinky," said Nancy. "Go tell your dad to bring in his toolbox."

"It's fine," I said.

"Smell it."

No need to sniff. The odor had a way of getting into my nose whether I wanted it to or not. I hadn't been the best at keeping it dry and the only place I sweated was in my cast. Now that it was seriously wet, it really smelled.

Fats poked and said, "It's soft and lumpy."

"Fine. I'll go in tomorrow and take care of it."

Nancy scoffed. "Our basement tried to eat you. I'll take it off."

"Well—"

"Don't worry about it. I've done it loads of times. My family specializes in broken bones. That peeping Tom upstairs has broken his arm twice and his foot once. This is a piece of cake. I'll just use some snips. Five minutes tops."

Nancy knew her stuff and had my wrinkly red arm out of its prison in no time and into a dry, non-smelly brace and sling. While she was working, my phone kept buzzing. Uncle Morty.

"Just answer it," said Nancy. "How bad can it be?"

"You don't watch the news very often do you?" I asked.

"I do, but it's your uncle."

"He's the smelly one and crabby and demanding."

She smiled and adjusted my sling strap. "Sounds like family. Are you forced to live above a spider breeding ground?"

"I said we'll clean it out," said Pat. "That stuff might be worth something."

"It's worth incinerating."

Pat threw up his hands. "I give up."

"Finally," said Nancy. "All set, Mercy?"

I stood and hitched up my tiger-striped leggings. "I guess. Thanks. I appreciate it."

"No problem," said Nancy. "You'll let us know what you find out about Maggie?"

"I will. Did you look in the box, Pat?" I asked.

Pat closed his toolbox, slowly snapping shut the latches. "You know, I was going to, but when I started to open it, I couldn't."

"Spiders?" asked Fats with a shiver.

He chuckled. "Yeah, it was the spiders."

Nancy went over and hugged him fiercely. "Go up to bed. I'll be there in a minute."

He hesitated and she shrugged. Pat nodded to us, slightly pink, and headed upstairs.

Fats produced a toothpick out of nowhere, snapped it in half and ate it. I will never get used to that. "Do I need to have a talk with somebody?"

Nancy sighed. "What good does talking do?"

"Obviously you've never seen me talk."

"I have," I said. "It leaves an impression."

"It's fine. He's a bit of an idiot, but he always manages to redeem himself," she said with a laugh.

"What does your husband do for a living?" asked Fats.

"We own Mullanphy Motor Works. Hence all the posters of you up in our garage."

"You're on posters?" I asked.

"I did a little modeling," said Fats. "Me with an engine is a surefire hit."

I didn't know what to say. I couldn't picture it. I really couldn't. Maybe if Fats was punching the engine.

"I believe that," said Nancy. "Pat has your entire collection. One of our distributors gives them to him."

"That can't be comfortable," I said.

"It's better now that I've met you two." Nancy walked us out to Fats' truck and gave us hugs. "Thank you for getting that box out of here and doing something about the murder. It's weighed on us for far too long."

Nancy got teary-eyed and so did I, mostly about being too big for mom jeans and covered in spider bites, but still it was an emotional moment.

We got in the truck and Fats said, "You're pathetic."

I blew my nose and snuffled, "I agree."

"They're just spider bites. How long before they go away?"

"No idea. And don't say 'just'. You ran. I know your Kryptonite now."

"What are you going to do?" Fats asked. "Carry a bag of spiders?"

"Don't tempt me."

"Answer your phone."

"I don't want to. We're late and I'm not going to dinner," I said.

She looked at me, produced another toothpick, and said, "I already canceled during the crying."

"Is Chuck pissed?"

"Who cares? I still haven't forgiven him for taking the side of that douchebag, Julia."

Fats peeled out and we careened through the streets until we merged on highway forty at nearly a hundred miles an hour. That's how I knew she was serious. Fats was a great driver, but that's where her anger came out. Julia was a cop who'd given me some serious problems during the case where I broke my arm and Chuck backed her, not me. He had his reasons and we were working on it. Fats still wanted to pummel him.

"Answer your phone," she said, snapping her toothpick in half dramatically.

"Fine," I said. "Hello."

"What the fuck did you do?" Uncle Morty yelled.

So many things.

"Nothing."

"Nothing? Screw that. You did something."

"I got Maggie's personal effects from her family," I said. "What's wrong with that?"

He thought about it. "Nothing. That ain't it. What else?"

"Tell me what's going on."

"It's lighting up like a friggin' Christmas tree over here."

"Huh?"

"I've got emails flying left and right. What did you do? I know it's you. Nobody kicks up a crap heap like you."

He wasn't wrong. I was a crap heap kicker, but that time it was totally innocent. About the time Fats and I were heading into Pat and Nancy's basement, the church started talking. Bishops to the archbishop and back. The priests at the cathedral to the priest at St. James. They were all talking about Sister Maggie's murder.

"How do you know?"

"I freaking tagged the bastards, of course."

"You mean you put a worm in the church's computers," I said and Fats raised an eyebrow at me. I raised my palms back.

"Like you're surprised. It's what I do and it's a damn good thing I did," said Uncle Morty.

"Why? What'd they say?"

The answer was not much and I mean that. They were talking about Maggie and Dominic, but they knew less than we did. Uncle Morty said that when he started poking around in the church records, he came up with nothing on Maggie. She was there, listed as a nun in Aunt Miriam's order, birth and death date. No details. Her murder had been glossed over. We knew that but didn't know that Father Dominic had been scrubbed. He wasn't listed anywhere. No pictures. He wasn't in the hospital archives. There were records from his home state of New York, birth, school, and where he was ordained. But nothing from St. Louis, not even a death certificate.

"He was never declared dead?" I asked.

"Not that I can find. What'd you do?"

I yawned. "I'll tell you when I get home."

"I ain't there."

Yes!

"How come?"

"I don't have to keep you on it. I gotta get you off," he said.

"Huh?" I said.

"I gotta get it done so we can leave."

I should've known, but I wasn't about to complain. I told him about the confirmed timeline and Father Bernard.

"That's interesting. I don't think the current guys have a clue about what went on."

"So what are they worried about?"

"What do you think? Looking bad *again*. You going through that box tonight?" Uncle Morty asked, but it was really more of an order.

"Maybe."

"Maybe?" He started a fresh rant and I hung up. I planned on curling up with a big dose of Tylenol and a new episode of *Outlander*, not some poor murdered woman's things. It was too depressing. I wasn't sure I even wanted it in the apartment. The smell of roach spray, mold, and misery pervaded the truck and I didn't fancy living with it indefinitely.

Fats turned onto my street and said, "What's going on here?"

We couldn't pull onto the street behind my building to park. There were construction vehicles totally blocking it up.

"Are they done?" she asked, leaning forward to look at the building behind mine.

"Not even close," I said. "Go around the front and drop me."

Fats parked illegally on the sidewalk, but I knew better than to warn her about a ticket. Calpurnia's people didn't get tickets or even a sideways glance. I got out and opened the front door for Fats since she was carrying Maggie's box. I was behind her when I heard Chuck's voice ring out. "Mercy!"

"What?" I kept a groan on the inside. I so didn't have the strength to deal with whatever his deal was. I barely had the strength to put on fresh Calamine lotion, which I sorely needed.

Chuck tried to get around Fats. "Did you get that worksite shut down?"

Holy crap. The rookie came through.

"Me? With what? My magical control of the building inspectors?"

"Goddammit, Mercy. Command is all over me on this."

"I didn't do it and, even if I did, it's not your deal," I said.

"You are my deal."

Fats dropped the box with a thud and radiated anger. "You got a problem?"

Chuck paled. "Hey, Fats. I...uh...no. I just need to find out what happened—oh my God what happened to you?"

"Spiders," I said.

I guess there was nothing to say about that because my hot boyfriend has never looked blank like that before or since.

"She was working on Sister Maggie's case and got attacked by spiders," said Fats. "And you want to talk about some douchebag construction site? Be my guest. Give that a shot."

Chuck woke up and squeezed past Fats to hug me. "Spiders? Seriously?"

"Yes. I was attacked by tiny carnivores."

"Where's your cast?"

"Had to cut it off."

"Are you mad?" he asked as he shifted from foot to foot.

"I'm mad," said Fats, squatting to pick up Maggie's box. "We've got things to do and we're not doing them." She stomped up the stairs, leaving a kind of heat behind that made Chuck nervous. I totally enjoyed that.

"Do you want me to carry you?" he asked.

"No. I'm fine, itchy but fine."

"But spiders. Were they poisonous?"

"We'll find out." I trudged up the stairs with Chuck fretting behind me and offering to go get me a Worf burger from Kronos. That sounded fantastic, but I was still wearing Fats' clothes, an unsightly reminder that I needed a salad with oil and vinegar dressing.

Fats stood at my door with the box, eyeing my boyfriend with expectation.

"Let me take that," said Chuck.

"About time," said Fats.

I opened the door and sniffed. No Morty stink. He really was gone. I led them in and Chuck set the box on the floor next to the TV. Skanky ambled in, probably wondering what was for dinner, took one look at the box, went up into spiky arch, and began a constant hiss. My sentiments exactly.

"What's in there?" asked Chuck. "It stinks."

"Sister Maggie's stuff."

"Really?" He went and got himself a beer. "Where was it? The convent?"

"Her family had it in their spider-infested basement," said Fats.

"And they just gave it to you? No receipt? No nothing?"

"Nope," I said.

He took a long swig. "Why? Families never just hand me their stuff. Half the time I have to get a search warrant and that's when they *want* me to catch the perp."

"The cousin has a crush on Fats and he wants it solved. There's a lot of family pain there," I said. "Nobody else is interested."

He nodded. "I get it. Now about that construction site."

"I didn't do it."

Chuck tried to approximate Aunt Miriam's stink eye, but he just looked constipated. It was oddly adorable. "Come on. You did something. You are all over this."

"The rookie did it," I said.

"What rookie?"

"Gordon and, before you ask, I did not ask him to."

Two spots of pink appeared on Chuck's high cheekbones and his voice went an octave lower. "Why?"

Fats sat down on the sofa and mimed eating popcorn, which made him scowl more.

I laughed and said, "He heard the guys calling me a skanky whore."

"What else?" Fats ground her toothpick to powder and her hands went to fists.

"Smelly slut," I said. "Among other things."

Chuck didn't say a word. He did an about-face and left, slamming the door. I ran after him and yelled down the stairs. "Where are you going?"

"I'm taking care of it!" he yelled back.

I groaned. Men. Nothing could stop it. If it wasn't the construction workers, it was guys on the street. I hated it, but I'd yet to find a cure for asshole.

And then it got worse. I went back in my apartment to find Fats on the phone saying, "Get me Calpurnia. I've got a situation."

I dove for the phone, but Fats stiff armed me. I did everything I could to get that phone, but it wasn't going to happen.

"Do not tell her. The rookie handled it," I said.

"That's not handling it. They'll be back."

"Chuck's on it."

She snorted. "Cops. You're under the Fibonacci umbrella and they will be made to understand that."

"I don't want to be under anything. No. Do not do it." I charged her and she batted me away, accidentally brushing my injured arm. I gasped and she let down her guard for a second, but a second wasn't long enough. I still missed the phone by a good foot.

"Give it up," she said, amused. "You can't best me."

"I can do it." I believed because Mom said that was half the battle.

"That's adorable."

I was starting to get the feeling my mother was wrong about a lot of things.

"Hang up."

"No," said Fats. "What was that? How long is the massage? Okay. I'll wait."

On the other hand.

"I won't talk to Tiny," I said.

Fats gave me a look designed to make a man think twice, but I wasn't a man. It didn't work on me. I knew she could pound me. I also knew she wouldn't.

"I love you and I love him, but I'm not owing Calpurnia for one more thing," I said.

"Hey, Cosmo," said Fats. "I might've found another angle." She paused and then said, "I'll call back if I need it. Thanks."

I tossed myself on the sofa and sighed. "Thank God."

"You're welcome." She sat down next to me and the springs underneath us groaned.

"Somebody's full of themselves. You may be built like you came from Olympus, but you are not a goddess."

She said nothing and knotted her hair up on the top of her head in a way that was perfectly messy and in style. When I tried that, I looked like I spent the night in the drunk tank. "You love me."

"When I say love, I mean you're alright," I said. "Let's not go overboard. We're not picking out china patterns here."

"Love means something in my world."

"Mine, too, but, keep in mind, I love Uncle Morty, so the bar isn't that high."

"You are my best friend," she said, not looking at me.

I thought about all the other women in my life. There was my friend, Ellen, who I rarely saw since she had kids, and of course, Claire, Mom, Aunt Tenne, my nursing school friends, and Aaron. I know he wasn't technically a woman but the guy didn't really qualify as a dude either. So, I wondered who was my best friend and how did you rate that anyway. I spent the most time with Fats and Aaron, but that wasn't so much by choice.

"I don't know who my best friend is," I said.

"Not me," she said with just the tiniest hint of sadness.

"We're new friends and we're always getting shot at."

She grinned. "If that isn't friendship, I don't know what is."

"You're weird and I don't understand you," I said.

"Have you seen yourself lately?"

"Point taken. Don't get me wrong. You're up there. Ellen's my oldest friend and she's been there through the parent stuff and the... other things."

"The boyfriend disappearing?" asked Fats and I jerked to attention. I didn't know she knew, which was stupid. Calpurnia had me researched. She probably knew what kind of tampon I preferred.

"Yeah. She knows it all," I said.

"For me, that's Gibson."

"I thought you didn't have any female friends."

She laughed. Gibson was her trainer and she started with him when she was ten. He was a sixty-five-year-old former middle-weight boxing champion from Detroit and he served as friend, surrogate father, confessor, and occasional punching bag. I thought that was sad, but she clearly didn't. To say she adored Gibson, who apparently didn't have a first name, was an understatement.

"Well, I'm not Gibson," I said.

"And I'm not Ellen."

But we were both there and that counts for a lot in the world of friendship.

"Let's go through that box," said Fats.

"Let's don't and say we did."

The door opened and Chuck sauntered in. I recognized that look. Somebody was pretty proud of himself. "Done. You will not hear another word from that site."

"Great," I said. "Now go out and yell at every dude with low self-esteem and a general dislike of women."

"What?" he asked.

Fats stretched and all the vertebrae in her back popped. It was disturbing. "She gets yelled at daily. Where have you been?"

"By who?"

"She just told you."

"Bastards."

"Pretty much," I said, getting up and laying a kiss on him. "But I like you."

"That's good." He nuzzled my neck.

Fats stood up and forcibly parted us. "Aren't you going to Kronos?"

Chuck looked at me and I weakened. "The usual would be great."

"I'll have two double Worf burgers, double cheese, cheese fries with that sausage Aaron makes, and an extra-large Metaphysical malt. Hot fudge and sprinkles on the side."

We gaped at her, but Fats didn't seem to notice. She went over and used a pen to open the top of Maggie's box, in case there were spiders at the ready.

Chuck mouthed at me, "Is she okay?"

I mouthed, "Long day." And then I said out loud, "I'm going to shower again and put on more Calamine lotion."

"Do that. Pink polka-dots are a good look," said Fats as she pulled a veil out of the box. "I don't know if there's anything useful in here."

Chuck left and I waited until he was definitely gone before I said, "I thought you didn't want anyone to know you're pregnant?"

"I don't." Fats looked up. "Why?"

"Two double Worf burgers? Cheese? You eat kale salads with dressing on the side."

"Is that going to give it away?"

"Only in a huge way."

Fats considered that and it was a conundrum. She wanted fat, a new experience for her. When Chuck came back, I cut him off from the barrage of questions that were coming and got him back out the door with his own sad little bag of food to go.

"Why am I leaving? I bought the food." he said. "I yelled at an entire construction crew."

I kissed him so hard and long, he didn't know which end was up or even what he was complaining about.

"You're right and I will make it up to you," I said. "It's a girl night tonight."

"How will you make it up to me?" he asked.

"I'll go look at houses."

Chuck grinned. "Yeah? Tomorrow good?"

"Aren't you working?" I asked.

"Dammit."

"I'll look at the new listings you sent me."

He grudgingly agreed and was on his way. Sadly, I went back to the hungry and hormonal. We sat up half the night, talking wedding plans for the wedding that wasn't happening yet and the baby, who for the record was a girl and would someday love boxing, her mama, and low-carb diets. I had a feeling that Fats was in for some tough times.

CHAPTER THIRTEEN

I couldn't move. I tried up, down, right, and left. Nope. Almost no movement and that's when the panic started. I didn't know where I was or why it was so damn hot. Then I heard a little wheezy snore to the left of me and I opened my eyes to see blackness, but it was a familiar blackness. Not in a good way.

I tried to lift my right arm, but it was pinned under Pickpocket's body and I'd worn my brace and sling to bed so my left arm was equally useless. I don't know when Chuck snuck in and brought his giant poodle to bed, but it was sometime after two in the morning when Fats finally got tired of surfing *The Knot* and watching *Say Yes to the Dress*. We picked invites, some bridesmaids, Fats' cousin Carla Jean and her partner, Jana, who could be easily mistaken for a man in broad daylight. Fats believed we could get Jana into a dress for the wedding. I bet fifty bucks that we couldn't. A woman that wears a bolo tie will not wear puffed sleeves and taffeta. It's just not happening. I didn't want to wear puffed sleeves and taffeta and I thought bolo ties were a plague upon fashion for both men and women.

Fats and I designed the entire wedding hoopla. It was an 80s theme, in case you couldn't tell by the puffed sleeves and taffeta, and I sincerely hoped Fats could be talked out of that when it came down to it. The one thing we couldn't figure out was how to get my cousin to propose without knowing about the future Ultimate Fighting Champion. Yes, that's on the list of future baby accomplishments. I agreed to talk to Tiny and hint that I was thinking about marrying Chuck immediately and ask what he thought about that. It wasn't going to help, but, without the proverbial shotgun, that's all we had.

Thinking about pretending to be getting married made me sleepy. It was all so exhausting. Everyone needed something. Even dead people needed something. I'd managed to put off looking through Maggie's box, but it was out there, waiting to ruin any peace of mind I might have. I snuggled down, comforted by Chuck and Pick's incredible heat and drifted off.

"Mercy."

I don't know if it was a minute later, but it sure felt like it.

"Huh?"

"The door," whispered Chuck.

"Why are you whispering?"

"It's Aunt Miriam."

I yawned and shifted my head so that Pick's ear slid off my face. "She can't hear through walls."

"Are you sure about that? Because I'm not."

I listened and nothing happened. "You were dreaming. Nobody's here."

"It's a nightmare and she is here," said Chuck rolling over and cuddling me.

"How do you know? Don't tell me you can sense the presence of angry."

"Wait for it."

A sharp—and yes, angry—rapping echoed through my apartment.

"See?" asked Chuck.

I burrowed into his chest, so warm and smelled heavenly. "Maybe she'll go away."

"Has she ever gone away?"

"There's always a first time."

More rapping. She was going to damage the wood with that stupid cane.

"Why is she here? Are you supposed to do something?" asked Chuck.

"Not until ten. What time is it?"

"Quarter till eight."

I knew Aunt Miriam believed in punctuality and by that I mean be early for everything, but this was ridiculous. "I'm not doing it whatever it is."

"You're going to do it. Just get up and answer the door."

The rapping got angrier. I know that sounds impossible, but I could totally tell.

"You answer it. Don't you have to go to work?" I asked.

"I'm flexing my time so I can sleep in with you."

"That's so sweet. Go get the door."

Chuck rolled away and put his hands behind his head to show off his exceptional muscular development. "She's your aunt."

"She hits."

"Toughen up, buttercup."

I sat up and slapped his rock hard abs. It hurt my hand and not him at all. "Don't quote my father to me and you only say that because she doesn't hit you."

"It's the perks of being an honorary Watts. I'm not blood. It's all you, baby."

"I might hate you," I said.

"I'm still not answering the door."

Dammit.

I would've used my so-called feminine wiles, but who had time for that? I crawled off the end of the bed and staggered to the door. It was Aunt Miriam, full of righteous anger and caffeine.

"Why aren't you dressed?" She stomped in. "We needed to leave five minutes ago."

"The appointment is at ten. I have a life, such as it is."

"What is this? What is this?" She poked my spider bites. "You look contagious."

"Spider bites and I wish it was contagious."

"What have you been doing? Never mind. Get dressed. Chop. Chop. Let's go."

I stepped back and put a breakfast bar stool between us. "It's at ten. I'm not sitting in a waiting room for two hours."

"It's at eight. I changed it."

"You didn't tell me or ask me, for that matter."

She snorted derisively.

"It matters. I don't need to go. I don't want to go."

"Get dressed. I need a ride."

"How'd you get here then?"

"Uber."

I raised my palms at her in the internationally-recognized symbol of duh.

"Don't make me call your mother."

Chuck yelled from the bedroom. "Go ahead. I just got called in anyway."

Aunt Miriam looked at me in triumph and I marched back into the bedroom, got dressed, and threw three shoes at Chuck. He didn't care. Somebody got murdered. I was off the list and he was out the door before me.

When I came out into the living room, I marched past Aunt Miriam and flung open the door. "Alright. Come on."

Aunt Miriam didn't move. She stood in the living room, frozen, clutching her cane and purse to her chest. Then I realized what she was looking at. Right in front of her was Maggie's box, her name scrawled on the side where it couldn't be missed.

"Come on," I said with my heart in my throat. "We'll be late."

"What is this?" she said softly.

"Um...late. Let's go."

She didn't answer and I got nervous. Aunt Miriam quiet was not a thing. "If we're late, they'll cancel and they'll still charge you fifty bucks for missing it."

That did the trick. Her innate cheapness always won out and she turned around to march out the door and down the stairs. I had to run after her. She was pretty speedy on those little scrawny legs and she beat me to Mom's car. Happily, the construction site was a ghost town and I didn't have to deal with being called a smelly slut in front of a nun. I know they would've done it. I once had a guy make obscene gestures at me in front of Nana and Pop Pop. There's nothing too low for dirtbags.

I got her in and drove to the doctor's building in an uncomfortable silence that made me clench my jaw so hard my teeth hurt. Aunt Miriam didn't look at me or say anything. I used to pray for that, but, like with most things, be careful what you wish for. Something was coming and it was going to be bad.

And it was. Bad. Uncomfortable. The kind of thing you would totally pay big bucks to have someone else do for you, like cleaning out your septic tank or lancing an anal abscess. Yes. I've done that. The doctor was too nauseated.

Aunt Miriam sat in Dr. Harrison's office with the full array of plastic female body parts on his desk while he tried to get her to say what her issue was. If I had to hear him say the word "vagina" one more time I would lose it.

When I was just about to climb out of my skin, my father called and, for the first time ever, I was happy about it.

"Excuse me," I said. "I have to take this."

Aunt Miriam started to protest, but I was out in a flash.

"Hey, Dad. Did you get one of those anti-aging facials yet?"

"What? No. Shut up," he said. "How's the case?"

"You did, didn't you? How about the eyebrow shaping because yours are off the hook wide."

"If you weren't my flesh and blood—"

"I know, I know. You'd kill me and dump me on a hog farm to be used as a snack. Whatever."

Dad took a breath and a different tack. "So, darling daughter, I heard you were nosing around on the Sister Maggie case. How's it looking?"

"Morty called you?"

"Yeah. Hurry up. I raced ahead, but your mother's going to catch up any minute."

"Raced ahead?"

"Focus, Mercy. You have to do this now and not just for the business," said Dad.

I walked down the hall and into an empty exam room. So many speculums. "Why's that?"

"Morty's talking crazy. He thinks Nikki will come back if he has a heart attack and he's going to the gym."

"I knew that."

"He's running on a treadmill, Mercy," said Dad. "He's trying to kill himself. You have to get to Greece."

"I'm doing the best I can."

"It's been two days."

"On the cold case from hell." I gave Dad the rundown and he almost sounded pleased, except for me not going through Sister Maggie's stuff.

"I've been wanting to talk to you about something."

Apologize for missing my birthday parties, driving my mother crazy, smelling like a corpse at my first communion—

"I want you to get your license and join the business," said Dad.

"What the hell?"

"That's not news. You love this work and what's more you're decent at it."

Decent?

"You're blowing me away with all that flattery, but I think I'll have to decline."

"Why? Your other *career* isn't working out. You have to earn a living."

"I'm a nurse," I said.

"Not right now."

"Thanks, Dad."

His tone changed. "Seriously, Mercy. It's our thing, our family thing and I...I need you."

"I want to be a nurse," I said. "I like it. I'm good at it."

"I wanted to be the FBI director, but things don't always go to plan. In fact, they almost never do."

"You wanted to be in the FBI? How come you turned them down when they asked you?"

Dad told me a story I'd never heard before, which was surprising, since Dad liked to talk when he was around. Straight out of college, he applied to the FBI and thought he had a good shot with a double major of psychology and criminal justice. He got through all the testing and they turned him down. No explanation. Said he wasn't suited. I'd never known my father to not get what he wanted, except for a perfect score on the SAT, but I don't think that counts. He'd spent his career making them want him so he could turn them down. A little bit obsessive and twisted, but, hey, that's my dad. He did accept consultation work and the occasional teaching gig. Being Tommy Watts, he worked those harder than anyone they'd ever seen.

"Do you see my point?" he asked.

"Not even a little."

He groaned. "It worked better this way. I got what I needed."

"To be a cop, instead of an FBI agent? I don't know about that."

"I got your mother and you, you dipstick. If I'd been in the FBI I wouldn't have met your mother. You think I'd give that up for the directorship?"

Not Mom. Me maybe.

"I guess not," I said.

"Are you going to come in with me?" Dad asked.

"I'll think about it."

"Good. Now get on that box—oh, shit, there's your mother." Dad hung up and I went back to the office, trying to think of an excuse not to go back in, but I wasn't fast enough. Dr. Harrison stuck his head out the door and said, "Miss Watts, can you come back in, please?"

I forced myself to go back in and it looked as though nothing had changed. Aunt Miriam sat there like an angry statue and the female reproductive system show and tell was still on the doctor's desk. Dr. Harrison sat down and picked up a cup of coffee.

I sat down next to Aunt Miriam and tried to find my patience, but it was MIA. "Why are we here?" I asked.

The doctor sipped his coffee and said, "I'm getting paid. I don't know about you."

"Definitely not getting paid."

Aunt Miriam started grinding her teeth and I said, "Fine. If you're not going to speak, I'm out. I've got things to do as I think you know."

Nothing. My family. Honestly.

"I'll call my mom. I swear I will."

Nothing.

"I already told my dad."

"What?" she gasped.

"Hallelujah," said Dr. Harrison.

"Quiet," Aunt Miriam hissed at him. "I'll deal with you in a minute. You told your father that I was...we were..."

"He knows about gynecologists. It didn't upset his delicate sensibilities. He doesn't have any." That wasn't strictly true, but it felt good to say.

"You should never have done that."

The cane went up, but I channeled Fats and moved fast, grabbing it and throwing it over my shoulder. Not half bad for a marshmallow Peep. "Look, we're having this out right now or I'm not coming back. Understand?"

"I can't say it," she said through clenched teeth.

"Don't make me get out one of those dolls they use with molested children."

"I have one," said Dr. Harrison, digging in a drawer.

"You are not amusing," she said. "Neither of you is."

I stood up. "As it turns out, I'm neither amusing nor amused. Let's go and move on with our lives, such as they are."

Aunt Miriam didn't move and Dr. Harrison looked pretty worried that he might have to carry her out. He probably knew about the purse bricks. "Sister Miriam, I am incredibly discreet. When you're ready to talk, I'm here, but I have to say this is just a waste of time for everyone."

He stood up to walk around the desk and I picked up the cane, thinking about when to call Mom.

"I have a lump," said Aunt Miriam in a strained voice that sounded like it belonged to someone else entirely.

The doctor sat down and between the two of us, we got it out of her. Aunt Miriam had a double prolapse, bladder and uterus. At least that's what we concluded. She wasn't quite ready for an exam of the "area" as she called it. I didn't really get it until it came out that she'd never had the "area" examined. Like never. Not a single pap smear. Nothing. I guess she didn't need anything until now and it was critical, but we couldn't get her to put on that paper smock. She wouldn't get close to an exam room. I started thinking Dad was right. Healthcare was not for me.

We made another appointment for Tuesday at ten and I promised to do something to prep her, although I had no idea how to do that. Dr. Harrison walked us out and gave me a thumbs-up and mouthed, "Good job."

Good job? What was good about it?

"Alright," I said to Aunt Miriam. "I'm outta here."

"I need a ride home."

So close.

"Why are you going home? Don't you have hospital business?"

Staff to harass. Candy stripers to terrify.

"I'm going to take a warm bath in Epsom salts," she said.

"Oh."

"Yes."

"Okay."

That's how I ended up driving out to the convent. Dad was right. Sometimes things do work out.

The convent sat on a low hill with a perfect blue sky highlighting the dark stone and lovely arches. When I was little I thought being a nun would be great if you got to live there. Then I found out about all the praying and became less enthusiastic.

Aunt Miriam was never enthusiastic, unless it was about wiping out sin or whipping me into shape. I'm happy to say she never came close on achieving the second one. But she had a good record on sin and her views were pretty progressive, considering her age. She had no issue with prostitutes or drug addicts. Dealers and pimps were her enemy and she went after them hard. Whole neighborhoods were cleared out just because the sinners couldn't bear to deal with her anymore. She helped the girls with therapy and the addicts with rehab, spending hours listening to what brought them so low. She didn't talk or lecture, not to them. The family was a different story.

On that day, Aunt Miriam stayed silent as she sat in the passenger seat and struggled with something. Her fingers tapped on her purse. She ground her teeth and sat so stiffly it looked like she had a corset on.

I had stuff to do and sitting in a parking lot forever wasn't on the list. "If you're going to yell at me, I wish you'd just get it over with."

Aunt Miriam swallowed and said, "I don't think I can get out."

Of all the things I had considered, that was not on the list.

"Do you want me to help you?"

"No."

Why can't it be easy?

"Do you want me to get someone else?" I asked.

"No."

Don't get mad. She's in pain, not just a pain.

"Alright. We'll sit here and waste gas. I heard that's good for the environment. We totally need those polar ice caps to melt."

"Don't be ridiculous," said Aunt Miriam.

"Look who's talking."

"I am never ridiculous."

"Wrong. How about this?" I asked. "Do you *need* my help?"

She pursed her incredibly thin lips and I took that for a yes. So I got out and went around to her side, opened the door, and maneuvered her out. My left arm was still in the sling and it wasn't the easiest of maneuvers, but I got her out without any crying, me or her.

"Are you sure you don't want to go back to the doctor?"

"Certainly not. Our appointment is on Tuesday."

Our appointment. Right.

I held her around the waist and half-carried her in. Where's Fats when you need her? She used dumbbells heavier than Aunt Miriam. This would be easy peasy for her.

It took me a half hour to walk her in and get her into her little apartment. I insisted she go straight to bed and she actually agreed. If

Mom had been in town, I would've called her immediately. Aunt Miriam going to bed at nine thirty in the morning. This was serious.

I tucked her in and made tea and toast. "Well then, I'm outta here. See ya."

"Wait."

I knew it.

"What?" I asked.

"I'm only going to say this once," she said.

I'll believe it when I see it.

"Go for it," I said.

"Don't do it."

That was it. Not another word.

"Illuminating," I said.

"I mean it."

"I'm sure you do, but I still don't know what you're talking about."

Her lips went white she was pressing them together so hard.

"Are we talking about telling Mom about your gyno situation or Maggie or something else altogether?"

"Don't investigate," she said. "Now leave and do not tell anyone about anything ever."

"That's a blanket statement and I'm not going to agree to it."

Then she pulled out the Dad card. "It's for the family."

I rolled my eyes. "I never bought that when my father said it and I'm not buying it now."

"I'm your family and I'm asking you not to."

I crossed my arms and said, "I'm your family and I'm asking you, why?"

She wouldn't say anything. I tried and tried. Maggie was her friend. A murderer escaped justice and probably killed somebody else. Dominic should be cleared.

That last one had the only effect. She clouded over, but it didn't change her mind and I ended up stomping through the apartment and into the hall, almost bowling over another nun.

"Oh, shit," I said. "I'm sorry."

"Never mind that." Sister Frances loomed over me with a Starbucks cup in one hand and a rosary in the other. "What's happening with Miriam?"

"Oh that. Nothing. She's fine."

Sister Frances' eyelids went to half-mast and she merely watched patiently.

"Alright. Alright. She had a thing, but it's fine."

"Come with me." Sister Frances turned around and walked briskly away. I briefly considered hightailing it out of there. I wasn't Fats fast, but I figured I could beat the oldest nun in the order, even if she was a fast walker.

Then it dawned on me that Sister Frances was the oldest surviving nun there. She would've known Maggie. I chased after her and we went into her little apartment. The senior nuns had little efficiency apartments, simple but comfy with a small kitchen equipped with the basics. She went in the kitchen and pulled out a frying pan. "I'm just back from the hospital. Long night. Poor Mrs. Wilkes. God is testing her, but she pulled through."

I had no idea who Mrs. Wilkes was, but I thought it best not to ask.

"Did you want to talk to me about something in particular?" I asked.

"Other than Miriam?" she asked.

"Yes."

"Yes," she said.

"What is it?" I asked.

"Go sit with Clarence. I'll make us a snack." Sister Frances cracked an egg into the frying pan and I turned around to find Sister Clarence tucked away in a corner with a paperback on her lap and a smile on her round face. The last time I'd seen her, Clarence had been a novitiate, but it looked like she was a full-fledged sister now.

"Hi," I said. "I didn't see you there."

"I try to be unobtrusive."

"I wish Aunt Miriam felt that way."

"Oh, no. Sister Miriam always knows the right thing to do. I don't, so I stay quiet."

I sat down on the love seat next to her chair. "I wish I understood why you like her so much."

Sister Clarence put her hand on her chest and her face flushed. "She's so good to me and helps me with all my endeavors. You are so lucky to have her. I never had an aunt like that."

Sister Frances glanced back at me. Sometimes a split second glance can say it all. Frances thought Clarence was nuts. For me, the jury was still out.

"So why are you here?" I asked. "Do you want to tell me something, too?"

She lowered her voice to a whisper. "Yes, I do, but it's very delicate."

"Oh, yeah?"

"Sister Miriam is ill and she's hiding it. We're very concerned."

"I know and I'm on it," I said.

Relief flooded over Clarence. "Oh, thank goodness. Are you taking her to a psychiatrist?"

"A psychiatrist?" *Not a terrible idea.* "Why do you think she needs a psychiatrist?"

Clarence and Frances knew something was wrong with Aunt Miriam, but they'd landed on the wrong thing. It was Clarence's job to clean Aunt Miriam's apartment. No trouble, she assured me. And during her cleaning she discovered a pile of papers to do with the Kansas burial ground, including photos (some gruesome), interviews of the men they'd already arrested, and news clippings. There was quite a lot.

"So you think she's crazy?"

"Not crazy," said Sister Clarence, horrified. "Troubled. She isn't sleeping and I think she may be taking drugs."

"Drugs? Aunt Miriam?"

"A sleeping pill called Ambien is in her cabinet and a bunch of painkillers that weren't prescribed to her."

Sister Frances brought over a tray with our snack. Fried egg sandwiches with plenty of Miracle Whip and Swiss Miss Hot Cocoa. I better not let Aaron smell that on my breath. It wouldn't be pretty. He considered himself to be my sole supplier of hot chocolate and I wasn't about to ruin that.

We ate our sandwiches and I have to say they were perfect, drippy egg and crispy edges. Yum. That I'd mention to Aaron. I just wanted to see what he'd do with a simple fried egg sandwich. No doubt it would be phenomenal. And fattening. So maybe I shouldn't.

"You don't seem concerned," said Sister Frances, dabbing at the edge of her mouth with a napkin.

"I'm not. I think I know why that's all happening," I said.

Sister Frances' eyelids went half-mast again. "Enlighten us."

Maybe I shouldn't have done it, but I told them about Dr. Harrison. I needed backup and who better than women who could understand her. Except that they didn't understand her. They'd both had pap smears and considered them just a normal part of life.

"Miriam," said Sister Frances. "Good gracious. I've never known anyone so ridiculously private. Did you know that she used to go out of her way to buy her sanitary products where none of us could see her buying them? As if she isn't supposed to be a real human."

"She could've trusted me to help," said Sister Clarence, tearfully.

"It's not about trust. She's embarrassed and in pain," I said.

Sister Frances started to gather the plates. "Hold on a moment. That explains the pain pills and you helping her walk in. What about the sleeplessness?"

"Pain isn't helpful for sleep."

"And the serial killer burial ground?"

"I was getting to that," I said.

Sister Frances sat back down and the nuns listened quietly. Well, Clarence got tearful again, but she was quiet about it. She didn't know about Maggie and the murder hurt her sweet heart, but what hurt her more was Aunt Miriam's pain.

"So Myrtle wants you to do it, so you're doing it," said Sister Frances with finality.

"But Sister Miriam doesn't want her to," said Sister Clarence. "What would Mother Superior say?"

"She won't say anything. She's at a conference in Maine. We will handle this and we're already handling it."

"We are?" I asked. "You just found out."

"Not exactly," said Sister Frances.

Uncle Morty told me about the traffic that kicked off after my visit with Father Bernard. He didn't mention that Sister Frances was contacted. They were so worked up, Bishop Tyler paid her a visit and got her out of bed.

"Why you and not Miriam?" I asked.

She snorted. "They don't know anything and I do mean not anything. That young man sat right where you are and asked why he'd never heard Maggie's name before."

"What did you tell him?"

"I told him the truth. Bishop Fowler had bigger fish to fry than catching a nun's murderer. He wanted an easy answer and Father Dominic jumping off that bridge gave him one."

"Do you think Dominic did it?" I asked.

The old nun got up and went to turn the kettle on for more Swiss Miss. Then she took off her veil and loosened the pins that held her white hair back from her face. Sister Clarence shifted anxiously in her chair, but I knew Sister Frances needed this ritual to give her time to think.

The kettle whistled and she made us more Swiss Miss. "I don't know. I want to say no, but I can't."

"Really? Father Bernard didn't think he did it. The Girls don't."

"He was a young man in love who wasn't allowed to be in love. I've seen men beat the wives they love for fear of losing them. Love and destruction can go hand in hand."

"Do you think they were going to run away together? Myrtle says yes."

"I wasn't that close to either of them, but I thought they might and that it would've been a mistake."

"Why?"

"They were dedicated to the church and its teaching. To give it up would have tainted their love, particularly for Maggie. She was absolutely devoted to her work. She would've been adrift without it."

"You think he killed her because she wouldn't go with him?" asked Clarence.

"If he did it, that's why. I can tell you that Miriam thought he did it."

I gasped. I actually did and it surprised all of us.

"You didn't know that?" asked Sister Frances.

"I told you she won't say anything about it. She's not going to iden-tify that medal. Can you do it?"

She shook her head. "No. I don't ever remember seeing it. The police came and searched her room after they found her body."

"Who did? St. Louis didn't take the case as far as I know."

The St. Sebastian police chief came up with a deputy. With the consent of the Mother Superior, they searched Sister Maggie's room. Sister Frances supervised and they didn't take anything. They were looking for the medal because Miriam reported that she always wore it and it wasn't on her body.

"Nothing? What about journals and things like that?" I asked.

"No." Sister Frances paused for a moment and Clarence looked at me with worry.

"What is it?" I asked.

"I spoke to that police chief and I remember it like it was yester-day." She swallowed hard. "I never told anyone what he said."

So many things went through my head. Did he make it sound like it was Sister Maggie's fault? What was she doing out there? She had one man. She might've had another. The awful things people say so it can't happen to them or those they love.

"What did he say?" asked Sister Clarence. "Was it terrible? Did he talk about how she died?"

Sister Frances looked up. "No. That was the odd thing. He didn't. He wouldn't. He said she didn't suffer and not to think about it anymore. He was very firm with me about that."

"She was strangled," I said. "That's suffering."

"I know. I thought it was very odd for him to say that."

"Was that what bothered you?" I asked.

"No. Not that." She took a sip. "First of all, he was drunk. I smelled it on him and he slurred. His deputy was embarrassed and kept trying to hurry him along."

"I can't believe it," said Sister Clarence. "How could he do a good job? Maggie was counting on him. We were counting on him."

"He couldn't," I said. If I told Dad, he'd lose his mind. Grandad, too. They had a thing about drunk cops, the stereotype. And on duty, forget about it. "What did he say to you? Was he rude?"

"No, not at all. A sad man, I thought. It was hard for him. But what he said, I think he meant it as a comfort. He said that Maggie's murder was nothing to worry about. These things happen. It was a small time crime."

"What does that mean?" asked Clarence. "She was murdered."

These things happen? Since when?

"That's unbelievable," I said.

Sister Frances developed a tremor in her hands and Sister Clarence took her cup from her. I don't think she noticed. "I can hear him saying it in my head. That slur and the sadness in his voice. Funny how some things stay with you. I can't remember who told me my father had died in Korea or my favorite nephew in Vietnam, but I remember the policeman telling me that about Maggie and I can't even say that I loved her. She was a casual friend, a sister, of course, but I didn't care for her like Miriam or Dominic."

"But you still couldn't talk about what he said," said Sister Clarence.

She shook her head. "I couldn't. It was awful. It made Maggie small, like she was nothing. Murdering her was similar to poaching a deer or jaywalking."

"Did he say anything else about crime in his area? Anything at all?" I asked.

That shook her out of her reminiscences. "No. Why would you ask that?"

"'These things happen.' Sounds to me like something was going on in St. Seb. Nobody minimizes murder, especially a nun's murder. I think the chief had a problem and he didn't have a clue what to do about it."

Sister Frances frowned and took her cup back. Her hands were steady. Her eyes intense and unclouded. "You got that from 'These things happen'?"

"It's a weird thing to say and 'small time crime'? Come on."

"He..." Sister Clarence trailed off.

"Yes?" I asked.

"I teach kindergarten and I say things like that to the children when they're upset."

Sister Frances stiffened. "I was an adult."

"Hold on," I said. "I think she's on to something. You say it to calm the kids down."

"Yes. They often make mountains out of molehills as the saying goes," said Sister Clarence.

"Maggie's murder was hardly a molehill," said Sister Frances.

I sat back with my Swiss Miss. "But he wanted it to be a molehill. What do you want to bet he'd said that before?"

"We do not bet, Mercy." Sister Frances sounded stern, but there was a twinkle in her eyes.

"Oh, no," I said. "I bet you do."

The nuns laughed and the tension instantly lifted.

"Money," said Sister Frances.

"You could bet something else," said Sister Clarence.

"Do you think I'm wrong?" I asked. "That the chief never said that about other crimes before Maggie's?"

"I don't. I believe you."

I had the feeling that Clarence would believe me if I said I was a virgin or hated dessert. "And you, Sister Frances?" I asked.

"I think you're right, but let's make it interesting anyway," said Sister Frances.

Aunt Miriam had been known to call Sister Frances a wily old codger and I had the feeling that I was about to find out why.

"What do you have in mind?" I asked.

"I will bet you two that the St. Sebastian chief of police never said that before."

"And?" Sister Clarence was suspicious. I wouldn't have thought she had it in her.

"And," said Sister Frances, "if I win, you two have to run the first two fish fries during Lent."

"Lent? That's forever away," I said.

She smiled. "I won't forget."

"You know I hate fish."

Sister Clarence grimaced. "You're not the only one."

"Is it a bet or not?"

Since I knew I was going to win, I thought what's the harm. That's a dangerous statement, if there ever was one. What's the harm? A lot of bad has come from 'what's the harm.' "Alright. You're on. What do we get? And don't say you'll pray for us," I said. "I know you pray for me already."

"How do you know that?" asked Sister Frances. "I don't pray for everyone I know."

"Aunt Miriam's your nemesis. You pray for me just to thwart her."

The old nun got miffed. "As if I would wish bad things to happen to my sister."

"Not bad things," I said. "Me. I bother her."

It took a second, but she broke down and smiled. "You do aggravate her and I have had to ask for forgiveness for enjoying it. She's just so much fun to bother."

"I understand completely."

"I don't," said Sister Clarence. "Sister Miriam is the best person I know. She helps me every day. I love her."

Sister Frances reached over and patted the younger sister's knee. "You are a special case. Your heart is so pure Miriam would never think of whacking you with a cane."

"Whacking me with a cane? She would never do anything like that."

Sister Frances and I exchanged a look, but we stayed silent. No point in ruining Sister Clarence's hero worship.

"So what do we get?" I asked. "Don't think I've forgotten that."

"I will break it to Miriam when it becomes necessary to tell her that you've continued to work on the case," she said.

"Done," I said. "But what about Clarence? That's not for her."

"It is. Truly," said Sister Clarence. "Sister Frances will know what to do. I couldn't possibly tell her and she'll be so upset with you that you can't."

"It's a deal then. But somehow I think I'm going to lose rather than win."

Sister Frances' eyes twinkled again. "Could be. So it's Miriam and fish fries."

"I wish I knew what you were up to with these fish fries," I said.

"Fish fries," said Sister Clarence rather loudly and then she clamped a hand over her mouth embarrassed.

"What? You know? Do tell."

"No. I just remembered. Sister Frances, you said the bishop had other fish to fry. What fish?"

Sister Frances frowned. She was a wily old codger. Hoped I'd forget. Well, I did, but thank goodness for Clarence.

"Sister Clarence, I'm liking you more every minute," I said. "Spill it, Sister."

The sister delayed by spilling her Swiss Miss, but Clarence and I would wait, all day, if necessary. "Oh, well. You're going to be disappointed."

"I'm used to it," I said.

She wasn't wrong. I was disappointed, but only with the lack of detail. But like Dad always said, you only need one thread to unravel the whole thing. Sister Frances gave me a thread and I was going to pull the hell out of it.

From the end of 1965 through the spring of 1966, something was happening in the diocese. There were meetings, not just meetings, panicked meetings. The Catholic church was not prone to panic, but the upper echelon was panicking to Sister Frances' mind. Hastily called meetings with closed doors. The nuns were completely shut out, which was unusual. Apparently, our diocese was an open and inclusive one. The archbishop, at the time, prized dialog and ideas, but all that shut down during that period. The male side of the house stopped talking to the female side and it was evident in every parish. Sister Frances had the impression that there was a flurry of words going on and they were words deemed unfit for feminine ears.

"What was it?" asked Sister Clarence fearfully.

Sister Frances pursed her lips and said, "I don't know. I never got a hint and then Maggie died. Nothing mattered for a long time after."

"Did the meetings stop after she died?" I asked.

Please say no. Please. Please. Please.

She shook her head. "I don't know. I don't remember. I think I remember Bishop Fowler saying that he didn't have time to deal with Maggie. I was so angry. What else could be more important?"

Thank you, Lord.

Sister Clarence eyed me in her sweet, inquisitive way. "Why are you relieved?"

"Because Mercy instantly thought that the church had a problem with Maggie and her death solved it," said Sister Frances.

"But why would that...oh. Mercy!"

"Everything's a possibility."

"Not the church killing a nun."

Desperate times.

"Maybe not," I said, turning to Sister Frances. "What do you think it was?"

She refused to say, but I had a good idea.

"You think it was about sexual abuse."

The nuns clammed up like I'd never seen anyone clam up. It was like they'd lost the power of speech. I suppose I understood it. The shame. The horror. And Sister Frances was a nun during the time that abuse had run rampant. I wasn't sure if that was the right way to describe it, but it felt like the right way. The church thought the institution was the important thing, not the victims. That sounded very familiar.

"You know I'm going to look at that as it relates to Sister Maggie, right?"

They nodded.

"I expect you to tell me everything you know about it."

The color flooded back into their faces.

"We don't know anything," said Sister Frances with relief. "But I don't want to talk about it."

"Secrets is what got you all into this situation."

"I have no secrets," said Sister Clarence earnestly.

I laughed and downed the rest of my cold Swiss Miss. "That I believe. And you, Sister Frances?"

"I will tell you everything I know about Maggie and that time period. It just so happens that I don't know what was going on. Only suspicions...in light of what has occurred since."

So plenty of secrets, just not about this stuff.

"There is one more thing," said Sister Frances. "Bishop Fowler retired not long after all that fuss."

"How long after?" I asked.

"In the summer, I believe."

I had to think about priests and retirement for a moment. "Was he old? For some reason, I got the impression he wasn't."

"He was in his sixties. Very young to retire. There were some eyebrows raised, but we were happy to see him go," said Sister Frances.

"That's interesting," I said. "You have my number, if you remember anything?"

"I'll call you and I'll do something else, too."

"What's that?"

Sister Frances set down her cup and steepled her fingers. "I will go to Miriam's next appointment."

"Really? Why? You're not exactly best buds."

"What makes you think it's for Miriam?"

"It's her appointment," I said.

"Miriam is always telling me how bright you are so I'm sure you'll figure it out at some point," she said. "Now go on and hop to it."

Sister Clarence timidly raised her hand. "I know what it is."

"Lay it on me," I said.

"She wants you to focus on Maggie and not be distracted."

"Very good," said Sister Frances. "I will, as they say, take one for the team, but I can't promise an exam. That is unreasonable given who we're dealing with."

"I understand, but an exam would be ideal."

"I'll do my best."

"Me, too," said Sister Clarence.

Aunt Miriam is going to be so pissed. This day just got better.

"I will do everything I can to figure out who murdered Maggie and the rest of it, but I can't promise anything either. It's been fifty years."

"But you will have tried," said Sister Frances. "That's important."

"It's the thought that counts?" I asked.

"That is a stupid saying. Thoughts don't mean anything. It's the effort that counts."

I sighed and sat back. Effort. Not my favorite thing.

"What are you waiting for?" asked Sister Frances. "I'm sure you have things to do."

"I'm tired."

"Then perhaps you'd like to relax for a while."

Why does that sound like a trap?

"Maybe," I said slowly.

She picked up her remote and turned on the TV, bringing up her Fire TV screen.

"Are we going to watch a movie?" asked Sister Clarence. "I love movies. Let's watch *Christopher Robin*. We need something happy."

"Is that happy?" I asked.

"Disney made it."

"They made *Saving Mr. Banks*. That was miserable."

Sister Clarence pursed her lips. "It was." Then she whispered, "I hated it."

Sister Frances held the remote aloft. "No happy movies. Those are for suckers and invalids, of which I am neither."

Oh, no!

"Come on, Clarence. That's our cue." I jumped to my feet.

"Aren't we watching a movie?" asked Sister Clarence.

"Yes," said Sister Frances. "And this is the movie."

She clicked a button and *Us* came up on the screen.

"I have a twenty-four hour rental."

"We'll see you in twenty-four hours or more. Don't wait up," I said, pulling Sister Clarence to her feet. "Come on, Sister. We're hitting the bricks."

"It looks like it might be interesting. That's a lovely young woman on a beach. What's wrong with that?"

I pointed at the screen. "'Terrifying and uncanny'"

"That sounds like horror," said Sister Clarence. "But—"

"It is and they like it. Trust me. You have to escape while you have the chance." I dragged the young nun to the door under the gaze of a smiling Sister Frances. "Who's they? Who likes it?"

"Sister Frances and Aunt Miriam."

"No. They're so sweet."

"What can I say? Sweet likes the evil." I pushed Sister Clarence out the door. "See ya, Sister Frances."

The old nun saluted and laughed. She definitely knew how to motivate me.

I said goodbye to the confused Sister Clarence and booked it down to the car. I only got lost once, which was a record for me. The convent was such a maze. I wonder if they did that on purpose. Every time I got lost in there, I'd find myself praying. It couldn't be a coincidence.

Before getting in Mom's car, I got out my phone and considered my options, trying to find a different one than the one that was obvious. Call Uncle Morty and go to St. Seb. I didn't want to go to St. Seb. Watching *Christopher Robin* sounded a lot better, even if it turned out to be miserable.

I sighed and dialed. A girl's got to do what a girl's got to do.

"Hey, it's me," I said.

"What'd ya want?" asked Uncle Morty.

"I just interviewed Sister Frances."

He started typing. "Oh, yeah?"

I opened the door and slid in. "Holy crap!"

"Good stuff?" he asked.

"Yeah, but not in a good way."

I think I prayed too hard.

Sitting in the passenger seat was Sister Clarence, who looked scandalized at my foul, foul language. "I've decided," she said primly.

"What?" I asked.

"Goddammit," said Uncle Morty. "What's going on? What've you got?"

"A nun in my car."

"Why?"

"I don't know. I really don't," I said. "I'll call you back."

Sister Clarence smiled at me the way only the truly good and inno-cent can. "I'm going to help you."

"How?" I asked. *By slowing me down? By freaking people out with your saintliness and veil?*

She held her palms up to the sky. "It will be revealed."

Dammit!

CHAPTER FOURTEEN

Try as I might I couldn't get Sister Clarence to believe that putting Uncle Morty on speaker wasn't a good idea. I also couldn't get her to let me drop her off at a hospital or fire station. She knew that was where people dropped unwanted infants, but she didn't make the connection.

What was I going to do? Clarence was sweet, unworldly, and utterly useless, unless I needed to teach someone to read or use the potty. I couldn't subject her to my life. Uncle Morty wasn't even the worst part. My own language wasn't exactly pristine and I slept with Chuck on a regular basis, unmarried. Aunt Miriam knew, I assumed, but she chose not to acknowledge it. That was the only time in my life, other than Maggie, that she kept her trap shut. And how could I explain Fats, unwed and pregnant, with her questionable connections and undercurrents of violence? She'd probably scare the little nun into being cloistered.

"I can take it," said Sister Clarence with confidence that she shouldn't have had.

"You don't understand. How can I make you understand?" I asked.

"I know that people use foul language."

"But Uncle Morty uses all the foul language. Sometimes in one sentence."

"I will get used to it," she said, smiling. "And I'll find a way to serve God while I'm helping you."

"He uses the 'C' word, Sister Clarence," I said, thinking that ought to do it.

"As long as he doesn't use the 'N' word, I'm fine."

I turned off of Kingshighway into the Central West End as a storm rolled in. Traffic was backed up and I had to get a nun out of my car. The cathedral. Yes. I'd lure her in on some kind of pretext and make a run for it. Not something that Aunt Miriam would approve of, but I knew she didn't want Sister Clarence with me. I wasn't good enough for her. She'd made that abundantly clear before I went to New Orleans. Something about crushing her spirit. Well, this case wasn't going to be good for anyone's spirit. I had a feeling.

"Uncle Morty would never use that word," I said.

"Then we're good to go."

"The 'C' word. Think about that. I don't like hearing it."

"You just used it," Sister Clarence explained patiently.

"The other 'C' word."

"There's another one?"

Oh, my God.

"Yes, there's another one," I said.

"What is it?" She leaned over to me. "You should whisper it so I know what it is."

Not going to happen.

"Let's skip that for now." I leaned to the side to see what the holdup was, but the problem was too far ahead. "I should've gone straight to St. Seb."

"Why didn't we?" asked Sister Clarence.

"I thought I'd pack a bag. I didn't want to have to drive back and forth. This isn't going to be quick." *Wait a minute.* "Oh, Sister, I'll have to take you back. I could be there for days."

"That's absolutely fine. We have a four-day weekend for training."

"Don't you have to, ya know, do the training," I said, trying to keep the hope out of my voice and failing.

"I did my training after work." She held up a Hello Kitty backpack. "And I packed a bag. I'm ready for anything."

You really aren't. 'Cause I'm not and I'm me.

"Look, I'm going to give it to you straight," I said. "This isn't for you. It's going to be bad. I have a sense about these things."

"I heard," she said solemnly. "I will deal with it."

"No, really. Bad stuff. Really, really bad."

Sister Clarence shifted in her seat and looked at me steadily. "The parents don't understand me."

I'm with them.

"Which parents?"

"All of them." She dabbed at the corner of her eye with a handkerchief that had kittens and rainbows embroidered on it. I'm not kidding. She was my age. Kittens and rainbows. She was so not ready for autopsy photos. "They've raised concerns."

"About what?" I asked.

"Me. They say that I can't understand the challenges and concerns that normal people face. But I am a normal person."

Well...

"What's that got to do with anything?" I asked.

She blew her nose so daintily I doubt she made a mark on her adorable handkerchief. "I need experience. Real life experience."

"This is murder we're talking about. It's not normal."

"But you know normal people," she said.

I thought about my people from Aaron to Grandad. Not normal. Nope.

"I wouldn't say that. No."

"But they're real people doing what real people do. My principal says I have to get out there and experience life beyond the convent and classroom. I didn't know how to do that. I was lost, but then I saw you going out there, fighting for justice, and I thought to myself, 'Gosh darn it all, Clarence, go out and don't be afraid. Nobody wants to hurt you.' So here I am. Ready to experience life and do God's work with you."

"You know I get hurt all the time, right? People literally want to hurt me and they are surprisingly good at it."

"I'll help protect you," she said happily.

"With prayer?"

"Yes."

"Awesome," I said. "We're all set then."

She put a soft hand on my arm. "You do pray, don't you, Mercy?"

"I'm praying right now." *That you don't get hurt.*

"Wonderful. Now you should call your uncle and find out if he knows something," said Sister Clarence.

I swallowed and told the Bluetooth to call Uncle Morty.

"Brace yourself, Sister."

"Consider me braced."

She wasn't braced. Not even close. Uncle Morty opened with the F-bomb and it was all downhill from there. I think Sister Clarence stopped breathing in case the air was tainted. I think it was. I caught a hint of sulfur.

"Shut up!" I yelled. "For the love of something I'm not allowed to say in vain, shut up!"

Uncle Morty took a much needed breath and asked, "What's your problem?"

"Sister Clarence is with me."

"Who?"

"Aunt Miriam's protégé. *Sister* Clarence," I said.

"Son of a...sea biscuit," said Uncle Morty.

"Hello, sir," said Sister Clarence. "Glad to be on the team."

"What the...something."

"That's right," I said, cheerfully. "Sister Clarence has four days off from teaching kindergarten and she's going to help us find the identity of a brutal murderer."

"That is not a good idea," he said.

"Don't worry, sir. I'm ready," she said. "What did you find out about Sister Maggie?"

"I...uh..."

"Go ahead," I said. "We're doing this."

"Why?" he asked.

"I don't know, but we are. What did you find out?"

"I got Maggie's death certificate."

Sister Clarence dabbed her eyes. "That's so sad. Her poor family. Do you know her family? I should speak to them. We could pray together."

Uncle Morty didn't say anything. He was at a loss for words. It was kinda worth it just for that. "Great idea, Sister. Morty, what's the cause of death?"

"Should I say it?" he asked. "For real?"

"Yes. Sister Clarence is on the team and she already knows anyway."

"Strangulation. But that ain't right."

"Isn't," said Sister Clarence.

"Huh?" I asked.

"Not ain't," she said. "Isn't."

Uncle Morty seethed. He was silent, but I could sense the seething.

"Let's leave the grammar alone for now," I said.

"Sorry," she whispered.

"It's fine. So, Uncle Morty, what's not right?" I asked as I inched the car forward. I should've gone straight to St. Seb and bought what I needed at Walmart.

"The death certificate. It's a duplicate. That don't happen."

"Doesn't," said Sister Clarence.

I looked at her.

"Sorry," she said.

"What did she say?" asked Uncle Morty.

"Nothing," I said. "What do you mean a duplicate? You can't find the original?"

"There is no original. The dup is all there is. It's the official death certificate and it's got friggin' 'duplicate' stamped on it."

"What in the world?"

"I ain't never seen that before," said Uncle Morty and Sister Clarence twitched. The "ain'ts" were hurting her. You can take the kindergarten teacher out of kindergarten, but you can't take the grammar out of the teacher.

I leaned to the side again and it looked like a three-car pileup. There was a break in traffic coming the other way and I did a quick u-turn, causing Sister Clarence to gasp. "Mercy, that was illegal."

"You'll get used to it," I said. "Morty, what are you thinking? It is fake?"

"Oh, yeah. I'm looking at the ME's signature and it's...messed up. I think somebody pulled the original and put this one in."

"Why? Anything else odd on it?"

"No. Standard issue. Says murder. Right date," he said.

"What's the date?"

"The day she disappeared."

"I wonder how good they were with that back then," I said.

"Pretty good. That hasn't changed much," said Uncle Morty. "Body temp, lividity, insects, tissue breakdown. It hasn't changed."

"We need the autopsy."

"Hell, sorry, yeah, we do. What'd you find out from the other one? What's her name?"

"Frances?"

"Yeah. Her."

I told him everything that Sister Frances said, causing Sister Clarence to tear up again. And Fats thought *I* was a marshmallow Peep.

"Got it," said Uncle Morty. "What'd you want from me?"

I asked him to find out about our drunk chief, if there were any other problems reported. Something in the St. Louis papers. Anything. And more importantly, what other crimes were going on in his jurisdiction. The so-called small time crimes that he alluded to.

"And if you can look into this duplicate thing," I said. "I bet they changed her cause of death. It's a duplicate because the coroner or whoever wouldn't sign off."

"Maybe," said Uncle Morty.

"Why?" asked Sister Clarence. "We know she was strangled. That's what Sister Miriam said."

"She said that because that's what she was told," I said.

"You think she wasn't strangled?"

This is going to be so bad.

"I think there's more to it and that's why the chief said that she didn't suffer."

"'Cause she suffered more? What the...something," said Uncle Morty.

"He was comforting himself or lying to himself, if you will. Give me a break. She suffered. The guy had to get drunk to search her room."

"I'll look into this guy," said Uncle Morty. "The average cop don't get hammered to investigate."

Sister Clarence grimaced at the "don't", but she said, "Remember the stuff with the church."

"What stuff?" asked Uncle Morty.

"Sister Frances suspects that the church's reaction, specifically Bishop Fowler's, was to do with sexual abuse. Something was happening that winter. See what you can find out. I know there's a database of pedophile priests."

He started scratching his scruffy beard. "I hate kid stuff. I hate it."

"I know. Me, too. But there's something there. The way the church treated Maggie and Dominic. I don't know. Something was definitely up. Sister Frances said the nuns were kept out of it. Lots of secret meetings. Fowler retired pretty soon afterward."

"If I knew I had a pedophile priest in the parish, I'd keep the ladies away," Uncle Morty mused.

"Yeah, right. We're delicate," I said.

"Not that. What do you think your aunt would do if she found out there was a pedophile preying on her parish?"

"He might not get out alive." *Maybe he didn't.* "See if any other priests retired early or moved unexpectedly during that time. That's what they did, right? Pass the trash."

"Yes," said Sister Clarence. "Shameful."

The way she said it, you'd have thought it was her personal shame.

"I'll look," said Uncle Morty. "I'll see if anyone else got scrubbed."

I could tell from the tone of his voice that he was thinking what I was thinking. It wasn't always the creepy old guys that preyed on children. Dominic was scrubbed by the church. Maybe the reason wasn't Maggie after all.

I drove into the alley behind my building, expecting it to be quiet. I really had to stop expecting. The opposite always happened. The construction workers were back, not en masse, but the ones that were there were highly pissed and arguing with a foreman on the other side of our parking lot. I hoped I could pull in unnoticed and get away. Like most hopes, it went unfulfilled.

I zipped into the spot farthest from them and said, "You stay here. I'll be right back."

Sister Clarence unbuckled. "But it's part of my education. How normal people live."

"Trust me. You need to stay here."

"But—"

"Please," I begged. "It's for your own good."

She nodded reluctantly, but those few seconds was just long enough for a couple of turds to spot my car from the second floor. When I got out, abuse started raining down on me.

"Hey, bitch, you call daddy?"

"You smelly shitbag, this is our livelihood!"

I recognized the voices as I ran to the door and keyed myself in.

Please don't notice Clarence. Please. Please. Please.

I dashed up the stairs, taking them two at a time, which is saying something for me. Sometimes I appear leggy in photos, but that's all photoshop. You can't be my size and be leggy. It's not a thing.

"Mercy!"

Come on.

Mr. Cervantes called out to me from his door, his face red and in a grimace. That stopped me cold. He was the nicest and calmest person I knew, despite his inexplicable admiration for Aunt Miriam.

"What's wrong? Are you feeling okay?" I asked.

"I am not," he said in a rush. "I heard what those animals have been saying to you."

"Oh, that. It's okay."

"It is not. You shouldn't have to put up with that."

"Yeah, well, ya know, it is what it is."

"Did they hurt you? What are those marks?" he asked.

"Spider bites. They're better."

He pulled back. "Goodness. What have you been doing?"

"Looking into a case. Can you take care of Skanky for a couple of days? I have to go away."

Mr. Cervantes sighed and his shoulders relaxed. "Good. Go away for a few days and we'll have this straightened out."

I was opening my door but stopped. "What do you mean?"

"We organized. The entire building is launching a protest."

"Are they...protesting me?"

"Of course not. It's not your fault. We're calling and emailing the buildings department and that company. Mrs. Winkle has a recording from yesterday. Her daughter attached it to an email and she sent it off. I must tell you. I couldn't listen to the whole thing. It was foul and I just heard them. They're at it again."

"I'm sorry."

"Don't apologize. We know it's not your fault. You don't smell. I'd lay odds that it was your Uncle Morty that smelled up that airplane."

I blinked back tears. Just when I started questioning the goodness in humanity, it was Mr. Cervantes to the rescue.

"Don't cry dear. We'll figure it out."

"Thank you," I managed to choke out and ran inside.

Skanky was stretched out on the living room floor, gnawing on a piece of plastic. I snatched it out of his jaws and tossed it in my new cat-proof trashcan—that means expensive—because that was the only way I could keep him out of it. I don't know where he got that wrapper. I'd taken to putting all my plastics straight into recycling, but still the little varmint found it somewhere.

He yowed complaints at me as I ran into the bedroom and started throwing stuff in a bag. Jeans, sweaters, panties. I grabbed the Timberlands that Fats gave me. She said she got a great deal on them and I'd decided to believe it wasn't a five-finger discount and that there was a credit card involved and not some truck heist out East somewhere.

After that, I filled my toiletries bags to the brim and grabbed some woolly socks and my favorite poofball hat. I almost left it at that, but I stopped in front of my armoire and took a breath.

I might need it.

I found my Mauser under some sweaters in the back and I grabbed an extra clip just to be on the safe side. I didn't like carrying a weapon and it did seem faintly ridiculous. Whoever killed Sister Maggie was probably long dead. If he wasn't Dominic, that is, and alive, he'd be at least seventy-five but more likely eighty-five or ninety, if I went by the average age of serial killers. I'd like to think I could fend off a geriatric killer, but I put the Mauser in my bag anyway and ran out to the living room, jumping over a grumpy Skanky cat. He'd be happy enough in the near future. Mr. Cervantes had the unfortunate habit of making my cat gourmet food and I expected to find him significantly fatter when I got back.

When I got to the door, I glanced at Maggie's box and considered leaving it. A cursory look said it wasn't helpful, but something made me grab it on the way out.

Mr. Cervantes was still in his doorway on the phone. "Buildings inspector. I'm on hold."

"Thanks!"

All those calls probably wouldn't do any good, even the FBI couldn't get the job done, but I appreciated the effort.

I jogged down the stairs and stood at the door for a second, holding Maggie's box like a shield and telling myself that it would blow over. I'd wait it out or, if it stayed at that insane level, I could sue the company. Something civilized.

Then I opened the door and civilized went out the window. Now when I say out the window, I mean it went out headfirst and landed on its head. The workers had assembled in front of my car and were laughing.

"She brought a fucking nun."

"That ain't no nun. She's a stripper. Show us your titties, your holiness."

The rest of their hooting insults can't be repeated. I've been catcalled since breasts happened, but nothing like that. They were surrounding her, pack-like and predatory. I shifted the box to my hip and stalked across the parking lot, putting my hand in my bag for my weapon. It slid into my hand so easily, but I didn't do it. Dad's training kicked in. Don't flash a weapon unless you're prepared to use it. I wasn't prepared to shoot a trio of construction workers although they were sorely in need of a good scare. I grabbed my phone instead and pressed my instant-record button.

Those idiots were truly idiots. Their boss was yelling for them to stop, but did they stop? No. No, they did not. They ramped it up, as idiots will, and unleashed a barrage that shocked even me and I grew up with Uncle Morty. He couldn't begin to compete with those three. They hated everyone, starting with women and Catholics and proceeding to calling me trailer trash. That's right. Dudes with third-rate tattoos—at least one of which was misspelled—mullets, and tee shirts that said things like "Boobs are two of my favorite thangs" hated trailer trash. Irony was not their strong suit.

I got it all on video along with repeated hand gestures that don't bear describing. I'm not going to lie. I started enjoying the absurdity after about thirty seconds and their boss? He was an idiot, too. Oh, yeah, he wanted to stop them now, but he'd seen what'd been going on since the airport story broke. He knew and let it go on. Only now did he care. I guess they'd finally gone too far or he'd heard about the complaints. Well, I'd make him really care. He'd care so hard he'd wish he'd never taken to construction.

When the hate trio paused for breath, I said, "Hey, morons. She is a nun. A real live Sister of Mercy."

"Fuck you. She's a whore, just like you!"

I didn't wait for the barrage to get going. I dumped my stuff in the back, got in, and pulled out of my parking space so fast I almost hit a panicked guy in a cheap suit running toward the morons waving frantically. I hit the gas and we peeled out, barreling into the alley, narrowly avoiding Fats' truck as she drove in from the opposite end. She hit the horn, but I passed her. I was getting away. I had to get away.

Fats did the fastest three-point turn in the history of turning behemoth trucks around and came after us. There was no hope. I couldn't outrun Fats Licata and I knew from experience that there was nowhere I could go that she couldn't find me.

I drove around to my parents' house and screeched to a halt in the alley behind. Fats was on my door in a second. She whipped it open and said, "Where the hell have you been?"

"What?"

"I came to get you for your aunt's appointment," she said.

"Why?"

"I'm helping you on this case."

Why is everyone always helping me?

"Aunt Miriam's appointment has nothing to do with it," I said.

"She knows about the case and has information. It behooves me to keep track of her and whatever she's got going on."

"You're not going to do something to my aunt, are you?"

"Do I look like I would do something to a nun?"

Well...

"No. Of course, not," I said. "Aunt Miriam got an earlier appointment. That's done and we're going to St. Seb."

Fats leaned to the side and said, "You picked up another nun?"

"I did. This is Sister Clarence." I looked back at the little nun and saw her for the first time since I left her in the parking lot. I don't know why I didn't look at her before. Maybe because I was driving or because she wasn't making a sound. I took silence as a good thing. It wasn't. Sister Clarence was sitting in Mom's cushy front seat, pale as porcelain, with tears streaming down her face.

"Oh, crap, Clarence," I said. "I'm so sorry. I shouldn't have left you out there. I never thought that would happen."

She sucked in a breath and whispered, "Mercy, I will pray for you."

Good thing? I wasn't sure.

"I'm going to fix it. I recorded them."

"You...does that happen to all women?"

"No. It's not normal. It's me."

Fats pushed in. "Hey, Sister. Fats Licata. Am I right in thinking you were just at Mercy's apartment?"

Sister Clarence nodded.

"Was something...unpleasant said to Mercy?" asked Fats with a muscle twitching in her jaw.

She nodded again.

No. No. No.

"So," I said quickly, "let's go to St. Seb. Got to get a police report, autopsy results. Exciting stuff."

"Sister?" asked Fats. "Did they say something to you?"

She nodded.

"Mercy, give me that recording."

"I don't want to. I have a plan."

"What's your plan? Calling the cops?"

"Actually, I was going to send it to the media. It's been a slow week," I said.

She held out an enormous hand and I sighed before handing it over. "My code is—"

"I know your code." She jabbed the keypad and took a quick look. "Get in my truck. We'll head out after I take care of this."

"Please don't. I can't owe Calpurnia anything else. I'm up to my eyeballs in debt as it is."

Fats waved me off. "This is about the church, not you."

Sister Clarence put a gentle hand on my arm. "Your life isn't what I expected."

"I think that all the time." I grabbed my bag and Maggie's box off the backseat. "We'll be taking Fats' truck."

"May I ask who she is?"

"A friend."

"Are you sure?" asked Sister Clarence. "She seems rather threatening."

I grinned at her. "Oh, she is. Definitely. But we won't be getting yelled at anymore."

"I bet nobody ever thinks she's not worldly."

"Probably not. No."

She smiled and looked positively saintly. "I'm going to learn a lot this weekend."

Yes, you are, and may God forgive me.

CHAPTER FIFTEEN

W e sped down Highway 44 into the storm. We had snow, sleet, and a short bout of hail before we reached Eureka. I was in the front seat next to the glowering Fats, who'd already had her grammar corrected three times and was now forced into silence. Sister Clarence never corrected me and don't think Fats didn't notice.

But, at least, the little nun was happy again. It only took one look at Moe, Fats' miniature dog who we picked up from her doggy day care where she'd just been groomed. Moe had pink bows behind her ears and a wardrobe of four coats in her own pink handbag. Sister Clarence thought she was adorable. She was not. Pink didn't go with her brindle coat and it somehow set off her bulging black eyes. She did love nuns and they played ball, fetch, and tug of war in the back seat. You could do that with a pocket dog. Even Wallace the pug was bigger than Moe.

"I love this dog," said Sister Clarence. "She has a wonderful spirit."

"I'm glad you like her," said Fats through her clenched teeth.

"Where did you get her?"

"Dead hooker."

"Fats!" I said.

"She said she needs an education in real life."

"That's not real life," I said.

Sister Clarence stuck her head between our seats. "How did this poor woman die?"

"Overdose," said Fats. "And it *is* real life."

"A little too real," I said.

Aunt Miriam was going to chase me down and beat me bloody.

"You're not afraid to get dirty. Maybe Sister Clarence isn't either."

"Please call me Clarence," she said. "Sister is so formal and I'm very new, compared to Sister Miriam and Sister Frances."

"What would Aunt Miriam say?" I asked.

She put her finger to her lips. "We won't tell her."

"I've corrupted you already."

"Principal Johns says that I've lived far too clean a life to be teaching children that won't."

Fats made a fist and her knuckles cracked. "I don't like him."

"He's a her and she's right. I was very sheltered."

"Homeschooled?"

"Yes by my wonderful mother. My childhood was practically perfect in every way, but I don't think it prepared me for the life I need to lead. What about your mothers? I know Miss Carolina and she is truly perfection."

I gritted my teeth. My mother was perfection and I sort of resented her for it. Mom never got spider bites all over her face or got the "C" word yelled at a nun. She'd never shot anyone or had a pug pee on her for fun.

"She never solved a murder either," said Fats.

"Huh?"

"I know what you're thinking. Carolina Watts, Mrs. Perfect USA. Did she ever solve a murder? Or a kidnapping?"

"She was too busy helping my dad do that. Besides, she hates the limelight and I keep thrusting her in it."

"At least she likes you."

Clarence and I exchanged a look. I couldn't think what to say. When Fats said girls didn't like her she meant it and it made me terribly sad. We hadn't been able to scare up anyone else to be in the wedding, just her cousin Carla Jean, and her partner. To be honest, I bet Jana would avoid it if she could, especially after she saw the dress.

"Nancy likes you," I said.

"What?" asked Fats.

"I was just thinking of all the women that like you."

Clarence raised her hand. "I like you. Do I count?"

A smile crept onto Fats' face. "You count."

"And you don't scare her. Right, Clarence?"

"Why would I be scared? You own darling Moe. Dog lovers are wonderful people." She sat back and started a new tug of war. Moe was extremely fierce. The nun didn't stand a chance.

"Thanks," whispered Fats.

"That's what maids of honor are for."

"You'll do it then?"

"Of course, I'll do it. There was never any question."

"What about Tiny? We're running out of time," she said.

"I'll think of something."

"Fast."

"Double fast." I leaned forward. "I don't know about this weather. We'll never be able to go out to the crime scene today."

"Where is it?" asked Fats.

"Outside of town. Uncle Morty couldn't give me an exact location. Let's hit the cop shop first off and then find a hotel that takes dogs."

Fats grinned, showing no teeth. "Already taken care of."

"Why does that make me feel nervous?" I asked.

"Because it's me. We're at the Miss Elizabeth's Bed and Breakfast."

I googled Miss Elizabeth and got an eyeful. "It's haunted. Why would you do that?"

"I thought it would inspire you," said Fats. "Plus, they have a killer breakfast, inspired by the last breakfast of Miss Elizabeth's victims."

"Ooh, that is creepy," said Clarence from the back. "Real life. I'm so excited."

"See," said Fats. "She likes it."

I twisted in my seat. "Alleged murderer. Nothing was proven."

"She confessed on her deathbed."

"To killing five men and stashing their bodies on the property," I said. "No bodies were ever found."

"Maybe you'll find one," said Clarence. "You find things."

Swell. Five more murders.

Instead of dignifying that hope, I messaged Chuck, who was less than pleased. The storm was only going to get worse and he worried. I mostly think he wanted to show me his listings. I promised to go over them on my tiny phone later and that calmed him down.

I hung up and Fats pulled off the main highway onto a rural route. Even through the snow I could see how pretty it was. Rolling hills with dense trees dotting the landscape and I started to think, against my will, about my great grandparents. They died here. Somewhere in these lovely hills their plane crashed, taking their secrets with them. I should go see the memorial while we were there if I could find it in the snow.

We drove past a Walmart at the edge of town and Fats asked her nav system to find the police station. She didn't ask me because I hadn't mentioned that I'd been there before. It wasn't a pleasant memory and most of it a blur. Just seeing the "Welcome to St. Sebastian" sign made me want to turn around instead of deal with the local cops again. Don't get me wrong. St. Seb was a lovely town once you got past the small section of urban sprawl with the fast food chains and rows of tract homes, disturbing in their sameness.

Downtown was another matter entirely, filled with 1930's bungalows, painted ladies of the Victorian era and a main street with quaint shops that probably hadn't changed since they were built. Fats parked at the former public library, complete with pillars, built in the 1880s, if I had to guess. They'd built a new library next door, all modern, but matching in style so that you had to do a double take to notice it wasn't original.

The police station occupied the old library and there was a jail in the basement. I gave my statement there after I was outed as the one who found the body of Janet Lee Fine in the city park, but I remembered few details of the interview, mostly feeling sad, exposed, and wanting to go home to forget all about it.

"Here we are," said Fats. "What's the game plan?"

"We're winging it."

"Why can't you plan? I have a plan."

"Okay. Let's do that."

Fats adjusted the super fuzzy fur-lined hood on her jacket. "My plan is to see a ghost, workout, and eat at Crabapple's."

"Crabapple's?" I asked.

"Don't worry. It's got great reviews."

Please don't be vegan.

"It's vegan," she said.

Dammit.

"What happened to cheeseburgers and malts?" I asked. "I was down with that."

"Over. The baby wants tofu."

Clarence stuck her head between us. "Baby? Who has a baby?"

For once, Fats was struck dumb with horror. She made a little finger point at me, but no way. I was not taking a baby for the team. "She meant Moe," I said. "She's her baby."

Clarence gave me a side eye, but she went with it. "Dogs eat tofu?"

"My dog does," said Fats. "Now go get that police report."

I agreed, but I had no idea how to do that, since I never had to do it before. Everything was online and if it was online, Uncle Morty could get at it. I couldn't remember much about the cops in St. Sebastian, but I didn't think they had a drunk in charge anymore.

"Put on some lipstick," said Fats, eyeing me with disappointment. As usual, her makeup was flawless. Mine was nonexistent. Aunt Miriam didn't believe in makeup or wasting time. I was lucky to get some lip balm on and it wasn't even tinted.

"It's in the back in a bag," I said. "I look okay. The bites are better."

"You look like Marilyn Monroe got an infectious rash. You've got to cover those bites and play up the sex kitten angle. They're cops. Give them a show."

I glanced back at Clarence, who was wide-eyed and slightly confused. "Won't they want to help?"

"Not as a rule, no," I said.

Fats got her purse out of the center console. "You're hopeless. It's a good thing you've got the face you've got or forget it." She pulled out concealer, powder, some kind of green glop, mascara, and a liquid liner that I would never have dared to try. No. That's not true. I tried liquid liner one time. It was bad.

"Do that cat's eye thing," said Clarence.

We looked at her.

She pinked up. "I saw it on one of the mothers at school. It was very striking."

I said I couldn't do it, but I was in luck. Fats could. I never had so much makeup applied to me so fast. Her hands were a blur. When I looked in the little visor mirror, I was in full Marilyn, Marilyn on the cover of *Playboy* Marilyn. It was amazing what Fats could do with spare makeup and a little hairspray.

"You are gifted," said Clarence. "Are you good with scars?"

"Scars?" asked Fats.

"There's a mother in my class." She went on to describe the mother's situation and I was left to wing it alone.

You'd think I'd have a leg up with my dad and all. Half the time I saw him growing up was in the shop as he called it. Mom would haul me down there when he had a break and we'd have a snack together. I think we were supposed to be bonding. Mostly, it was just weird and Mom stopped taking me after a pedophile in holding took a liking to me. I heard Dad might've smacked him around, but I've been careful never to ask him directly.

I flipped up my hood and rushed inside while my team discussed that green glop that Fats had decided against spackling me with. A bored-looking deputy, sitting at the front desk, looked up from a magazine and dropped his coffee. Mission accomplished, Fats.

"Good afternoon," I said, briskly walking up to the desk and leaning on it. "Who can I talk to about a police report from 1965?"

"19—what?" The young cop sopped up his mess with an entire box of tissues.

An older woman wearing sergeant's stripes walked in and said, "Not again, Dallas. This is getting embarrassing."

"Sorry, Sergeant Stratton," said Dallas. "She came in and I don't know what happened."

Stratton gave me the once-over. She knew what happened and she wasn't happy about it. Maybe I should've stuck with my spider bites and lip balm. "What can I do for you, Miss Watts?"

"You remember me," I said.

"You're hard to forget."

"In a good way?"

"No."

"Oh, um, I like to see someone about a police report from 1965," I said.

That surprised her and I got a zing of pleasure from the consternation.

"What crime?" she asked.

"A murder. Victim's name was Margaret Mullanphy."

"We don't get a lot of murders in St. Seb." Dallas tossed his wad of Kleenex in the trash and hitched up his belt. He was pretty handsome in a slightly scruffy way and I gave him my help-me-out smile. He liked it. A lot.

"You got this one," I said. "Do you think you can help me out?"

"No," said Stratton. "You don't have standing."

"How do you know?" I asked.

"Because, during the dry spell, you came into our town without a heads-up and started digging, making us look like half-witted yokels that couldn't find a body that was right under our noses."

This is going well.

"That was never my intent. I didn't want credit."

She crossed her arms. "You got it. Headlines for a month. 'Hot Body Solves Cold Case'."

"An anonymous tip led you to the body. I gave zero interviews," I said.

"You were seen at the burial site digging. The family found out and told everyone," said Stratton.

"That's their right." I crossed my own arms. "Their little girl was kidnapped and murdered. They can do whatever the hell they want. I didn't enjoy the coverage, but I wasn't going to throw a hissy fit about it either."

We eyed each other for a minute and she finally said, "Your father's a good man. He's getting a raw deal from the FBI."

"Yes, he is," I said.

"How's your mother?"

"Recovering. Slowly."

Stratton clicked her walkie. "Hey, Chief. Guess who I've got up at the desk?"

The walkie crackled and a tired man's voice said, "The abominable snow man."

"Mercy Watts."

No answer.

"I'd duck if I were you," said Stratton.

Dallas winced as we listened to someone pounding down the stairs, paused, and then marched into the foyer. I'd like to say I recognized him, but I didn't. The chief wasn't memorable in any way. A casting director could put him in any generic cop role and he'd fit perfectly. Dad had at least three bosses that could've been confused with that hefty bald guy with a bristly mustache and a network of broken veins on his cheeks. I assumed he wasn't one of Dad's old bosses by the way he was looking at me. Dad's bosses usually liked him even when he was driving them nuts with his obsessive work ethic.

"I knew you'd turn up again," he said.

I tilted my chin down and gave him the smile that got The Girls to order a pizza instead of making it from scratch. "I tend to do that. It's not intentional."

"Like you didn't intend to dig up that girl?"

I actually didn't, for the record, but there was zero use in saying it. "I didn't intend to cause you an issue."

"Oh, yeah?"

Sometimes I can't help myself. I do things that, even while I'm doing them, I know it's a bad idea. Mouthing off to my dad about chores and the fact that he never did them. Telling my algebra teacher that she made *another* error while grading my test. And I did it just then, right at that critical moment. 'Cause I'm stupid.

"Why don't you ask whoever was the chief in 1999, why they didn't notice someone burying a child and her bicycle in the dried up lake bed four hundred yards from the town fair?"

"I was the police chief in 1999," he said with a snarl.

I will never learn.

"Well, what's the answer?"

Wow. I really won't.

I waited, literally biting my tongue. It was my only hope. The Chief, Gates, according to his name tag, just stared at me.

"Miss Watts," said Dallas, hesitantly, "wants to know about a murder in 1965. That's before you."

Chief Gates shot the kid a look that should've melted the heavy coating of pomade in his hair. "Yes, Deputy Mosbach. That was before I was chief, seeing as I'm fifty-five years old."

"I just meant—"

Stratton shushed him and said, "I told her she doesn't have standing to request the records."

"Good. Don't let the door hit you." He turned around and marched out.

"Wait." I dashed after him and caught him three stairs up. He wasn't the fittest cop out there.

"I'm sorry about saying that. I don't know what came over me. I do it with my dad. It's crazy and it never works out for me."

Through his irritation, I saw a flicker of amusement. A very tiny flicker.

"Miss Watts, I don't have time for this," he said. "Why you chose to show up in the middle of a blizzard to ask about a fifty-year-old unsolved case is beyond me, but the city manager's on vacation and nobody can find the key to the snowplow facility. I've got things to do that might just include using the jaws of life to get the plows out."

"It's not unsolved," I said.

Exasperated didn't begin to describe his expression. "You're joking?"

"No, really. It's considered solved. There was a suspect who died, but I have a very good reason to believe that he didn't do it. There wasn't any real proof, just a little wishful dot connecting."

"What was the case?"

"Sister Margaret Mullanphy."

"You think we made a mistake on a murdered nun?" he asked.

I took a breath and thought fast. "Not you. Not anyone currently in your department. Something was going on here in St. Sebastian, a crime wave, I think. The chief back then couldn't handle it. He was in a bad way."

Someone behind me cleared their throat and I glanced back. Stratton and Dallas were in the doorway. He was freaked and she was giving me the hairy eyeball.

"What makes you say he was in a bad way?" asked Gates. There was a warning in his voice, but because I'm me, I didn't heed it.

"I spoke to a witness this morning that described him as sad and drunk while on the job and in the middle of searching the victim's rooms at the convent."

He put his hand on his nightstick, never a good sign. "What was his name?"

"Actually, I don't know. There's nothing online and the death certificate was faked."

"Oh, Lord," said Stratton.

"What?" I asked.

"Do you want me to tell you his name?" asked Chief Gates.

Please don't say Gates.

"I'm thinking maybe no."

"His name was Chief Woody Lucas."

Whew!

"Okay. Thanks for telling me. Now about Sister Maggie's file, what do I need—"

"He was my grandfather," said Chief Gates.

I took a step back. "Tell me you're joking."

"No, ma'am. He died in 1972."

Ten bucks it was alcohol-related.

"Liver failure?" I asked.

Shut up.

"Forget I said that."

He smiled the coldest smile I'd ever seen outside of Hunt Hospital for the Criminally Insane.

"I won't forget." Chief Gates went up the stairs. He might've been stomping. It was hard to tell.

I turned around. "That could've gone better."

Stratton shook her head. "It's like you've never done this before."

"I haven't."

She screwed up her mouth and then said, "You're all over the news. Didn't you jump off a bridge in Paris to chase a terrorist?"

"I never had to ask for a police report before," I said.

"How is that possible?"

I walked down the three steps and looked out a window. Ice pelted the glass. They say when it rains it pours. When it's me, it sleets.

"Everything's online and accessible normally."

"So you get what you need illegally."

I smiled. "I wouldn't say that."

Stratton sighed. "Well, beat it. We're the last two here and I'm sure we'll be heading out any minute."

"Can't I just see that file?" I asked. "It won't take long. Autopsy. Photos."

"Miss Watts, you didn't just fall off the turnip truck."

I grinned at her. "And that's why I think you might just give me a peek."

"It's gone," she said.

"As in..."

"We've been flooded over the years." She pointed to her left. "The Missouri River is less than a half mile away."

"Where do you keep your files?"

"Used to keep what survived in the basement. Then our pipes burst three years ago, Dallas can tell you, we were five feet deep."

Dallas nodded, but he wasn't quick about it.

"Dallas, did you have burst pipes?" I asked.

"Oh, yeah. It was bad. My first winter on the job. The plumber redid our plumbing. He didn't insulate or something."

"Like I said," said Stratton, "we couldn't give them to you anyway. You're not family or a defendant's counsel, are you?"

"No," I admitted. "But I know the family. They could request."

"They could, but all the old stuff is gone."

I groaned.

Stratton laughed. "Sucks to be you."

"You have no idea."

Her radio crackled. "Hey, Candace. Arnold's in the ditch."

"Oh, man," said Dallas. "Already?"

She answered. "Dallas is on it."

"Bring some chains. He doesn't have his," said the radio.

"Will do."

Dallas went over to the coat rack and started layering up, muttering about every time it snows. Stratton went to the desk and gestured to the door while answering the phone. I sighed and put my hood back up. I was halfway out when I stopped and turned around.

"Hey, Stratton," I said.

"For the love of God, what?"

"So if I was family, you'd have to let me have evidence, if it survived?" I asked.

She put her hand over the receiver. "You aren't family."

"Like I said, I know the family. They like me," I said.

A faint look of worry crossed Stratton's face. "I doubt that."

"Then you'd be wrong."

She waved me away, annoyed.

I waved back. "What if I were family and it wasn't murder, officially?"

"Officially?"

I stepped back inside. "Let's say it was ruled an accident."

She raised her eyebrows. "You said she was murdered."

"A different case."

"An accident?" she asked.

"Yeah."

"Are you talking about a car?"

"Not exactly."

"Then what are we talking about?"

"Nothing for the moment."

"Why are you interested in a fifty-year-old solved case anyway?"

I put my hood back up. "I'm not family, but it's a family thing."

"Ah, crap," she said.

"I'll be back."

Stratton sighed. "I figured. Yes, yes, Ethel, I heard you. Who's at the mailbox?"

I went back out into the storm hoping to catch up with the foot-dragging Dallas, but I didn't see him. I could barely find my way to the truck. When I got in the passenger seat, I almost sat on Clarence.

"You're in the back," said Fats.

"I moved up," said Clarence. "That took a long time."

I got in the back with Moe, who wasn't nearly as pleased to see me as she was Clarence. She kept barking and charging at me.

"What is up with this dog?" I asked.

"She's protecting us," said Clarence. "Let her sniff you."

Moe didn't sniff me. She tried to pee on my lap. What is with me and little dogs? I thrust her out the door to pee into the sleet. She came back in popsicled.

"Let's go," I said, plucking the ice off Moe's tail.

Fats put on her hazard lights and slowly pulled out of her space. "I don't see a report. What went wrong?"

"Everything," I said. "A deputy just left. Did you see where he went?"

"Hell, no," said Fats.

"Hey! Clarence is right next to you."

The little nun looked back at me with her cherub face lit up. "Fats is teaching me all the words and emoticons. Do you know what an eggplant means?"

I'm so going to hell.

"Let's talk about that never," I said. "You didn't see where he went?"

"I can barely see the police station. We're going to the bed and breakfast." Fats popped a toothpick out on her lip and drove out onto the road at a snail's pace.

"I have to get the St. Seb Sentinel at the very least."

"Don't speak to me. I'm driving here."

It took us thirty minutes to go the half mile to Miss Elizabeth's Bed and Breakfast. I could've gotten out and walked faster. I might've frozen to death, but it seemed a reasonable alternative, considering how many times Moe bit me.

Then we drove into the driveway and Miss Elizabeth's brick Victorian mansion loomed over us and the biting became preferable. I've never felt worse about a place and I stayed at Cairngorms Castle. People really did die there.

Miss Elizabeth was clearly not into giving a good first impression. The sign was hanging half off. No cheery windows welcomed us. A couple were boarded up and, if there wasn't a pair of eyes staring at us from behind a tattered curtain, I was completely paranoid. Hint: I wasn't completely paranoid.

"It really does look haunted," said Clarence happily.

Yes, it does.

CHAPTER SIXTEEN

"A re you ready for a haunted evening?" a woman's voice rang out as we walked into the foyer.

Clarence took my arm and cuddled up close. "This is so exciting. Wait until I tell Sister Frances."

"She can never know. We stayed at a Hampton Inn or something," I said.

"I couldn't possibly lie."

"It's for her own good." *Or mine. Either way.*

Fats stomped on the rug and looked around. "Hello!"

"Be right there!" said the voice.

"Is there a Hampton Inn in town?" I asked.

Clarence squeezed my arm and said, "I always heard about bed and breakfasts. This is exactly what I imagined."

The crazy thing was that she was right. Miss Elizabeth's was creepy as hell outside, but inside it was warm and cheery with polished woodwork and lovely antiques. It smelled like baking bread and chocolate chip cookies.

We took off our ice-encrusted coats and hung them on the fancy twisted wood coat rack and Moe dashed around sniffing and wagging her curly tail.

"Hello. Hello." A woman with curly short grey hair and wearing a huge apron came out from the back, carrying an enormous mixing bowl and a batter-coated wooden spoon. "Mary Elizabeth?"

"Yes, ma'am," said Fats, taking out her ponytail and shaking her light brown hair out. It fell perfectly. I don't understand how she did that. My hair was a wreck. I didn't need to see it to know.

"I didn't realize you had two guests with you."

Clarence stepped up. "I'm a surprise addition. I hope you have room."

Our hostess smiled. "Plenty of room. You're our only guests. I'm Irene. My husband, Lefty, is out in the woodshop, working on a new window frame. I have hot chocolate on the stove. Would you like some?"

She didn't have to ask Clarence twice. We dropped our bags and followed Irene to the back of the house to a large addition with an eat-in kitchen and blazing wood stove.

Irene poured us mugs of thick hot chocolate that would've done Aaron proud and asked Fats, "You seem familiar. Are you a pro wrestler?"

"I dabbled a little," she said with a sly smile.

I could not picture Fats in an over-the-top costume, not that her normal wardrobe of cheetah leggings and neon wasn't the tiniest bit costumy. "I can't see that."

"I'm sure you were wonderful," said Clarence. "The best ever."

"They fired me," said Fats with more than a little pride. "I was less restrained than required."

"Pink the Impaler," said Irene. "Lefty loved you. Those men didn't stand a chance."

"You fought the men?" I asked.

"You're surprised?" asked Fats.

"On second thought, no, not really."

My phone buzzed and I glanced at the screen. Uncle Morty.

"I'll be right back," I said and went into the hall, away from talk of choke holds and body stockings.

"What's up?" I asked Uncle Morty.

"Don't ask the St. Seb cops about the old chief," he said in a rush.

"Too late."

"Son of a bitch. How'd you get there so fast? 44 is a parking lot."

"I guess we beat it."

He began typing and said, "The current chief ain't a fan of you."

"I got that and then I made it worse."

"Yeah, you do that. Called his grandpa a drunk, did ya?"

I sat down on a squat Victorian chair and almost slipped off the horsehair upholstery. "Yep. I also called him sad and implied that he faked Maggie's death certificate."

"Going for broke then."

"Always. Why'd this take so long? You're usually superfast with this kind of thing."

He grumbled and admitted that he'd gotten distracted by some more pictures of Nikki, happily flouncing around Greece. He found a pic of her in a swimming suit and declared that he would never eat pizza again. Right.

"So what did you find on the old chief?"

"Well, I ain't surprised that you hit a nerve. The guy was sad. Drank himself to death. Cirrhosis of the liver. 1972."

"I guessed that."

"Jesus, Mercy," said Uncle Morty. "Do ya want to never get to Greece?"

"It popped out."

"Stop popping and start thinking. You want the rest?"

I did and I didn't. But what I wanted really didn't matter. He was going to tell me no matter what. Chief Woody Lucas was a St. Seb native, born and bred. He graduated from the Catholic high school and fought in WWII, where he served as a Marine in the Pacific. Married. Two kids. The daughter, Melanie Lucas Gates, was police chief from 1972, taking over after her father died until she retired to open a florist shop in 1992. That's when the current chief took over.

"So I stepped on the family business," I said.

"You stepped in it alright."

"How's our current guy?" I asked. "Not the healthiest specimen. He was sober, but from the weight and veining on his cheeks I'd say he's following in Grandpa's footsteps."

Uncle Morty typed so that it sounded like three people were typing instead of just one.

"Hello?"

"Got his financials. He's screwed."

"Anything we can use?" I asked.

"No. You nailed it. He has a whiskey habit and he likes the good stuff. Up to three or four bottles a week. Divorced. Kids with the ex in Kansas City."

"I don't think that helps us. Any good news?"

"He's solid cop. Straight shooter. Crime rates' down, not that it was ever high. Does a lot of community outreach."

"How's that good news for me?"

"A good cop is a hell of a lot better than a bad one. He'll do the right thing."

I didn't know about that. He was hating me pretty hard and I couldn't blame him.

"What else have you got?"

"Crime rates prior to the murder," he said. "You'll like this."

"Define like."

I did like it. Uncle Morty pulled the stats from a variety of resources and, despite the stats not being terribly specific about little podunk towns, he came up with a trend that backed me up. St. Seb's county had seen a rise in small time crime prior to Maggie's murder. Property crimes, thefts, and arson were all up.

"Not violent crime?" I asked.

"No. I got the insurance data. It ain't real specific, but we've got more claims coming out of that county during the five years prior. Looks like a slow trend up."

"And after?"

He chuckled. "I wondered if you'd ask that. After the murder, it went down. We got a nice little cliff with Maggie at the top and a severe drop-off after."

An involuntary shiver went down my back. "Do you feel as bad about that as I do?"

"Damn straight and what do you want to bet that old chief felt it, too?"

"I'd bet the farm, but he didn't do anything about it," I said.

"You got to get that report," said Uncle Morty.

"Not gonna happen. The sergeant told me that the old files were destroyed three years ago after some pipes burst. It wasn't the first flood. The river got some of them before that."

"Let me check." He went at that and I let my gaze settle on the pictures opposite me. I wish I hadn't. They were ghost pics of the house I was in. Grainy apparitions on the stairs and next to beds. Framed newspaper clippings and magazine articles. Miss Elizabeth had been busy. Swell. I thought about our family cat, Blackie, the one that showed up when something tragic was about to happen. Seeing him a couple of times was enough to make me think that there might be something in the Miss Elizabeth legend.

"Goddammit," said Uncle Morty.

"So no files or evidence, I assume?" I asked.

"They did flood. Morons kept using the basement. You got to get something. We're ass out."

I groaned. "I can take another run at Aunt Miriam, intervention style, get Mom and Sister Frances to gang up on her. If she'd just ID that medal, I'd be off the hook."

He snorted. "Miriam don't care what people think and you wouldn't be off no hook. Myrtle wants you to do it."

I slumped back and nearly slipped off the chair again. Who thought horsehair was an awesome fabric? It's not. It sucks. "It's not looking good."

"You want the rest?" he asked.

"Is it better?"

"Eh."

That wasn't a good sign and his info wasn't terribly helpful. He checked into the odd duplicate death certificate and couldn't find another one like it. All his hacker buddies agreed it was hinky. That wasn't good news exactly, but his other info was decidedly worse. There were twelve clergy with substantiated claims of abuse in the sixties. That meant a lot of kids, but Uncle Morty couldn't connect any of that to Sister Maggie or Father Dominic or Bishop Fowler. None of them was accused of anything to do with the sex abuse scandal and

Fowler supposedly retired for health reasons. If something was going on during the period leading up to Maggie's death it was well hidden and the church hadn't stepped up.

"Is the diocese still talking up a storm?" I asked.

"It's settled down," said Uncle Morty. "The current crew doesn't get what the hell went on and they're pissed that something was hidden."

"But they don't know what?"

"Not a friggin' clue. Nobody understands what went on with Maggie and Dominic. They're looking at him hard, but there ain't nothing there."

I mulled that over for a minute. What do people get worked up over? Sex and money.

"So if it wasn't a sex crime they were dealing with that fall, that leaves money. Follow the money," I said.

"Money? The church is loaded."

"Let's see. Lots of meetings. Nuns kept out of it."

"That sounds like they had a molester on their hands," said Uncle Morty.

"Except they didn't."

He started typing again. "That bishop covered it up. Protected somebody."

"Let's assume the diocese did come clean with the sex abuse."

"You go ahead and do that. I'm looking again," he said. "Keeping chicks out still makes it look like sex."

"I know, but I bet it was money, not kids," I said. "You can give it to one of your accounting gurus. A numbers puzzle from the sixties, they should love that."

He grumbled but agreed. "You going to the paper next?"

I looked out the window. "I don't see how. It's snowmageddon out there."

"Where are you holed up?"

"Miss Elizabeth's B and B."

"The haunted hotel? What the fuck?"

"It was available and close."

"That place is notorious," said Uncle Morty. "My guy, Howie, stayed there with his wife before doing the wineries in Augusta."

"And?"

"They left at two in the morning and needed new underwear."

"Are you telling me you think this joint is really haunted?" I asked.

"I think you know Howie," he said. "He scare easy?"

Howie? I scrolled through my index of dudes and came up blank. There weren't a lot of Howies running around.

"Old guy. Firefighter," said Uncle Morty. "Runs the Gruesome Ghouls Haunted Firehouse."

"Grisly Gus?"

"Yeah. His real name's Howard."

I knew that guy and there was a reason why he ran the charity haunted firehouse. Grisly Gus was terrifying, a true ghoul, missing half a hand, multiple burns, and a limp, not to mention his laugh. Think chicken bone in garbage disposal. Some grandparents threaten their grandkids with the bogeyman if they won't go to bed or eat their broccoli. Grandad threatened me with Gus. I totally went to bed. I didn't sleep. But I was in there.

"Grisly Gus ran out in the middle of the night? *He* gave *me* nightmares."

"That's what I'm saying."

"What happened to Gus? Grandad never told me. He's pretty beat up."

"Howie wasn't a fan of safety equipment. It didn't work out for him."

"Wow."

"It was the seventies. Guys were crazy," said Uncle Morty. "I sent you a map. Get over to the Sentinel."

"I'll have an accident and freeze to death."

"It's six blocks. Suck it the hell up."

He hung up on me and I took a look at the map. Go out the front door and take a left. Six blocks. Fats did have a stupid big truck and snow tires. It was three o'clock, if I didn't go, the day was basically wasted.

I went back in the kitchen and found it empty. The mugs were gone and two fresh loaves of bread were cooling on a rack. "Hello?"

"Yes?" whispered a voice.

I spun around. No one was there.

Don't freak out.

"Fats? Clarence?"

"They went upstairs," said no one.

Breathe. You didn't hear anything.

"Yes, you did," said the voice. "You heard me."

I took off, running out of the kitchen, bouncing off walls, and grabbing the newel post to whip around and run upstairs. "Fats! Clarence!"

At the top of the stairs, a man stepped out, but I was going too fast and I rammed right into him. I'm not going to lie. I've never been so happy to plow into an old man and knock him off his feet. He was real, solid, and landed on his bum with an *oomph*.

"Well, that's a fine how do you do," he said, looking up at me with twinkling blue eyes under shaggy white brows.

I gasped and collapsed against the bannister. "I'm so sorry. I just. I was."

He chuckled. "Don't worry yourself. It's not the first time. Nor will it be the last."

"Let me help you." I gave him a hand up. "Are you okay?"

"I didn't break a hip," he said. "I look that old, but I'm not. I trust you've met Miss Elizabeth."

"I didn't see anything."

"Well, you wouldn't, would you." He adjusted his woolly grey cardigan and ran a hand through his hair that was as shaggy as his brows. "I'm Lefty, part owner and fixer of all the stuff that breaks for no good reason. Are you here for the tournament?"

"Tournament?" I asked blankly.

"Basketball. It's a big deal around here."

"Um...no. I'm Mercy Watts. I'm here with my friends. Do you know where they went? I was on the phone and when I went back to the kitchen, they weren't there."

He patted my shoulder. "Did you just have an...experience?"

"I think maybe."

"Just breathe. It's alright. I take it you didn't get the spiel."

I sucked in a breath, but my heart was still racing. "Where are they?"

"Irene put them in the Blue Room. No offense, but our furniture is antique. I don't know if the bed will hold Pink the Impaler. She's a whopper, bigger than I imagined."

"Thank goodness."

He patted me again. "Try not to panic. It just encourages her."

"Um...who?"

"Miss Elizabeth. Stay calm and she won't pester you."

Irene came down the long hall carrying a pair of wool blankets. "What nonsense are you talking, Lefty? Don't get her worked up. I haven't had a chance to give her the spiel yet."

"And you're already too late," said Lefty.

"You can't be—" Irene looked at me. "Oh, dear. I'm so sorry. Were you in the kitchen?"

I nodded.

"I was afraid of that. She does not like that kitchen. We put on the addition and I have not heard the end of it." Irene put her arm around me and herded me down the hall. "We'll have you tucked up with warm cookies and feeling better in no time. Oh, Lefty?" she called out.

"Yes, dear?"

"The faucet's running in the yellow bathroom again."

Lefty muttered something and went in the opposite direction.

"It's fine," said Irene. "One of her little jokes. She just loves to bother him."

"Miss Elizabeth?" I asked.

"Who else? You wouldn't believe our water bill."

There was a clang from down the hall, followed by a whoop of joy.

"See," said Irene. "Fixed already. Here we are. I gave you all the triple, since you girls want to be together."

"We do?" I asked.

She wrinkled her nose and whispered, "I recommended it. She might think you're sad."

"I'm not sad." *I'm freaked the hell out.*

"Trust me. Alone is not good. Happy couples are the worst, but let's not take any chances." Irene opened the door with a flourish and there were my investigating partners. They were in bed with face masks on, eating cookies and listening to jazz noir.

"What are you doing?" I asked.

Clarence waved her cookie at me. "It's like a slumber party."

In hell.

"We've got stuff to do." *Like find some other place to sleep.*

Fats stuffed an entire cookie in her mouth and shook her head. "Bwizzard."

Irene put the blankets on the foot of their beds. "Now if you want those pedicures, just let me know. Mrs. Cleary is right next door and she's in for the day."

"No pedicures," I said. "I have to go to the newspaper office."

"Whatever for?" asked Irene.

"Research."

Clarence dunked her cookie in a glass of milk. "We're investigating a murder."

"Not helping," I said.

Irene looked at me like I'd lost it and I was pretty close. "In St. Seb, murders aren't our thing." She leaned over to me, whispering, "I don't think Miss Elizabeth murdered anyone. She just wanted to. She didn't like men very much." Then loudly she said, "It's a good thing you're all ladies."

"I can't believe this is happening."

"We get that all the time," said Irene. "But trust me, it's happening, but what am I saying? You already know. Ladies, can I trust you to tell Mercy the rules?"

Fats stuffed another cookie in her face and nodded.

Clarence crossed her heart. "I promise."

"Can I have the truck keys?" I asked and got a snort for my trouble. "Fine. I'll walk."

Irene went to the door and called out, "Lefty, I've got a customer for you."

He trotted in, rubbing his hands together. "Where are we going? Walmart? The Chinese buffet?"

"The Sentinel," said Irene.

"That's only six blocks," he complained.

"Take it or leave it."

Lefty grinned at us. "Who's ready to take a ride on my brand new

Gator?"

"What's a Gator?" I asked.

"It's a pointless mini truck that we do not need," said Irene.

Lefty stood up straight. "It is an all-terrain vehicle with snow tracks. We won't ever get snowed in."

"We're in the middle of town. We've never been snowed in."

He held up a finger. "Climate change. It's happening."

Irene sighed. "Do you have boots, Mercy?"

"I do."

"Put 'em on. He's been known to roll that thing."

Lefty grinned. "That's why I got the upgraded roll bars. Come on. To the snow."

"Where are your boots?" asked Irene, looking at my bag on the third bed.

I went over and got out my Timberlands. "Give me a second."

"Those aren't snow boots. Come with me." She marched out and I looked at Fats.

She shrugged and ate a third cookie. She hadn't swallowed the second one yet and it wasn't pretty. "What happened to you?"

Fats muttered something while picking out a fourth cookie.

"Have fun," said Clarence.

I would not be having fun. That much was guaranteed.

CHAPTER SEVENTEEN

I rene had boots. She also had military-grade cold weather gear, including an enormous parka that hung down to my knees. I put that thing on and instantly started sweating, but Irene insisted. She dressed me like we were going to Antarctica in the bad season. By the time I got out the back door, I had a stocking cap, earmuffs, a hood, thermals, ski pants, boots that came up to my knees, fat mittens, and two extra-long scarfs. Lefty looked like he was going to a beach compared to me.

"Can you walk?" asked Lefty.

"Maybe," I said between layers of scarf.

"Quiet," said Irene as she opened the door and a gust of icy wind blew in, glazing the kitchen in white. "We've lost enough guests. This one is not getting frost bite."

"It's six blocks." Lefty stalked out into the howling storm.

"Lost?" I asked.

"You'll be fine," said Irene.

"I didn't get the rules."

"They're more like guidelines." Irene pushed me out the door and I wished I'd taken the ski goggles she offered. My eyes smarted and watered with the wind in my face. Lefty waved at me from the other end of the yard next to a building that I could barely make out.

I waddled toward him, hoping I didn't get blown over. I'd be like the little brother in *A Christmas Story*, unable to get up and wailing like a two-year-old. A couple of gusts did push me off what was supposed to be a path. It had been shoveled at some point, but the wind had drifted the snow back over. I was looking down trying to get through a drift when something dark came at me. I screamed and fell over. Actually, it was more like rolled over as I was shaped like a beach ball. A screaming beach ball.

Then Lefty was there, trying to hoist me up but ended up kind of rolling me to a weird little truck that reminded me of those mini cars people bought kids, only super-sized for adults with a snowplow bolted to the front and four odd-looking track things instead of wheels. They looked like they'd been taken off a tank and miniaturized, then splayed out, giving the impression of a waterbug standing on a pond.

Lefty stuffed me in the cab, literally using his foot while holding onto the roll bar to force my rotund form inside. I filled up most of the space and I wasn't sure he would fit. Lefty wasn't a small guy, but he managed to wedge himself in, smiling happily despite the mini icicles hanging from his brows. "Ready!" he yelled.

It wasn't a question and I got the impression if I said no, I would've been ignored. Lefty slammed the lever on the dash into drive and hit the gas. I was thrown back as we hurled onto the street, cutting off a snowplow and almost sideswiping a parked minivan.

"Woohoo!" Lefty yelled. "How do you like them apples?"

Again, not a question, and I couldn't answer. I was screaming because we left the road and went into somebody's yard and took out their mailbox.

"I'll pay for that!" He was still smiling when we crossed the road between two moving cars and hit the snowbank in the yard opposite. The second car slid and did a 360, hitting the snow bank a second after we got over it.

"Stop!" I yelled. "They might be stuck!"

"That's Monty Lurman. He's a trooper."

"What does that mean?"

Instead of answering, Lefty went for another snowbank. We hit it full tilt, spun sideways and rolled over, bouncing sideways. The world was white and upside-down, then right side up. Lather, rinse, repeat. We must've rolled three times before landing right side up in another yard at a severe tilt. Lefty gunned the engine, but my side's track spun uselessly and his side just turned us in a useless circle.

"High-centered!" yelled Lefty. "Get out!"

I couldn't get out at that angle, but I didn't have to. A man appeared at my side yelling, "Son of a bitch, Lefty. You're insane."

"You know you want one!" yelled Lefty.

"Hell, yeah!" he yelled. "Having fun?"

"No!" I yelled. "Help me!"

The men laughed and two teenagers joined us. They pushed the Gator off what I would later find out was a Barbie Princess Playhouse and then we were out of the yard, sliding into the street and I was screaming again. Lefty hit every snow drift and snowbank like he was magnetically attracted to them. My throat was burning and I was longing for my Dad's driving. He might've been needlessly aggressive and we had taken out a mailbox or two, but we never rolled. My standards had been significantly lowered.

"There it is!" yelled Lefty. "We made good time!"

"We made a mess!"

He laughed and cranked the wheel to the left so hard, I flew out like a cork out of a champagne bottle, tumbling ass over teakettle until I hit a parked car and threw up. I laid there in a new and special mixture of snow, sleet, and not a few hailstones, and I prayed. Not that Lefty would come and find me. I prayed he wouldn't. The world was spinning. The vomit wasn't projected so much out of me but into my scarves so my face and neck were coated. I was okay with it as long as Lefty didn't come back.

My prayers were not answered.

"Whoa," he said. "You can really roll. Impressive."

Not a compliment I ever wanted to hear, but he acted like I'd really accomplished something, patting me on the back and saying, "I hope somebody recorded that. We'd get so many views."

"Swell," I said.

He shoved me upright and dragged me toward the Gator.

"No! I'm not getting back in that thing." I pulled sideways and we both went down in the icy parking lot. It took serious effort to get back on our feet. That parking lot was sheer ice under six inches of snow.

"I'll have to plow this again," said Lefty as he shoved me forward.

I hit the wall next to a door that had St. Sebastian Sentinel printed on it in black. The door was frozen shut, but Lefty found a snow shovel from somewhere to hack away at the ice until he got it to budge.

"Success." He forced the door open eight inches and tried to kick me inside. Literally. He kicked me. The good news was that I barely felt it, but still it was kind of embarrassing and it didn't work. I didn't get halfway in. I was closer to eight feet wide than eight inches.

"What the hell are you doing?" yelled someone and a man got in my face.

"Help!"

He grabbed me and between him nearly pulling my arm out of socket and Lefty kicking my giant butt, I tumbled into a reception room with a cracked linoleum floor and battered metal furniture. I lurched into a desk, thrusting it three feet into a wall, knocking off a bunch of framed headlines.

"Lefty! Only you would come out in the biggest storm we've had in twenty-five years," said the man.

"That was rockstar." Lefty whipped off his balaclava and shook out his mane of white hair. "I rolled it."

"How many times?"

"Three, I think. Could've been four."

"Nice."

"You want to take a spin?"

"I would, but Mallory would kill me."

"I hear that," said Lefty. "Irene isn't thrilled, but she'll be singing another tune when everyone's calling us to get to the pharmacy tomorrow."

"I'll take your word for it." The man turned to me and frowned. "Who in the world is brave enough to get in that Gator with you?"

The world was still off kilter and I couldn't answer. There was just now one of him. A skinny man, wearing two flannel shirts and a greying ponytail.

"She had to get to you," said Lefty. "She's investigating a murder."

The skinny man got rigid. "We had a murder?" He snatched up the phone he had clipped to his braided leather belt and keyed in a code.

"Old murder," I croaked. My throat was killing me.

He stopped. "How old?"

"1965."

"Well, you weren't kidding when you said old." He walked over and stuck out his hand. "Tank Tancredi."

I gave him my fat mittened hand. "Mercy Watts."

"Really?" Tank leaned in to get a closer look at the only part of me that was visible, my eyes, but he wrinkled up his long nose and pulled back. "Did you..."

"Barf? Oh, yeah."

"For God's sake, Lefty," said Tank. "The girl's covered in vomit."

Lefty had peeled off his layers and was standing by the door in a pair of red long johns and woolly socks. "What's that?"

Tank unwound my scarves and grimaced. "Egg sandwich?"

"With Miracle Whip," I said.

"How about some peppermint tea?"

"Yes, please."

Tank turned on Lefty. "You've got Tommy Watts' kid covered in barf. Help her while I get the tea going."

Lefty came over curious but unapologetic as he helped me out of my coat and ski pants. "Well, I got you here."

"I can't deny that," I said, accepting a box of tissues and wiping off my chin and neck.

"So who's Tommy Watts?"

Tank leaned in through a doorway. "Only the most famous detective in Missouri history. Come in. It's warmer."

We went into the main newsroom, a decent-sized office with beige walls and the same battered metal furniture. There were four desks and a small office with Tank's name and editor printed on the door.

"I sent everyone home," said Tank. "Maybe I shouldn't have, since you came out in a blizzard."

I sat down on a sturdy sofa in Tank's office and said, "I didn't know what I was getting into."

"You had fun," said Lefty.

"Fun is subjective," said Tank and he handed me a box of wet wipes. "I have these for Taco Tuesdays."

"Now it's egg sandwich Thursdays," I said.

Tank's phone rang and he glanced at the screen. "It's Irene. Call your wife."

Lefty sighed. "Did Brooke Boothe call her?"

"Did you take out her mailbox again?"

"No."

Tank waited with the expression of a veteran newsman who knew not to rush things.

"Alright. I hit Caden's Barbie Princess Playhouse. I'll fix it. I can fix anything."

"We hit a little girl's playhouse?" I asked. "You're a menace."

"Caden's a boy, but yeah."

I crossed my arms. "That's unforgivable. We could've just driven straight like normal people."

"I don't have a Gator to be normal," said Lefty. "Where's the fun in that?"

"I barfed and little Caden hates you."

He screwed up his mouth and got out his phone, saying, "It's me. I'll fix it."

Lefty went out into the newsroom and started defending himself against what sounded like an onslaught of recriminations.

"Well, that'll take a while," said Tank. "What can I do you for?"

"I need to see your back issues from 1965. Please tell me you keep them."

"Back then it was all microfiche, but yeah, I got 'em."

Microfiche. I'd heard of it, but the only time I'd seen it was on *The X-Files*. It looked like a huge pain in the ass.

"You don't look happy," said Tank.

"I've never used microfiche."

He gave me a mug of peppermint tea and said, "I get it. You're a Google girl. Probably don't remember a time before email."

"Ridiculous, huh?"

"Not really. I showed my kid a rotary phone once and he couldn't figure out how to dial it. He was ten and in the gifted class."

"I'm not alone."

"Not at all," said Tank. "What murder are we talking about?"

"Sister Margaret Mullanphy in December 1965."

He nodded. "I heard about that."

"Still a topic of conversation?"

"Only because of the school."

"Did they name a school after her?" I asked.

"Not a bad idea, but no, they didn't."

"What are we talking about?"

Tank put down his own cup and said, "Hold on." He left and came back a few minutes later with a stack of newspapers.

"No microfiche?" I asked.

"These are recent. Last few months." He leaned on his desk and held the papers protectively to his chest.

"Are you planning on showing me those or what?"

"First, I want you to know this is a genuine newspaper, not a rag like the *National Enquirer* or *The Globe*."

"I assumed that," I said.

"How much do you know about St. Seb?" he asked.

"Almost zero."

He frowned. "You found Janet Lee Fine and you didn't look into the town? Your father didn't?"

"My dad had nothing to do with that situation and as far as I can tell the town had nothing to do with it either."

"She was brought here."

"Yes, she was."

"Who do you think killed her?" he asked. "There must be a pretty good reason that you ended in our dry lake bed."

There was no way I was going to tell him how that happened. It defied explanation and I'd done my best to forget it ever happened.

"Mercy?"

"It's unsolved and I have no earthly idea who did it," I said. "I'm here about Sister Maggie."

"Oh, I know and that's interesting."

"Is it?"

"In St. Seb, interesting things happen," he said. "I like interesting."

"What's your point?" I asked.

He had a point and I wasn't crazy about it. St. Seb was known for a lot of things, being charming, proximity to the Katy Trail and the wineries on the other side of the river. It was also known for having a high number of odd occurrences. Miss Elizabeth wasn't the only ghost in town. The gas station had a ghoul that liked to overflow gas tanks and turn on people's wipers. Regular sightings of a body hanging from a tree in the small park across from the hospital were so common that nobody got excited about it. A steamboat called the Arabian Queen had been sighted gliding down the river every June tenth for 150 years. That was the day its boiler blew, killing everyone onboard. It wasn't unusual to have a see-through cop directing traffic on Fifth Street or have every single alarm clock in town go off at four o'clock in the morning for no apparent reason.

"I could go on," said Tank.

"I'd rather you didn't."

"You know about Miss Elizabeth?"

"She's been mentioned," I said.

"Did Irene tell you the rules?" he asked.

"Not yet."

"Get the rules. You want the rules."

I sipped my tea. Why did I decide to come here? This was not a good idea.

"So about the school?"

"Do you want to know?" he asked.

I didn't, but it was necessary. Ten years ago the local Catholic Church bought a plot of land on the edge of town, intending to build a new high school. They started building eight years ago. The building site had a tremendous amount of problems, everything from a termite infestation to steel headers bending with no weight on them. The school council tried to keep it quiet, but that wasn't possible and Tank did report the odd occurrences, reluctantly. The stories were tame by national news standards and he didn't sensationalize it. I appreciated that, since pretty much everything about me got sensationalized. But there was no way to explain why a two-year building project went through twelve construction companies and took seven years.

"It's done now?" I asked.

"It's done. The school opened in August." He handèd me another paper. "Possible Vandals at St. Seb Catholic" was the headline.

"Not vandals?" I asked.

There had been vandalism. The principal would open the doors and every locker would be open and the contents strewn everywhere. The water fountains went on during lunch and caused a flood. Toilets overflowed. Doors locked and unlocked. The school nurse's office kept getting switched with the football coach's and when that happened the amount of supplies doubled. One time a sofa showed up, brand new, and a brand new set of Grey's Anatomy books were on the bookshelf. The football coach lost his desk and his cushy reclining chair turned into a stool.

Students reported feeling a presence, particularly when they were upset. Sometimes their backs were rubbed or they felt like someone hugged them. A boy, who was a known bully, had ice water thrown in his face twice when he'd cornered a kid from the Science Olympiad. A group of girls were in the bathroom when the words 'You are what comes out of your mouth' appeared on the mirror in red lipstick. The school chapel smelled like honeysuckle and it wasn't unusual to get a tap on the shoulder when you weren't paying attention to the morning prayer.

I want to go home.

"Why are you telling me this?" I asked. "If it's to freak me out, then mission accomplished."

Tank crossed his arms. "The plot of land the school council bought belonged to the Snider family and they made a pretty penny off that sale. People weren't happy about it."

"So?" I asked slowly.

"That's where your nun's body was found. People around here thought those woods were sort of sacred."

"And haunted?"

"Obviously, but not in a bad way."

"There's a good way to be haunted?" I asked.

"The woods were exceptionally lovely. Flowers like you've never seen. Birds, squirrels. The wildlife loved it."

"Did you go there?"

"Sure. It's kind of a thing in high school to go there at midnight to see if you can spot her."

"Maggie?"

"Yeah."

"And did you?"

Tank laughed. "No. Kids claimed to have seen her, but I think it's BS. The most I ever experienced was calmness."

"Is that really something to get excited about?" I asked.

"I'm not a calm person. Never have been. The first time I felt it, I literally didn't know what it was."

I looked through Tank's papers again and found that, although Sister Maggie's name was mentioned, there was nearly nothing about the nun herself or her murder.

"So what do you know about Maggie's death?" I asked.

A look of consternation came over Tank's narrow features. "Not much honestly. I was looking into it at the time the first construction company up and quit."

"You *were*? What happened?"

"I haven't thought about that...since it happened."

I waited. You have to let people go to certain places in their own time and Tank did go. Slowly, because he felt guilty. The first construction company left in a hurry, citing vandalism, and it certainly looked like it. The cops had investigated thoroughly. Sugar in gas tanks. Wires cut. Tires slashed. The site manager would come into the project trailer and switch on the lights and every bulb would blow. His laptop with all the project plans and timetable burst into flames. There was a picture of a smoking laptop on Tank's front page.

The cops never found a single fingerprint. Surveillance cameras covered the area completely and they didn't show anything. They didn't glitch or go out at a critical time. Nothing happened. Nothing visible anyway. A vehicle would be driven up and parked at the end of a shift. A camera would be trained on the area for the next twelve hours and the next morning there was sugar in the tank.

"That's it?" I asked, looking at the paper covering that incident. "What were you supposed to do? That stuff's hardly your fault. You covered it."

"Not that," said Tank. "People were getting pretty worked up with everything that was happening. They were questioning why the chief and Stratton couldn't find anything."

"They thought it was Maggie?"

"Of course. This is St. Seb. Once you see a Confederate regiment marching through the hospital, you suspend your disbelief pretty quick."

"That's weird," I said, "but what's it got to do with Maggie?"

"Nothing. People were talking about what to do. You know, should we abandon the site and build somewhere else. But nobody was going to take that land off the church's hands after everything that was happening and they couldn't afford to buy another parcel. So I started wondering about the nun. What happened and how it happened. Nobody talked about that. My mother would not speak about it and I found that to be prevalent in all the locals who were here at the time. Even people who moved away wouldn't talk."

"Did someone threaten them?"

"Not that I could tell. I'd say it was a shared horror about the incident that kept them quiet."

"Fear that it was someone local?" I asked.

Tank shrugged. "No one ever said that, but I think it must be. Whenever I mentioned the murder, that priest, the one in St. Louis, was quickly named as the killer. Almost like a talisman against the fear."

"Were you threatened?"

"I didn't think so at the time, but looking back, maybe."

Tank told me about how he investigated the murder. He started with the locals that he knew and was stonewalled by everyone. Next, he went to the cops and they wouldn't give him the files, citing the same stuff Stratton told me without the flooding story. Then Tank started calling out-of-towners and combing through his microfiche.

He handed me a paper. Not his. The headline read "Arson at the St. Seb Sentinel investigated."

"Someone set you on fire?" I asked, looking around.

"Yep. There'd been a couple of fires around town at the time and at the school job site. Somebody kicked down our delivery door and threw in some Molotov cocktails. If Merv Whitman hadn't been out walking his Rottweiler, we'd have burned to the ground."

I had a feeling. It was so strong I was glad I was sitting and the peppermint tea didn't hurt either. "When did that happen? What time?"

"Two in the morning. Merv has insomnia something fierce, lucky for me."

"Cops never found who did it?"

"Nope. I didn't have surveillance cameras. Never thought I needed to. We cover traffic accidents, weddings, and the fair. I'm not running the *New York Times* here."

"And that's the incident?" I asked.

"That was the first incident," said Tank. "Because of the other fires, everyone, including the cops, thought this was some kids messing around. Nobody got hurt. The sites seemed to be picked because they were empty. A gazebo in the park. Places like that."

"You didn't connect it to you personally?"

"God, no, but I installed cameras everywhere and got the destroyed area rebuilt."

The feeling was getting stronger. Something was so not right.

"I bet that distracted you from the high school story and Maggie's murder," I said.

Tank grimaced. "You know your stuff. Yes, it did. I had shit to do. Insurance to deal with. My own contractors, the lazy bastards, and to top it off my electrical work wasn't up to code and had to be completely redone."

"How long?"

"Nearly a year to get back to normal. In the meantime, two more

contractors at the high school project quit, but I wasn't paying attention until we were back to full speed."

"Then you got back to Maggie?" I asked.

He looked away. "I did. Started following up on the out-of-towners
first. Nothing exciting. I was kind of worn out and the community was
over the whole thing by then and had decided it was the church's fault
for buying that land."

"And?"

"My house burned down."

There are a lot of things that cause incredible stress in life. Divorce,
moving, losing a job, but I'm going to say having your house burn down
with your two dogs inside beats those hands down. Tank and his family
had gone to Disney in Florida, leaving their dogs at home for the first
time ever. They usually put them in the kennel, but Tank got tired of
paying the high price and the dogs hated it. They lost weight and their
fur would start falling out, so he decided to leave them at home and have
a neighbor's kid look after them. Emma did a great job, by all accounts,
and her mother happened to be with her on that last day, checking on the
plants. The dogs were walked, fed, watered, and locked in for the night.

Sometime after they left, the air-conditioner malfunctioned.
Because it had been installed too close to the exterior wall, the house
caught fire. The Tancredis lost everything.

"It wasn't arson?" I asked.

"Ruled an accident."

"But..."

"But you came in here asking questions and I'm thinking about
why I stopped looking at the murder and the school."

"You never went back to it?"

"No. I don't think I even thought about it until the school opened
this fall and everything started happening," he said, his voice tight with
guilt. "My kids were traumatized. My wife would barely speak to me
for six months. She couldn't see a dog without crying. We had to

rebuild and buy new land because the family didn't want to go back. It was a mess."

"Stuff kept happening at the school though?" I asked.

"It did, but I gave the job to Milo. He's a solid guy and he covered it appropriately."

"No interest in Maggie I take it."

"Milo isn't a deep thinker, a just-the-facts kind of reporter and the other things that happen in St. Seb, he ignores it."

"Does he believe it?"

"I couldn't say. We've never discussed it."

"You never discussed Confederates in the hospital?" I asked.

Tank's face cleared slightly and he chuckled. "What's to discuss? Things happen in St. Seb."

"But that's why you question how I happened to find Janet Lee Fine's body?"

"It is." He smiled. "Care to go on the record?"

"I can't," I said. "It's not my story to tell."

"You have me intrigued."

"And you'll be staying that way."

Tank snapped his fingers dramatically. "I figured. Are you ready for the joy of microfiche?"

"First, tell me what you know. You were researching the murder when your house conveniently burned down," I said.

"Honestly, I don't remember much. I don't even know what I did with my notes. That period was so miserable. I almost got divorced."

"Anything will help."

"She was found in the woods by some locals." He took his ponytail out and ran his fingers through his hair. It hurt him to remember that time period. "The names are on the tip of my tongue."

"Were they suspects?" I asked.

"I doubt it."

Lefty knocked and walked in, looking like he'd taken a severe tongue-lashing. "So that was a nightmare. I have agreed to build Caden a princess treehouse and a pirate stronghold." He looked back and forth between us. "What happened in here?"

Tank swallowed. "I was telling her about the fire."

"Which one?"

"The one here and my house."

"Ah, crap," said Lefty. "What's that got to do with the price of tea in China?"

"Maybe nothing," I said.

"I should've known something was up. I thought it was an accident," said Tank.

"Maybe it was."

"The house?" asked Lefty. "It was, wasn't it?"

I took a long drink of tea, grateful for the calming effect on my stomach. "I think it may have something to do with an investigation Tank was doing at the time. Sister Margaret Mullanphy's murder."

"The nun? That was a priest in St. Louis."

"That's not a sure thing," I said.

"You're looking into that murder?" asked Lefty. "Why? Because of the school?"

I gave him the bare bones. A family friend asked me to and that there was zero evidence that the priest did it, other than he ended up going off the Eades Bridge.

Lefty made himself a tea and poured a little whiskey in from a small flask he had hidden in his coat pocket. "Well, if you think that priest didn't do it, then you should look at Bertram Stott."

"He's new in town," said Tank.

"And a convicted murderer," said Lefty. "Google him."

I did google him. No microfiche necessary. Bertram Stott was convicted of murder in 1975. He stalked a woman in Tennessee and murdered her. He served twenty-three years and was released for good behavior. He managed to avoid the death penalty because stalking wasn't so much a crime then and his lawyers were able to shift blame to the victim, saying she incited him to lust and caused him to strangle her with her teasing ways. The prosecutor wasn't allowed to bring in evidence that Stott had harassed other women mainly because he was a clean-cut kid of only twenty-six with no other arrests. Since his release in 1998, he'd been clean as far as I could tell.

"See," said Lefty.

"There's no connection," said Tank. "He didn't live here. He's from Tennessee."

"I heard he was connected and that's why he moved here when he retired."

Tank got on his computer and started typing in a way that reminded me of Uncle Morty. "Well, he did strangle that woman. Where'd you hear that rumor, Lefty?"

"Oh, I don't know. Some ladies in church back when he joined the congregation."

"That guy goes to church?" I asked.

"He shows up occasionally. Keeps himself to himself though. We're used to him now."

"So he hasn't done anything weird?"

Lefty sipped his spiked tea and thought for a minute. "Well, he's odd and creepy, I suppose. But he hasn't bothered anyone that I know of. The ladies kept a pretty close eye on him for a long time, but he's not such a fast mover now."

"What happened?" asked Tank.

"Congestive heart failure. He was in the hospital for a while and now he lives at Shady Glen, the retirement home, uses a wheelchair, so I guess they don't think he's much of a threat anymore."

"When did that happen?" I asked.

"Oh, I don't know. Last year, I guess. He's not a spring chicken but young for Shady Glen."

"He'd have been seventeen or eighteen back in '65," said Tank. "That seems a little young for murdering nuns."

"Hold on." I texted Uncle Morty about Bertram and he sent me, "On it."

"What was that about?" asked Tank.

"I know a guy."

"A guy that can give you everything on Stott?"

"Maybe."

Tank went quiet and I got the feeling he was cooking up a plan, but I wasn't worried. The newspaperman was on my side. He'd help me, even if it was only to assuage his guilt for letting his investigation drop, not that I blamed him. If something happened to Skanky and I thought it was my fault, I don't think I'd care about anything for a long, long time.

"You want to go over to Shady Glen now?" asked Lefty hopefully.

"I saw that whiskey," I said. "I barely made it here when you were sober."

"I'm sober. It was barely a drop."

"Still, I think I'll hit the microfiche, if I may," I said.

Tank stared at his computer screen and didn't respond. I walked around his desk and took a peek. It looked like a fire investigation report. "I never put it together. I had two fires a year apart and I never put it together."

"No reason you should," I said.

"Wasn't the fire here kids?" asked Lefty.

"That's what we thought," said Tank.

"There you go."

He shook his head and tapped the paper on the desk. "I just checked the numbers. There were four fires before the fire here and one after. That's it."

"So what?" asked Lefty. "The kids wised up or they got bored."

Tank flicked a glance at me and I bit my lip before asking, "Were they all Molotov cocktails?"

"Yep."

"What were the other targets?" I asked.

We had the gazebo, an abandoned shed next to a house that was being torn down, a dumpster fire, and some decrepit playground equipment at the park that the Jaycees had been raising money to replace. I vaguely remembered the equipment and the gazebo he was talking about. They were both by the lake where I found Janet Lee Fine.

The only incident after the Sentinel fire was a pile of sport equipment at the public high school that had been left out, tackling dummies and tires for foot work.

Tank sat back and folded his hands over his stomach. He watched me and waited.

"I'm getting that this is important, but so what?" asked Lefty. "It's good they didn't torch the Burger King or the high school itself, right?"

"It sounds like the cops thought it was the same person," I said.

"Definitely," said Tank. "Same beer bottles, gas, rags. Always happened about two in the morning."

"And places where there weren't any cameras."

"So it was all the same," said Lefty.

"Except here," I said. "Here our guy kicked in the door and threw the device in. More than one?"

Tank nodded. "They estimated three."

"Very different," I said. "I'd say the other fires were distractions. Your fire was the point. The cops should've figured that out."

"Maybe they did. I didn't get much out of them, except the whole kids idea and then it stopped. We had the sports equipment and poof, it was over."

"Until your house went up."

"But that was wiring," said Lefty. "Nothing like the other ones."

Tank looked at me again. "I'll find my notes from back then. I'll give you access to my microfiche and anything else you want."

I sighed. "In exchange for what?"

"I want the exclusive and I want it to be a five-part story with total access."

"You were going to let me have the microfiche anyway."

He smiled. "That was when it was just a fifty-something-year-old murder. Now it's my arsons. You need my microfiche. Your guy can't get the stories any other way."

"I don't know why my life has to be hard," I said.

"It won't be hard from my end," said Tank. "I'll make it as easy as possible."

I rolled my eyes. "Really? I've heard versions of that before."

"Look. My wife has been quietly pissed at me for six years. I would very much like to know that it's not my fault our dogs are dead."

I stuck out my hand. "You had me at dogs. Deal."

CHAPTER EIGHTEEN

For the record, I don't like microfiche or microfilm. It is evil and must be destroyed. Tank put me in the basement in front of a machine that looked like a crappy super-sized version of the computer Grandad had set up in his man cave "just in case".

Since Grandma J wasn't there to look after it, Tank's monstrosity was covered in thick oily dust and the area smelled like cat pan, very old cat pan. Tank used an old sweatshirt to wipe it off, sort of, and showed me how to use it. He had cabinets full of little boxes labeled by month and year. That sounds easy enough, I know, but it wasn't. The Sentinel had been publishing for over 150 years and organization wasn't their strong suit. Tank took over after the internet became a thing and didn't really pay attention to the basement and the piles of clutter down there. It took us an hour to find the little boxes for 1965 because, you guessed it, he pulled all the relevant stuff on the murder and put it somewhere where he wouldn't lose it.

That place was a shelf in the toilet room. Why? We'll never know.

Then he showed me how to use the rolls of film and little sheets of film. Whoever was in charge couldn't make up their minds, so we had both. It's hard to say which was worse. I started with the film and the

sight of the paper whizzing across the screen made me crazy nauseated. Plus, the machine wasn't exactly kept in good condition, so it
kept unfocusing and that isn't a good thing. By the time I found the
articles, I wasn't sure I cared anymore and wanted to put Tank or Lefty
on it, but Lefty had gone to help a neighbor out of a ditch and Tank
was off searching for his notes, which he was certain held critical information. I don't know if they did. He never found them. Tank found
that suspicious. I found it likely, considering the whole storing important stuff by the toilet idea.

By the time I found the first article about Maggie I felt gross and
barfy. The article didn't improve things. It was published the day after
her body was discovered by a couple named Desmond and Mary Shipley, who were out mushroom hunting. I didn't know you could find
mushrooms in the winter, but Desmond and Mary were described as
experienced and they were looking for a variety called Turkey Tail
when they happened upon Maggie's body. They didn't know her identity at that point and the body was described as female, mid-thirties,
and partially nude. It was out in the open, next to some brush that
Chief Woody Lucas said was loose and showed signs that it had been
over the body at some point and then removed. Chief Lucas also said
that the woman had to be from out of town because no one had been
reported missing and no one at the scene or morgue recognized her.

The brush next to the body was an interesting point. It sounded to
me like the killer used it to conceal her, so he could visit, and when he
was done with her, he removed it. That fit with Maggie's medal being
found in the Kansas graveyard. Visiting was a serial killer thing.

The chief didn't come to that conclusion. He said the wind had
most likely blown it off. When questioned about the uptick in crime in
the county, he said the words I was waiting to read. "It's nothing but
some small time crime. It'll pass."

Then the reporter, one Barney Scheer, asked if murder was a small
time crime. I thought I heard some sarcasm in that question, but the
chief apparently didn't. He said, "These things happen. It won't affect
our community as a whole." I took that as a yes and so did Barney
Scheer who reported that the chief wouldn't answer any more questions about the murder and started talking about the weather.

Perhaps more interesting was the interview Barney did with the mushroom hunters. Mary described finding the body as ghastly and said everyone should lock their doors. Something I noticed the chief *didn't* say. She was described as very upset and unable to speak more about it. Her husband was made of sterner stuff. Desmond said that the body had been there a while, but less than ten days because that was the last time he'd been out to the area with Mary. Most important of all, he said he couldn't tell how she died because the body had been abused.

Abused. Odd choice of words. Not something like animals got to it or decomposition made it hard to tell. Abused. It must've been extensive, too. Strangulation was generally pretty easy to identify. Maybe the killer was trying to cover that up, but why bother? He put her where she'd be found.

There were pictures of the site, sheet over the body, and I got a good look at that brush. It was a big pile of loose fir branches with the needles still on and a bunch of regular branches. The wind didn't blow it anywhere. It was too bunched up. The chief made it sound like that brush might be incidental. It just happened to be there. Yeah, right. Desmond didn't think so either, and he gave the impression of a man who knew more than just mushrooms.

Barney Scheer interviewed everyone and their brother about those woods. It was a popular place for walking in the fall because it had gorgeous fall color, but the leaves were long since gone and only a few people were out in the area. One family said they walked right by the spot while searching for a Christmas tree to cut down and another group of women were birdwatching, looking for the elusive yellow cardinal. Neither group noticed anything amiss or smelled anything either. Barney reported the daily temperatures as not above thirty-six with a low of twenty-four in a heavily treed area, so decomposition wasn't an issue.

He was thorough, that Barney. Nobody saw anything unusual in the area, except a man with a house adjacent to the Snider land said he thought he remembered flashlights in the woods during the time in question, but thought it was kids. Davis Snider, named as the head of the Snider family, said none of his family had been out to the woods in some time and said anybody could've been out there. No trespassing signs were posted, but no one paid them any mind. His family lived in town so they had seen nothing.

It took two days to identify the body and after that the reporting took a sharp turn. Before, Barney had been investigating. After, he was giving facts as he was told by Chief Lucas. There was a generic statement by the church and a picture of Bishop Fowler entering the police station. Then it was silence until Barney reported that Father Dominic was the police's suspect and that he had jumped to his death off the Eades Bridge. No evidence connecting Dominic to the crime was mentioned. Barney said an autopsy was being done but didn't report the cause of death until after Maggie was identified. Then he called it "simple strangulation." That wasn't even a normal term and, from what Desmond said, there wasn't anything simple about it.

I zipped forward, scanning the months after the murder. A cursory glance said things slowed down like Uncle Morty said. In June, Barney did an interview with Chief Lucas talking about the crime rate going down substantially. No reasons for the change were given and the murder wasn't mentioned.

Then I went back to before the murder. What did Uncle Morty say? Arson, property crimes, and thefts.

Wait. Arson?

I found the first incident in June 1965. Someone poured kerosene on the front doors of the high school and lit it on fire. The doors were destroyed, but, since the building was brick and neighbors smelled the smoke and reported it early, the damage was minimal. Then there were several dumpster fires, starting with a variety of accelerants from kerosene to heating oil to gas. That went on through the summer. In September, a Molotov cocktail was thrown through the plate glass window of a local bar called Dark Sparks, burning the place to the ground. The owner said there was a fight earlier in the night between regulars and a crowd of high school students who wanted to be served and were refused. Another cocktail was thrown into an open garage with the family at home. That one took out the garage and part of the house. They tried again at the high school, throwing cocktails in through the windows of the science lab and English literature department, but the principal had fire alarms installed, which apparently wasn't mandatory at the time and that had pissed off the locals who thought it was a waste of money. Not so much as it turned out and the clamor was so loud that neighbors heard it and called the fire in. Those school fires and the house fire all happened in November. The last one was the day before Maggie disappeared. Yet another Molotov cocktail was hurled through the window of the Liquor Mart. It had no alarm and burnt to the ground. The owner reported that he had some trouble with some high schoolers who wanted beer earlier, but said they left without a problem. The teenagers weren't named in either the bar or Liquor Mart, but it couldn't be a coincidence. The high school was hit three times. Who gives a crap about high school unless you're in it?

The odd incident was the house. The family was home. All the other places were empty and hit in the early morning hours. The house happened at nine in the evening. The family was awake at the time and heard the explosion, calling the fire department seconds after it happened.

I went back to the articles on that fire. If my hunch was right, there'd be a teenager in the family and it would be a girl. Arsonists were by and large male, so I was looking for a disgruntled guy and I doubted he'd be that pissed at another dude and make sure he wasn't hurt. No. It had to be a girl that broke up with him or something of that nature.

I scanned the initial report and only got the name of the family, Coulter. There were a few follow-ups, but I didn't get actual family members until there was a town meeting the night before Thanksgiving, a week after the Coulter fire.

Chief Lucas called for the meeting, but he didn't have a clue who was setting the fires or doing the break-ins. There'd been a rash of property being stolen out of unlocked cars and houses. Apparently, nobody locked their cars or houses back then. People had lost car stereos, wallets, purses, cash, guns, and TVs. It could be teenagers. It's not like the thefts were hard to pull off.

The locals were hot. Barney Scheer reported yelling and raised fists. Mr. Coulter spoke and said his family had never experienced anything like that. He said that they'd been egged and TP'd in August, but his daughter, Kathleen, age seventeen, knew the boys that did it and it was just a prank. Mr. Coulter was a divorce lawyer and it was suggested that his fire was related to his work and nothing to do with the other fires at all.

I leaned back. "And there it is."

Tank walked in, carrying a stack of folders. "There what is?"

"Kathleen Coulter, age seventeen."

"You can't be saying that a girl killed Sister Maggie."

"Not at all. Did you know that there was a rash of arsons in 1965?"

Tank froze and then his face curved into an intense frown. "No, I didn't."

"Have you heard about any other suspicious fires in the area other than your own?" I asked.

"No. Our last fire was over a year ago and it was down to an aroma therapy candle."

"Molotov cocktails?"

"Are you kidding?" he asked and I showed him the Coulter articles.

"I can't believe I missed that."

"You weren't looking for other crimes," I said.

"Why were you?"

I told him what Sister Frances said about Chief Lucas and then showed him the chief's comments on the murder.

"He sounds overwhelmed," said Tank. "And he might've been sick already."

"Oh, he was sick already without a doubt."

"That's right. You're a nurse."

"I am and it takes a good while to cause cirrhosis of the liver."

Tank sat down in a folding chair next to me. "Did you find any fires after the murder?"

"No. My guy said there was a steep climb in crime leading to Maggie with little after. The paper confirms the stats."

"Nobody was arrested?"

"I can't find that Chief Lucas had a lead much less an arrest."

Tank slumped down and gripped the folders in his lap for dear life. "Was he just a terrible cop?"

"Please tell me you're not his grand-nephew or something. I already pissed off your current chief today."

"You talked to Will?" he asked.

"Yeah, and it didn't go well," I said.

"If you brought up his grandfather, I wouldn't think so. Will's uptight about the family."

"Ah, crap. You *are* family. I cannot catch a break."

He forced himself to relax, stretching out his long fingers and dropping the folders in his lap. "I'm married to his sister Mallory, but we go way back. Played football in high school together."

"You do not look like a football player," I said.

"It wasn't my idea. My dad loves the game. That's where I got the nickname."

"Because you were a tank on the field?"

He laughed. "Because I wasn't. Anybody could run me over like a tank. I decided to embrace it, like you and your name."

"I didn't so much embrace Mercy as it was just what I was always called. I screamed a lot as a baby and my dad kept saying 'Have Mercy!'"

"There you go," said Tank.

"Yep."

"So we've got arsons back then and arsons when I was looking at the murder."

"I don't think it's just a coincidence." I told him my theory about the high school students.

He nodded. "Like I said, they thought our fires were kids. But if it's the same guys, they wouldn't be kids now."

"People go back to what works for them." I tapped the folders. "What'd you find?"

"Photos from the murder. Might help. You never know."

We spread the photos out on the floor, but I couldn't get oriented. "Do you have a map?"

"Like a map map? Paper?" asked Tank.

"Yes. I can't picture where this is."

He went off to find a map, thinking they probably had one since they weren't into throwing things away, and I looked at the pictures. We had tire tracks in a muddy area, the body, the brush pile, pictures of a house, and a road. There weren't any notes and the articles didn't say anything about tire tracks. The pictures were sharp, still in black and white like the newspaper, but I could make out a lot more details. Maggie was on her back. I could tell from her feet pointed up under the sheet. I would guess that she wasn't displayed in any particular way, just sort of lying there. Most importantly, there wasn't any blood anywhere and I was pretty sure I could tell even in black and white.

"I found a map." Tank walked in as he unfolded an old school map and laid it on the floor next to the pictures. "Are you having a hard time looking at these because I am."

"Not too much. I've seen worse." I'd caused worse. The picture of Richard Costilla falling down the stairs in New Orleans, his face exploding and spraying blood up the wall, bloomed in my mind.

"Mercy?" He squatted next to my chair and tentatively put his hand on my knee. "Okay?"

I took a breath, using the calming techniques I'd been taught. It worked, but I hated that I still needed them. "I'm fine and it's good that you're bothered. This should never be easy."

"I'm glad Barney didn't get a picture of the body."

"It would've been extremely helpful."

He nodded. "She probably wasn't killed in the woods, right? He just dumped her there."

"I think so, but that whole reference to the body being abused is bothering me."

"Me, too, but probably not for the same reason."

I patted his hand. "So where's the area we're looking at on your map?"

Tank got a red felt tip marker out and circled a wooded area and then put a dot in the center. "That's the woods on the Snider land and the dot is where the memorial used to be."

"There was a memorial?" I asked. "What happened to it?"

"I have no idea. I never thought about it."

"You might want to."

"Then you do believe that it's Sister Maggie that's haunting the school," said Tank.

I leaned over and looked at the picture of her body under that sheet. "I believe that people had a place to remember what happened to her and now they don't."

"I'll find out what happened to that memorial." He got out a green felt tip and drew on a road next to the Snider property. "That's the road in Barney's pictures. I recognize the trees." He picked up the pictures of the tire tracks, looking at them from all angles. "I want to say that the tracks are here." He drew two short parallel lines near the dot.

I got down on my knees and ran my finger from St. Seb down the road to the tire tracks. "It's not that close to the body. Why stop there?"

Tank showed me a picture of the woods where you could see the body in the distance. It wasn't apparent from close up, but there were rocks to climb over from that angle and they were reasonably steep. I took a blue pen from him and made dots on the map. "So rocks here. Surrounding the area?"

"Yes, unless you approach from the creek on the other side."

"That doesn't make sense. It would be really far out of the way," I said.

"Right. I think this picture was taken from the walking path. It wasn't an official trail, just a path that everyone naturally used over the years." He pointed at an area a ways away on the map. "I used to park here. There's a dirt area next to the road with space for a few cars. We'd just park there and party back in high school."

"That's where the path started?" I asked.

He drew a line from the parking spot through the woods, sort of around Maggie's area in a big circle. "That's a rough guess. It was probably around three miles all told. The views over Indian Creek were beautiful. Will and I used to camp there with the kids when they were little. The school built a parking lot."

"That sucks."

"It does. They really ruined it."

I looked back and forth between the pictures and the map. I imagined just the body, no sheet, in that dense woods. There was quite a bit of undergrowth and rocks.

"If you were just walking on the path, how close would you get to the body?" I asked.

"On the path? Oh, I'd say no closer than fifty yards. Why?"

I traced my finger over the trail. "He put her in the center of the walking path loop. People were out there, walking around her, but nobody noticed until he removed the brush."

"What are you getting at?" Tank asked.

"It was very deliberate and it took effort," I said. "These rocks. Hard to climb?"

He frowned. "Not real bad. I did it plenty of times."

"Could you get to the memorial without climbing over at least some rocks if you're coming from the road?" I asked.

Tank looked through the photos and thought about it for a minute. "I don't think so, but like I said, it wasn't hard, not a cliff or anything."

"Did you ever carry your kid up there?"

"Sure."

"How?"

A look of frustration passed over Tank's thin face and he said, "I don't know. In a kid backpack. I'm telling you it wasn't hard."

"How big was the kid?"

"Jesus, I don't know. I probably carried them both at one time or another. They were fat kids. Thirty or forty pounds maybe. I didn't carry them after they turned three. So flipping heavy."

"So he leaves the road and the tire tracks stop here." I pointed at the lines and then the body dot. "And Maggie was found here."

"Yes," said Tank, getting thoughtful.

"He stopped driving, presumably because there were rocks in the way. How'd he get her to where he left her?" I asked.

Tank threw up his hands. "He obviously carried her."

"For a minimum of fifty yards, over a good amount of rocks, and at night because nobody saw it happen."

"Where there's a will there's a way."

I shook my head. "I don't think there was a way. I've seen pictures of Maggie. She was tall, well-built, and not a swizzle stick. I'd guess she weighed at least 130, more like 140. Can you imagine carrying 140 pounds of dead weight? According to my dad, corpses are hard to carry. I tried to haul a kid I was babysitting out of a playground sandpit when she was trying passive resistance. It was exhausting and she was seven."

"But you did it," said Tank slowly.

"I didn't do it. A mom took pity on me and helped."

Tank ran his hands over his face. "He had help."

"I think so."

"Maybe he was just really strong."

"You look fit. Could you carry me that distance? I'm short, but I weigh about the same."

"No, not over those rocks. I'd have to drag you. Maybe that's what Desmond Shipley meant by 'abused.'"

We went through the pictures again, looking closely for signs that something had been dragged. Tank broke out a little magnifying glass he used for tying fishing flies when work was slow and we couldn't find that the moss on the rocks was disturbed enough to make it plausible. There certainly wasn't any flattened area around the tire tracks. Plenty of what was probably footprints, but we didn't have a close up, so they weren't distinguishable. Could've been one set of shoes or five.

"So two guys, at least." Tank was visibly sad and I was about to make it worse.

I pointed at the dot. "And this isn't an accident."

"Huh?"

"This road? Where does it go? St. Seb to where?"

"It's kind of a back way to Hermann. Lots of farms out there."

"Not a main road? Not even back then?"

He got to his feet, knees creaking, and sat on the folding chair. "100 is direct and it's been there all my life."

"These guys knew the area and they knew it well," I said.

"Locals. Chief Lucas lied."

I picked up the tire track photo. "With access to a truck."

"Is that important?" Tank asked. "Everyone has a truck out here. It's farm country."

"I can tell you who didn't have access to a truck and didn't know where to put a body where people would be walking around it and never see it until he wanted them to."

"The priest?"

"Bingo."

CHAPTER NINETEEN

I don't know when the Sentinel bought the printer photocopier combo that Tank showed me how to use, but I'd seen Smart cars that were smaller and they made less noise, too. I did get the hang of that monster and printed out all the articles on the murder, break-ins, and the arsons back then and the recent ones, too. I copied the photos and tried calling Uncle Morty for a third time. I knew he was distracted, but this was getting ridiculous. One minute it was all about getting to Greece and the next he was mooning over pictures and not getting my info. I had to know about Bertram Stott. That guy fit the profile so hard, murderer, teenager then, and in town when Tank's fires happened. But I needed to place him in St. Seb in 1965. The cops weren't going to help me, especially since I'd have to show them the connections that said a local killed Maggie. Stratton wasn't stupid. She'd know the old chief would've seen it, if he'd been doing his job instead of drinking his ass off.

To be fair, I guess my idea that it was a couple of teenaged boys wasn't a lock. They could conceivably be unconnected and back then people didn't think kids did serious crimes. Arson wasn't connected to serial killers like it was now. That wasn't the old chief's fault.

"You know what I didn't look at?" I asked, mostly to myself.

"I'm afraid to ask." Tank looked up from labeling my articles.

"Really?"

"My Great Aunt Patsy lives in Shady Glen."

I wrinkled my nose. "Well, we don't know it's Stott and he is pretty sick."

"That's the only thing keeping me from taking her home tonight."

"Would she go?"

"It'd be a fight. All her friends are there. It's perpetual coffee klatch. She loves it."

"She's probably fine."

"Probably." Tank was not convinced.

"Ten years and no bodies. I think she's fine," I said.

"Would you leave your Aunt Miriam in there?"

I pictured Aunt Miriam and her lethal purse with the brick inside. "Yes. He'd be in more danger than her."

"I thought you said she was a nun."

"Yes, but a dangerous one. You want to hear what I didn't look up or not?"

He grimaced, but I told him anyway.

"Dead or missing pets," I said.

"Now?"

"Then. Serial killers sometimes start with animals. The state stats wouldn't keep track of that and nothing popped out in the articles I read. Nothing in the town meeting."

"Who said anything about a serial killer?" asked Tank, stepping back like I was contagious.

"Oh, well, there might be a reason to think that," I said.

"Because Bertram killed that woman in Tennessee? That's only one."

That we know of.

"Because we have arson, a dead nun with some kind of disturbing abuse to the body, and a good amount of planning." *And her medal in a serial killer graveyard, but we won't talk about that.*

"This just keeps getting worse."

"It usually does," I said. "Can you look that up? I'd like to get out of here. Anything from Lefty?"

Tank checked his phone. "Heading back now. He pulled six people out of ditches and plowed half of downtown. Irene is never getting rid of that Gator."

I laughed. "I guess not."

"When will you get that information on Bertram Stott?"

I glanced at my phone in case I missed something. "I should've had it already. Usually, he's lightning fast."

"Maybe he can't find anything," said Tank.

"Oh, he'll find something. There is no way that guy stalked women, killed one, and never ever committed another crime. That just isn't a thing that happens."

He tucked my photocopies in a folder and said, "I should stop talking to you."

"It's not me," I said.

"You're like a harbinger of doom. I was happy this morning. Nothing but this storm was happening. Our last crime was a purse snatching at Walmart and Mallory was making Italian beef for dinner. My favorite. Now I don't have an appetite or Tylenol PM in the house. I think I need both."

"But you have the exclusive."

"Exclusives don't put a guy like me to sleep at night." His phone buzzed and he said, "Lefty found another person stuck in the Frick's parking lot. It'll be a little longer. You want to look for dead animals?"

"I really don't," I said. "How about more tea?"

"Done."

We took my research upstairs and my phone went off. Destiny's Child blared out of my phone, bouncing off the walls as I scrambled to mute it. "Wishin' you the best, pray that you are blessed."

"What was that?" asked Tank.

"My mom, I hope," I said.

"You hope?"

"Sometimes my dad uses her phone so I'll answer."

We went back to Tank's desk and he refilled our mugs before popping them into the microwave. "You don't like your dad? He's a pretty amazing dude."

"He's amazing alright."

Tank grinned at me. "Not easy to live up to him, I guess."

"And even harder, if you don't try."

"Are you telling me that you *haven't* been trying?"

I sat down and kicked my feet up on his desk. "I have not. I've been trying to be left alone. It hasn't worked out for me."

"That's an understatement."

"It was inevitable that I would be sitting here with you, I guess. I've been going to crime scenes since I was a baby," I said.

Tank tilted his head to the side and I could see that he was trying to work out how that happened.

I laughed and said, "My mom was getting her hair done and Dad had me, which was rare. There was some murder and he took me to the scene in a backpack."

"He adapts and overcomes," said Tank. "Your dad's a character."

"It wasn't even a kid backpack. He stuffed me in a hiking pack and zipped me in. There's a picture of me looking around with blood spatter in the background and Dad taking pictures."

"Nobody stopped him?"

"Are you kidding? Tommy Watts? Not gonna happen," I said with a snort.

"So you aren't going to call—"

My phone went off again and against my better judgement, I swiped the green button.

"Don't panic!" said Mom.

"What?"

"I said not to panic." She went on to lecture me for a minute about panic. I don't know about anyone else, but if someone says not to panic, it totally means there is something to panic about. Don't panic is the sister of calm down. Each has the opposite effect and both pissed me off.

"Mom, for God's sake!" I said, trying not to yell and failing a bit. "Just tell me what happened."

"We can't get there. We're snowed in." Mom was slurring hard. The more she talked the worse it got.

"What happened?"

"Your father is talking to John, but he says there's no way."

Breathe. Do not yell at the mother.

"Mom, can you hear me?" I asked.

"Of course, I can hear you. I'm talking to you. Now call Fats and take her truck. I'm sure you can make it."

"Make it where?"

Mom took a breath and said, "On second thought, have Fats drive. She's good in a crisis."

I'm not?

Tank dropped a tea bag in my mug and sat down behind his desk, checking his computer. "44 is still shutdown."

I nodded. "Mom, listen, I'm in St. Sebastian."

"What in the world are you doing out there?" she asked.

"Um...wineries."

"In the winter?" Her voice went high and I imagined her on the edge of tears. "You have to get back."

"Give Dad the phone."

"He's out. Nobody's there, Mercy. I can't call Aunt Miriam. She can't go out in this weather. She's old. She could break a hip."

So not Aunt Miriam. Can't be Grandad and Grandma. Oh, no.

"Is it Uncle Morty?" I asked.

"Aren't you listening?" asked Mom.

"You didn't tell me, Mom. *You're* panicking."

She went quiet and I could hear her taking a calming breath.

"It's Morty. They've taken him to the hospital, but they won't tell us anything. We're not actually family."

Say he wasn't at the gym.

"Mercy, he was at a gym. What was he doing at a gym?"

Dammit.

"Did he have a heart attack?" My heart wasn't in my throat. I felt like it wasn't anywhere in my body.

"I don't know. He was on a treadmill and he went down. They called me because I'm his emergency contact. Why would he be on a treadmill?"

"Well..."

"Mercy?"

"He's upset that Nikki's living the high life with hot guys and he's fat," I said. "I told him not to do it."

"You knew about this?"

And so did Dad.

"I did, Mom. I tried to talk to him, but he's freaking out."

"And you left him? You know he's a big baby," said Mom. "What are we going to do? His mother and brother can't get there. The airport's shut down."

"What about Chuck?" I asked.

"He's working."

"Screw that!"

"Mercy!" exclaimed Mom.

"We're not doing Dad all over again. This is more important than work."

"What are you doing in St. Seb then? Hanging out with the ghosts, I suppose."

"I'm trying to get Uncle Morty to Greece."

"I don't see how," she said.

"It doesn't matter," I said. "Is he at SLU?"

"Yes, he is."

"Okay. That's good. You call Chuck and tell him to go."

"Mercy, we don't know what case he's on," said Mom.

I balled up my fists and said, "I don't give a crap if it's the Kennedy assassination. Tell Chuck to go. I'm calling Pete. He's always at work."

"Chuck won't like that," said Mom.

"Not important."

Mom agreed and I hung up. I told Tank what happened and called Pete. He didn't answer, but he was in the hospital, so I had him paged. Tank made me more tea, even though I'd barely touched the mug I had, and called Lefty who was still MIA.

After a few tense minutes, my phone played the *Scrubs* theme song.

"Hello? Pete?" I said all squeaky and weird.

"What happened? Are you okay?" asked my old boyfriend, Pete, in his super calm way.

"I need a favor. I'll watch Wallace," I said.

"Is it your dad? You know he threatened to shoot me once."

"What? No. It's Uncle Morty."

"That's worse."

"Worse than a shooting?"

"I might survive a shooting," said Pete.

"I don't know what to say to that, except that Uncle Morty had a heart attack and I'm in St. Seb and Mom is at Cairngorms Castle. I don't know what to do. We're snowed in." I sucked in a breath.

"When did they bring him in?"

"I...I don't know."

"I'll call you right back."

I hung up and practiced my calming breaths. They were so not working.

"So is this uncle your guy with the information?" asked Tank.

"He is." I started crying like a big wuss while texting Mom that Pete was on it. "And I'm here. I'm supposed to be there."

"It sounds like he wanted you here."

"He did, but he's crazy. This crime is fifty years old."

Tank nodded. "I've been wondering what the rush is."

I told him about Uncle Morty stinking up the plane and being put on the No Fly List. And Nikki. And hot guys in Greece. I blubbered the whole time. It wasn't pretty and I already smelled like vomit.

Tank put a blanket over my shoulders and then sat down, getting very quiet.

"And there you go. That's why I'm here and I have to sleep in a haunted mansion tonight. I don't need that. She already talked to me."

"It really is a serial killer," said Tank, handing me a box of tissues.

I blew my nose six times. I could've gone a seventh, but it was getting embarrassing. "Sorry I left out the medal before."

"We might really have a serial killer living at Shady Glen."

"Maybe," I said as Pete's theme played again. I answered with "Is he alive?"

Uncle Morty was alive and angry that the gym called my mother. He'd had what Pete called a cardiac event that caused a panic attack that made him pass out while running on the treadmill. He was stable, but they were keeping him sedated—probably more for the anger than anything else—and were running a ton of tests. Pete thought he'd be okay, but his lifestyle of concentrated sitting had to change and his cholesterol was through the roof. Next was looking at a blockage at the heart, which Pete thought he had and would require a stent.

"Thank you so much, Pete," I said before blowing my nose the seventh time. It was unavoidable.

"You are taking Wallace. Honestly, I think you should take her twice."

"What did he do?"

"He's out of it."

"And?"

"He may have threatened to wipe my degrees and board certification," said Pete.

"Why?" I asked.

"He thinks I dumped you. Did you tell him that?"

I had to smile. Uncle Morty was alright. Making unreasonable threats and demands was his normal state. "No. He knows I'm the scumbag on that score."

"I wouldn't say that."

"I would."

Pete laughed. "If you insist. I have to go, but I'll check on him after he gets out of the cath lab."

I thanked Pete again and told him to tell his mother I was her new pug sitter. Tank stood up and said it was time to get started on the next day's edition. His staff of three had sent in their stories and he had to do the layout.

"Will I be in the way?" I asked.

"Not at all." He started in on his layout and my phone rang. Predictably, It was Dad. Unpredictably, he was incredibly upset. I did my best to calm him down with Pete's assessment.

"I didn't take you seriously," he said. "I was thinking about the FBI and getting our life back. I'm an asshole."

I didn't know what to say to that.

"No comforting word, huh? That's fine," said Dad. "I don't deserve them."

"It's not your fault," I said, "and it's not mine. I told him not to run."

"He's losing his woman. I know how scary that is."

"It's not because he's fat. Nikki didn't care."

"I don't know what to do. I can't get there."

"Is Chuck going?" I asked.

Chuck was going. He left the scene of a murder suicide, handing it off to Nazir, and was currently making his way across the city at five miles an hour. That almost made me cry again. He wasn't my dad. It wasn't going to be my mom's life all over again for me.

"Are you up to helping me?" I asked.

"Did you get to the police station before the storm hit?" asked Dad.

I told him what happened and that cheered him up. Me being a blockhead always did.

"Well, you're ass out there. You'll have to get to the paper tomorrow."

"I'm there."

"Oh, yeah?"

I heard Dad straighten up. Tommy Watts was now awake and on fire. He came to the same conclusions I did without seeing the map or the pictures. It was like he could see it, like he knew it on instinct. I could say two words and he'd finish the sentence. It would've been annoying if it hadn't been so damn impressive.

"So," Dad said, assuming his lecturer voice. "What is bothering you about this?"

"Everything," I said.

"Be specific."

"Simple strangulation and what Desmond Shipley said."

"We need to know a little more about Shipley," said Dad. "But Morty's out obviously."

"I've got an idea about that."

"Good. Handle it."

I'd never had Dad trust me to handle something like that. He usually wanted details and to tell me I was wrong and possibly an idiot. "Okay. I will. I know a guy."

"I figured. You don't always use Morty."

"I don't."

"Good. Get him or her on Bertram Stott, too. I have a feeling about him."

"What do you think about the abuse thing?" I asked.

Dad had a theory. It was one that had occurred to me, but I did my best not to think about it. The killer had visited the body. We knew that from the brush being moved, but that wasn't all. Dad thought that he, or they, might have been practicing on the body. He thought they'd been testing different types of killing.

"That's really horrible," I said. "I can't...we can't tell anyone that. Myrtle and Millicent or Aunt Miriam. They couldn't take it. I can barely take it and I didn't know her."

"It is horrible, but don't think about how you feel. Think about what it tells us," he said in a very gentle tone, the one I hadn't heard since David disappeared.

"They're young. Inexperienced. No conscience, for sure."

"Right. And they had time to do it. Not a lot of obligations."

"And they didn't know her," I said.

"Not that. Knowing her doesn't mean they couldn't carve her up. Either she didn't mean anything to them or they were punishing her."

"Punishing her? She was dead, I hope."

"She was dead from the time she disappeared."

"Why do you think that?" I could tell Dad was smiling and, for once, it was nice.

"The same reason you do. You've got skills, Mercy. Instincts," said Dad. "Go ahead. Tell me why."

I told him that I thought she'd been taken at the asylum on her way to the bus stop for her meeting with the bishop.

"So?" said Dad.

"So that's impulsive and high risk. Who kidnaps a nun in broad daylight where it's easy for someone to hear or walk by? You'd have to restrain and silence a full-grown woman and have the equipment to do it. That says plan. Maggie lived at the convent. It's super quiet and isolated. Only women and it's not well-lit even now. If I wanted to kidnap Maggie and make sure I got away with it, I'd take her there. I think something happened. One of our guys reacted and he got lucky."

"Only one of our guys was in the parking lot?" asked Dad.

"Two makes it a plan. There was no plan."

"You are my kid."

"Did you doubt it at some point?" I asked. "Mom won't be thrilled with that."

"I didn't doubt your paternity. You always seemed to be your mom's kid and I was incidental."

"You weren't around a lot."

"I know and I'm sorry about that," said Dad.

Time to change the conversation.

"So what's up with that 'simple strangulation' comment?" I asked.

"It happened after the crime had been supposedly solved, right?"

"Yes."

"Take it apart. Separate simple and strangulation," he said.

I thought about that. Strangulation was easy. It was what it was. Simple. Now that was just plain odd. "I don't know. It's weird."

"Think, Mercy. What do people mean when they say simple? What's simple?"

"Um...easy. Over. It's over. Nothing to get fussed up about."

"That's my girl," said Dad. "Mr. Barney Scheer was told to stand down. So he had to make that sound reasonable. Simple. Easy. No big deal. Just like the whole small time crime thing."

"Do you think he really believed Father Dominic did it?"

"Probably not but believing gets easier over time. People tend to take suicide as an admission of guilt and you said the crime rate went off a cliff. There certainly weren't any other murders. That all backs up the story."

"I don't think Father Dominic killed himself," I said.

"Neither do I. It's too convenient and he was a priest. Damnation is a pretty strong deterrent."

The door to Tank's office banged open and a snow beast walked in. "Ready to go?" Lefty asked.

"That's my ride, Dad. I have to go."

"Mercy, thanks for calling me."

Er...I didn't.

"Sure. Thanks for helping."

"You never asked me for help before."

"Well...I..."

"I know. Talk to you later." Dad hung up and I was left confused. What did he know? That he was a huge pain in the ass? He was pretty chill if that was it.

Tank got out of his chair and tried to persuade Lefty to peel off some layers to warm up. It was a no-go and Lefty didn't need to warm up. He was running on hot adrenaline and plenty of it.

"Gotta get back and refuel. Gas station is closing and I expect to get more calls." Lefty waved at me. "Suit up! Irene is making steak and Guinness pie."

"Aren't you a bed and breakfast?" I asked, going over to pick up my barf scarf.

"Restaurants are all closed. Besides, Irene has a new recipe. She likes guinea pigs other than just me."

"Sounds delicious."

"It will be," said Lefty. "What about you, Tank? Need a ride?"

"Thanks, but I'm working on the morning edition for a while longer."

"It's pretty bad out and getting worse."

"I've got the Jimmy. I can get through anything," said Tank. "Mercy, is there anything else you want me to look into besides the animal thing?"

"Animal thing?" asked Lefty.

"We've got a problem, my friend, and I'm not just whistling Dixie here."

"With that old murder?"

"Mercy can fill you in," said Tank. "Is there anything else?"

I wound the barf scarf over the mostly clean scarf and considered. It was a can of worms and I'd already opened a barrel full.

"I can see there is," he said. "Please don't say rape or child molestation."

"What the hell has been happening here?" asked Lefty.

"It's not that," I said. "It's actually unrelated to Sister Maggie."

"Well, normally I'd say we're not a haven for crime, but given what I now know, I won't. Lay it on me," said Tank.

I told him I was interested in a plane crash that happened in the eighties and wanted any articles he might have on it.

"A plane crash?" asked Lefty. "Are you sure you have the right town? We're not exactly Lockerbie, Scotland."

"It was a small plane with just two people on board and it did go down around here," I said.

"Oh, right. There's a pretty little memorial out near the Westin Dairy."

"That's the one," I said.

"It was an accident?" asked Tank.

"Cause undetermined."

"How do you keep coming up with these old crimes?" asked Tank.

"My great-grandparents were on board."

The men went quiet and helped me on with my boots, gloves, and hat. Tank took the earmuffs and opened them up. "You asked Will for the police report?"

"That would've been destroyed in the flood along with everything else," I said.

He nodded. "I'll find those articles for you. Now, Lefty, don't forget to tell Mercy the rules. She's had a hell of an afternoon with you nearly killing her and whatnot. The last thing she needs is to have Miss Elizabeth taking an interest in her."

"No problem."

"What do you mean by 'take an interest'?" I asked.

"Talking to you. Being what she considers helpful. Or, you know, other stuff," said Lefty.

"Other stuff?"

"As long as she doesn't talk to you, you're all good," said Tank.

"Um...what if she does?" I asked.

"Then you'd be interesting. You don't want to be interesting." He popped on the earmuffs and pushed me out the door into the storm.

Crap on a cracker. I'm interesting.

CHAPTER TWENTY

We made it back to Miss Elizabeth's Bed and Breakfast almost without incident. Almost. Lefty was tired from pulling cars out of ditches and he did his best just to drive straight. Unfortunately, driving straight wasn't in the cards. Forty mile an hour wind gusts pushed us around on a sheet of ice. While I was at the paper, we'd gotten a lot of sleet, which put a thick crust of ice on everything. The Gator would ride on top of the snow and then break through and we'd have to plow our way out. It took an hour to go six blocks. I'd gotten a theory of the crime and even a suspect, but it wasn't worth it. I could've waited a day.

After Lefty finally got the Gator into the garage, we had to shovel before we could close the door because the wind instantly blew a three-foot drift in behind us. By the time we staggered into the back door, I'd lost the feeling in my butt. You know it's bad when you can't feel your butt.

"Finally!" exclaimed Irene as she bustled over from her stove. "I was thinking about calling out the National Guard, but Will called and said he saw you plowing Minnie Lake's front yard."

Lefty hung up his frozen stiff clothes and started clawing the ice out of his eyebrows. "I didn't plow anyone's front yard. He must've had a couple for the drive home."

"Don't even say that."

Lefty raised a brow but said nothing.

Irene helped me unbundle and saw the scarves. She wrinkled her nose. "Oh, Lefty. What did you do?"

His eyes shifted to the right. "Nothing. She wanted to go to the newspaper. I got her there in one piece."

She held up the barf scarf. "I don't call this one piece."

"You'd be wrong then," said Lefty. "And I bet she'll give us a great review on TripAdvisor, too."

I said I would, a stellar review, the smell of steak and Guinness cinched it. I was starving.

"Hold on," said Lefty. "What is that noise?"

"Huh?" asked Irene.

"You didn't tell those ladies the rules, did you? Irene, good God, people will start avoiding us if we can't control the situation."

"I told them." She listened for a second and I heard it, too. A loud rhythmic thumping. "That's not her. It's Fats. She's exercising."

"Why?" asked Lefty.

"She ate cookies," I said.

"She wanted them," said Irene, rather defensively.

I took off my ski pants and my butt started to tingle. It wasn't pleasant, but at least it wasn't going to turn black and fall off. "It's not your fault. She has issues with food."

"She attacked those cookies with a vengeance."

"That's how she does everything." I flexed my fingers and toes. Not bad. A little blue, but that's what you get for being a Watts. "I'll calm her down."

That's what I said, but Fats was uncalmable. I'd never been able to distract her from exercising or feeding me steamed vegetables. Steamed cauliflower is gross, but I ate it.

"Wait," said Irene. "You need the rules."

"Got it," I said. "Don't be interesting."

"Well, yes, but there's more to it than that," said Irene. "First, make sure—"

A loud thump followed by a scream interrupted her. Lefty took off running and Irene pointed her spatula at the door. "Go!"

So I went running through Miss Elizabeth's house, but I didn't know where I was going. Lefty was fast.

"Fats! Clarence!" I turned three corners and ran into Lefty's back nearly taking him out.

"What the hell?" He stumbled forward and caught himself on the newel post.

"She fell!" yelled Clarence from the top of the stairs.

I darted around Lefty to run to Fats, but then I saw her. If she fell, she had an awfully interesting way of landing. Fats was balanced on her hands, knees on elbows, halfway up the stairs on the landing. The PJs were gone and she was back in spandex.

"I didn't fall," she said. "I jumped."

Lefty clutched his chest. "Thank goodness."

Fats brought herself up into a full handstand and arched her back until her body was in a graceful curve and her heels touched the narrow space between two framed family photos. Then she snapped her legs back and she was upright without breaking sweat.

"What is wrong with you?" I asked.

"I ate six cookies. One after another," said Fats as she hopped down the rest of the stairs in the squat position.

"What's wrong with that?" Lefty asked. "Irene's cookies are the best."

"I haven't eaten that many cookies in the last six months."

I crossed my arms. "Six months?"

"Okay. A year." She reached the end of the stairs and asked, "How far is Crabapple's?"

"You're not going out for tofu tonight," said Lefty. "They're closed. Irene is making dinner."

"Tofu?"

"No."

"Broccoli?"

"Maybe."

I threw up my hands. "It's steak and ale pie and it smells fantastic."

Fats started doing squat thrusts. "I have to get ahold of myself."

"I agree, but I don't think my meaning is the same as yours."

"Is this normal?" Lefty asked.

"It depends on your definition of normal," I said.

"I have a gym setup in the basement."

Fats rocketed to her feet. "Where?"

He pointed at a door.

"May I?"

"Knock yourself out."

She dashed for the door and I yelled after her, "Not literally!"

We stared after her and listened to the pounding down the stairs and the "Hell, yeah," when she saw the equipment and then a metallic thwack of weights being put on a bar.

"It guess it takes a lot of focus to stay in that kind of shape," said Lefty.

I grinned. "I wouldn't know and I don't want to."

"Do you think she's okay?" Clarence asked.

"She's okay for her." I turned to Lefty. "Do I have time for a bath before dinner?"

"I'm sure you do. Dinner should be in about an hour."

I thanked him and tromped up the stairs, my body feeling heavier and heavier by the moment. My arm was aching something fierce and I hoped I hadn't messed it up. When Nancy cut off my cast, I never expected to go tumbling into snowbanks at high velocity. I should've known better.

"Are you okay?" Clarence asked when I finally got to the top of the stairs and stooped to pick up Moe, who was chasing her tail to no avail. "You look as though something terrible happened."

"My Uncle Morty had a heart attack," I said. "And Lefty tried to kill me with fun."

"Is he okay?"

"For now. I see some lifestyle changes in his future. It's not going to be pretty."

"Did you find anything out about Sister Maggie?" Clarence was wringing her hands and her cherub-like face had transformed into a mask of worry. She wasn't her cheery self at all.

"What's wrong?" I asked.

"Oh, well. I shouldn't worry you."

"Consider me worried."

"It seems that Sister Miriam knows where we are," she said.

"Is that all?"

Clarence let loose a torrent of fears as we walked down to our room. Would Aunt Miriam be very angry? What would she do? Did she feel betrayed?

I couldn't muster one ounce of give a crap. I smelled. My arm was burning, and I was interesting to a ghost. And it could get worse. It would get worse. It was me.

"She's always angry with me, so I'm not so much worried about it." I opened the door to our room and there in the center all Sister Maggie's belongings were out. And I mean out out. Her things were stacked in a tower with her clothes floating in the air above. A whole outfit. Skirt, shirt, sweater, and veil, full, like someone was wearing them and holding a book in front of themselves.

I slammed the door shut and bit back the mother of cursing rants, my heart pounding.

"What's wrong?" Clarence asked.

"I...uh..."

Moe growled and yipped as she wiggled, struggling to get to the door. Not going to happen. Clarence couldn't go in there. I wasn't sure she was ready for real life, much less the afterlife or whatever that was.

"Moe hasn't gone out, has she?" I asked with a bit of a pant.

"No. Do you think she needs to?"

"Yes. Yes, I do. Can you take her? I've got to do a thing and stuff."

"Um...okay." Clarence hesitated but then carried the pocket dog down the hall.

I waited for her to turn onto the stairs, knowing she would look back to check on me. She did and I waved with a pasted on smile. She frowned but went down the stairs.

Breathe, Mercy. Just breathe. It's not what it looks like.

Wrong.

I opened the door and I was not seeing things. Everything was still there. Stacked up in a precarious and, dare I say, impossible to maintain tower, or floating with no strings attached.

"Mercy?" Clarence called out.

I didn't think. If I had, I sure wouldn't have done what I did. I dove for Maggie's things, launching myself at her veil. I half-expected to connect with something solid, but it was just air and musty clothes. I snatched the veil out of the air and the whole tower collapsed back into the box. I landed on the balls of my feet and tumbled forward to my knees, whacking my good arm on the edge of the box.

The door opened behind me and Clarence said, "Do you want me to—what are you doing?"

I looked back, veil in hands, and drew a blank. "Nothing."

"You don't have to hide that from me."

"Er...what?"

"You don't have to go through her things alone. I can handle it," said Clarence stoutly. "I have to toughen up and, besides, we're honoring her by caring."

"Okay. I just didn't know." I got to my feet with the veil still in my hands. "I am going to take a bath though."

"Good. Would you like some hot chocolate? I think Irene has a fresh pot."

"That would be great. Thank you." I laid the veil on the top of a well-used notebook and rubbed my arm.

"Okay. I'll be right back." Clarence left and I said, "Knock it off."

"No," said the voice speaking inside my head.

Hearing voices isn't a good sign for anyone at any time, but I'd seen on Irene's website that Elizabeth occasionally talked to the guests, so I decided that insanity wasn't looming. Besides, what choice did I have, stop investigating? I had a feeling Elizabeth wouldn't be keen on that, so instead of calling for a psych consult, I filled up the six-foot-long claw-foot tub in the big bathroom off our bedroom. It was seriously luxe in there with double sinks, a glassed-in shower with about twenty spray nozzles for massages, and a reclining chair that had a foot bath attached.

I plugged the tub and filled it with steaming water and a generous helping of bubble bath. The room filled with lavender-scented steam and I sank into the tub. I might've been just a little scalded, but it was worth it.

At least it was worth it until I put my head under the water and came up with a song in my head. I'm not talking about an ear worm like when you can't get some catchy lyrics out of your head. I'm talking about hearing music. Hearing it, like there was an Alexa in the room, which there wasn't.

"John Brown's body lies a-moldering in the grave. John Brown's body lies a-moldering in the grave."

That's right. It wasn't even a song I liked or written in the current century. I'd spent the whole day thinking about death. A little break would've been nice, but it wasn't happening. The song kept going in a loop. It was probably Miss Elizabeth's favorite. I assumed she was from the 1880s like her house, but I might be wrong on that. She loved the hell out of that song.

Because I'm me, I decided to ignore it and picked up my phone when it sounded off with a generic ringtone. I almost didn't answer because usually generic means loser stalker that got my number somehow, but I needed a distraction so I swiped green.

"Hello?" The instant I spoke the music volume went down. Elizabeth was just trying to bother me.

"Mercy? This is Tank Tancredi."

"Oh, hi. How's it going? Do you have Italian beef yet?" I asked.

"Eating isn't in the cards for me tonight," he said.

I sank down until the bubbles were over my chin. "Bad news, I take it."

"You were right."

"About?" I asked, but I already knew from the sound of his voice. Animal lover that he was, this would be hard to bear.

"The animals." Tank was choked up and it took a minute for him to continue. "A bunch of pets went missing."

The music stopped abruptly and I mouthed, "Thank you."

"You're welcome," said the voice in my head.

The animal thing was so upsetting, the voice didn't even bother me.

"Were there articles in your paper?" I asked.

"Yes, but they were after the murder."

Tank had shown his investigating skills with his incredible thoroughness. He went through every edition for six months before and after Maggie's body was discovered. No mention of animals before. All the coverage was on the fires and escalating thefts and break-ins. He went back another six months. No fires, but there were plenty of thefts and break-ins. Those went back about two years and Tank made an Excel spreadsheet to track them. Once he had it all down in a handy color-coded graph, he could see the trends. The crime rate with regard to thefts had steadily been rising for the two years before Maggie's murder. At first, the thefts were far apart, but as time went on they got closer and closer together and became bolder. The thief or thieves came in while families were sleeping and stole things right under their noses. Interestingly, violent crime didn't change. For St. Seb proper, that meant no violent crime at all. Zero. Not even a domestic. Outside the city limits, yes. They had various problems, but not a lot. Inside, nothing. Tank said this was normal for them.

The most interesting thing about Tank's graphs was that they showed a dramatic uptick during the two summers prior to Maggie's murder and there were also bumps on holidays.

"That says kids to me," I said.

"Definitely. They've got the time to do the crime," said Tank.

"So what happened after with animals?"

Tank took a breath and told me that there was a lot just outside of town, past the city limits sign, where a family had made a grisly discovery during the summer after Maggie's murder. An old farmhouse had been left to fall into ruin and a local dentist's family had gone out to look at the location. They were thinking of building a new house and the property had a nice setting. While they were there they found a series of what looked like small graves, complete with crosses. They didn't think much of it, assuming it was a family plot for the farm and back in the day, infant mortality was high. But then they went inside the dilapidated house and found animal skins nailed to the remaining walls. Cats. Dogs. Even a few hamsters and Guinea pigs. There was a cobbled together table made from the farmhouse's old front door and it looked like it was stained with blood.

"How many?" I asked, feeling as barfy as when I rolled out of Lefty's Gator.

"Twenty-six total."

"That's a whole lot. Nobody reported missing pets?"

"If they did, it wasn't covered in the paper."

"We need to know when that started."

"We do," he said with a shake in his voice.

I waited while Tank got himself together. Then he told me that Barney Scheer had reported on the discovery and had done a pretty bang up job. Some animals were identified by their owners and he determined that the first one to go missing was a dachshund that belonged to Mrs. Louisa Henderson. He found the missing pet ad Mrs. Henderson put in the classifieds in the June before Maggie died. A lot of the missing animals were in the classifieds. Thirteen in total. As far as Tank could tell until the discovery at the farmhouse, all the owners thought their animals had simply gotten lost. Every single animal that had a known owner disappeared between June and December 1965.

"None after?" I asked.

"Not that Barney found. I saw a couple of ads for lost cats in the six months after, but they weren't on the list."

"That six months is very important."

"Looks like it," said Tank.

"Nobody connected it to the fires that were happening at the same time?" I asked.

"Not that I can see. Of course, if we had the police report, we'd know more."

"That flooding is awfully convenient for the cops."

Tank took a deep breath. "You think they're lying about the files being lost?"

"I think it's weird that they kept putting files in a basement in a flood zone."

"That's a yes."

"It's a maybe," I said. "You know the chief, how much does he hate me?"

"I give you an eight out of ten. He was nearly replaced after you found that little girl. A lot of questions about his competency came up."

"What about his liver?" I asked.

Tank went quiet and I could feel the struggle going on by his breath and the needless shuffling of paper. Family loyalty versus the truth was always a tough choice.

"Yes," he said finally. "How did you know?"

"I'm a nurse, but a career in medicine isn't really necessary. Your brother-in-law isn't looking good and the family history is a red flag."

"He's got a problem. Mallory tries to talk to him about it, but he denies it completely. He says he only drinks socially."

"I have it on good authority that he's up to three or four bottles a week."

"Shit."

"It's not good, but I'm more interested in whether you think Stratton would lie to me. She said it first and the deputy, Dallas Mosbach, looked a little uneasy about it."

"Dallas is a good kid. He worked for me in high school, covering football games."

"Do you consider him a liar, in general?" I asked.

"Not at all. He'd lie to you, but it wouldn't come easy, and he'd only do it if he was told to."

"What about Stratton?" I asked.

"She's Will's girlfriend."

"Well, there you go."

"Don't get me wrong. I like her a lot. She's about our only hope of getting Will on the wagon. Candy doesn't drink at all. Her father had a problem."

"It was an instant reaction when I asked for the files. Do you think they discussed what to say to people who came in?"

"I doubt it," he said with a chuckle. "Mercy, you are a known troublemaker. They don't want you around, making people take another look at Will."

"Like I'm going to go away just because there was a flood," I said.

"I'm not saying it's a good plan," said Tank. "On another note, I copied all the articles on that plane crash. Do you want me to email them to you?"

I gave him my email address and asked, "Anything interesting?"

"Well..."

I got barfy again. "What?"

"Nothing earth-shattering. It was a small plane crash, deemed an accident. Faulty wiring or something. Plane was coming in from New Orleans and supposed to land in St. Louis. They almost made it."

Almost.

"Nothing about it not being an accident?" I asked.

"No, but Melanie, Will's mom, she was the chief then, didn't investigate. Our cops just secured the scene and I guess Jeff City took over."

"Why not St. Louis?"

"I have no idea. No one seemed bothered by it at the time."

I swirled my free hand through the bubbles. Agatha and Daniel. Nobody was bothered. "Sounds straightforward."

"There's nothing in our coverage to say it wasn't."

"Why did you sound funny when I asked if there was anything interesting then?" I asked.

"There are photos of the crash site."

"Pretty bad?"

"Have you seen the photos of the Buddy Holly crash?" Tank asked.

"No." I'd heard of that crash, but only because Grandad loved a song about it and insisted on telling me where he was when the music died whenever he heard it. In bed is the answer, but he heard about it on the playground at his elementary school. According to him, tag was never the same after that.

"Do you want to know more right now?" he asked.

"I don't think so," I said, but I needed to know more. Agatha and Daniel died for a reason. Something they had with them or something they knew, but that could wait. It had to wait. "Is there anything else?"

"There is, but it's just interesting."

"Okay. Consider me interested," I said.

"Chief Lucas' comments on the animals."

"Let me guess. He called it a small time crime."

"Nailed it. Now he did express horror and said he would work with the ASPCA, but that animals weren't people after all."

"I bet that went over well."

"Like a lead balloon. He barely held onto his job. Frankly, it looks like nobody else wanted it, dead nuns and somebody killing family pets doesn't look like a fun gig."

"But that was all over," I said.

"He notes that in his statement and he was right. It was over. No other animals were ever found and just the normal amount wandered off after that."

"No suspects, I suppose?"

"It was suggested that your priest came down and was stealing people's pets to practice before he killed Sister Maggie," said Tank.

"Seriously?" I asked.

"Well, that's a hell of a lot better than thinking it could be your neighbor and it ended with Maggie's death, so it kind of makes sense, if you really want to think he did it."

"I guess so," I said, feeling sad and worn out. I needed to call Spidermonkey, but I found the prospect of interrupting his family reunion with my big fat mess a seriously unpleasant thought.

"Do you have anything else for me?" Tank asked. "Don't forget we have a deal."

"I haven't forgotten."

"How's your uncle?"

"Good, I think. Waiting on results."

We said goodbye and I looked at the phone for a second, trying to make myself call Spidermonkey. I couldn't do it and set the phone back on the tray. The second I did, the music started up again. No rest for the wicked as my mom would say.

"Oh, come on!" I exclaimed.

Clarence appeared in the doorway. "What's wrong?"

"Nothing!" I yelled over the music in my head.

"Why are you yelling?"

"Am I?" I tried to lower my voice, but that's pretty damn hard with John Brown's freaking body a-mouldering in your flipping head. "My ears have water in them."

Clarence set a mug on my tray and said something I couldn't make out. Then she went over to the vanity and started rifling through the toiletries. The music got steadily louder. I had to get out of that house. But where could I go in the middle of a blizzard? Tank's house? Maybe he hadn't left yet.

I picked up my phone and the music vanished so suddenly I jerked and made a big splash over the side of the tub. "Oh!"

Clarence spun around. "Mercy? Oh, my goodness." She covered her eyes and I looked down. I was up and out of the protective bubbles in all my glory. Mom better never find out I flashed a nun and I didn't even want to think about Aunt Miriam. "I'm sorry. My...um...ears cleared." I sank down. "You can look."

"I'm so sorry, Mercy. I didn't mean to. Oh, my goodness."

"It's fine. We all have them," I said.

The fiery flush cleared her cherub cheeks and she said sweetly, "I don't think that's quite accurate."

"Well, you know what I mean. Breasts are"—in my peripheral vision I could see Maggie's things going into another tower—"holy crap."

"Men think so, I believe," said Clarence, walking toward me with a box of Q-tips.

"No!"

"What? What's happening?"

"Stay there."

Clarence started panicking. "What's wrong? What happened? What did I do? I didn't mean to see."

"I...uh...had an idea. I have to think about the idea that I had. Don't move."

Maggie's clothing was hovering as if someone was inside of them again. If I hadn't seen our cat, Blackie, not to mention what happened out at the lake with Janet Lee Fine, I would've had my own cardiac event. It's not the kind of thing that gets better the second time around. Clarence couldn't see that. She thought breasts were "Oh, my goodness."

Think of something. Think of something.

"I'm going to get out of the tub." I'd get everything back in the box and stash them in another room. There we go. "Close your eyes or I'll scar you for life."

Clarence covered her eyes. "Is your idea good? Is there a new clue?"

"Yes, actually there is." I set my phone on the tray and new music blared.

"Mine eyes hath seen the glory of the coming of the Lord."

The Battle Hymn of the Republic? What the hell?

I stood up and started to step out as the music got louder, but then I got an idea. I reached for my phone and the music got softer. I pulled my hand back and it got louder.

Very subtle, Elizabeth.

A burst of laughter echoed through my head and I picked up my phone before sitting down. The music shut off in the middle of "Hallelujah," and a wave of water went over the side of my tub again.

"Are you out?" Clarence asked.

"I'm in and there's just enough bubbles."

She lowered her hand tentatively and said, "I don't understand."

"I'm beginning to," I said. "I'm supposed to call someone."

"Who?"

Mom? Dad? Pete?

"I don't know."

Clarence perched on the vanity's tufted stool and asked, "Can I help?"

"Maybe," I said.

"The hospital to check on your uncle?"

"No, Pete will call."

My phone went off with Mom's theme and I quickly answered, "Hi. How is he?"

"He's still fine," said Dad. "Pete called. I said I'd call you. I'm starting to like that guy."

That's too little too late.

"Do tell?" I asked.

"He's not half bad. Morty's out of the cath lab and he's got a blockage, but he's stable, so they're going to wait and see how his numbers look tomorrow."

"Sounds like a plan," I said, leaning back and sinking into my luke-warm water. "Are you and Mom okay?"

"We are. Did you call your guy?" Dad asked.

"Not yet."

"What are you waiting for? A sign from God?"

I glanced over at the hovering nun's outfit and said, "I think I already got one, sort of."

"Well, then get on it." Dad railed at me over lollygagging and then hung up so he could have dinner with my mother, who'd had a good cry and was now trying to figure out if it was possible to charter a helicopter to get them back in the morning, since every highway in the state was blocked. So much for the not panicking.

"Was it bad?" Clarence asked.

"It's fine. I mean, as fine as a heart attack gets. They'll probably have to do a stent or a balloon angioplasty, but those are pretty routine."

"But there's no one there with him."

"Chuck will be there eventually and my old boyfriend, Pete, will watch over him," I said.

"That's not the same as family," said Clarence.

I smiled at her. "No, it's not. Nothing's like family."

"What will you do now?"

"I'm going to wash my hair and call my super snoop," I said.

"Your what?"

"I have a hacker that's pretty fantastic at finding things out."

Did you hear that, Elizabeth? I'll call him.

She must've heard because I set down my phone and nothing happened. So I dunked my head and, when I came up, Clarence was heading for the door. "No!"

She jumped and slipped on the wet floor, falling with a thump on her rear. "Ouch!"

"Oh, Clarence. I'm sorry. I just…"

Happy now?

Maggie's belongings tumbled back into her box while Clarence slipped around, trying to get to her feet. Fats dashed in and yanked her upright. "What happened in here?"

"Nothing," said Clarence. "I slipped."

I gave Fats the something-freaking-happened look and she took Clarence out of the bathroom, saying she needed to change her wet skirt. They went back and forth about I don't know what while I washed my hair and didn't bother to condition. I'd pay for that.

As soon as I stepped out of the tub the music started again.

"Twas in the merry month of May when green buds all were swelling."

It was soft this time, a little reminder that Elizabeth hadn't forgotten. I dried off and wrapped the towel around me before picking up the phone. The music stopped just when the story was getting good. I was tempted to set it down to see if Sweet William died, but I didn't for fear that the Battle Hymn would come back blaring.

In the bedroom, Fats had Clarence changed and was shooing her out of the door.

"There's nothing I can do?" Clarence asked.

I smiled reassuringly at her. "Can you check on dinner? I'm starving."

The little nun grinned and said she would.

Fats closed the door and said, "Alright. Let's have it."

"Go have a shower. You're dripping."

"I worked out. You should try it."

"Pass," I said. "The way you look right now is not a good advertisement."

Fats popped a toothpick out on her lip. She must store them in her cheek like a giant hamster. "So?"

I folded the top of Maggie's box together and put it in the enormous Victorian wardrobe. "So I have to call Spidermonkey."

"That's it? You skipped conditioner for that?" Fats never skipped conditioner or manicures or shaving her legs. I, on the other hand, was hairy with snarled hair and chipped nails.

"I may have had a little trouble with Elizabeth," I said.

She gave me the stink eye. "Define trouble."

"She spoke to me."

Fats threw up her hands. "You have to follow the rules. What did you do?"

"I don't know. Nobody told me the rules, except don't be interesting."

"Well, you can't do that," she said.

"I know."

Something rustled in the wardrobe and we both turned our heads to look, slowly like you see people do in movies.

"Do you know what that is?" Fats asked.

"Probably," I said.

"Do I want to know?"

"Hard to say."

"Have you had your own coronary event?" she asked.

"Two or three."

Fats chewed on her toothpick and said, "I say we leave it."

"Good call." I opened my duffle and pulled out some leggings my mom had secretly tried to throw out because the knees were all baggy. "Are you going to turn your back?" I asked.

"I'm going to take a shower."

"Well, go ahead."

"What's going to happen?" Fats asked.

"Beats me. Probably nothing."

"I don't like surprises."

Bummer. 'Cause Elizabeth does.

"I'm right there with you."

"I'm going in," said Fats, but she didn't move.

"Go for it."

Still no movement.

"Are you, Fats Licata, afraid?" I asked.

"I'm prudent. I don't want to bring a knife to a gun fight," she said.

"There's no weaponry."

"No?"

"Music and some other stuff, but no weapons."

"All right then." Fats went in the bathroom and shut the door. Fear vanquished. I wish I had that easy of a time coping with fear. My heart was still pounding and my cortisol levels had to be through the roof.

The shower started running and I got dressed quickly as the wardrobe doors rattled. "I'm hurrying. Give me a break."

"No," said the voice.

"Awesome. That's swell."

Nothing. I'd say that was good, but the Battle Hymn started up so it really wasn't.

I have to get out of here.

"No," said the voice.

"I don't like you," I said.

"I know."

I sat on my little twin bed and tried to unsnarl my hair while calling Spidermonkey. The second the phone began ringing the music and the wardrobe rattling stopped.

"Mercy?" Spidermonkey asked. "Thank God it's you."

"Really?"

"Hold on," said my hacker. "I have to take this."

"What's going on?" I asked.

What was going on was Spidermonkey and Loretta were trapped in South Carolina on Sullivan's Island during a tropical storm. It wasn't bad enough to leave, but no fun to stay. Think twenty-four hours a day with family for a week with nothing to do but board games and Netflix. Spidermonkey loved his family, but he was this close to crazy. There were babies. A lot of babies and they all had great lungs.

"I do love them," he said.

"I believe you."

"Help me."

"I don't think I can actually get you out of there," I said.

"You can give me something to do," he said. "You're the only one Loretta will allow. I've been praying you'd call."

"I have got something for you, but I didn't want to interrupt."

"I'd pay you to interrupt. Another baby's crying. I don't remember our babies crying like that."

"Were you really around that much?" I asked, thinking of my dad.

"I guess not. What have you got? Oh, wait. Hold on," said Spidermonkey.

"Mercy, it's Loretta. Tell me you need us and we have to leave."

A laugh bubbled up out of my incredibly tight chest and I let it loose. The wardrobe wasn't so scary anymore. Neither was the music or the voice. It could be worse. Loretta's voice assured me of that.

"You, too? Aren't you Mom? Mom's love this family stuff," I said after I stopped laughing.

"My daughters-in-law are fighting about vaccines again and they're on the same side."

"Anti-vaxxers?"

"Yes. It's insane. Dillon is fifteen. He isn't going to get autism."

"I'm with you," I said.

The clinic had dealt with their share of anti-vaxxers and it was nuts. I've never seen so much fear about the wrong things. Measles kills people. It does. Fact.

Loretta harrumphed and said, "They were vaccinated and they're fine. What the crap?"

"I don't know. It's a thing right now."

"Maybe you can talk to them."

Not just no, but hell no.

"I'll just tell them they're crazy and should vaccinate their spawn."

Loretta started laughing and told Spidermonkey about the spawn.

"Thank you. I needed that. Now what can we do for you?" asked Loretta.

"Are you sure? It's dark," I said.

"Isn't it all?"

She wasn't wrong, but Maggie's death was worse. I could feel the horror in my skin, a sort of an unhappiness shroud of worry and dread. This wasn't a small time crime and I couldn't imagine how anyone, even a drunk, would say that.

"This is different."

"If it's about a child, then I can't hear this," said Loretta.

"No child victims."

"And it's not to do with The Klinefeld Group?"

"No, but I have something new about Stella," I said.

Spidermonkey took the phone, sounding grumpy. "I've been waiting for you to contact me about that."

"You told me not to."

"The landscape is different."

"You mean rainy."

"And angry. The girls are talking about peanut allergies now," said Spidermonkey.

"Does someone have one?" I asked.

"No, but it sounds like they want one of the kids to have it so they can be in the in-crowd."

"I don't know what to tell you."

"This is your generation."

"Do not lump me in with anti-vaxxers. That's a low blow," I said. "I'm vaccinated and if I were to spawn, my kid would be, too."

Spidermonkey's soft South Carolina accent began to purr and soothe. "I know you're reasonable, even when you're not being reasonable."

"I don't know what that means."

"It means I don't understand you and the risks you take," he said. "Okay. I've locked the door and my laptops are ready. Let's start with why you aren't using Morty for this."

"He had a heart attack."

And the typing began. With a vengeance.

CHAPTER TWENTY-ONE

"I've got him," said Spidermonkey.

"Who? What?" I asked.

"Morty. ICU. Got him."

I should've known he'd go straight into the hospital and grab up Morty's chart, but it startled me anyway. My mind was on Maggie and the dread of telling the two of them her story was weighing on me, especially with Elizabeth sharing her opinion if I took a wrong turn.

"Okay. Great," I said.

"What do you want? I've got results."

"Lay 'em on me."

Spidermonkey gave me all of Uncle Morty's numbers, so fast I could hardly absorb them. He had damage, but it was recoverable. That much I understood.

"Anything else?" Spidermonkey asked.

"No. That's good. Thank you."

"He's okay, isn't he?" That soft voice nearly brought me to tears again. He cared. Uncle Morty considered Spidermonkey a mortal enemy. Competition was not acceptable. Period. But even with that, he cared.

"I think so, but he'll have to change," I said.

"That's a tall order for Morty."

"You said it."

"Now let's talk about this case, you obviously didn't go to Greece."

"I wish." I gave him the lowdown on what happened, leaving nothing out, and listened, as I spoke, to the comforting sound of keys being struck and information being gathered.

"What do you want first?" Loretta asked. They were on speaker, but I could barely hear her over the rain. We were all in storms of various types.

"First. Hm. Let me think. Let's go with Bertram Stott."

"Got it. Anything specific?"

"I want to know his connection to the area and if he was here in 1965. If you can see what he was up to after his release that would be helpful."

"You're thinking other crimes."

"I doubt he was reformed in the prison system, especially back then," I said.

"Agreed. You're thinking what? Other murders? Rape? Stalking?"

"All of the above, but I think he learned from his conviction and got better. The best you'll probably find is his name on interview lists, suspicions but nothing concrete. If you find a living cop who liked him for something, I can have my dad make a call."

"Hold on," said Loretta. "Tommy's on board?"

So I did leave something out, but I did it on instinct. Hiding what I was up to went right to the bone. "Yeah. He knows I have someone for research besides Uncle Morty. He told me to call you."

"I'm surprised. Tommy's all about the family from what I'm told."

"He is, but the family usually means him."

"That's a bit harsh, don't you think?" Loretta asked.

"But accurate. He's working on it and he'll talk to whoever we need info from," I said.

"Well, that's unexpected," said Spidermonkey. "Tommy is a great resource. There's only so much I can get from the internet and it's not like you can hop over to Tennessee to charm them."

"Not this week," I said with a laugh.

"So about the church, you said Morty cleared them on the pedo stuff. I want my beloved to recheck. Is that a problem?" Loretta asked.

"Nope. Do it. He wasn't exactly focused. Once he saw Nikki with that guy, it was really over. Brain off. Crazy jealous monster on."

"And there was money," said Spidermonkey. "I like that. I've got a feeling that's what we're going to nail them on."

"We're not trying to *nail* the Catholic Church," said Loretta.

"If they caused a nun to be murdered, you bet your pretty little britches I am," said Spidermonkey.

"I'm sure they wouldn't do that on purpose."

"Really? You're sure?" he asked.

"Don't get sarcastic with me."

The two of them started bickering about the church and the pedophile coverup. Even though they weren't directly affected, it pained them both in many ways and the discussion gave me time to think, but Elizabeth wasn't having it. The wardrobe began rattling.

"Alright," I said. "Alright."

"What was that?" Loretta asked.

"Oh...um, I was thinking out loud. There's just so much to research."

"And here we are talking about unrelated crimes."

"Might not be unrelated," said Spidermonkey.

"You're determined to think the worst."

"I wonder why."

"It's a good thing you're so attractive," said Loretta.

The wardrobe's doors burst open and Maggie's box looked like it had a couple of wild dogs fighting inside it. "The asylum!" I yelled and the box went quiet.

"Oh my God, Mercy," said Loretta. "Why are you yelling?"

"I'm excited?"

"Are you asking us?" Spidermonkey asked.

"No. I'm excited. I...uh...thought of something. Can you find the layout of the asylum where Maggie worked?"

"I should be able to. What specifically? The interior?"

"No. More exits and the nearest bus stop. I want to see how it would've gone down, assuming I'm right."

"But it could've happened at the Cardinal Rigali Center since Maggie was going to her appointment there," said Loretta. "If Bishop Fowler knew Maggie was about to report something that he didn't want reported, that's another possibility."

"If you can get the layout for the Center, too, it would be good, but my dad and I both think this was a spur of the moment thing. Lying in wait says plan." I explained what Dad and I were thinking, including our theory on the body being abused. It turned out to be too much for Loretta. She left the room under the guise of checking on a crying grandbaby, but I wasn't fooled and I didn't blame her. Excusing myself from Maggie's case sounded like a swell idea.

"Is she okay?" I asked.

"She will be," he said. "This is a lot different than watching *48 Hours.*"

"Or *20/20.*"

"If they do one more story that trashes you, I will give them a virus that they won't soon forget."

I laughed and laid back on the bed. "Don't do that. They might trace it to you."

He snorted the way Uncle Morty did but somehow made it sound elegant and I pictured my handsome hacker sitting in a wicker chair all silver-haired and buttoned up. "That will not happen, rest assured."

"Don't tell me. I don't want to know."

"Deal. I'm pretty good with taxes. I'll get the church's filings and see what I can make out. That's where it shows."

"And the asylum," I said. "That was probably a non-profit."

"Yes, yes. Now we're cooking with gas," said Spidermonkey. "And this Bishop Fowler was involved, plus the doctor."

"I forgot about him."

"The doctor?"

"Yes." I told him about my feeling on the doctor's untimely accident four days after Maggie disappeared. "I originally thought she would've been with him, but in light of his health and the accident, I doubt it."

"Let's see where Dr. Desarno practiced," said Spidermonkey.

"I'm sure he had an office at St. Vincent's."

"He probably did. I've got the obituary and the newspaper story on the accident. Would you look at that? Green Dodge pickup."

"I need to be taking notes. Two pickups so far."

"Or one," said Spidermonkey, just a little bit ominously.

"Do you have a feeling?" I asked.

"I don't think it's a coincidence that we have a truck at both scenes four days apart at the same place."

I got the pictures that I printed at the Sentinel and looked at the tire tracks. "Is there any way to identify tires from that far back?"

"Not to a specific model of truck, if that's what you're thinking. But we might be able to tell by how big they are. That will tell us which models they'd likely have been on."

The pictures were good but not that good. "I can tell they're big, obviously not for a sedan, but we don't have a closeup on markings."

"I can try. Do you have a scanner?" he asked.

"I'll ask if they have one, but trucks aren't rare, even if we think the truck used to dump Maggie was a Dodge that doesn't mean it's the same Dodge."

"Sometimes I forget how young you really are," said Spidermonkey. "Back then trucks were tools. They weren't stylish. The average man didn't drive one just in case he needed to carry home a bag of dirt. Trucks were for farmers or contractors. People who needed them for work."

"So?"

"There weren't a lot of trucks running around downtown St. Louis in the 60s. That came later when trucks got comfortable. You've got a truck at two related crimes within a week. That's not a coincidence."

"Tank said everybody had a truck," I said.

"Well, you're in farm country, aren't you?" he asked.

"Definitely. So we need to know if Bertram Stott had access to a truck, too," I said.

"You feel that strongly about him?"

"I do and so does my dad."

Spidermonkey kept typing away. "I'll find every vehicle he's ever had. Don't worry about that. What else did your newspaper guy say?"

"We're starting to think the flooding excuse is a little hinky." I asked Spidermonkey to look into that and gave him the names of Candace Stratton and Dallas Mosbach. He was particularly interested in Dallas, since he showed a hint of displeasure.

"And let's take a look at Barney Scheer, our reporter at the time," I said. "He changed his tune. I'd like to know why."

"Mercy, you are my favorite person right now," said Spidermonkey.

"Oh yeah? That seems unlikely."

"This is a pile of work."

I'd just been thinking I'd gone way overboard and there might be a family issue. "Your kids won't be happy."

"Are you kidding? They barely know I'm here. I'm the swimming, bonfire-building grandpa. Right now I have no use."

"It's a lot of stuff."

"And we're not done."

"No?"

"You haven't filled me in on that historian, Dr. Wallingford," he said and, despite his soothing voice, I could tell he didn't like being out of the loop, even though he asked to be.

"So you have been working," I said.

"Perhaps a smidge."

I snorted. "A smidge? You've been checking up on me and The Girls."

"It's what I do," he said.

"I don't know if you have the time," I said in a self-sacrificing tone. "What with all those babies crying."

"Mercy Watts, tell me what was said or I'll—"

"What? What are you going to do, Mr. Cashmere Sweater?" I asked with laughter.

"You don't think I'm tough," he said petulantly.

"I think you're elegant and brilliant. That's better."

"Alright. I won't freeze your bank accounts. Today."

"Thanks. You're swell."

"I think so."

I teased him for another minute until Loretta came back and demanded to know what the historian found. I gave them the short version of how I connected the initials C.M.B. with Bickford House.

"We have to look into that family," said Loretta.

"Dr. Wallingford knew a few things about them." I told them what he said and they were particularly interested in the break-ins like I was. Spidermonkey said he would see if he could get the *Kindertransport* lists for the Bickford House area, but he doubted they would help us with identifying Constanza Stern.

"Why not?" Loretta asked. "She was a child, Jewish, and that's the time."

Spidermonkey kept typing and talking. His ability to split focus was amazing. I could barely spell and talk. "Because Constanza was special. Josiah and Stella didn't pick out some random girl and take a photo with her."

That was true and how Constanza became intertwined with the Bleds fascinated me nearly as much as The Klinefeld Group and whatever they were looking for.

"I want to know how that little girl ended up in Auschwitz," said Loretta. "She was safe in England. Why on Earth would she ever leave?"

"That's the million dollar question," said Spidermonkey. "I think Bickford House is our way in. The earl leaving his ambassadorship in November 1938 tells us that."

"We need to know why," I said.

"I'll see what I can do, but you need to talk to Dr. Bloom. Find out if the earl or his family showed up in his research on the Resistance."

"I will when I get a chance." There was a timid knock on the bedroom door and I glanced at the clock. "Dinner time," I said. "I have to go."

"Good luck," said Loretta.

"Mercy?" Spidermonkey asked.

"Yes."

"Do you have a weapon with you?"

"I brought the Mauser."

"Do me a favor and keep it on you."

I agreed to carry the Mauser any time I left Miss Elizabeth's and a knot formed in my stomach. Spidermonkey had never asked that of me before. He had a feeling and it wasn't good.

CHAPTER TWENTY-TWO

C larence poked her head in timidly. "Are you ready for dinner?"

"I am, but Fats is still in the shower," I said.

She chose that moment to walk in. Actually, Fats doesn't really walk, not like regular people do. She does a kind of march mixed with a sashay. Zena: Warrior Princess should've looked like her. How do I know about Zena? Chuck. She was his adolescent fantasy and I've been forced to watch the show and be told how awesome it is. Nope. But, I will admit, it's great at putting me to sleep.

Irritated, wet, and wearing a towel that barely covered the important bits, Fats growled, "I'm done."

"Oh, my goodness." Clarence closed the door and scurried away.

"You need a bigger towel," I said. "Maybe a bath sheet."

"Do you see this?" She pointed at herself.

Carved muscle. The flat stomach that I never had.

"Give me a hint?"

"Look." She dropped the towel. Yes, she did. Fats Licata was naked and I saw it. Oh, my eyes. The burning.

I fell backward and put my good arm over my eyes. "Oh, my God. What in the hell are you doing?"

"Look. Look at this," she demanded.

"No. You can't make me."

"You're a nurse."

"I'm not doing it."

She did her sashay march thing over to the side of the bed. I could sense the anger and the naked. So much naked. There has never been so much naked.

"We're practically family. Just look."

"Uncle Morty is practically family and I've never seen him naked."

"Never?"

"No. What the...is your family crazy?" I asked.

"We're not uptight and inhibited, if that's what you mean," she said. "I walked into the pool house on vacation and my dad was in there changing."

"You weren't scarred for life?"

"Sure, but who isn't."

"Okay. Fine. I walked in on Uncle Morty in the shower when I was little. That was probably his first heart attack."

"See. You're fine."

"He had a really hairy back. That's all I remember."

"I think it's a good thing you don't remember anything else."

"When I think about it I can still hear the screaming," I said.

"Yours?" she asked.

"His. He was hoarse for a week."

Fats poked me hard on the hip. "Okay. So we've waltzed down memory lane. Look at me. I think I'm showing."

"You are," I said.

"The baby, you moron."

I groaned. "You're not showing. You won't show until at least four months."

"I do everything early. Walking, talking, winning."

"You're not going to gestate fast. That's not a thing."

She poked me again. "Think about it. This is my baby."

"So?"

"Mine and Tiny's."

"Okay," I said slowly. "What are you getting at?"

"He was fourteen pounds."

I nearly dropped my arm. "Holy crap that's a big baby."

"And he was two weeks early," said Fats.

"You might have a problem."

"Look at me or I'll tell Lorenzo Fibonacci you want to get with him."

Lorenzo was Calpurnia's nephew, incredibly beautiful, sleazy, and frighteningly seductive.

"You wouldn't." I was pretty sure I had the strength to resist the hotness that was Lorenzo, but I wouldn't want to chance it.

"Try me," said Fats with a growl I heard her use on serial rapists and a shiver of fear went down my back.

"Alright. Just cover up, will you?"

"You are a prude."

"I'm good with it." I gave her a pillow and she retrieved the normal-sized towel that was a hand towel on her.

"Come on, you wuss," she said and I peeked over my arm. The view was out of some men's fantasies, the world's buffest woman barely covered. I needed to do sit-ups. A lot of sit-ups. "I am, aren't I?"

I sat up and tried to think of what to say. The short answer was no, not by any normal standards was Fats showing. But...

"I knew it," she said and spun around to disappear into the bath-room with a slam.

Clarence knocked on the door and did not open it this time. "Are you two okay?"

I got up and said to the angry door, "I'm going down to dinner." I know. I know. Doors can't get angry. Wrong. That door had anger written all over it and I was not opening it. Ever.

"I'm coming," I said and put on a pair of comfy slippers that Irene left for me and opened the other door, the good door. Clarence was hovering three feet away, red-faced and kind of hunched over.

"Look at you," I said. "It's fine."

I put an arm around the formerly innocent nun and guided her to the stairs. "Fats is just having a time."

"With what?"

"Weight. She's been a pro bodybuilder and super fit all her life. It's hard to gain an ounce. It's not you or me." *It's Tiny. He better propose soon or I don't know what.*

"That's good to hear," she said. "Fats looked so angry." Clarence whispered, "I can see why some people are afraid of her."

"Well, you shouldn't be. I'm not. Most of the time."

We joined Lefty and Irene in the kitchen, where the wood stove was blazing and a good thing, too. With all the windows in the addition the howling wind was particularly noticeable. Snow was piled up against the glass and I started to feel like I was in Alaska.

"It smells fantastic," I said. "I hope we didn't keep you waiting too long."

"No. It's fine," said Irene. "I had a chance to make some calls on your behalf."

I took a seat at the oval oak table and accepted a large glass of red wine from Lefty, who looked slightly embarrassed. "Something wrong?"

"I may have told her about Bertram Stott," said Lefty.

"May have?" Irene asked. "You called me from the Sentinel."

"And there's that."

I smiled and took a large sip of wine. "It's fine. I don't think it's a secret that Stott is a convicted murderer."

"No, but it's news that he may have something to do with the nun's death." Irene had been busy, making a dinner worthy of Aaron, and called everyone she could think of to see if anyone knew if Stott had been in town in 1965. She came up empty-handed, but I appreciated the effort.

"Where's Fats?" she asked.

"Getting dressed," I said. "She's feeling a little heavy after those cookies. Don't expect her to eat that pie. Until recently, I've only seen her eat veggies and tofu."

Irene shook her head sadly. "That's no way to live."

"More for us," said Lefty happily and he began cutting generous slices.

Irene piled our plates high with rosemary-roasted potatoes and a salad with generous chunks of stilton cheese, walnuts, and pears. "I made a dump cake for after."

"What's a dump cake?" Clarence asked after agreeing to have a thimbleful of wine. Lefty literally put her wine in a shot glass. No joke.

"It's a treat," I said. "You'll love it."

"You dump all the ingredients in. Dump cake," said Irene. "So many calories, but oh so good."

"Should we wait for Fats?" Lefty asked.

If we want to starve.

"Let's not. She's probably doing a thousand sit-ups and I don't want it to get cold," I said.

The food was as good as it looked. So good I texted Aaron about it and he asked for directions. I was a little afraid the weirdo might hit the road in the middle of a blizzard on a food hunt, but there wasn't anything I could do about it.

"It's a bummer that nobody remembered Stott from back then," I said.

"I'm not surprised. My friends are all too young to have known him. Teenagers all look the same when you're in the third grade," said Irene. "Nobody is happy to have him here and we all heard the rumors about a connection to St. Seb, but no one can remember who said it."

"Anybody older you can ask?"

"Let me think about it."

Lefty topped off my wine and said, "What bothers me is that guy is living at Shady Glen."

"Tank said he's in a wheelchair," I said.

"I know, but still."

Clarence passed me the potatoes. They were so good I was going to split a seam. "What is Shady Glen?"

"A retirement village and it doesn't come cheap," said Lefty. "How does a jail bird afford that?"

"That," I said, "is an excellent question."

"Is it supplemented by the church?" Clarence asked. "I believe the diocese is very active."

"Not Shady Glen. Private all the way. Tom Altemueller had his mother in there. He said it was almost six thousand a month."

Irene whistled. "Stott must have family money."

We're always ending up at money.

"Mercy?" Clarence asked. "Did you think of something? Sister Miriam says you're always thinking. She acts like it's a bad thing, but it can't be, can it?"

I patted her hand. "My thinking has a history of causing her a problem, but you're right. I was thinking that money keeps coming up everywhere I turn."

"How do you mean?" Lefty asked.

I told him about the pedophile angle with the church that we'd all but ruled out and that left money. Murder almost always came down to love or money. Serial killers were the rare exception. They killed for the pleasure of it.

"That's it?" Clarence asked. "Just the church's money?"

"It's not...I don't know. I just keep hearing it. Maggie was supposed to be meeting with my godmother to talk about donations and fundraising for St. Vincent's, for starters."

"Was that place in trouble financially?" asked Lefty.

"State budget cuts hurt them. There was never enough money," I said.

"Anything else?" Irene asked.

"The first thing I heard about the land that Maggie was found on was that the family was wealthy. Tank talked about how much money he lost on the fires."

"A bundle for certain." Irene offered me more pie, but I couldn't fit it in, no matter how much I wanted to.

"Thank you," I said. "Also, the newspaper articles on the high school quoted how much money the project lost. I keep hearing about money. It's probably not related, but I can't help but notice."

"The high school is a disaster," said Irene. "Tank brought that up?"

"He did. You weren't happy about the land being sold either?" I asked.

"We were not. Those Sniders. Always out for a buck."

"Now Irene. That was the old generation. Robert Junior's a good man and he's making us proud."

"He sold that land and he knew what it meant to the community," said Irene.

"He probably needed money for his campaign."

Our hostess got up and started cleaning. I recognized that reaction. Angry cleaning was something my mother specialized in. "That is ridiculous and you know it. We all saw Angela's new BMW."

"The woman can get a new car. It's their money," said Lefty.

"Their money? Vultures, the whole lot of them."

Lefty drained his wine glass and explained that his feisty wife was not a fan of the Snider clan and for good reason, in my opinion. Having dealt with The Klinefeld Group, I knew that some things did not fade with time and, according to Lefty, St. Seb had a long memory.

Back during the Great Depression a lot of farmers struggled and went under when the banks called in their loans. The Snider family went in and offered just over what the farmers owed to sell their land to them instead of going into foreclosure. It was a terrible deal, but Irene's grandparents took it because a little money was better than no money. The Sniders held that property and sold it later at a huge profit. The Sniders were a wealthy family to begin with and feeding on the farmers was seen as the worst kind of opportunism. They, also, went after friends and neighbors, repeating the pattern with store owners and even some houses in town were bought that way. Irene estimated that by the time the depression had ended during the war, the Sniders owned around forty percent of the property in and around St. Seb. They gave no money to charity or any church and were regularly seen wearing fur coats and driving brand new cars when everyone else was struggling to put food on the table and sending their sons off to work for the WPA after Roosevelt was elected.

"That wasn't Robert Junior," said Lefty. "It wasn't even his father."

Irene snapped her dish towel. "You think they're different now?"

"I think he's different."

"How is he different?" Clarence sipped her wine. It would take two hours to drain that shot glass.

"Robert Junior is going to be president someday," said Lefty. "He's the change we need."

Irene threw up her hands. "You drank the Kool-Aid. Robert Junior is no different."

"He works for charity. He's putting in his time in the State House."

"A politician?" I asked.

"Yes, and a good one, too." Lefty explained that Robert Junior was a lawyer that had been elected as a state representative and was now looking to move up to better things as the state attorney general. He was well-liked and had a good approval rating. But whatever Lefty said, Irene countered. She was biased, but her words had a ring of truth. Robert Snider Junior sounded like a guy who figured out how to be popular after losing his first election when he tried for alderman. Lefty admitted he changed his tune on some key things and managed to get into the House. It sounded to me like the property sale for the high school was a misfire, but Robert Junior was now popular enough that he didn't care. From what both Irene and Lefty said, he wasn't terribly bothered about the disapproval.

"So where'd the money come from originally?" I asked.

"Slaves," said Irene.

Lefty slapped the table. "You don't know that."

She scowled at him. "They came from the South after the Civil War and were loaded. Where do you think it came from?"

"I don't know."

"It can't be worse than slaves," said Clarence, looking rather shaken by the conversation. I bet her homeschooling mom never talked about people using their neighbors to line their own pockets or politicians lying. Clarence was too sweet to have been exposed to more than the common cold.

"Well," said Irene, "I guess bank robbery is better."

"That was just a rumor," said Lefty.

"Yes. I'm sure a mysterious aunt died and left them a fortune out of the blue."

I took a drink and chuckled. "That's straight out of a romance novel."

"That's what my great grandmother said they said. When the money got low, back in the day, old Daniel Snider went to visit this dying aunt in Decatur and came back with a suitcase full of cash."

Clarence surprised me by drinking the rest of her shot glass and asking for more before saying, "Strange things do happen. Mercy was born in the Bled Mansion and nobody knows why."

Lefty and Irene turned to me.

"Really?" Irene asked.

I shrugged. "It's true. How did you know that, Clarence?"

The little nun blushed. "Sister Miriam told me."

"She thinks it's odd?"

"Oh, yes. She certainly does."

Aunt Miriam had never mentioned that to me and she was a big mentioner. I'd never known her to hold back and she had a cordial, if somewhat restrained, relationship with The Girls. They were never tight like Myrtle and Millicent were with Grandad and my parents.

"I might have to ask her about that," I said.

"Please don't."

"It's not a secret." *Not that anyway.*

Clarence clutched her shot glass. "I shouldn't have said anything. I don't want to cause trouble for your family."

"I can't imagine you causing trouble," said Irene. "And that Snider money isn't just odd. It's downright suspicious."

"Why?" Clarence asked, glad for the change in subject.

"Because the weekend Daniel Snider was in Decatur just so happened to be the one and only bank robbery in the town's history. Beat that, Lefty."

"It's coincidence. That's all."

"Oh, you think so?"

"I do."

"Care to bet?" Irene asked.

Lefty rolled his eyes. "There's no way of settling it. That happened over a hundred years ago."

Irene pointed at me. "We have Mercy Watts at our table. I googled her. She's not just some pretty face."

"Thanks," I said.

"You're welcome. She's a real detective. Her father is Tommy Watts. He worked for the FBI."

"So the hell what?" Lefty asked. "She's here about the nun. Why would she spend her time answering a question that has nothing to do with anything."

They were about to really go at each other when I said, "Because I'm curious and this is the kind of thing my dad loves."

"Really?" Lefty was aghast and more than a little bit worried. Losing a bet to Irene probably wasn't something to be taken lightly.

Irene put her hands on her hips. "What can you do, Mercy?"

"I'll make a call and see what my guy says about the Snider finances," I said.

"That sounds like an invasion of privacy," said Lefty.

"A little bit, but if you want to know, that's how it goes."

"I'm in," said Irene.

"You would be," he said. "You just hate the Sniders."

"I don't trust the Sniders. You didn't grow up here. You don't understand. There's something off about them."

"They've had their troubles like anyone else."

Clarence leaned forward. "What troubles? Are they in need of counsel?"

"It was a long time ago now," said Irene.

"Still bad," said Lefty.

"Not for the reason you think."

Fats walked in, dressed in fresh spandex, and looking like she might just have done five hundred sit-ups. "I have to hear this."

Lefty and Irene told two versions of the same story. I suspected that was a reoccurring theme in their marriage.

The facts were simple. The interpretations were not.

In 1999, Robert Junior's father was killed in a hunting accident. The Snider family went out turkey hunting as people did and Robert Snider, who wasn't wearing safety orange, accidentally got shot and died just after the paramedics showed up on the scene.

That was Lefty's version. A simple accident. Family tragedy. Nothing more.

Irene wasn't so convinced. Robert Snider, according to her, was the family black sheep. He had a business degree but couldn't hold a job. He drank and had multiple accidents that the family paid to have swept under the rug. His wife was seen with bruises and the occasional black eye. She moved out a few times but was convinced to come back with what Irene described as bags of cash. The family bought Robert a car dealership that he ran into the ground and in the months before he died he was admitted to the hospital for what the family called exhaustion.

"He had a breakdown," said Irene. "And it was a humdinger."

"Dr. Johnson told me it was exhaustion," said Lefty.

"He's on the payroll. What do you expect? Mercy, do people get exhaustion or is that code for freaking crazy?"

"Irene!"

"He was in Walmart yelling that someone should just kill him because they were out of his favorite yogurt and started peeing in the front yard. Daily."

Fats forked a piece of steamed broccoli and said, "I'm going with freaking crazy."

"People have been known to work themselves into the ground," I said. "It can have dire consequences."

"There," said Lefty triumphantly.

"Exhausted himself doing what?" Irene asked. "He didn't work. His brother, James, had taken over the dealership. How hard is it to lift a bottle?"

They went around and around about the merits of crazy versus alcoholic or lazy or entitled. Robert was seen as guilty of pretty much every vice there was. I had a feeling Irene was right. Maybe the Snider family had a problem and they decided to solve it. It was coldblooded, but they sounded special to begin with.

My phone buzzed and I excused myself to answer it.

"I made it," said Chuck.

"To the hospital?" I asked. "Just now?"

"Fifteen minutes ago. It was a nightmare. I've never seen roads that bad. I took a cruiser and slid off the road. I had to hitch rides with snowplows."

"Are you okay?"

"I've had better days, but I'm fine."

"Have you seen Uncle Morty?"

He paused. I don't know if it was for effect, but he had me worried.

"Chuck?" I asked.

"He's okay."

"What did he do?"

What didn't he do would've been the better question. So far, he'd tried to escape the ICU, pulled out his IV, yelled at everyone, and stolen three phones in ill-advised attempts to call Nikki in Greece. He didn't know the number and kept calling 911.

"It gets worse," said Chuck.

"Worse? He didn't...hurt someone, did he?"

"He...cried when I walked in."

I waited for the rest, but it wasn't forthcoming. "And?"

"He cried, Mercy. Morty Van der Hoof cried. On me."

"Well, he did have a heart attack and they're talking about a procedure tomorrow. He's probably terrified. I would be. Can I talk to him?"

"No. They shot him up with something. Thank God."

"Okay. So it's fine," I said.

"It's not fine. I can't unsee that. I'm going to have to burn this shirt. It's covered with snot and old man tears."

"He's not that old."

"Missing the point, Mercy," said Chuck.

"What is the point? You didn't think it was so bad that my dad cried about my mother's stroke."

"That's different."

"How?"

"I didn't see it."

I rolled my eyes. "You'll probably survive. I did."

"Real sympathetic," he said, sounding like a petulant little boy.

"I know. I really appreciate you going in this terrible storm, but some family had to be there."

"It's a good thing I love you like I do."

"Why's that?" I asked.

"I just realized that Morty is going to be my family forever," he said.

"He has been since my uncle adopted you."

Irene came over and gave me my newly filled wine glass and gave me a motherly look that I really needed.

"It's different now," said Chuck. "The family's going to call me. Nobody calls me."

"I call you," I said.

"That makes it all worth it."

"That's a good man you've got there," said Irene after I'd hung up.

"I think so," I said.

"A girl like you needs a good man."

"A girl like me?"

"You're in the spotlight. All that press and it gets pretty nasty. Your father's famous and you've got that face. You need a man that will have your back, not try to get in front."

My eyes welled up. "He's working on it."

"Not easy?"

"He's a police detective."

Irene hugged. "Know where you are and it will be fine."

"We're figuring it out."

"It takes work, even if you're a bed and breakfast owner with a ghost that prefers your husband nine days a week."

I wiped my eyes. "Elizabeth likes Lefty better?"

"Absolutely. Come in and have some dump cake. It cures the blues."

"You just want me to call my guy and find out if Daniel Snider robbed that bank."

"I wouldn't say no."

We laughed our way back into the kitchen to eat dump cake and watch Fats weigh her second course of steamed cabbage. It was the calm in the middle of the storm.

CHAPTER TWENTY-THREE

There are bad nights and then there are bad nights. That was a bad, bad night. It started off well-enough though. We did the dishes and curled up in front of the wood stove with more wine and chocolates. I say "we", but it was everyone except Fats who decided that was the time to do her kickboxing routine. Clarence was fascinated by my bodyguard for two reasons. Firstly, because Fats could do the splits while standing on one foot. And second, that she thought it looked like a good activity for what she called her "Troublesome Trucks." Little kids were a handful at the best of times and even the calmest ones needed to get out their endless energy. By the time we went to bed, Fats had devised a training regime that wasn't totally insane and parents might like. It included a fifteen-minute stretch and warmup that should be able to drain the spazz out of the most active kid.

While Clarence and Fats talked kids, I messaged Spidermonkey about the Snider family and its dubious history. He questioned the wisdom of getting off on what he called a tangent, but I insisted. It wouldn't take long and I was curious about the bank robbing theory. There was something appealing about getting dirt on a family that had been rubbing people's noses in it for a hundred years.

I admit I probably wasn't thinking straight. The wine and excellent food had dulled my senses. I actually called my dad for backup. Only a copious amount of wine could've gotten me to do that and it totally worked out. Dad was on the Sniders so hard. He started calling his old contacts at the FBI and we were off to the races. Literally. Dad against Spidermonkey. Both wanted to beat the other to the answer. I had to mute my phone to avoid the one-upmanship.

Dad did ask one question that rolled around in my mind long after I muted him. "How old was Robert when he died?"

I asked Irene and the answer was fifty-one and she said it with a good deal of scorn. Fifty-one was long past time to get your crap together and, for once, Lefty agreed. We left it at that and I had more wine. Through the talk of St. Seb's many spectral occurrences and family stories that we shared, numbers, names, and dates kept coming back at me. Fifty-one. Twenty-three. 1999. 1965. Thirty-two. December third. December seventh. And the money. Always the money. Maggie. Stott. Dominic. Myrtle and Millicent. Robert Snider. Dr. Desarno. Kathleen Coulter. The bishop. Aunt Miriam. Chief Lucas. Barney Scheer. Janet Lee Fine. Tennessee. Kentucky and, of course, Kansas. It was a spiderweb with threads going every which way, but I couldn't bring them together. I couldn't see it.

We went to bed at midnight and I fell instantly asleep. It lasted an hour. That's how long she gave me. An hour. Then Elizabeth started playing "John Brown's Body" and rattling the wardrobe. I'd doze off and wake up with a fresh chorus.

Fats and Clarence slept through it. They barely moved. Fats snored lightly and Clarence muttered Hail Marys every once in a while. The wardrobe was rocking and rolling. I don't know how they didn't hear it and they sure didn't see the eyes. I'd read on the website about some eyes in the dark. People tried to see them. They booked certain rooms, not ours, in hopes of catching a glimpse. Let me just say catching a glimpse of a pair of backlit eyeballs at three in the morning is highly overrated. I'm not going to lie. I peed a little when I rolled over and there they were, floating by the window. No body. No flipping eyelids. Two eyeballs. I think they're what I saw in the window when we arrived so it wasn't a strictly nighttime thing and they really were

there. I turned on the light and they stayed. Eyeballs. I wished I had a
tennis racket. I totally would've given them a whack.

Fats and Clarence didn't wake up with the light on and I didn't
have the courage to turn it off again, so I tried talking to Elizabeth. I
begged her to go away and leave me alone.

No answer.

So I sat there, clutching my pillows in front of me, listening to
"John Brown's Body", scared out of my mind, and watching those
eyeballs in case they decided to, ya know, do something.

They didn't. They just were there, looking right at me. And people
think that paintings with the eyes that watch you are creepy. That ain't
nothing. At one point I couldn't hold it anymore. I absolutely had to
get up and go to the bathroom. Those eyes watched me go and they
watched me come back. I seriously considered waking up Fats, but she
was halfway to crazy town as it was. I didn't want to push it. Clarence
was never going to happen. She'd taken off her veil to go to bed,
releasing masses of light brown curls that made her look about twelve.
Scaring her was not an option.

I thought about going into another room. Surely Irene would
forgive me, but I made the mistake of checking on which room was
ghost-free. The only one that didn't have stuff was ours. Awesome.
Perfect. Fan-freaking-tastic.

I stayed and at some point I must've drifted off only to be jolted
awake by all our phones' alarms going off at four. That woke up Fats
and Clarence. They fumbled with their phones, swiped off the alarms,
and fell back into what I can only describe as a stupor. You might ask
why I didn't say anything. I did.

I said, "Look. Look. Look." And I was pointing to no avail. They
didn't look at the eyeballs or the rattling wardrobe. Nope. That was all
for me.

When Fats woke me at seven with a none too gentle whack to the
shoulder, she said, "What in the world, Mercy? That is not funny at
all."

I opened my eyes to slits and looked out over the edge of my
pillows. "You see them?"

"Yeah, I see it. I'm not blind and neither is Clarence. She ran out of here like I flashed her. She actually thinks something went on while we were sleeping."

"It did," I said, glancing at the window. The eyes were gone. Bastards.

"Stop thinking you're funny. You aren't," said Fats as she put her hair up in two little buns on either side of her head.

"Funny?"

"I'm not saying that doesn't take talent but save it for daylight."

I sat up and opened my eyes fully. The music was gone and the wardrobe was quiet. It took me a second to see it and when I did, the hair on the back of my neck prickled to the point of burning.

"Oh, crap," I said.

"Yes. You scared a nun. Congratulations."

"I didn't do that."

Fats stopped with one bobby pin in her mouth and another one positioned to be thrust in her right bun. She didn't move. Her eyes slid to the left to the tower of Maggie's belongings, precariously balanced in a kind of Pisa-like structure on top of the box, which was upside down. Her clothes were laid out on the floor, not floating, thankfully.

"You didn't do that?" Fats asked.

"No. Nobody could do that," I said. "Notebooks don't typically hold up dictionaries like that."

"I thought it was odd." She finished her bun and assessed the situation. "Elizabeth?"

"I hope."

"What does that mean?"

I told her about the eyeballs and she was hot. So pissed I thought she would start sizzling. Fats wanted to see those eyes. She wasn't happy when Irene put us in the no eyeball suite.

"I can't believe you didn't wake me up," she said. "Why do you think we're here?"

"To solve a murder."

She waved that away. "Yeah, yeah. I meant here in Miss Elizabeth's. We were supposed to have a ghostly evening."

"I did. Trust me, it sucked. I'm exhausted," I said.

Everything hurt. It felt like a flight to Australia where you didn't sleep a wink. I needed a deep tissue massage and half a gallon of coffee just to put on my pants.

Fats, on the other hand, was feeling just fine. She walked around the tower, examining it at all angles. "This means something."

"It means Miss Elizabeth hates me."

"You don't listen at all. These things happen when you don't follow the rules."

"Nobody told me the rules," I said. "Thanks for that."

"No? Well, them's the breaks."

"You're all heart."

"Why are you complaining? You got to see the eyes," she said.

"That's not a good thing. It was scary as hell."

"You mean, cool as hell. Now what about this tower. I didn't read about this."

I got out of bed and stretched. I could hear my joints complaining. "She just wants to annoy me."

Fats raised an eyebrow. "This isn't the first time?"

"Hardly."

She flicked me on the forehead. Hard. "The rules, Mercy."

"Son of a bitch that hurt. What rule has to do with that kind of thing happening?"

Fats went on to tell me the rules, two specifically. The first and foremost was don't think of anything supernatural in Miss Elizabeth's house. Check. Did that, not five minutes in. Second, if she gives you a job, do it. I didn't think I got a job, but when I told Fats about the music that ended when I called Spidermonkey, she thought it fit. Elizabeth bothered people when she wanted them to do something. Change clothes. Take a bath. Get out of her house. Call their mother. Those were just some of the examples. I wasn't the first to get the music, but, according to Fats, I was the most dense.

"What do you think I'm supposed to do?" I asked, looking at the tower.

"Something," she said.

"Helpful."

"Was it like this before?"

"Not exactly."

She gave me the stink eye and I told her about Maggie's clothes floating as if someone was in them. She did a fist pump. "That is the most amazing thing. Did you take a picture?"

"I was trying not to poop my pants," I said.

She shook her head. "It's a wonder nobody has killed you."

"Hey! I kick some butt."

"You've got balls and you're lucky. Butt kicking is my department."

She had a point but it still stung. "What do you suggest? There isn't a butt to be kicked."

"It's obviously about Sister Maggie. You haven't gone through this stuff yet, have you?" Fats asked.

I hadn't and I didn't want to. Maggie's stuff made her a real person, not that I didn't think of her that way. I just didn't want to know too much about her life because I was about to know way too much about her death.

"No," I said.

"What are you waiting for?"

For it to go away.

"Nothing."

"You know there's a clue in here, right? Elizabeth wants you to find it."

"Maybe. Or maybe she wants me to be miserable," I said. "Last night was miserable."

"Because you didn't do what you're supposed to do."

"Swell."

"Alright," said Fats. "I'm going to get coffee. You get started."

"No coffee for you," I said, a tad vindictively.

"Irene has decaf. I checked." Fats walked out and, the second she did, Maggie's clothes filled up like a person was inside.

"Fats!" I yelled.

"What?" She poked her head back in. I couldn't say anything. I couldn't. I thought I might get used to it. I didn't.

"Mercy? What?" Fats came back in and froze. "So that's happening."

"Yes," I whispered.

"I see what you mean about the pooping."

"Glad to hear it."

"You better figure out what clue Maggie left us. Pronto."

"Definitely."

I edged around what I thought of as a body and plucked a book off of the tower. It didn't collapse and it should've. The book was a textbook. *The Handbook of Clinical Psychology*. I sat on the edge of my bed and leafed through it. Maggie had underlined things, but nothing seemed relevant. The stuff she was interested in wasn't about criminal behavior and there wasn't anything like "Hey, there's a guy who wants to kill me" written in the margins.

I moved onto other books, paperback classics like *Pride and Prejudice*. *Wuthering Heights, Anna Karenina, A Room of One's Own,* and *The Second Sex*. I can't really say if I liked Maggie before I saw those books. It wasn't a question I asked myself. She was a victim and beloved by those I loved. That was enough. More than enough really to bind me to her. But those books brought her to life and I knew why she was beloved. Maggie was my kind of girl. She liked the fun, witty romance of Austen and didn't mind thinking about the hard questions in *The Second Sex*. And I wondered if she longed for her freedom and was she about to leave the male-dominated Catholic Church. Maybe Aunt Miriam would talk to me once I solved it, once she knew that it wasn't her fault. Maybe she would sit with The Girls and remember the way Maggie should've been remembered, not closed off and in pain the way it happened back then.

I went through the tower faster, driven by an engine, my eyes scanning for something Elizabeth wanted me to see. But I didn't see it. I had her novels, so many novels, some textbooks, a teddy bear, extra clothing, a crucifix for the wall, a notebook, and her bank books, checking and savings. Both were modest and Maggie spent little. She had a cat apparently and bought little gifts for friends and family. The last year of her life only had twenty-seven entries. Not a lot going on when you didn't have a car or regular bills. There were a few church documents pertaining to her christening and becoming a nun, but they weren't unusual and didn't have a single name that I recognized. Lastly, there was a little photo album with pictures of her and her fellow nuns. Aunt Miriam was there, smiling and sunny as I'd never seen her. That photo was taken three months before Maggie died. The last photo in the album was of a group of people in front of a set of large institutional doors, the asylum maybe. Maggie, The Girls, several priests, doctors, an elderly woman, a middle-aged woman with an incredible beehive, and a bald man missing a leg. The expressions alone were fascinating. They ranged from apprehensive to joyful. The Girls, Maggie, two priests, and the old lady were in the latter category. Maybe the rest just weren't crazy about getting their pictures taken. Grandma J was like that. She hated photos.

I pulled the last photo out of the little black triangles that held it to the page and flipped it over. The date was on the back. Ten days before the murder. No names were listed. I could ask Myrtle who was there. She might remember.

Fats came in with extra-large mugs. "What did you find?"

"Nothing, except a photo of people who may or may not be at the asylum," I said.

She looked down at Maggie's clothes and I saw a chill go through her.

"I feel like that would go away, if you'd found it."

"Me, too." I took the coffee and gratefully sipped.

"No diary?"

"That would've been too easy," I said.

"No letters?" Fats asked. "There has to be letters."

I sighed and closed my eyes. "You'd think so, but no. I guess she didn't need to write. Her family was just a few miles away and The Girls saw her all the time."

I could hear Fats going through the books and making little dissatisfied noises. "It has to be here."

"Unless Elizabeth is just messing with me."

"That could be. She does take a dislike to some people and she drives them out," said Fats.

"You sound kinda jealous," I said, opening my eyes and seeing her examine her mostly flat stomach. "You really shouldn't be for multiple reasons."

"I am," she said. "You got the eyes."

I pointed at the clothes. "That's not nothing."

She raised a muscle-bound shoulder. "It's beyond creepy, but I wanted a little more."

"Well," I said. "It's breathing."

Fats looked over and I saw the first twinge of fear I'd ever detected in her.

"That could go away and it would be okay," she said.

It didn't go away. The sweater and blouse moved up and down with the rhythm of a living, breathing person and my hands went a little numb from the chills going up and down my arms.

"You aren't easy to please," I said.

She grinned at me. "Tell me something I don't know."

"How about you tell me? Can we get out of here today and do some interviewing?"

"Still snowing, but the wind is down. Lefty's already out plowing," she said.

Clarence spoke to us from the hall, but we couldn't see her. "Would you like breakfast now?"

"I think so," I said. "The tower is gone by the way."

"So it's okay in there?"

Not in the slightest.

"It's fine. But we're coming down," I said.

Clarence peeked in to see me next to the books and stuff on my bed. She couldn't see the clothes behind Fats' bed and it was a good thing. They were...panting.

"Let's go down now." Fats went out and turned Clarence around in case she got any ideas.

"I'll change and be right there," I said.

That's what I thought. I was wrong.

I washed my face and checked my spider bites. Better, but I covered them up with powder anyway. Not bad. I sucked down the rest of my coffee and threw on some warm clothes in anticipation of going out into what looked like a frigid morning. I took a picture of Maggie's photo and sent it off to Myrtle. She probably wasn't up yet. The Girls reveled in snowy days and were known to stay in bed until noon, watching episodes of the *Mod Squad*, a show that they for some unknown reason associated with bad weather.

I almost went downstairs but remembered that I'd muted Dad and Spidermonkey last night. I took a look and smiled at the last message from Dad. "I still think you're right." I was totally saving that one.

Dad and Spidermonkey's messages told the same story. Yes, there was a bank robbery in Decatur. It was unsolved and 100,000 dollars in cash and securities was never recovered. Dad's FBI contacts said it was an open case and had slipped him the suspect list. Guess who wasn't on there. Daniel Snider. That didn't mean a whole lot to my dad, but his cheapness showed up and he wasn't willing to cough up any dough to Uncle Morty's contacts when my guy was already going to do the research. Most importantly, he thought I was on to something. I loved that.

And Spidermonkey agreed. It didn't take long for him to discover there was something off about the Snider family money. They'd moved into a smaller house and sold their general store in St. Sebastian before that bank got robbed. Afterwards, they were sending kids to college and buying boats. It was easy enough to trace the family tree and there wasn't any wealthy aunt in Decatur. No family whatsoever.

The robbery, as described by the FBI and the newspaper accounts that Spidermonkey found, was so straightforward, I couldn't believe nobody caught the guy. And it was one guy. He walked into the bank five minutes before closing at noon on Saturday, stuck a gun in the lone bank teller's face, and had him load up a large suitcase. That poor guy was the only one there. Everyone else had hit the road for the day, so he had no choice but to give the robber what he wanted. No alarm was sounded. The bank didn't have one. The teller cleaned out the strongroom and let the robber tie him up. The guy left through a back door and was never seen by anyone else. If the teller hadn't been gagged and tied up, the cops would've thought he did it. There were suspicions that it was an inside job and the teller, Jimmy York, had to be in on it. He lost his job and fell on hard times, ending up as a handyman and the town drunk.

The unfortunate York said the robber never spoke a word. He had all his instructions written out crudely on a sheet of paper. The man wore dirty clothes that smelled like a pig farm, had a red bandana over his face, and a small-billed cap that York called Irish. That led the local cops and the FBI to think it was an Irish hood out of St. Louis and their main plan was to watch and wait for some Irish dude to start flashing a load of cash or rob another bank. They were still waiting.

There it was again. Money. But what did it mean? If I assumed Daniel Snider did rob that bank, so what? The Sniders were dirtbags? Not really. The Bleds broke the law like crazy during Prohibition and who knows what else. That didn't say anything about The Girls to me.

I just couldn't make the connection. Maybe all these things that seemed too coincidental to be coincidental, were just that. Coincidences. Maybe Maggie's murder was a crime of opportunity and the killer happened to have hiked on the Snider land once so he put her there. Maybe the arsons in '65 had zero connection to Tank's fires. Maybe. Maybe. Maybe.

I flipped over Maggie's box and dropped her textbooks inside. "And don't bring those out again," I said. "I'm done. I did it."

Irene walked through the door, smiling. "You should know that Elizabeth doesn't follow orders."

"Figures," I said.

"Are you coming to breakfast? I made a nice casserole, lots of sausage and cheddar."

"I am." I must've sounded dejected, because Irene came in, the smile sliding off her naturally cheerful face.

"You'll get there," she said.

I yawned. "I'm so tired and there's nothing here. There's supposed be something here."

"What makes you think that?"

I pointed at the floor and she came around to see Maggie's clothing, still breathing on the floor. I don't know what I expected Irene to do. Maybe roll her eyes or sympathize. That is not what happened.

"Elizabeth, how dare you!" Irene exclaimed. "That is sacrilegious and wrong. You've gone too far."

The clothes instantly dropped to the floor and I got the strangest feeling that Elizabeth was gone, too. I didn't realize I felt her presence until it left.

"I thought you said she didn't follow orders," I said.

"She doesn't, but she has a sense of propriety. Normally anyway. No wonder you were up all night." She folded the clothes and gave them a sniff. "These could do with a wash. Musty."

"The clothes were bad, but it was the eyes that kept me up."

"Where did you go?"

"Nowhere."

She frowned. "The eyes were in here?"

"All night," I said.

"Well, aren't you Miss Popular. They've never been in here before. Interesting."

"Can you get her to knock it off? That was off the hook freaky."

Irene started looking through Maggie's books. "That isn't Miss Elizabeth."

"Say what?"

She shrugged. "We don't know what or who that is."

"That's...disturbing," I said.

"They won't do anything but watch you."

"You sound like that helps."

"It's all I've got. I can say that they're really rare. I don't think we've had a sighting in a couple of years," she said.

"Swell." There were shivers racing up and down my spine. "Why don't you get one of those paranormal investigators in here?"

"You think we haven't tried?"

"So?"

"Total waste of time. Miss Elizabeth was insulted. They got nothing and made it clear that they thought the whole thing was bunk and, as soon as they left, she filled our toilets with crickets. It was a nightmare. We had to close down for a month."

"That's really...weird," I said.

"And loud. Incredibly loud. We won't be doing that again." Irene scanned the books, files, and knickknacks on my bed. "So did Miss Elizabeth give you a hint as to what's in here?"

"Nope." My phone buzzed and I glanced at the screen. Spidermonkey. He had info. "I did find out that you're probably right about Daniel Snider."

Irene did a fist pump. "I knew it. Those Sniders are all about money. I don't care what Lefty says."

"That doesn't say anything about the Sniders today," I said. "The sins of the father and all that."

"They're no better now. Selling that land for the high school was just the latest thing."

"Didn't Robert Junior need that money for his campaign?"

She snorted and went to the door to peek out. "Don't tell Lefty I said this, but that's not true. It was ten years ago. He wasn't running for anything more than alderman. Who needs a war chest for that? The Sniders sell off land when they need to pay some bills, they've been doing it since forever. That land was the last thing they had other than the houses they live in. My husband is a huge fan of Robert Junior, but what small town lawyer drives an S class Mercedes?"

Money again.

"That is questionable. I just wish I knew what it had to do with Maggie's murder, if anything," I said, picking up the copy of *Pride and Prejudice* and flipping through the dog-eared pages.

"You need to eat," said Irene. "Going through these things on an empty stomach won't help. Besides, even if there is cash involved somehow, it wasn't hers. Nuns aren't known for having vast sums of money."

Vast sums.

"No," I said slowly.

Irene was reaching to haul me to my feet but stopped. "She didn't, did she? That would be suspicious."

"She didn't. Most of these books are second hand." I picked up her checkbook and double-checked the balance. Maggie had a grand total of fifty-two dollars and sixty-three cents in her account. Her savings had just under three hundred. Definitely not vast sums, but there were vast sums, just not in her accounts. "Hold on." I dug around and found the notebook.

"What is it?" Irene asked.

"I'm not sure." I opened it and started looking through the pages.

Numbers. Lots of numbers. I hadn't paid attention before. It was written in pencil and the writing had faded and was hard to make out. I had a similar notebook on my coffee table. I liked figuring out my bills on paper as opposed to using a calculator and I just thought Maggie did, too. But those numbers didn't match her accounts. What she wrote in that notebook were vast sums. Thousands upon thousands of dollars. The whole book was filled with pluses of as much as $50,000 down to as little as $250. Little notations appeared, like "January 1962" or "bed linen March". There didn't seem to be any particular organization to how Maggie put the math in. Like my own notebook, it looked like she opened it to a page and started working things out. The first five pages had no notations at all. Then there was "Electricity 1962 October." The next page had "Laundry—children" with no date. It was mixed up with 1965 stuff between 1958 and 1960. All kinds of expenses were mentioned from a trip to the zoo to rat traps with big additions of cash and lots and lots of question marks.

And then something jumped out at me near the back of book, "M&M Ask them." That wasn't about the candy. It was next to $25,000 and several question marks. So hard to see, but "M&M" appeared several times next to large sums. Other names were there, too.

Irene bent over the notebook squinting. "I can't see a thing. What is it?"

"Money," I said. "Vast sums."

"Did she have family money?"

"No. This looks like the asylum's money."

"But she wasn't an accountant, was she?" Irene asked.

I shook my head. "No, but she was involved with administration and fundraising for the asylum. The day she disappeared she was supposed to have a meeting with my godmother about 'St. Vincent affairs'."

"And that means what? Money?" she asked.

"Charitable giving has always been important to the Bleds." I took out my phone, ignoring the messages from Spidermonkey, and I called Joy. "Hold on. I'll come down in a moment."

Irene nodded and left me alone to cross my fingers that the house-keeper had stayed over because of the storm.

"Hello?" Joy was not happy to be awakened and I felt a twinge of guilt that was easily ignored.

"It's Mercy. Sorry to wake you, but it's important."

"It better be."

"Are you at the house with The Girls?" I asked.

"Yes. I didn't want to leave them with just Rocco in this storm. They were making hot buttered rum, light on the butter."

"Are they awake?"

"It's a snow day, Mercy. What do you think?"

"I need some information," I said.

Joy got up and rustled around. I imagined her putting on a robe and slippers that she kept in her room for emergencies. "What kind of information?"

"I want to know if The Girls donated to the asylum where Maggie worked."

"I'm sure they did. You know how they are."

I ran my finger over the first "M&M" in Maggie's notebook. Milli-cent and Myrtle. It had to be them.

"I need to know how much, when, and if she asked them anything about the amounts," I said.

"Right now?"

I hesitated. "I can have my guy look into it, but only The Girls know what they discussed with Maggie. I've got sums here. I think Maggie was on to something. I want to know where to look or even if I should look."

"Okay. I'll get Myrtle up," said Joy. "Mercy, do you think you've solved it?"

"Let's not go that far, but there's money popping up everywhere."

Joy sighed. "Sex and money. Isn't that always the way?"

"They thought it was sex," I said. "But it's not. I'm almost positive. This was money."

"Good God. A nun murdered over money. She probably didn't have two dimes to rub together."

"It's not Maggie's money I'm talking about."

"Then it's the church's."

"In a manner of speaking." I heard Joy knock, wait, and then open a door.

It took a few minutes to rouse Myrtle and get her situated. I began to feel more guilty for getting her up, but she asked me to do this. I was damn well going to do it.

"Here she is," said Joy.

Myrtle took the phone and I told her what I'd found. Once I mentioned the numbers she was fully awake.

"Yes, dear, of course we donated to the asylum. They were having such trouble financially."

"Were they?"

"Oh, yes. But once Maggie took over the fundraising it got better."

"Better how?"

"They were able to buy the children new beds and expand the staff," said Myrtle.

"Is that because of you?"

"Partly, but there was never enough. So many children and the illness side also took up a lot of funds. The government had begun cutting mental health programs and it wasn't giving much at all for the patients there."

"Is that why St. Vincent's closed? Money?"

"That's why the mental hospital closed," said Myrtle. "As for the children, caring for them shifted to foster care, but the money situation didn't help."

"Do you know how much you gave?" I asked.

Myrtle chuckled. "Not at the moment, but we have our account books in the library."

In the background, Joy said she would go get them.

"Was it a lot?" I asked while we waited.

"Not especially," she said. "I wish you were here, Mercy. It's a snow day."

I smiled and pictured the last time we had one. Aaron came and we had five kinds of hot chocolate and made ourselves sick. It was awesome. "Me, too, but I'm on to something here."

"You think Maggie's death has something to do with our gifts?" My godmother's voice was fearful. I hadn't thought of that interpretation. Of course, they would think that. I should've known.

"It is not your fault," I said. "Someone did this. It's entirely their fault. I'm just looking for the motive."

Myrtle went quiet for a moment. "And it's not Dominic?"

"No. I've ruled him out conclusively."

"You're sure?"

"Positive. He didn't have access to a truck and there was a truck involved. Plus, he had no connection to St. Sebastian. It was a local I'm pretty sure."

She breathed out a long held breath and I had the impression that it had been in there since 1965. "Thank you, dear. Even if you don't find out who did it, we will be forever grateful for that."

"Oh, I'll find out. I have a feeling."

"You and your feelings."

"It's a good thing," I said. "We might not have enough to prove it in court, but you will know why and who."

Myrtle sniffed and then blew her nose. "Thank you, dear. I wish you would accept payment."

"Not a chance," I said.

She chuckled a little. "Here's Joy. That was quick."

Joy and Myrtle went through the family expense ledger from 1965 that the meticulous Mrs. Perkins kept. It showed all allocation of funds, right down to how much the milkman was paid and how many stamps were bought in January as well as charitable giving and large purchases, such as cars or plane tickets. The Girls had their own separate accounts for personal use and the money that went into those accounts was noted as well.

The funny thing about The Bleds, as incredibly wealthy as they are, never much bother about their own money, keeping it, expanding it, or hiding it. I knew from when I was young exactly what was going on and how much they were giving. That was the important thing. Giving. My grandad, on the other hand, would burn his checkbook before showing it to me. He gave to charity, but it was considered a private affair. Money was almost a taboo. Not so with The Girls, and Myrtle didn't mind one bit about telling me exactly what was going on in 1965.

We added up the donations to the asylum and the numbers fit what I found in Maggie's notebook. All total $120,000. That would be nearly a million in today's money and a pretty big dollar amount, considering at the time a house cost something like $20,000.

"Why were you giving so much to the asylum?" I asked.

"It wasn't that much. We gave considerably more for cancer research and the Red Cross."

"Trust me, it's a lot."

"They needed it," said Myrtle. "Perhaps we should've given more."

"Did Maggie ask for it?" I asked.

She didn't ask for the money. Myrtle said the asylum had been in money trouble for years. The building was old and needed constant repairs. The state wasn't giving any funds for the mental patients and the need kept going up with the state institutions closing down. Birth control was just becoming acceptable and there were still a lot of out of wedlock births. Children needed care and the church was trying to provide it.

The Bleds had donated to the asylum for years before Maggie started working there, but they had never visited. Maggie urged them to come and see for themselves and they were appalled by the state of the place. Myrtle and Millicent increased their donations and began serious fundraising on the asylum's behalf. Things improved and a lot of good came of their efforts.

"Did Maggie ever talk to you about the asylum's money? Where it was going? How it was being spent?" I asked.

Myrtle thought about it and said, "Maggie wasn't comfortable talking about money. She thought it was rude."

"That sounds familiar."

"I know a lot of people feel that way."

"So she didn't talk to you about it?" I asked.

"Well, now that you mention it, I think she asked something about how much we gave or when we started. Something like that. I don't really remember. Maggie was a nun. Money was only important because of the children."

"I understand. But did she ever seem upset or concerned about it?"

"Oh, dear, I wish I could tell you, but I had little to do with it. She

and Millicent may have discussed it more. They were thick as thieves.
I do know that she wanted to expand."

"Expand? The orphanage or the mental hospital?" I asked.

"I don't know, but they weren't going to, I don't think."

I looked down at those numbers and one name, in particular.

"Do you recognize the names Harvey Kotts or G.T. & S.?"

"No. Who are they?" Myrtle asked. "Wait a minute. I'll ask Joy."

Joy took the phone. "I don't know about Harvey Kotts, but G.T. &
S. is a construction company. My brother worked for them after he
dropped out of college."

Construction? Oh, right.

"Thank you so much," I said. "This is it."

"What?" Joy asked.

"I just…I think I know. Is Myrtle's phone there?"

"It is. Why?"

"I sent her a picture. See if she can identify the people in it and
where it was taken," I said.

The ladies went back and forth. I had to smile at hearing Joy basically interview Myrtle, asking all the right questions. The picture was
taken at the asylum as I thought. One of the doctors was Dr. Desarno.
I looked at Maggie and the old man in a lab coat next to her smiling
shyly. They were living on borrowed time and it made me sad to see
their faces next to Bishop Fowler. He was the corpulent priest at the
center, looking sweaty for November and like he was smiling because
he had to. Myrtle thought the rest of the people were probably staff or
board members, but she didn't remember taking the picture at all.

"What was the meeting about?" I asked Joy.

"The Girls were going to join the Board of Governors in the New
Year," she said.

"But they never did."

"No."

"I'll call you back." I hung up and dashed down the stairs. Money.
Money. Money. All about the money.

CHAPTER TWENTY-FOUR

Spidermonkey picked up on the third ring. "Where have you been?"

"Someone was stealing from the asylum and Maggie found out about it," I burst out as I ran down the stairs.

"What? No. That's not right," he said.

"It is and I can prove it."

My hacker was totally befuddled. He'd been up half the night going through the taxes and found nothing off. Nothing. Not a dime out of place. The asylum was a charitable institution that depended on donations and the church to survive. They were barely doing that in 1965. In short, there was nothing to steal.

"They were stealing Bled money," I said.

He shuffled some papers. "Yes, they donated. I wrote it down. Ten thousand a year since the asylum's inception."

"Nope," I said.

"What do you mean? Did The Girls say something different?"

I told him what I found out and he booted up his computer. "$120,000? There's no record of that."

"No kidding."

"You think that's why Maggie was murdered?"

"Yes. Absolutely," I said.

Spidermonkey began typing and calmly said, "That doesn't make sense to me. Everything you found out points to a serial killer, not a financial motive."

I came into the kitchen and slapped Maggie's crucial notebook on the breakfast table and everyone jumped a foot, except Fats. She wasn't there.

"It can be both," I said.

"Can it?"

"I don't know how, but yes. It's both a serial killer and a financial thing." I sent him Maggie's picture and gratefully accepted a fresh cup of steaming black coffee. "Irene, do you know any Shipleys?"

"There are some Shipleys at church. I don't personally know them, other than to say hello."

"Can you find out if any of them are related to Desmond and Mary Shipley?" I asked.

Irene said she would find out and Spidermonkey said, "Shipley? The mushroom hunters?"

"Yes. I want to know if they told their family anything about Maggie's body."

"I can find descendants."

"Irene's on it."

Irene gave me a thumbs-up and grabbed her phone. Clarence raised her hand. "What happened? Did you find out who did it?"

"Not yet. Hold on," I told her. "Where's Fats?"

"In the gym. She ate a croissant."

I rolled my eyes. "Spidermonkey?"

"I'm here, looking at those taxes. Myrtle really confirmed that they donated that money?"

"She did," I said. "Are you doubting my detective work?"

"This is big, Mercy."

I went over to Irene's fab casserole and breathed in the heady scent. Delicious. "I think so. Totally worth being kept up all night."

"Someone in the church stole that money," Spidermonkey said.

"Maybe."

"There's no maybe about it. I'm looking at this photo you sent. It was taken in front of the asylum. I recognize the doors."

"I figured. The Girls were supposed to join the board. Maggie's death put a stop to that. Whatever happened to her started with that money and turned into something else. I have to talk to the Shipleys. Maybe I'll get lucky."

"Mercy, this photo says a lot. Look at it."

I looked and piled a plate high with casserole. Oh, the calories. "I've seen it. The church ran the asylum. I get that, but an accountant may have diverted the funds, right?"

"Sure, but the church is all over this. They ran the place. Bishop Fowler is right there at the center. You think that man didn't know how much the Bleds were giving to his institution?"

I forked the best casserole ever into my face and looked down at the picture. The answer was maybe. Fowler could be a trusting idiot and let others handle things, but his behavior after Maggie disappeared was off. He came off like a man with something to hide.

"So he knew Maggie was onto the money," I said. "Can you look at him? Money-wise, that is."

"I'm on it, but the clergy doesn't pay taxes. I'll have to find his bank accounts. If he took the money, he spent it on somebody."

Irene wrote down a number on a pad and then dialed again. She smiled and nodded at me. I had a team and it felt good.

"How about the board?" I asked. "Can you find out who they were?"

He already had and could name everyone in the photo, except the man with the missing leg.

"That's interesting," I said.

"He might be the husband of the woman next to him, Helen Smith," he said. "Neither of them look very happy."

"What's her deal? Please tell me she was loaded for no good reason."

"I wish I could. I can't nail down who Helen Smith is."

"Seriously?"

"Smith is the most common name in Missouri and don't get me started on Helen," said Spidermonkey.

"Well, I'd think she'd be from St. Louis," I said.

"Then you're thinking wrong. The old lady is from Hannibal. There's a boatload of Helen Smiths."

"Swell."

"What can I do?" Clarence asked.

I gave her the picture and asked her to send it to Sister Frances to see if she could identify the beehive and amputee in the photo. The little nun got right on it, happy to be useful.

"What else did you find out?" I asked Spidermonkey.

"Well, the church is in the clear on the pedophile question. I can't see that they held anything back and they are worked up about your investigation into Maggie's death. I guess you visited some old priest and stirred the pot."

I'd forgotten about my visit to Father Bernard and I quickly gave Spidermonkey the rundown on it. "What are they saying?"

"They're worried that they'll look bad and they don't have a clue about why Maggie was treated the way she was."

"That's what Uncle Morty said," I said. "He didn't get to Stott. Anything there?"

Spidermonkey hadn't spent too much time on Stott. He was more concerned with the church. He did find out that Stott had never owned a truck, green or otherwise, and he had no connection to Missouri before ten years ago. That didn't mean that Stott didn't live there in 1965. There just wasn't a record of it.

"No connection?" I asked. "Parents were never here. Grandparents?"

"Grandparents were dead by that time."

"He had to be here. I just know it."

Spidermonkey kept typing and said, "I believe you're right, but I'm not seeing it. You have to find people who were around at that time. You said people thought he was there."

"We're trying, but fifty years is a long time."

He laughed. "Tell me about it."

"Can you look at his finances for me? Maybe there's something there."

"Already done. Nothing."

Damn and double damn.

"I guess I'll just start asking random old people if they know that dirtbag."

"You could start with that nursing home he's at," Spidermonkey said.

Stop the presses.

"How much money did he have?"

"Stott?" Spidermonkey laughed. "What do you think? He was in prison for a lot of his working life."

I was so tense I had to put down my plate and I really hated to do that. "No money?"

"No. He trained as an electrician in prison and did that until he retired and moved to St. Sebastian."

"Electricians make good money," I said.

"Not ex-cons. Nobody wants a felon in their house. He did industrial work when he could get it. Stott was barely scraping by."

"Shady Glen costs $6,000 a month and you know Medicaid isn't forking over the whole amount."

The typing went from fast to furious. "I can't believe I didn't think of that."

"Somebody's bankrolling him," I said.

"I'll follow the money and get back to you."

We hung up and I slumped down into a chair. Money. So much money and it was getting clearer. Sort of. Spidermonkey was right. Bishop Fowler probably knew about the money, but he didn't kill Maggie. He was waiting for her in that meeting and pissed that she missed it. I shoveled in the rest of my casserole and looked at the picture. One of those people either did it or knew who did.

"Mercy?" Clarence sat down next to me. "Sister Frances doesn't recognize anyone, but she's going to go through her pictures and see what she can find."

"Thank you. That's great."

"What now?"

Irene walked over with the coffee pot and a slip of paper. "You've got a meeting."

"A Shipley?"

"Yep and do they want to meet you." Irene grinned at me while she refilled my cup. "The word is out. St. Sebastian wants to solve a murder."

"Where do you think you're going?" Fats staggered into the kitchen as I wound the barf scarf around my neck. Irene had washed it, but Ode de la Barf clung to the fuzzy yarn.

"The Shipleys' kid wants to meet me," I said.

"What about me?" Clarence asked. "I'm supposed to be helping."

We all grimaced. I wasn't sure what the Shipleys' son had to say, but, if he had details, Clarence shouldn't hear them.

"You can help me make lunch," said Irene, her eyes darting around for something to hand the nun.

"After," I said, "you can work on some case stuff, if that's okay."

"What stuff?" Fats asked as she put her hands on top of her head to catch her breath.

"Um..."

"I want to really help. Don't give me something silly." Clarence was onto me. I couldn't get away with having her cold call people out of the phone book.

My eyes fell on Maggie's notebook. "This stuff. Irene, do you have a magnifying glass?"

"I have the standing one that I use for stitching."

"Perfect." I showed Clarence Maggie's entries. I could make out enough to put it together, but not everything was clarified. We needed all the money that Maggie noted, as a plus noted, dated, and identified. Maggie had done a lot of work. I didn't want it to go to waste.

"Why are we doing this?" Lefty said through a mouthful of casserole. He'd come in from plowing the high school parking lot and was all about taking me to Dwayne Shipley's house. He'd heard Dwayne had taken up blackberry winemaking and wanted the skinny on the results. "Didn't you prove the stealing?"

"I did, but I doubt it started up magically when Maggie came to work at the asylum. It must've been going on for years."

Fats popped her back in a series of disturbing twisting motions and said, "You found a motive when I was in the basement?"

I pounded some more coffee and told her the good news.

"You're right," she said. "That doesn't start up overnight."

"I wonder how Maggie knew," said Clarence. "She was a nurse, not a businessperson."

"The math wasn't hard. She knew The Girls. They told her what they were giving." I pointed at a page with the cost of bed linen written on it. "We can tell from Maggie's math that there wasn't enough money for the linen. Look at the question marks."

Everyone bent over and we looked at where Maggie had written a donation of $2,000 with some initials next to it, not The Girls' initials though. There should've been money for bed linen from that donation and there wasn't.

Clarence smiled grimly. "I will do it."

"Great." I gave her Spidermonkey's number. "Tell him who you are and, once you're organized, send him the initials and dates. I bet he can find those other donors."

Her smile became more grim as she scanned the page. "You think the church stole from orphans and the mentally ill?"

"I think someone in the church organization did or, at least, knew what was happening."

"I...I...hate this."

I hugged her. "I know. But this is how they made it. I have no sympathy for thieves."

The nun nodded and went off with Irene to get the magnifying glass.

"You're not going without me," said Fats.

"Wrong. You stink and I'm out."

"I don't think the Gator can handle all three of us anyway," said Lefty.

"We'll take my truck," Fats said.

He shook his head. "I don't know. We got an extra five inches since midnight and it's still coming down."

"I have chains," said Fats. "My job is to watch you, Mercy. Don't forget Calpurnia has an interest."

"Who's Calpurnia?" Lefty asked.

"An independent businesswoman."

Lefty frowned but didn't question that odd answer. "Well, I've got to go. If you're coming, let's do it."

"No," said Fats.

I pulled on my poofball hat and mittens. "Yes. You can catch up. I'm not waiting for chains. That's a pain and a half."

Fats eyed me and popped out a toothpick, chewing it slowing. "We're talking about a serial killer."

"I know. I told you," I said.

"The reporter's fires were ten years ago, so that means he's still active."

"If it's related, maybe. Ten years is a long time. Things change. He's an old man by any calculation."

Fats thought it over. "You need a weapon. Can you handle my Python?"

"Are you kidding? No. But I don't need it." I pulled my Mauser out of my coat pocket and showed it to her. "I'm covered."

"Is it loaded?"

I rolled my eyes.

"Is it?"

"Yes. It's loaded. Wouldn't be much use if it wasn't."

"You can't blame me for asking. It is you."

"Thanks."

"I call it like I see it," said Fats. "I'll be right behind you. Do not go anywhere else but to the Shipley house."

"Fine."

Fats went to shower and Lefty opened the back door for me. "What would she do if you did go somewhere else?"

"I don't plan on finding out," I said.

Lefty agreed that going against Fats Licata was probably not the best idea, but he wasn't ready to let the question of Calpurnia drop. He pelted me with questions as we got in the Gator and rolled out into the street that seemed like it hadn't been plowed despite the big piles of snow on either side.

"You know I'm going to google this woman, right?" Lefty asked.

"Of course."

"You want to tell me?"

"Not a chance."

He grinned at me and hit the gas. "So I heard you saw the eyes."

We went through my night of terror and Lefty shared stories of other guests who'd been scared out of their wits. He took a lot of pride in the number of people that left in the middle of the night, usually without packing. He had a referral agreement with the Motel 6 so his "Chicken Littles" got a discount and usually weren't too pissed. They did get bashed on TripAdvisor every so often, but Lefty relished those reviews. Nothing brought in guests like "I wet the bed."

None of this was making me feel better about a second night in Miss Elizabeth's House of Creepy, but it did keep Lefty talking and on the road. We made it to Dwayne Shipley's split level in thirty minutes and only my feet and hands were numb. My standards for successful transport were going way down.

"Is there anything I should know about Dwayne Shipley?" I asked.

"Like what?" Lefty asked.

Should've asked this before I ditched Fats.

"Drunk? Crazy? A history of violence?"

"You live in a different world."

"Same world. Different view," I said. "So?"

"I think he teaches economics at the junior college," said Lefty.

"That it?"

Lefty shrugged and blocked a minivan in the driveway before booting me out. I landed face down in a snowdrift and the kids building a snow fort next door laughed their faces off. I pelted them with snowballs until I heard laughing behind me.

A man wearing two sweaters smiled at me from the doorway of the split level and waved us in. Lefty couldn't resist and did a Kamikaze run with a lump of snow the size of a toaster oven. He got completely destroyed before jumping over the snow fort to drop the lump on the kids' heads.

The squeals and protests followed me inside a toasty warm house that was much more modern on the inside than the outside. That house had looked the same since probably 1984. Inside, it was all *Fixer Upper* with cool greys and rustic accents.

"Glad you made it in one piece," said the double sweater guy. "I've heard Lefty isn't the best driver."

"It depends on what you want to be the best at." I stomped on the oversized mat to try and get the snow off. It was hopeless. That snow was the super sticky kind. Great for snowballs and caking on clothes.

"Let me help you take those off." He gestured to a bench and squatted in front of me to yank my boots off. "I'm Dwayne, but I guess you know that. My wife Amy's in the kitchen."

"Hello!" a woman called out from the second floor. "Do you want some coffee?"

"I'd love some. Thank you!"

Dwayne got me out of Irene's snow beast get up and Lefty knocked on the door to bring in a fresh wave of freezing and snow. I went upstairs while Dwayne helped Lefty, asking him about the possibility of the basketball tournament going ahead.

Amy brought me into the living room and we sat down next to a wagon wheel coffee table. I'd seen a wagon wheel coffee table in Mom's favorite movie, *When Harry met Sally*, but I'd never seen one in real life.

"She's looking at the table, Dwayne," said Amy.

"It's an heirloom," said Dwayne.

She leaned over to me and I got a whiff of her Chanel No. 5. "I wanted to hide it before you got here, but he wouldn't let me."

Dwayne and Lefty came up and Dwayne crossed his arms. "Dad left us that table."

"Because he hated me," said Amy.

Dwayne sat down in a kind of modern wingback chair upholstered in pale paisley fabric. Super stylish and it didn't go with that wagon wheel at all. "My father loved you. He brought this wagon wheel back from the war. It meant a lot to him."

"He did not bring it back from the war. How would that even happen? It's huge."

I have to give that one to Amy. It's not like a wagon wheel fit in a duffel bag.

"So your dad was a veteran," I said.

"A combat medic," said Amy.

There you go. Desmond did know about bodies.

"Sounds like an interesting man."

"Don't get me wrong. Des was the absolute best. He just didn't bring back this wagon wheel."

"Enough with the wagon wheel," said Dwayne. "Dad said he brought it. I believe him. You know he never lied."

Amy sighed and poured us some coffee. "Well, he was a little off at the end."

"Dad was sharp right up until the day he died."

Amy gave me the look that all wives give when they think their husbands are off their rockers and I decided it was time to get away from weird war trophies.

"When did your father pass away?" I asked.

"Three years ago. He was ninety-two." Dwayne picked up a photo album and showed me his father, a tall, thin man with a gentle smile. He didn't look like he'd be a combat anything the way Stella didn't look like she could possibly be a spy. Looks aren't everything.

"Where did he serve? The Pacific?" I asked.

"No. The European theatre. He dropped in behind the lines on D-Day and won the Bronze Star with two oak leaf clusters." Dwayne's voice broke and I thought of Chief Gates. Loyalty to the WWII generation ran strong.

"Did your father know Chief Woody Lucas?"

Dwayne opened his mouth but had a hard time speaking so Amy took over. "Des did not like that man. Oil and water."

"Dad would never say anything like that," Dwayne protested.

"Mary, Dwayne's mother, told me. We were always close. She died ten years ago." Amy took the album and pointed out a pretty woman, who looked like she'd rather not be having her photo taken.

"Did Mary say why Des didn't like the chief?" I asked.

"I heard he was a drunk," offered Lefty as he added a copious amount of sugar to his coffee.

"He was," said Amy. "Des didn't approve."

"Dad respected Woody's service," said Dwayne.

"He didn't respect that drinking afterward."

"Woody really went through something over there. Dad wouldn't tell me what, but I know it was bad. They were good friends in high school. They almost joined up together when Pearl Harbor happened, but Dad wanted to be a medic and the Army offered it to him."

Amy threw up her hands. "We're not talking about Woody's service. Miss Watts is here about the nun and you know Woody botched that big time."

Dwayne shook his head. "We don't know that. Dad never said it was Woody's fault."

Amy rolled her eyes and sat back, eyeing her husband over her mug.

"By the way, please call me Mercy," I said. "I'm curious about what your parents told you about the murder."

"That's easy. Nothing," said Dwayne.

Crap on a cracker.

"It sounded like you had some details."

"Not details, details."

"Please tell me what you know," I said. "I've got some good leads, but there's conflicting information."

"I'll tell you everything I know," said Dwayne, "but I don't think it will help you."

Dwayne Shipley was thirteen years old in 1965, a seventh grader. He confirmed that his parents were avid mushroom hunters and, since his father was a mailman, he worked early and had his afternoons free. He and Mary would go out hiking and hunting for mushrooms on a weekly basis. The Snider land was a favorite spot since the woods were dense and had lots of fallen trees where the fungus liked to grow.

Dwayne remembered coming home to hear his mother sobbing in the bedroom and his father loading a revolver on the kitchen table. Des said that they had found a body in the woods and his mother was very upset. He wouldn't give any details, except that it was a woman and that they didn't know her. Mary wouldn't say anything about it, but she sent Dwayne's sister over to live with their grandparents for six months and starting locking the doors. Both parents told the two kids not to go with anyone they weren't very good friends with and never to go into the woods at all. Desmond Shipley was a mild-mannered man and not a fan of guns, despite his service, but he bought two more handguns and taught the whole family how to shoot over Christmas break. Although he never said it, Dwayne understood that it was because of the murder.

"Your parents were scared," I said.

"You should know that Des didn't scare easy," said Amy. "He was sweet, but tough. We got carjacked down in St. Louis right after Dwayne and I got married. Des didn't bat an eye. He took care of us all, got us out of the car, and handled that maniac like he was returning a library book or something. Cool as a cucumber."

Dwayne flipped through the album and showed me an old black and white photo of Des and Mary. The couple was middle-aged and dressed like they were going into the Outback with floppy hats and vests covered in pockets. They both carried baskets filled with mushrooms and Des had a large camera on a strap around his neck. Grandad had that same model that he inherited from his own father.

"There they are. Out mushroom hunting." Dwayne smiled sadly. "When I think of them together I always picture them like that." He took the photo out and looked at the back. "1964."

"You have no idea why they were scared?" I asked. "Chief Lucas said it was an outsider and I saw in the paper that it was reported that the priest in St. Louis did it."

Amy shook her head. "Mary didn't believe that."

"What did Mom say?" Dwayne asked.

"Not a lot. Just that it had to be some insane person because it wasn't a lover's quarrel like Woody said."

"Why insane?" I asked.

"She wouldn't say, but I can tell you this. Mary was still scared and, keep in mind, this was thirty years later when she told me that. She said it was horrible and she still had nightmares about it."

"Poor Mom," said Dwayne. "I didn't know that."

"She didn't want to upset you. I don't think she even told Des."

"Dad knew she was upset."

I leaned forward. "How do you know that?"

"My sister told me some stuff after Mom died. I don't know how true it is."

"Carrie's no more a liar than Des was," said Amy.

Dwayne poured himself a cup of coffee and rolled it between his hands. "Well, she was really upset about Mom dying. Dad was trying to give away her clothes and Carrie was mad at him. I thought she was sort of embellishing. She does do that."

Amy nodded. "I suppose she does. She's an artist, after all. So what did she say?"

"That Mom was mad at Dad and wanted to move away after the murder. Dad wouldn't do it and he didn't care if Mom was miserable. She heard them fighting," said Dwayne. "But my parents never fought. Never. I don't think I ever heard my dad raise his voice. So I don't think a real fight could've happened."

"Did your sister remember what they were saying exactly?" I asked.

"I didn't want to hear it. We'd just buried Mom. It was a miserable time and Carrie was making it worse."

"Oh, Carrie," said Lefty.

We all looked at him and he reddened with embarrassment.

"Sorry. I just figured it out. Carrie Norton's your sister?" Lefty sounded astonished and was trying to hide it.

Dwayne laughed. "People are always surprised. There's Carrie and then there's me."

I looked back and forth between them as they laughed together. Carrie must be something. Not normal, I had to assume.

"Sorry, sorry." Amy pick up a different album and showed me a picture of the family together. I almost laughed. It was like *Sesame Street* and that song *One of these things is not like the others.* Carrie Shipley Norton was not like the others and I liked her on instinct. In the first picture, Carrie was a hippy, like an all-in hippy. Flowers in her hair. Bellbottoms and barefoot when the rest of the family was wearing suits and Mom had on a nice print dress with a bow at the neck.

Amy took me through the decades. Carrie in the seventies. Farrah Fawcett hair and Daisy Dukes. In the eighties she went punk rock, then came grunge and oddly a mohawk. Dwayne's sister currently had blue dreads and seemed to like overalls a whole lot.

"She's fun," said Dwayne. "Just about killed my mother until she got married. Mom thought she'd die alone."

"That's just silly," said Amy. "She always had boyfriends."

"And they were all crazy. Until Yuki showed up. He calmed her down."

"If you can call that calm."

"Mom did," said Dwayne. "Yuki is very focused and he got Carrie together. They own the restaurant, Crabapple's. It's vegan, but surprisingly good. Carrie gives art classes and they're really popular."

"She's a lot younger than you then?" Lefty asked.

Dwayne laughed again. "Wrong. Everyone thinks that, too. Carrie's older, but she's got a young spirit as Dad used to say."

"How old was she back then when it happened? I asked.

"She was sixteen."

Please. Please. Please.

"Did you know your sister's friends at the time?"

"Sure." He showed me a picture of Carrie with a group of girls dressed up and showing lots of leg. His sister was the wildest of the bunch by far.

"What about boys?" I asked.

Lefty smiled and helped himself to more coffee. "I bet Carrie will know that guy Irene mentioned. She knows everyone in town. First name basis."

"That's our Carrie," said Amy. "Social butterfly. Who are you asking about?"

"Bertram Stott," I said.

Dwayne and Amy exchanged a look and shrugged.

"Still doesn't sound familiar to me," said Dwayne. "But I was her little brother. She barely acknowledged my existence."

"Me, either," said Amy. "What kind of name is Bertram? Is he British?"

"He's a murderer living at Shady Glen," said Lefty with relish.

"That's him?"

Dwayne and Amy had heard the rumors, but they hadn't paid them any attention. It was a small town. People talked and truth was subjective.

"So you're saying he really is a murderer?" Amy asked.

"Definitely."

"Do you think he killed the nun?" Dwayne asked.

"I think it's a possibility."

Lefty held his cup aloft. "It's a sure thing. That dirtbag showed up right before the fires started up again at the paper and Tank Tancredi's house."

Dwayne and Amy fiddled with their cups and shifted in their seats. We'd gone from fifty years ago to right now and the thought wasn't close to comfortable until Amy had a thought. "What fires? Were there other fires?"

I told them about the series of fires in 1965, but neither of them remembered anything about it. They did remember the pets going missing and the remains being found. That particular story got more traction than Sister Maggie and people were still careful about their pets years later.

"How many fires were there?" Dwayne asked. "Seems like I'd remember that."

"Eight," I said.

"Nobody got hurt though, right?" Amy asked.

"No. They seemed to be designed to avoid that. There was a lot of damage though. One family's house would've burned to the ground if they hadn't been home at the time."

"Who was that?"

It took me a second to remember. There'd been so many names in such a short time. "The Coulters' house. They thought it had something to do with their daughter."

"Kathleen," Dwayne said. "I remember now. Somebody set their garbage on fire."

"Actually, they threw a Molotov cocktail in their garage," I said.

"Jesus. They could've killed someone." Dwayne took the photo album and flipped it back to the page with his sister and her friends. "That's Kathleen there in the boots. Isn't she pretty?"

Kathleen was pretty, amazingly pretty, with waist length hair, big eyes, and an open, happy expression that drew the eye to her. I could believe that boys would like her in a huge way and that might turn dark as it seemed to have done.

"Is Kathleen still in town?"

"Oh, no. I think she moved a long time ago. I don't know if she even graduated from high school here," said Dwayne. "You can ask Carrie."

"Would she mind being interviewed?" I asked.

"Are you kidding? It'll be the highlight of her week," said Amy. "Should I call her?"

"Please do." I turned to Lefty. "Do you have to get back to plowing?"

"I know you're joking," he said. "I'm not missing this."

Amy went to get her phone and someone knocked on the front door.

"It's probably my..." I never knew what to call Fats. Friend? Bodyguard? Genetic freak of nature? I settled on friend because she'd decided we were friends and that's not something I was going to shake off.

"What friend?" Dwayne asked.

"Pink the Impaler," said Lefty.

"Who?"

"Pro wrestler." He leaned over to Dwayne and said, "Mercy says they're friends, but I think there's more to it."

"Oh," said Dwayne wisely. "That kind of friend. I see."

"No," I said. "*Not* that kind of friend."

"You're a lesbian?" Amy asked. "I didn't see that coming."

"I'm not a lesbian."

"It would be okay if you were," said Dwayne.

"Good to know, but I'm not."

"It takes all kinds," said Amy. "We don't judge. You can be yourself with us."

God help me.

"I appreciate that. Still not gay. I have a boyfriend."

"Of course you do," said Dwayne with a calm, understanding voice.

"You do you," said Amy.

Lefty nodded. "We embrace the rainbow around here. Our mayor is gay."

What is happening?

"Can you hear me?" I asked. "Not gay."

They all nodded and there was more knocking.

"I'll just get that," I said.

Amy propped the phone up on her shoulder and gave me a double thumbs-up, for crying out loud. I threw up my hands and jogged down the stairs to the front door. Fats was standing outside with Moe tucked under her arm, looking like she was considering punching her way in.

"What took so long?"

"They think we're gay," I said.

"What?"

"Lefty thinks we're not really friends, which apparently makes us gay."

Fats stopped midway to setting Moe on the floor. "What do you mean we're not really friends?"

"We're friends. We're friends," I said quickly.

"Really good friends," said Amy as she came to the staircase. "Oh, my."

Fats whipped off her sunglasses, ate the toothpick that had been dangling on her lower lip, and said, "I can't speak for Mercy, but I'm not gay. I'm going to marry her cousin, Tiny. Let me assure you that he is all man."

"What do you mean you can't speak for me?" I asked.

"I can't. What you do on your own time is no concern of mine," said Fats.

"That's not close to helpful."

"I absolutely believe you, Miss..." Amy was rigid like she was in front of a firing squad.

"Licata, Fats Licata. Do you mind my dog coming in?" She said it like there was the remotest chance they would say so if they did, which they wouldn't.

"Of course, not. We love dogs," said Amy, still rigid.

"I thought as much." Fats kicked off her boots and hung up her coat.

"I hope we didn't offend you, Miss Licata," said Dwayne, leaning over the bannister.

How come nobody ever worries about offending me?

"Hello," I said. "I'm still here."

They glanced at me blankly and Amy invited Fats to come upstairs. Fats leaned over to me. "Sometimes it pays to be scary."

"Try all the time. You get believed and I'm gay."

Dwayne called out, "I knew it!"

Dammit!

CHAPTER TWENTY-FIVE

B
lackberry wine is a thing in St. Sebastian and I got to hear all about it while we waited for Dwayne's sister, Carrie, to snowshoe over. That's right. Instead of letting Lefty pick her up, she was walking in a negative ten wind chill. Carrie had gotten snowshoes and was thrilled to try them out on the half mile trek to Dwayne's house, giving me ample time to learn the intricacies of berry maceration.

Fats and Amy were no better. They were discussing the advantages of Lycra versus Spandex. Fats was an expert on stretchy fabric. No surprise there. And Amy had a six foot niece with, from what I gathered, an unfortunately large rear, who was having trouble finding pants that fit. They were pretty excited about stretchy pants. I was not.

Since neither topic was scintillating, I took Dwayne's vast collection of photo albums and started looking through them. At first, I was looking for more pictures of Kathleen Coulter. I found a few, but none had boys in the pictures and were mainly girls doing girl stuff. Not helpful. But then I started going through the other albums, acquainting myself with Dwayne and Carrie's parents. I found a very old album from Desmond's high school days with a lot of pictures of him with a beefy kid that looked suspiciously like Chief Will Gates.

Someone had written dates and names on the back of the pictures and the boy was Woody Lucas. They were best friends, Woody and Des. The album was littered with pictures of Woody and, surprisingly, he was still there after the war. Picnics, camping, and the town fair. Woody and Des were in the Jaycees and the volunteer fire department. This didn't jive with what Mary had told her daughter-in-law about Des and Woody. Their falling-out wasn't the war and the drinking. Or, at least, if it was, it didn't happen for some time.

"Amy?" I asked.

She jumped, startled to find me still there. "Oh, I'm sorry, what is it?"

"Do you have some paper I could use?"

"Is there something in the albums that suspicious?" Amy asked.

"Not suspicious, but there's something...I just need to work it out."

She got me a legal pad and went back to discussing jeans with the most give. I went through the albums searching for a change between Des and Woody. The last picture I found of Woody was in 1972 at a D-Day event, celebrating the thirtieth anniversary. Woody was in a wheelchair and looked like he was on death's door, which he was. The most interesting thing about the picture was that the two veterans weren't together. It was a picture of Des and Mary. He was wearing his uniform and she had a forties dress on. They were straight up adorable and Woody was in the background. The camera caught him glancing at his old friend with a combination of resentment and sadness. Maybe Des had everything and Woody envied him. I looked again. No. That wasn't quite right. In all those pictures through the years, Des had Mary. He was always happy and Woody didn't seem to mind, even though the woman I took to be his wife vanished from the album sometime in the fifties. His kids went, too, but Woody was still in the thick of it with Des, clearly sick but welcome. What happened?

I went through and wrote down dates. The albums were mostly chronological, but some years were mixed up, 1961 had some 1963 snaps in there. Carrie wasn't the best at snowshoeing and I had time to confirm my theory. It was the murder that broke up a friendship that started in childhood and made it through war, alcoholism, and divorce. The last picture of Woody and Des together and happy was at Thanksgiving in 1965. Woody sat at their family table between a young Dwayne and a woman noted as Aunt Bette. The next picture was at the reunion seven years later. I knew that Woody hadn't done a bang-up job on the investigation and with the odd death certificate there was possibly a cover-up. Des severing a lifelong friendship suggested that he knew it and Mary sending her daughter to live with the grand-parents said she knew it, too, and thought she had to protect her daughter. Like everything else, that said local.

"Where did your grandparents live?" I asked.

It took a second but Dwayne changed his focus from the best carboys to people long dead. "Oh, um...Union. Why do you ask?"

"Did Carrie change high schools after the murders?"

"No. Grandpa just drove her in and picked her up every day," he said.

Ding. Ding. Ding.

"That's a lot of effort for an elderly person," I said. "How far was it?"

"Oh, I guess it was about twenty miles to their house. Not that far."

"Are you kidding?" Amy asked. "Twice a day? That's eighty miles. Why would they do that?"

Fats smiled at me. "That's the question, isn't it?"

"It is for me," I said. "How long did Carrie stay with your grand-parents?"

Dwayne shrugged. "I don't know. Sometime in the summer, I guess."

The doorbell rang and Amy ran down to let Carrie in. She did not disappoint. Carrie Shipley Norton was one of a kind. She wore a ski hat that looked like something a jester would wear and a knitted face mask that was a long curly red beard. When she peeled off her over-sized Carhartts, she had on a pair of camo pants, black lace top with a hot pink bra underneath, and her hair had lost its dreads but was now purple and super curly.

"Hey there," she called up at me. "So glad you called. Have I got a story for you."

Carrie dashed up the stairs, hugged us all twice, and settled down with both a cup of coffee and a chai latte that Amy whipped up for her.

"So should I start or do you? I've never been interviewed by a famous detective before."

Usually, people weren't all that happy to see me and I was taken aback for a second.

"I guess you should go ahead," I said.

"My granddaughter is so excited that you're here. She and her girl-friends are over today, making mug cakes and watching those hot guys that hunt demons. What's that show?"

"*Supernatural?*"

"That's it. But they are so excited that I have evidence in a murder. It really is unbelievable." Carrie opened the Hello Kitty backpack that was exactly like the one Fats had and pulled out a yearbook. "Amy said you wanted to know about Bertram Stott?"

Oh, my God!

"Is he...in there?" I could barely breathe. The thought had never occurred to me. Stott graduated in Tennessee.

"Damn straight he is." She flipped open the book and there on the page in black and white was one Bertram Stott. He was an average-looking dude and I wouldn't have picked him out as a future inmate. Real estate agent, yes. Murderer, no. Stott pretty much looked like everyone else on the page. Dark hair parted on the side and controlled with what I assumed was Brill Cream. He had a rather large nose and a small mouth that had a forced smile, not inconsistent with being made to take a school picture. His eyes were narrowed and sort of mocking, but, if you didn't know what he was, you wouldn't have guessed it.

"But he didn't graduate here," I said.

"That's right. He left after the first semester," said Carrie. "I guess the yearbook staff just forgot to take him out."

"I'll be damned," said Lefty. "You got him. He did it."

"Did the murder?" Carrie asked. "I wouldn't be surprised."

Nobody else was surprised either after what she told us. Bertram Stott showed up during the summer. Carrie didn't know exactly when and he was an ass. Her first contact with him was walking home from the town pool. He drove by and made obscene gestures at her and her friends. That happened every time she saw him, even in school. He was rude and occasionally drunk in class. Stott got suspended at one point for carrying a bottle of whiskey in his backpack and another time for patting the rear of a student teacher. He had a gang of friends, all as badly behaved as he was. Stott was the leader and the group became known as the Wolfpack. They were aggressive to everyone, especially girls, and being groped in the hall became just another part of Carrie's day. Stott was definitely the worst of the bunch and she thought that half the other guys in the group were only trying to be cool and wouldn't ever have done the things they did if Stott hadn't been there egging them on. The girls and the faculty breathed a sigh of relief when he left and even members of the Wolfpack seemed to feel the same way. The group ceased to be a problem by the end of the year and lots of parents complained when Stott turned up in the yearbook. How that happened was never really explained.

"What car was he driving?" I asked.

She shrugged. "I don't know cars. Some rusted out old beater."

"It wasn't a truck?"

"No."

"Are you sure?"

Carrie frowned at me. "I'm sure. It was kind of a joke. He thought he was badass, but he drove that thing. It had fins. Fins were not cool in 1965."

"Did any of his friends have a truck?" I asked.

"Maybe. There were a lot of farm kids."

"Any trucks stand out to you?"

"Sorry, no," she said. "Is that important?"

"Yes, but I'm not surprised that you don't remember one," I said. "Did your friend Kathleen Coulter know Stott?"

"We all knew him whether we wanted to or not."

"Did Kathleen have a particular problem with him?"

Carrie was somewhat bewildered. "I don't think so. Why?"

"Someone tried to burn her house down," I said.

She paled and started tugging on her long purple locks. "I forgot about that."

"Who did they think did it?" Dwayne asked.

"I think everyone thought the Wolfpack did it, but nobody got in trouble that I know of. It never happened again."

"You don't remember Stott having a crush on Kathleen?" I asked.

"Not really. Kathleen was very popular. Half the school was in love with her, but she had a boyfriend." Carrie took back the yearbook and showed me a picture of the all-American Thomas MacIntyre. He was tall, blond with a square jaw and there was nothing shifty in those undoubtedly blue eyes.

"Did Thomas have a problem with Stott?"

Carrie laughed. "I don't think you understand. Everyone had a problem with Stott. Everyone."

Everyone. That was a lot of people with a problem. I had no doubt that if I could get ahold of the police report from the bar fire that Stott and his crew were the high school kids kicking up a fuss about not getting served. It was probably the same deal with the liquor store. So if Stott was causing problems from A to Z why would anyone protect him when it came to the murder?

I looked up at Carrie and asked, "Dwayne said your parents moved you to your grandparents after the murder? Why'd they do that?"

"You think they told me? No way," she said. "Mom and Dad were completely freaked out. Mom shaking and crying. Dad would barely speak and the next thing I knew I was hauled off to Union."

Dwayne set down his cup with a thunk on the wagon wheel coffee table. "I can't believe they didn't give you a reason. What did Grandma and Grandpa say?"

"Nothing. Just that it was for the best or something," I said. "Oh, I was pissed, but nobody cared what I thought about it."

We were all quiet for a moment. I don't know about anyone else, but I was thinking about all the things parents do for your own good. Sometimes it makes sense later on. Sometimes it doesn't. This time it totally did.

"When did you come back?" I asked.

"August. Right before school started. I missed most of the summer. Mom wouldn't allow me in town. I had to go to the pool in Union. Sometimes my friends came over, but mostly I hung out with my grandparents. It was the worst summer of my life." Carrie tilted her head to the side and said thoughtfully, "I really hated them for that. Mom and I hardly talked for years."

"They must've been terrified," said Amy. "Des and Mary didn't go off half-cocked."

Carrie nodded. "I can see that now. God, I haven't thought about this stuff for years."

The murder was in December. Stott left, but Carrie stayed in Union.

"Your parents weren't afraid of Stott," I said.

"Sounds like everyone else was," said Fats.

They all nodded and I looked down at the photo albums. "Stott left. He was gone and you never saw him again?"

"Not until he came back to town, what was it, about ten years ago," said Carrie.

"Did he say anything to you? Did he come in the restaurant?" Dwayne had puffed up. Brother was thinking of getting a shotgun.

"I saw him in the Piggly Wiggly a couple of times, but he didn't say anything to me. Hell, I didn't recognize him. Cheryl at checkout told me who he was. That guy did not age well. He looks like he's in his late eighties."

"Decades in prison will do that," said Fats. "Have you heard of any problems with him?"

"People weren't happy to have him back, but nothing happened," she said.

Lefty threw up his hands and said, "I'm confused. Did Stott kill the nun or not?"

I thought about it and in the end I went with my gut. "Not."

Fats made a fist. "He fits the profile. He's a murderer. He was here. What's not to like?"

"He didn't drive a truck," said Amy. "Is that it?"

I shook my head. "It doesn't help, but no. It's that your parents, who had intimate knowledge of the crime, didn't think he did it."

"Dad wouldn't know," said Dwayne. "He was a mailman."

"He was a medic during the war and he said the body had been abused. Your father wasn't some no-nothing schlub. He saw what I saw in the crime scene pictures. There was a truck. The body had been revisited."

"Ew," said Amy. "Revisited for what?"

Carrie patted her sister-in-law's knee. "I don't think we want to know."

"You don't," said Fats grimly.

"So you're saying that Desmond knew what? That it was a local and it wasn't this Stott character? How?" Lefty asked.

"I don't know, but Des and Mary believed strongly enough to make their daughter very mad at them."

Carrie agreed. "And it wasn't like them at all. We always talked about things before that. Why the rules were the rules. Things like that. It annoyed me, but I was a teenager. Everything annoyed me."

"You told me after Mom died that they fought about it," said Dwayne.

"They definitely did," said Carrie.

"*Our* parents were yelling?"

She rolled her eyes. "Not yelling yelling, but I could tell they were fighting. It was tense in the house after the murder. Don't you remember? Dad bought guns and made us go target shooting. Mom would check the locks five times before she'd go to bed and half the time Dad slept on the sofa. With a gun."

Dwayne's eyes went wide. "I don't remember Dad on the sofa."

"You were such a dufus," she said, affectionately. "But I love you."

"Carrie, did your mother want to move after the murder?" I asked.

Carrie sneered at her little brother. "I know Dwayne doesn't believe me, but I heard them fighting about it. Dad thought we could hold out and Mom wasn't convinced."

"Hold out?" Fats asked. "Like it was a siege."

I picked up the album that had most of 1965 in it. "They did hold out until August."

"What's in August?" Lefty asked. "Just the fair."

"I didn't come back for the fair," said Carrie. "I got to come back between that and the start of school."

I flipped through the pages of photos. Something happened in August 1966. I came to the part of the album that had the first photo of the year. A birthday party for a grandparent. There were lots of photos of mushrooms and scenery. Let me just say you've seen one mushroom in black and white, you've pretty much seen them all.

The rest of the group kept trying to figure out what happened to make Des and Mary relax and I took the opportunity to call Spidermonkey.

"I've got good news and bad news," I said.

"Same here," he said with a chuckle. "Pretty fascinating stuff though."

"I like fascinating. You first."

"Bertram Stott has a trust fund," said Spidermonkey.

My jaw dropped. Literally. Amy told me I was going to catch flies.

"I thought he didn't have any money."

Stott didn't have any money and neither did his parents or grand-parents. Solidly lower middle class was the best way to put it. But now Stott's fees at Shady Glen were being paid by a trust in his name. It had also paid for his house and a car. An allowance was dropped into his account like clockwork every month.

"Who set it up?" I asked.

"I can't tell, but Wells Fargo is the trustee. I'm working on breaking through their firewall, but it's a good one. It will take some time. Morty's better at banks than I am."

"When did the trust fund happen?"

Everyone looked at me and stopped talking.

"Ten years ago." Spidermonkey was smirking. Sometimes you can just tell.

"About the time Stott moved to St. Seb?" I asked.

"The very month."

"He's blackmailing someone."

"Looks like it. Must be his accomplice on the murder," said Spidermonkey.

"Is that all your news?" I asked.

It wasn't. Spidermonkey had found the layout of the asylum and confirmed that the most likely route to the bus stop was through a large parking lot. He took a look at the location of Bishop Fowler's office, too. The bus would've dropped Maggie just down the street. It was a straight shot to the office, so it was unlikely that Maggie was taken there. Also, Dr. Desarno had an office nearby where he saw most of his patients, making it unlikely that he was out at St. Vincent's the morning of the murder. Spidermonkey felt that cleared the elderly doctor. I'd already taken him off my suspect list, but it was good to know I was right.

"And my bad news is that Bishop Fowler wasn't a wealthy man when he died," said Spidermonkey.

"Figures. Why can't it be easy?"

"It's you."

"Swell and guess what? I have worse news. Stott didn't do it," I said.

I had to do some real convincing to get Spidermonkey off Stott once I'd conclusively placed him in St. Sebastian at the time of the murder. He was perfect. A real dirtbag, but I was fairly sure he didn't kill Maggie.

"Alright. Alright," he conceded. "I believe you, but he has to know who did do it."

"Sure and I wish I knew how Des and Mary ruled him out."

"Desmond Shipley had skills," said Spidermonkey.

"You sound like you knew him."

"I did a check like you asked. Airborne medic. That man came back from the war with a chest full of ribbons and medals. His photos from the campaigns he was in were published. He won a few awards for combat photography."

"He switched to tamer subjects after the war," I said.

"Mushrooms. He won a contest for that, too."

I looked down at the photos in front of me. Mushrooms. Hiking trails. All beautifully composed and a feeling started. A kind of déjà vu.

"Dwayne?" I asked. "Your father took photos during the war?"

"Yeah, he did. Who is that you're talking to?"

"A friend who's gifted at finding things out," I said. Then I told Spidermonkey I'd call him back.

Carrie rubbed her hands together. "Ooh, a hacker. The plot thickens."

"Do you have any of those photos from the war?" I asked.

Dwayne plucked another album off the shelf. It was beautiful. Dark blue leather covers with gold embossed military images, a ship, bomber, tanks, and aircraft. "Dad documented the whole war. He sold quite a few pictures, too. Some are in museums."

I opened the album and leafed through. It was hard not to go through each page and study it. Desmond's war, every bit of it, was there and it got pretty ugly. Bodies on the beach. Dead children in a Dutch house. There were also men together, smiling during the misery of Bastogne. It was simply an extraordinary album.

"Why would Dad's service matter?" Carrie asked.

I reluctantly handed the album back to Dwayne and turned the other album to the picture of Des and Mary mushroom hunting. "Because your father has a camera."

Everyone was blank, except Fats, who nodded. "Of course. My Uncle Moe is our family's shutterbug. He always has his camera. You never know when the perfect shot will appear."

Dwayne and Amy were confused. Carrie wasn't. She nodded and said, "They fought about that."

"What?" Dwayne asked.

"I was never totally sure, but I think Dad might've taken pictures at the crime scene."

By the time Carrie got done recounting her parents arguments about destroying something that was "sick", I was convinced Des had done what he'd done during the war. He documented and his wife wasn't thrilled. She didn't want "that" in the house in case the kids saw it. As a kid that did see some horrible things that her father had documented, Mary was right on the money. Once you see that, you can't unsee it.

But Des was more careful than Dad. Carrie remembered seeing him carry a hefty lockbox out of sight a few times right after the murder. She found it tucked away under shoeboxes in the back of her parents' closet. Since she was a nosy teen with an axe to grind, Carrie tried to pick the lock but didn't get inside.

"I can't believe you did that," said Amy.

"Are you? Really?" Carrie laughed. "I figured at the very least Dad had some dirty magazines in there. He'd grounded me again and I thought maybe those would give me some leverage."

"That's disgusting."

She shrugged. "Desperate times. Plus, I was curious about the murder. Everybody was. It was pretty hush hush."

"You wanted to see what had been done to that poor nun?"

"It's hard to believe, but I did," said Carrie. "It didn't seem real somehow. How could something like that happen right here in St. Seb?"

"It's like how people slow down to look at an accident," said Lefty. "They want a glimpse."

Amy wrinkled her nose and leaned into her husband. Dwayne had gotten quiet and was looking down at all the mushroom pictures. I watched him but decided to let him stew on whatever he was thinking.

"What happened to that lockbox?" I asked.

"I wish I knew," said Carrie. "I thought we'd find it after Dad died, but I looked and it wasn't there. Dwayne?"

Dwayne fiddled with the buttons on his grandpa sweater and didn't answer. Unless I missed my guess the stewing was about to boil over.

Amy took his hand. "Honey, what is it? Did you see those pictures?"

He shook his head. "No. I didn't know...I didn't have any idea that Dad would've done that. What color was that lockbox?"

"Did you throw that thing away?" Carrie asked. "I will kill you."

"Carrie!" exclaimed Dwayne.

Color flooded Carrie's cheeks. "Green. Kind of a military shade and it had a little padlock on it."

"I saw it."

"When?" Amy asked.

"1974 at Christmas."

We waited, but Dwayne was having a rough time. Sweat broke out on his temples and he had to take off a sweater.

"Lefty said that you think the nun might've been killed by a serial killer," he said finally.

"There's reason to believe that." I couldn't imagine where he was going. St. Seb didn't have murders. Maggie was the only one and she was only dumped there. "Is there a particular reason why you remember seeing that lockbox when you did?"

There was a very good reason and my fingers started itching to call Spidermonkey back. Dwayne came home from college at Christmas in 1974. When he pulled up in the driveway, his dad and a man were coming out of the front door. The man wasn't much older than Dwayne and wore a wide-collared suit with an ascot and had hair over his collar. Dwayne didn't recognize him and he was way too young and hip to be a friend of his father's.

Des handed the man a green lockbox and they shook hands. Dwayne heard the young man say, "Thank you, Mr. Shipley. This is really going to help. You won't regret it." Des said, "You're welcome" and they parted. Dwayne and the man passed each other on the walkway to the house and said hello.

When Dwayne asked who the man was, Des said it was just a reporter who wanted to talk about the war. Dwayne asked if he gave him some pictures and Des said he did.

"Oh, my God," said Carrie. "A reporter has the pictures."

"I feel sick," said Dwayne.

"Why?" I asked.

Amy squeezed Dwayne's hand. "Was it *that* reporter?"

Dwayne nodded and Amy put her hand over her mouth. Lefty, too, had lost his normally jolly expression and muttered, "Son of a bitch."

"What reporter?" Carrie asked.

"The one that disappeared."

Crap on a cracker.

CHAPTER TWENTY-SIX

S nowplows are slow and wide. Every turn we made, another snowplow. St. Sebastian was serious about clearing the roads. I guess that tournament really was important, but the snow kept coming down, so I didn't see it happening. Plus, it was freezing. Even blasting the heater couldn't combat the cold and Moe jumped into my lap and did a spin on Carrie's yearbook, trying to find the most comfortable spot, which happened to be pressing against my coffee-filled bladder. That was extra awesome when Fats drove up on side-walks full-tilt and bounced us around like popcorn kernels in a Whirley-Pop.

"Stop that. I'm going to pee myself," I said as I held onto Moe and the oh-shit handle above the door for dear life.

"You could've used the bathroom at Dwayne and Amy's," said Fats.

"I didn't have to go then."

"Well, you're out of luck now."

"Thanks, Mom," I said.

Fats smiled, her eyes crinkling behind her mirrored Wayfarers. "That was mom-like. I'm going to rock this parent thing."

"Not if you don't start eating."

She whipped off the sunglasses. "What do you mean?"

"You're growing a human. That takes food."

"I'm giving her food. I ate a croissant and Irene's casserole. That had to be a thousand calories."

"How many did you work off after?" I asked, tapping her Fitbit.

She grimaced and put the glasses back on. "Call Spidermonkey. That new body is news."

"Fine, but you need to go on a real pregnancy diet."

Fats yanked the wheel to the left and we passed a snowplow blind, scaring the crap out of me and poor Moe started shivering.

"I'll tell Tiny." It just slipped out and Fats slammed on the brakes. Thank goodness for seatbelts or I would've cracked my head open. Moe would've been a curly-tailed pancake.

"Tell him what?"

"That you're not taking care of yourself," I said, rubbing the painful stripe left against my chest.

"I am."

"Fats, you're not Pink the Impaler now. You're Mom. It's a totally different gig."

"I don't want it to be," she said after a moment.

"Bummer," I said. "Can we go? It's freezing."

"This baby's going to change my life," said Fats.

That was somewhere between a question and a statement, so I let it lie, and instead said, "We don't know that we have another body."

She snorted and hit the gas, dodging into traffic, if you could really call it that. We were going twelve miles an hour and there were exactly three cars on the road. "Where do you think that guy went? The Bahamas?"

"I don't need any more bodies."

"Bummer."

"Fine," I said. "I'll call."

Spidermonkey didn't answer, but Loretta did, sounding just as harassed as before if not more.

"Do you have any information on the flu vaccine?" she asked.

"Er...like what?"

"Did the flu shot cause an outbreak a couple of years ago?" Loretta asked.

I sighed. We'd heard all about this so-called theory at the time. One woman with the flu told me all about it in the ER, angrily blaming the shot for how ill she was. Had she actually gotten the flu shot, you ask? No, but it was still somebody's fault. "The CDC never said that happened."

"Thank you. I just...I'm losing my mind. I don't care if there is hurricane force winds, I have got to get out of here."

"Don't do that," I said. "It can't last forever."

"Minutes are like hours in conspiracy-theory hell. My grandson just accused me of eating a peanut butter cup," said Loretta.

"Did you?"

"Yes, I did and I'll do it again. He's not allergic to anything. Nothing. Four years old and calling me out. I'll find myself a hickory switch and I will beat that little—"

"I think you've gone to the bad place, Loretta," I said. "Can we talk murder?"

"You'd think that would be worse, but it's not. What have you got?"

"Two things and they're big."

"How big?"

"A new murder." I told Loretta about the strong possibility that Des documented the scene and then gave the pictures to a reporter named Kenneth Young in 1974. Young was a grad student studying journalism at Mizzou. During the summer before he disappeared he worked at the Sentinel with Barney Scheer as an intern. He was in St. Seb during the 1974 Christmas break for a few days and was last seen in town at a gas station.

Dwayne, Amy, and Lefty remembered the disappearance, but it wasn't a big story at the time. Young was from Iowa and it was assumed something happened on his drive home for Christmas, most likely an accident. Dwayne knew Young was the man he'd seen talking to his father, but only because the new police chief, Melanie Gates, showed up to interview Des, and Dwayne was fascinated by a female police chief, not an everyday occurrence in the seventies. He knew his parents were upset by the disappearance, but he thought they were overreacting. His father's revolver had come back out and Mary was checking the doors again. By the time Dwayne came back for Easter, he'd forgotten all about it.

"So what got him thinking about it?" Loretta asked.

"Tank Tancredi covered the disappearance again after I found Janet Lee Fine's body and bike in the lake bed. Two disappearances linked to St. Sebastian is unusual and there isn't a whole lot to report around here. Tank's story got people talking, but nothing came of it," I said. "What's Spidermonkey doing?"

"Hold on." Loretta had a conversation with her husband and came back with some news. "He's working on identifying some donors from Maggie's notebook. That nun you have with you is a sweetheart. I hope this isn't too hard on her."

"It probably is, but there's nothing I can do about that now," I said. "Anything on that yet?"

"He says he's got a back door. Whatever that means. But we do have something for you on that reporter," said Loretta.

"Young? Already?"

"No, the other one. Barney Scheer."

Loretta's news wasn't exactly helpful, but it was illuminating. Barney, like Woody and Des, served in the war, signing up immediately after Pearl Harbor. He was a Marine in the Pacific, serving with Chief Woody Lucas in the same platoon. They were drinking buddies after the war, but Barney seemed to have gotten it together after his kids were born. Unlike Woody and Des, the two veterans stayed close and Barney gave the eulogy at Woody's funeral.

"Woody must've asked his old friend to back off and he did," I said.

"Not a very good reporter," said Loretta. "But a loyal friend, I suppose."

That didn't rub me the right way. Des and Woody were super close, but Maggie's murder killed their connection. Why didn't it kill Barney and Woody's? Did being comrades in arms mean so much that Barney would ignore his profession and his conscience to help Woody? Why would Woody need help at all?

"We have to rule out Woody Lucas," I said. "It seems he went through a lot of trouble to keep Maggie's murder quiet."

"We're already looking," said Loretta. "He didn't own a green truck. We know that already."

"That's good, but something's definitely going on."

Fats took a hard turn into the Sentinel parking lot and we slid ten feet nearly hitting a telephone pole.

"I'm at the Sentinel," I said. "I'll see what I can dig up."

"Wait a minute," said Loretta. "Now this is going to help."

I smiled. "I'm all ears."

Fats parked and took Moe from me, raising an eyebrow. "Hurry up. She's a frozen pup."

Loretta's information was good. Spidermonkey had outsourced to an up-and-comer in the hacking world and the kid was a whiz at gathering deleted texts. Once he heard cops were hiding something, he was all up in it and came back with the current chief, Will Gates, being a big, fat liar.

There was flooding periodically. That got confirmed. But the new guy, like me, thought it was odd that the cops wouldn't have taken steps to protect their files and evidence. It turned out, in the late eighties, shelving had been purchased after a record flood and it was noted that it was to keep records off the floor in case of the river coming over its banks again, which it did two more times.

"So they were flooded and records were lost?" I asked.

"Our guy doesn't think so. That flood was minor compared with the ones that came after. The water made it to the police station, but the water was only a couple of inches deep. The shelving they bought was to keep everything up a minimum of two feet, so those other floods shouldn't have touched the files and evidence."

I tried to remember what the flood stories I'd read had said about depth, but I couldn't. "There was the burst pipes. That can ruin everything."

"It could, but he doesn't think it did," said Loretta.

Fats got out and went around the truck to pull me out into the icy air and pushed me toward the Sentinel's door. I dropped the yearbook and it went fluttering away in the wind. Fats pounced on it before it slid into some slush created by an excess of salt and scowled at me as I tried to hear Loretta over the wind and crunching of the snow.

Our new guy decided the best way to know what the cops were up to was to see what they told their spouses and, it turned out, those burst pipes picked a great day to do their thing. Deputy Dallas Mosbach was on duty when it happened and that guy was pretty flipping dedicated to duty. A little too much, in my opinion. His wife went into labor with their first child and, instead of going to the hospital post haste, Dallas stayed in the basement of the police station to "save the files". That's right. Files over labor. His wife's sister had to take her to the hospital when the contractions got five minutes apart and he wasn't there for another two hours until his wife started threatening him saying, "Nobody cares about those old ass cases. If you don't get over here, I'll divorce you and take the Camaro."

Old ass cases.

I don't know if it was the threat to the Camaro or what, but he left saying, "The guys will get the rest" as if his wife cared at that point.

We stumbled into the reception area of the Sentinel and Tank sprang to his feet from behind the desk. "Thank God. I was about to call Will. I thought you had an accident."

"I'm about to. Bathroom?" I ran to the bathroom and told Loretta I'd call back when I had something.

When I came out, the whole area smelled delicious and Fats was eating a huge, drippy sandwich. Her Fitbit was on the desk and Moe was next to it with a bowl of meat all to herself.

"That smells amazing," I said as I began to drool.

"My wife's Italian beef," said Tank. "It cannot be beat. Want some?"

"Do you really have to ask?"

He laughed and served me up a sandwich. I had to tell Aaron about this recipe. He would love it and then pump it up to the stratosphere.

Tank waited patiently until we got half our sandwiches down before sliding a copy of his story across the desk. Actually, it was a series on missing persons in Missouri and how investigations had changed over time. Kenneth Young's case was used as an example and it was a sad one.

What Dwayne and Amy had told me was true. Young was in town doing something at the Sentinel that wasn't specified, other than research. I think we knew what that was. Maggie's murder. He said goodbye to Barney Scheer, gassed up his car, and was never seen again.

When he didn't turn up at his parent's house in Iowa, they reported him missing, but it took a while for the investigation to even start. The police said he ran off with a girl or was partying. They weren't concerned, but when he missed both Christmas and New Year's, they got busy. It was another week before enquiries were made in St. Seb. A few people were interviewed, but Barney didn't report any particulars on the interviews. There was no mention of Desmond or his pictures, and Maggie's murder certainly wasn't brought up.

"Do you have the original stories?" I asked.

"On your favorite," said Tank.

I groaned. "Microfiche?"

He made a shooting motion at me. "Do you want to go down and look at them?"

Want is putting it strong.

"I guess I better."

Tank picked up Carrie's yearbook. "Why do you have this?"

"I thought I might take a look later and see if there are any other pictures of Stott that might help us know who he was friends with," I said.

"We can do that right now." Tank looked at the index in the back. "Nope. Bertram Stott. One page."

"He might be somewhere in the background."

"Grasping at straws, aren't we?" Fats asked.

"You never know," I said.

Tank set the yearbook down. "Bedtime reading for you."

"It's not like I'll be sleeping."

"Miss Elizabeth having fun with you?" Tank asked.

I wrinkled my nose. "You have no idea."

Fats picked a stray piece of beef off her paper plate and said, "Mercy has all the luck."

"If that's luck, it's all bad," I said.

Fats and Tank disputed my definition of luck, since I'd gotten Maggie's financial insights out of it, but I wasn't persuaded. Those eyeballs didn't give me anything but an all-over exhausted ache.

Tank got me some Tylenol and we finished our sandwiches, got mugs of tea, and some brownies before heading down into the basement of the Sentinel. In hindsight, that was a really bad idea.

Microfiche, film, or whatever is bad enough when you've slept. It's brutal when you haven't. I got nauseated right off and Tank had to take over, even though he was practically cross-eyed from looking it at half the night.

It took nearly an hour to find the little box with the appropriate year in it and another fifteen minutes to find Barney Scheer's rudimentary articles about his missing intern.

Tank was not happy. Especially after I told him what Spidermonkey and his guy had found out about the flooding and Chief Lucas.

"Will lied," he said.

"How surprised are you?" I asked.

"My brother-in-law is a good cop and Woody Lucas was supposed to be, too."

Fats did a series of stretches and said, "Things have changed."

"I don't know how I'm going to tell Mallory," he said.

"No reason to tell her anything yet," I said.

"It's going to come out," said Tank. "We're talking conspiracy here and it's my wife's family. I almost wish you'd never come to town."

"I get that all the time."

"I bet," he said. "Here we go."

Tank read the articles about Young's disappearance and it wasn't good. He didn't say anything, but it showed in the set of his thin shoulders and the way he kept reading the words over and over again. Fats and I exchanged a look, not daring to interrupt the newsman's concentration. Whatever he was seeing was probably not something that we would pick up.

Instead, we waited, making a nest for Moe in Fats' coat and, I'm not ashamed to say, looking on Amazon for a Santa costume for her to wear at Christmas. Okay. I'm a little ashamed. Dogs should not be made to dress up for the amusement of humans, but she was such a weirdo, it was going to be adorable.

"We should buy one for Skanky," said Fats.

"He'll probably just eat the fur and throw up all over," I said.

"There's something wrong with your cat."

"You'll get no argument here."

We both jumped when Tank's ginormous printer beast fired up and attempted to deafen us.

"I'll print you some copies," said Tank, not looking at us.

"Okay. Thanks," I said.

Eventually, the behemoth finally spit out copies of the stories Tank had been pouring over. He handed them to us and leaned on the desk with crossed arms, watching. I felt like I did when I thought I was going to fail the AP Physics exam spectacularly and everyone was going to know. I did and they did. Tank looked like my teacher when he asked what I got. Prematurely disappointed.

I read the article twice, looking for one of those ah-ha moment things and not finding it. The articles were disinterested at best. It was possible that Barney really didn't like Kenneth Young. Just by reading the articles you never would've known that he knew the kid personally. It was that impersonal. I know. I know. The news isn't supposed to be biased, but this writing was more like a traffic report. I expected something like a plea for help. Barney Scheer was talking about a missing twenty-three year old that had worked all summer in the very basement we were in and he couldn't have been less intense.

"Am I missing something?" Fats asked. "So he's a crappy reporter, so what?"

"He's not a crappy reporter," said Tank. "The articles about Maggie's murder before the switch were insightful and caring. You can hear the compassion for her right in there with the facts. He did that without saying how he felt in so many words. Barney was good."

"Well, there's not much here," I said. "Barney sure wasn't on the hunt to find out what happened to that kid."

"Maybe he already knew," said Fats.

"If he figured out what Young was working on, then it's not a stretch," said Tank.

"But Barney Scheer didn't kill him, if any of these basic facts are right," I said.

"No?"

"No. Barney names himself as the last person, other than the guy that pumped his gas, to talk to Young before he left town and he says that two more members of the staff were here at the time. That puts Barney right in the mix."

"He knew when Young left," said Fats. "Following isn't hard."

"I'm sure the staff members alibied him."

Fats glanced at the paper and read, "Kenneth Young left the Sentinel at approximately twelve-thirty. A member of the staff, Ralph Sullentrop, walked him out and saw him get in his 1971 VW Beetle and drive away."

1971 Beetle.

"He still could've done it or tipped someone off," said Tank.

1971 Beetle.

"Sure, but I'm saying Barney felt secure in his own position, but that doesn't mean he didn't have a suspicion about what happened to his intern. These articles show feeling, just not the ones we'd expect," I said. "Let's see how Young did as an intern. Can you see if he has any articles?"

Tank went back to the summer, the months whizzing by and then jolting to a stop on May. He zipped around looking for Young's name and I had to step away. The movement got to me in a huge way and I paid for it. Fats made me stretch and then do some lunges. She said it was good for me, but she didn't do any lunges. Then I had to do some squats by myself, but I drew the line at up-downs. Not going to happen.

I was sensing a theme with me working out and Fats not. The next six months was going to be rough, but the rhythm of the workout freed my mind to roll around on the case. I had to go through that yearbook page by page. If it didn't reveal any connections to Stott, I'd start googling classmates. Carrie was a sophomore in 1965, but she said her friends didn't really hang out with seniors. She would make some calls for me. Maybe that would help.

I wanted to concentrate on Stott, but no matter where I wanted my mind to go, it kept coming back to that 1971 Bug and I didn't know why it sounded so familiar. It couldn't possibly have anything to do with Maggie, but still, there it was, popping up into the forefront. The connection was right on the tip of my brain. I could almost reach it. Almost.

"He liked him," said Tank.

"Huh?" I asked.

"Young. Barney Scheer liked him."

Fats and I went over and looked at the screen. Tank had an article about the fair up. Young had done a three-part article on judging irregularities during the livestock showing. I know that doesn't sound exciting and it isn't. I read the articles. Young alleged bias, bribes, and downright cheating with the scales. Tank assured us that this was a big deal in the farming community. Having a prizewinning steer could give a farmer a leg up with their breeding program and the extra income could make the farm profitable in a bad year.

"So he trusted Young to investigate this," said Fats. "I wonder why. He was only in college."

Tank sat back. "Kenneth Young was gifted. His prose is wonderful and he doesn't embellish. He's just good. Barney was happy to have him here. More than happy."

"You got all that from an article on dirty cattle judges?" I asked.

"That and this." Tank zipped the pages back to June and an article on Kenneth Young appeared. It included a photo of Young, smiling and leaning back on his Beetle. I couldn't stop looking at that face, young, hopeful, handsome. Gone. And his car. It felt like déjà vu, but that was just stupid. I'd seen a thousand Beetles. More even. They weren't exactly unique. But 1971. I couldn't get it out of my head.

"He wrote an article on his intern? Don't interns usually get kicked around and ordered to shut up and make coffee?" I asked.

Tank smiled. "I did. On my first internship, the biggest story I got to write was about people not picking up their dog's poop. Young got a half-page spread with a picture. He was recommended by the head of the journalism school and several professors."

"They thought he was going places," said Fats. "No offense, but was the Sentinel a hot gig for Young?"

"Sure," said Tank. "If you want to work and get a lot of bylines. The big papers will give you scut work. Barney let Young have free rein."

"That's probably how he found out about Maggie's murder," I said.

"Young was clearly cut out for investigative journalism. He would've been looking for a good story."

"A murdered nun definitely fits the bill," said Fats.

"Look at this story." Tank zipped over to a human-interest story on veterans and combat stress. "Young could write anything. He had real heart."

"And not bad looking," said Fats, glancing at me. "That probably opens doors."

"It closes them, too," I said. "But he looked to be in the sweet spot of not too good looking."

Tank scratched his chin. "A guy like that, he would've been popular with the ladies."

"Maybe we can find someone he dated," I said.

"I imagine that'd be a wide field. Take it from me, a guy like that could've had any girl he wanted."

"Not any girl," said Fats. "I wouldn't have been interested."

Tank and I looked at her.

"Seriously?" I asked. "What's wrong with Kenneth Young? You went out with Lorenzo Fibonacci. He might be gorgeous, but what a moron."

"I like a man who knows how to take care of business."

Tank and I frowned simultaneously.

"How on Earth can you tell if that kid couldn't take care of business? Is it the eyebrows?" Tank asked. "My daughter's big on eyebrow maintenance. God knows why."

"It's the car," said Fats. "A man that won't maintain his vehicle, won't maintain himself. It's a deal breaker."

"What's wrong with his Beetle?" I asked.

"It's damaged and has rust."

"Do you have some sort of rust detection sensor? That photo's in black and white. And it's hella grainy."

Tank held up his hand. "She's right. I think I saw that." He went back to the photo and I got the weirdest feeling. Déjà vu, but stronger.

"Where?" I said with a strangled voice.

Tank glanced at me, frowning, but then zoomed in on the rear wheel and bumper. Sure enough, it was damaged. The panel over the wheel had some discoloration and the bumper hung down too far. The feeling got stronger.

"Mercy?" Tank asked. "Are you okay?"

"That's a 1971 Beetle," I said.

"Yeah."

"What color would you say it is?"

Tank and Fats looked at the screen for a second and Tank said, "White, I guess."

I looked up at Fats, the human rust sensor, and she shook her head. "It's beige."

Crap on a cracker.

"That's a 1971 beige Beetle with rear end damage."

"Yes," said Tank and Fats, in unison.

"I think I know where that car is."

Tank looked back at the screen. "That car? You couldn't possibly. It's been missing since '74. You weren't even born."

I looked at Fats and watched her put it together. She took a deep breath and said, "It could be a coincidence. Millions of Beetles were sold that year. Beige was a popular color."

"But only one ended up where Maggie's medal was found," I said.

"Are you talking about that serial killer graveyard?" Tank asked. "They found a car?"

"Not just a car," said Fats. "A 1971 beige Beetle."

"With rear end damage," I said. "Chuck showed me a picture. That damage was the only thing they had to go on. The VIN was pried off and the car was clean, not so much as a plastic straw was found inside."

Tank ran his fingers through his long hair. "So they're looking for murder victims who had that car."

"That could take a while," said Fats. "Or forever, depending on whether that damage was on the original police report."

"It still might not be the car," said Tank.

Moe jumped up out of her nest and started barking.

"Even the dog knows we're on to something," I said.

"This is going to kill Mallory. Her grandfather, mother, and now her brother let a serial killer skate?" He put his head in his heads. "Nightmare."

Moe went nuts, spinning in a circle and yipping.

"Does she need to go out?" I asked, even though Moe was a calm dog when it came to it. I'd only seen her go to the door and stare at it. No barking at all.

"Maybe." Fats grabbed her coat. "I'll take her and you call the rookies."

I drew a blank. The rookies?

"You're done, Mercy," said Fats. "They wanted you to find something to reopen Maggie's case, this is it."

"I can't just leave it," I said. "I promised Myrtle."

She put on her coat and popped out a toothpick. "And Morty's in the hospital. Throw the guy a bone. Get yourself off the No Fly List and his blood pressure goes down."

It was selfish of me, but I didn't want to do it. This was my case now. Mine. I wanted to solve it for my godmothers, for Maggie, for Kenneth Young, and Father Dominic. It wasn't just about getting to Greece anymore.

I started to tell her that, but Moe went batshit crazy and Fats said over the clamor, "Do it, Mercy. You've got an uncle in the hospital and a wedding to plan."

Not the wedding.

"Fine," I said, pulling out my phone. "I'll give it to the rookies."

Fats nodded at us and held out her arms to Moe, who normally would've jumped in them to go outside. But that time she ran around Fats and went up five stairs. Her brindle fur rose up to hackles and she bared her pointy little teeth.

Fats snapped her fingers. "No."

Moe growled in response and her hackles got pointier.

"Is she normally like that?" Tank asked.

"No." Fats went into dog training mode that had worked so well before, but Moe charged her, snapping at her hand as Fats reached for her.

I jolted to my feet. "Something's wrong."

"No kidding," said Fats. "She's lost her mind."

Moe darted around her owner and leapt at her ankle, snagging the fabric of Fat's legging and yanking it back.

"What the hell are you doing?" Fats yelled, stumbling backward.

"She doesn't want you to go upstairs," I said. "Tank, call the chief."

"Because the dog—"

"Do it." I pulled out my Mauser and took off the safety.

Fats pointed at Moe and said, "Stop."

Moe sat and went silent. Fats got her Python out of her backpack and crept toward the stairs. Moe growled. She stopped and an explosion ripped through the floor above us, bringing down the ceiling and turning the world black.

CHAPTER TWENTY-SEVEN

I could smell the flames, but I couldn't see them. The lights were out and the only illumination was from the exit sign next to the collapsed stairs. I dug my way out from under the acoustic ceiling tiles and hit my head on something. Fire alarms were going off and it sounded like there were a hundred in that basement alone. Then the sprinkler system triggered and a heavy spray hit my face.

"Fats! Tank!"

Fats grabbed me from behind and hauled me to my feet. She had Moe under one arm and a face covered in blood. I tried to see where she'd been injured, but she pushed me away. "Fire exit!"

"Where?" I yelled.

She shoved a trembling Moe into my arms and pointed at an egress window beyond the tall shelving that had fallen over like dominos. Its exit sign was blinking, but I wasn't leaving. Tank was still in there under the debris and I didn't have my Mauser. Talk about a sitting duck.

"We have to find Tank!"

"Go now."

"You think this is an accident?" I yelled. "He's out there."

"I lost my Python! Do you have your Mauser?" Fats yelled.

I shook my head and set Moe on a tile. "Tank has to be near the desk."

We squinted in the dim light and saw a pile against the wall. The destruction was worse over there. Not just the tiles had come down. Beams, insulation and I was pretty sure a bookcase from upstairs was there.

"Look for your Mauser!" Fats yelled. "I'll find him."

"I'm the nurse!"

"You gonna lift those beams?"

She had a point and I got down looking for my weapon. "Find the gun, Moe! Find it."

I'll be damned if she didn't. Moe alerted on a pile of tiles next to the collapsed stairs and I found my Mauser underneath. "Good dog!"

I kissed her little noggin and climbed over to Fats, narrowly missing being hit by a beam she tossed aside like a Lincoln Log.

"I got him!"

Tank lay face down, not moving, and there was blood. I couldn't tell how much, but I could smell it and then I could feel it, wet, sticky, and warm. That red light wasn't helpful in finding the source.

"Should we move him?" Fats asked.

"Let's roll him."

I assessed his neck and back and didn't find anything obvious. I had to check his airway so there was nothing for it but to go ahead and turn him over. I supported his head and neck and Fats moved his body. We got him on his back and I checked his vitals. Erratic. He had a head injury, where I thought most of the blood was coming from, a broken collarbone, and a hand that looked like someone dropped a safe on it. It wasn't bleeding like the head injury, so I didn't do a tourniquet.

"We have to get him out of here!" I yelled.

There wasn't a lot of smoke, but I was coughing and so was Fats.

"Do you hear that?" she asked.

"What?"

"Sirens!"

"Thank God!"

Fats gave Moe a pat and said, "Stay with him. I'll go out."

"Be careful!" I gave her my Mauser and it disappeared in her big hand.

She nodded and climbed over the shelving with the balance of a Flying Wallenda before ripping the egress window off. I'm not kidding. Fats ripped it off the wall and tossed it aside. Then she waved and somehow stuffed herself through. That window was not chosen with Fats Licata in mind.

Tank groaned and his eyes fluttered.

I bent over him. "Stay still. We'll have you out of here in a minute."

"What..." he trailed off and lost consciousness again. Not a good sign.

The sprinklers kept going and the temperature dropped precariously. I was soaked to the skin and started shaking violently. The fire alarm cut out suddenly and I could hear the sirens wailing close by. People were yelling and I yelled back.

And that's it. The rest is a blur.

Chief Gates was pissed. The kind of pissed that a father might get after he has to pick up his daughter at his own police station at two in the morning after she snuck out to go joyriding with a neighbor's nephew's cousin who's eight years older and might've stolen a BMW.

I regret nothing. Yates Digby was hot in a Leo DiCaprio in *The Wolf of Wall Street* kind of way. Funnily enough, he is now serving five to ten for insider trading and don't think I haven't heard about that three and a half million times.

I do regret being yelled at in front of Chuck, who happened to be doing an overnight ridealong with some of my dad's friends and witnessed the bellowing of "You've shamed the family, Mercy!"

Dad didn't yet realize that I had no shame. None. Zero. That really helps when you're standing at a crime scene wearing bubblegum pink sweats with elastic at the cuffs in extra-extra large. My transformation to actual marshmallow Peep was complete.

So when I turned up at the smoking crime scene and Chief Gates bellowed, very dad-like, "You should be ashamed of yourself. You wreck people's lives and turn everything to shit," I yawned. I did not apologize for getting firebombed. I wasn't taking that. He could bite me.

Chief Gates kept yelling in a vain attempt to cow me and I considered taking my Mauser out of the pink puffer jacket I'd been forced to buy at the hospital gift shop and pegging him in his big booze-soaked butt. He wasn't in the ICU with a head injury like Tank or getting sixteen stitches without a painkiller because you're pregnant like Fats or dressed like an idiot with a broken nose and a refractured arm like me.

Nothing had happened to Chief William Gates, but it was about to.

"I want you out of my town today. Now. I don't care if Highway 44 is shutdown, you can get the fuck on it!"

I turned slowly to him and said, "This is your fault and I figure you've got until 44 clears before the FBI is on you like white on rice."

He stopped mid-obscenity and made a gagging sound. Stratton came running over and got in my face. "How dare you! How dare you! Tank is—"

"Your fault," I said, walking past her to the Sentinel's door. Wisps of smoke rose like thin twisting branches up into the gently falling snow.

The crime scene laid out pretty easy. Someone opened the unlocked door and winged a couple of explosive devices down the hall. Lucky for us, the guy must've thought we were in Tank's office, because that's where he aimed, way down the hall and away from where we were in the basement. One device went straight through an open door into the loading dock where it destroyed a delivery truck and the other one hit the wall. That end of the St. Sebastian Sentinel was a wreck. The other half wasn't so bad. The reception desk, books, and coffee machine were intact, just blown over, and the fire had never reached them.

Tank's upgrades after the arson ten years ago had done their jobs very well. He'd put in fire retardant materials wherever he could and it showed. The fire didn't spread and was quickly put out by the sprinkler system. No one else was in the building at the time and it could've been a lot worse.

Chief Gates continued to yell behind me and Stratton came up to stick the crime scene tape across the door. "You need a psych evaluation, if you seriously think this is our fault. You brought this to town."

"It was already here," I said. "Unless I miss my guess, it's been here since 1965 and that's on you. The law enforcement in this town needs a serious second look and it is going to get one."

"I don't know what you're talking about."

"You lied to me," I said, pointing at the charred loading dock door. "And here we are."

"I never lied. Will doesn't lie." Stratton had nothing in her eyes but fury and a good amount of self-righteousness.

I snorted and rolled my eyes. "You don't have the files. The files from 1965 and my great grandparents plane crash were destroyed. Tough luck for you, Mercy Watts."

"They were destroyed." Stratton turned to go to the chief who was yelling at everyone. The fire chief and Lefty were trying to calm him down, but that guy was tanked. There would be no calming down.

I grabbed Stratton. "You want to rethink that stance."

"It's the truth."

"It's a lie," I said. "What did you think I would do? Throw up my hands and go away?"

"There's nothing to do. That case is closed."

"There was a good reason to think the suspect didn't do it and I told you that. So you lied and I had to do it the hard way. Look around Stratton. This is the hard way. If you'd given up the files when I asked for them or even told me they were there, I'd have had a head start. We wouldn't be here, looking at this."

"You didn't have the right to look at those files. You're not family."

"But I know the family. They would've given me access. They're talking to a lawyer right now, so don't get any bright ideas about torching them."

"I'm telling you those files are gone. Destroyed."

"And I have evidence that Deputy Mosbach was moving those files to safety on the day of the burst pipes and he wasn't the only one doing it. The Mullanphy family is using that evidence right now to get a court order to give me those files."

Stratton stuttered and her eyes darted around, looking for an out.

"I'm not trying to bring you and your boyfriend down. I want to solve this case."

"He's not my boyfriend," she said hastily.

"For God's sake, Stratton. I know he is and I know he's drunk on duty right now."

"Don't be—"

I put my hand up. "Enough. Wake up and smell the vodka, Stratton. Will has a problem and it's the same one his grandpa had. You're not helping him and you're sure as hell not helping me."

"We think it was probably kids. They're off school and have time on their hands."

I stared at her. "You think kids with nothing better to do tried to murder three people to liven up their day up?"

"Maybe they thought the building was empty."

I pointedly looked at the two vehicles parked next to us. "Oh, yeah? You think that?"

She turned and looked at her boyfriend slip and go down on his butt. Two deputies rushed over to hoist him to his feet and the fire chief slapped his forehead. "I don't know."

"I do. I understand that Sister Maggie's murder seems like it's too long ago to matter, but it matters. This is the third time Tank's been hit and this time they meant business."

"Third time? Those other two times—"

"Don't say kids, I swear to God," I said.

She put her hands on her hips and I could tell I was finally making some headway. "Fifty years is a long time, no matter what you say. Whoever did it is probably dead and buried."

"Possibly, but it didn't die with him, even if he is."

"But why do this? Killing you would just put a spotlight on why you were here. It's so impulsive. And I know you say not kids, but that sounds like an immature person to me."

"I'll give you that, but they also wanted to destroy everything we had," I said.

"What did you have?" asked Stratton.

I gave her a quick rundown and she took notes. I like notes. Notes were a good sign.

"You have proof that Bertram Stott was here at the time of the murder? I can't believe it. We looked when he showed up. People were concerned."

"Naturally," I said. "We looked, too, and nothing said he was here. I still don't know why he was. I need to know who his friends were. Carrie Norton is making some calls for me."

"There's usually stuff like that in the yearbooks," said Stratton. "Where is it?"

I looked back through the door. "In there. I think we left it on the desk."

Stratton asked the harried fire chief if we could go in. He said no and she said, "Screw it."

In we went, not too far, just to the desk. Deputy Mosbach joined us and we went through every scrap of paper in the reception area, but I knew five minutes in.

"He took it," I said.

"The bomber?" Mosbach asked. "Why? There are other yearbooks. He can't destroy them all."

"If you know where one is, I'm all ears," I said.

Mosbach grinned. "The high school had the whole set when I went there."

"Where were they?"

"Some were in the office.

"Where are the rest of the yearbooks?" I asked. "The ones not in the office?"

"They were in a storage room in the basement with the old files. We used to look through them. Eighties hair was freakin' crazy," said Mosbach.

"I take offense to that," said Stratton. "My boyfriend's mullet was awesome."

"I seriously doubt that," I said. "Can we get in the school?'

Stratton shook her head. "Sorry. Closed for the weather today."

"But the Turkey Shoot's tonight." Mosbach checked his phone. "Teams start arriving in a couple of hours."

"They're still having the tournament?' I asked.

"Basketball is big here. We've been our division champs for five years running. It would take a whole lot more than snow to stop the Turkey Shoot." Stratton flipped through her notes. "Dallas, I want you to go over to Shady Glen and see what Bertram Stott has been up to today."

Mosbach shifted from foot to foot. "Why? What for?"

She told him why and Dallas got worried. "What about the chief? He's not a fan of Miss Watts."

We looked over at Lefty, who had the chief in the back of a squad car and was pouring coffee down his throat.

"Let me worry about him," said Stratton. "You make sure Stott hasn't been out today and find out if he's had any visitors. If he'll agree to a search, search his room."

Mosbach made a face. "He's not gonna let me do that. He's an ex-con."

"You never know."

He turned to go and I said, "Hold on."

"Yeah?"

"Tell him we found his medal," I said. "Watch what he does."

"Like a military medal?" Mosbach asked.

"A St. Brigid. The FBI found it at that mass grave site in Kansas between two victims of a serial killer."

Mosbach went pale for a moment, but then he hitched up his pants and headed out muttering, "It's never boring in St. Seb."

"It seems like one of us should be questioning Stott," mused Stratton.

I shrugged. "I doubt it matters. That guy isn't going slip up for you or me or anyone, unless he wants to, but it will give Mosbach a little experience."

"Serial killers make mistakes. We've figured out how to talk to them. I've read the profiles."

"All that data is based on the ones we've caught," I said.

"That doesn't make me feel better," she said.

"Oh, I know. Believe me."

The fire chief came walking up with a couple of his guys. His craggy face had irritation in its many lines and folds.

"What's up, Bruce?" Stratton asked.

"I just got off the horn. The FBI is coming down and they're bringing an arson and bomb squad with them," said Bruce. "I guess we can't handle it."

Stratton turned to me. "You weren't lying."

"Nope."

Bruce eyed me. "Lying about what?"

"FBI coming," said Stratton. "Shit. I figured you were full of crap."

I smiled and it hurt my nose. "Sometimes, but not today."

"Isn't your father persona non-grata with the FBI?" Bruce asked. "Will's been going off about you and him."

"My dad is," I said. "I'm not."

"You were sent here by the FBI? But you're not an agent. You're not a...I don't even know what you are," said Stratton.

You and me both.

"I have an unofficial relationship with the FBI," I said. "They gave me a tip and here I am."

"I wish you would've said that in the beginning."

"Would it have made a difference?"

Stratton admitted it wouldn't have. I'd screwed over the chief by finding Janet Lee Fine's body. My leeway was zero.

Another firefighter cleared his throat, garnering our attention, and Bruce snapped into focus. "Oh, right. We think we know what the bombs were. We might be volunteers, but a few of us have been around."

They had been around. In fact, they'd been around far away in Vietnam, Iraq and Afghanistan. Two of the volunteers were demolition troops and they recognized the blast patterns. They thought our guys tossed a couple of grenades in the Sentinel.

"I don't know if that's better or worse," said Stratton.

"At least he didn't make them," said Bruce. "He's not at home cooking up more fire power."

"And he's not an expert. Anybody can pull a pin," I said.

"Where'd he get them?" Stratton asked.

Bruce shrugged. "Black market. I've got a buddy who brought back a couple from 'Nam as souvenirs."

"Why would anyone do that? Is he crazy?"

"More importantly, is he in town?" I asked.

"No," said Bruce. "New Hampshire. I'm just saying people can get them."

"That's just great," said Stratton. "This guy could have a suitcase full of grenades and here we are, waiting for the FBI."

"They'll get here when they get here. Arson team has to fly in from D.C. and Lambert's having an ice issue."

Stratton groaned and looked at me. "Well?"

"What?" I asked.

"You called the FBI. What did they say?"

"Nothing useful. They're coming when they can. 44's a wreck and they can't take a helicopter. Poor visibility."

I'd called the rookies from the hospital right after I called my dad, Chuck, and Spidermonkey. My people were freaked. The rookies were not and I wasn't in the mood for high-fives. My X-rays confirmed that I'd gotten a shiny new hairline fracture in my bad arm, so I was just about as pissed as I could be, but the rookies couldn't have been happier. Were they helpful? No. Were they thinking about their future promotions? Yes. The most I got was that they'd take me off the No Fly List and some sage advice not to shoot anyone or get shot. Darn. I was totally planning on getting shot.

"I don't know what to do," said Stratton. "I've done all the training, but we've never had a murder much less a Unibomber."

"Whatever you do, leave Will out of it," said Bruce.

Stratton grimaced. "He's upset. Tank's his brother-in-law."

"Jesus, Candace. Will's lit. The only thing he wants to investigate is where his flask is."

"Bruce!"

Bruce held up a silver flask with the initials WL engraved on the front. "I took it off him."

"Oh, my God." Stratton put her head in her hands and Bruce shook his head.

"We all knew he had a problem. I didn't expect him to show up at a fire, belching vodka, but I should've."

"I don't know what to do," she said again. "He's the chief."

"Not today," said Bruce. "That would be you."

"Ah crap."

"You'll be fine."

"Not that," said Stratton. "Look who's here."

I turned and saw a woman with red hair and no jacket slip around on the ice as she got out of a Toyota Camry.

"Who's that?" I asked.

"Mallory, Tank's wife."

This is going to be so bad.

I braced myself for impact. How many people blamed me? All of them was my guess, but Mallory Tancredi didn't come for me. She stalked across the parking with as much dignity as she could muster on ice and went for the squad car where her brother, Will, was sitting. That tiny woman yanked the chief out of the backseat and proceeded to smack the crap out of him yelling, "You drunken idiot. You're not content to ruin your own life. You have to ruin mine, too."

The firefighters and deputies managed to get Mallory off the police chief but not before she gave him a bloody nose and a black eye. While that was happening Fats pried herself out of the Camry and watched with grim amusement before coming over to me with Moe tucked under her arm.

"I like her," she said and Moe yipped in agreement.

"You're not alone," said Bruce. "I warn you, Candace. Don't arrest Mallory for this. It will not go over well, especially after it all comes out."

"After what comes out?" Stratton asked. She was still trying. God bless her.

"I heard Miss Watts say you lied about files and the FBI guy I talked to said this has to do with a serial killer that's been live since the sixties. You have got to come clean and deal with it. I recommend you do that before the FBI gets here and takes over, unless you want a repeat of the Janet Lee Fine situation."

"I told you I don't know what to do."

Bruce inclined his head toward me. "She does. I vote you let her do it."

The fire chief left and Stratton took a breath. "Okay. Miss Watts, what's next? The high school?"

"Is it open?"

"Not yet."

"How about those files?" I asked.

She took another breath and nodded. We got in Fats' truck and drove out of the Sentinel's lot without saying a word to anyone. Mallory watched us go, her eyes lit up. I gave her a nod and she nodded back. We were good and it was more of a relief than I would've thought. The bombing wasn't my fault. I didn't throw those grenades, but when I came to town, somebody noticed.

CHAPTER TWENTY-EIGHT

Fats was tragically low on gas, meaning a fourth of a tank, and we made a quick detour to the very gas station that was there in 1974, Harvey's Fill 'Er Up. Now you pumped your own gas and Fats got out, garnering double-takes for more than just her size. Some of her stitches were on her face and she had considerable swelling. I knew she had to be in pain, but Fats Licata did not show pain. I, on the other hand, wanted Chuck there to rub my feet and feed me ice cream while I groaned dramatically.

Fats and I looked bad, but the good news was that Tank was awake and talking. He recognized Mallory with no problem and he told her the news that her family had been involved in something shady to do with at least one murder, possibly more. Mallory didn't take it well. She found Fats in the ER and brought her to me. Tank said I needed protection and Fats was it. There was a lot to like about Tank's little firecracker of a wife. Her brother was lucky there were witnesses or I didn't like his chances.

"What do you hope to find in those old files?" Stratton asked.

"The coroner's report, interviews, an ID on the type of tire on the truck that they used to dump Maggie would be nice. Time of death is important and Desmond Shipley saw something he didn't like. I want to know what that was."

"The abused thing you mentioned," she said. "Do you think she was raped?"

"You know what? I doubt it," I said. "But hopefully, we're about to find out."

Stratton looked around from the front seat. I noticed she had her revolver on her lap. "Do you think he's watching us?" she asked.

"Maybe, but he's sneaky. He's not going to lob a grenade at us at the Fill 'Er Up."

She nodded. "It's still broad daylight. When are those agents going to get back to you? They know we're down here with a nut job on the loose, right?"

"It's hard to know what the FBI knows. It's even harder to know what their intentions are. Mostly, my guys are working on getting Maggie's case reopened and more importantly getting themselves assigned to it."

"Bastards."

"Remind me to tell you the rest of the story later," I said.

A phone buzzed and Stratton handed it to me. It was Fats' phone. Mine was somewhere in the depths of the Sentinel basement.

"How are you feeling?" Spidermonkey asked.

"I'm fine. Tell me you have something to connect Stott to Kenneth Young so Stratton can go arrest that old codger," I said.

"I wish I could, but I do have some news."

Spidermonkey was decidedly more helpful than the rookies, who were no longer answering my calls. He'd identified several donors to the asylum through the initials Maggie used and other Catholic charities that had accurate books and taxes. He estimated that at least thirty to fifty thousand had been stolen from the asylum before Maggie joined the staff. That was a lot of money in the sixties.

More interestingly, Bishop Fowler's sister had paid a boarding school a sizable tuition every year for a boy that wasn't her son or any relation at all that Spidermonkey could see. She also gave a woman named Nora Connery a salary for housecleaning when Nora lived in Oregon. Nora the fake housekeeper once worked in St. Louis at the Cardinal Regali Center. That accounted for half the money stolen. The rest remained a mystery. If we could find that money, we could find Maggie's murderer.

"Maybe it's in Stott's trust fund," I said.

"Possibly, but my instinct says Stott had nothing to do with that money. He was a kid at the time and no financial genius or any kind of genius. As far as I can tell he was in Tennessee at the time of Young's disappearance, working as a delivery boy. That's how he targeted the victim he went to prison for."

"But you can't rule him out?" I asked.

"No. We just need something to rule him in," said Spidermonkey. "There's nothing that says he ever came back to St. Sebastian between 1965 and ten years ago."

"But he *did* come back. Why would he do that?"

"Fond memories of being a young psychopath?"

Fats knocked on Stratton's window and she put it down.

"The credit card pad isn't working. I have to go in," said Fats and she jogged off through snowflakes that were starting to get fatter.

"Mercy?" Spidermonkey asked. "You still there?"

"Yeah...I was just thinking about something. We're at the gas station that Young was at before he left town," I said.

Stratton turned in her seat. "We don't change much. Just got pay at the pump and it hardly ever works."

Pay at the pump.

I frowned at her and my nose burned under its splint and heavy bandages.

"What?" she asked.

"I don't..." I looked out at the other people attempting to pay or gassing up or running inside with their credit cards in hand.

Credit cards.

"So Stott was only here like six or seven months. There has to be a better reason than that for him to come back," I said. "The trust fund would send the money anywhere he wanted. Why St. Sebastian?"

"Serial killers like to visit the places where they killed their victims," Spidermonkey said.

"Sure, but if he didn't kill Maggie there's no reason to visit," I said. "Her body isn't here either."

"But he was in on it. That's why he had her medal."

He had that medal. He was in Kansas.

"She was important to him. He was the accomplice. He kept her medal," I said softly. "He dropped it or purposely put it in a grave in Kansas."

"I know what you're thinking, Mercy," said Spidermonkey. "I checked. Stott didn't leave any paper trail to Kansas or St. Seb."

"He had to drive them to Kansas," I said. "You can't check a body."

Fats got in and pulled out of the gas station. "This town needs a tech update."

"Tell me about it," said Stratton.

"Everybody uses credit cards," I said.

Fats turned around and both women raised their brows at me.

"Gas is expensive."

"Yes, on a good day. Outrageous on a bad," said Stratton. "I hate filling up."

Fats started to say something, but I held up my hand and asked Spidermonkey, "Stott didn't have any money until that trust fund kicked in."

"That's right. What are you thinking?"

"I'm thinking how did he afford it, if he didn't use a credit card? Gas from Tennessee and back or, hell, wherever he was killing people," I said. "Hotels. Food. It all costs. Did he have a credit card?"

"He did," said Spidermonkey. "The interest was criminal, which he deserved."

"Did he use it?"

"Not much."

"You're a numbers guy. You tell me how he afforded driving halfway across the country to bury victims in Kansas," I said.

Spidermonkey went quiet and all I heard was typing. We fishtailed on a turn but drove into the police station parking lot unscathed before Spidermonkey answered, "He couldn't, not from the numbers I'm seeing. Of course, he could've been working under the table. That's a possibility."

"What kind of car did he have?" I asked.

"The last one was a 2002 Mercury Cougar. The trunk's pretty big. You could definitely get a body in there."

"Where is it?" I asked as we got out and slid across the parking lot to the door of the station. A deputy opened it for us and I handed her Moe, much to her surprise.

We took off our coats and the deputy at the desk eyed my marsh-mallow Peep outfit. I like to think she was envious of how I was self-confident enough to rock it, but she was just horrified. I explained how I ended up wearing those sweats. It didn't help. My street cred, if I ever had any, was zero.

Stratton got us mugs of truly terrible coffee and led the way up to the station's attic while Spidermonkey continued to type in my ear.

She paused outside a door and glanced at the deputy. She was about to prove that she lied and it wasn't easy for her to stomach.

"Patton, we're going to need you to help us go through the files and look for everything we've got on Sister Margaret Mullanphy."

Patton blinked her wide blue eyes. "I thought those were destroyed in the flood."

"We made a mistake. Those old files were moved up here."

"Oh, great. That will really help with your investigation, Miss Watts," said Patton. "Do you think it's tied to the bombing and the fires Mr. Tancredi had? I always thought something was off about those. Why would kids try to set fire to the Sentinel? They pretty much cover the fair and local sports."

Two spots of pink formed on Stratton's cheeks, but she remained dignified. "New evidence has been uncovered and that's what we're trying to determine."

"How exciting. Maybe we'll end up on *20/20*," said Patton.

I'd rather have a colonoscopy.

"You never know," I said. "Let's get at it."

Stratton unlocked the door and revealed what could only be described as a craptastic mess. Aftermaths of hurricanes looked more orderly.

"What the hell is this?" Fats asked. "I'm ashamed to be on your side this time."

"This time?" Stratton asked.

"You heard me." She stomped into the attic and sneered. "It's a wonder you've caught so much as a purse snatcher."

"We've caught criminals," said Patton indignantly.

"Do they march in and confess? No wonder you told Mercy the files were gone. They might as well be."

"We meant to organize it, but..." trailed off Stratton.

She didn't have to say they had a drunk leader and no motivation. At least she had the decency to look ashamed about it.

"What's wrong?" Spidermonkey asked.

"We have access to the police files," I said. "Now we have to find them."

"Should I let you go?" He had a funny twinge in his voice.

"Are you okay?" I asked.

"Yes. I just...I made a mistake."

"Lay it on me."

Spidermonkey's mistake was another person's oversight. Heck it wasn't even that. My hacker didn't think to take a hard look at Stott's car. I didn't think of it either, so it was hardly his fault.

Stott bought his Cougar in 2005 and drove it until he moved to St. Seb ten years ago when he traded it in on a brand-new loaded Cadillac that the trust fund paid for. It had 29,000 miles on it when he bought it and 92,000 when he traded it in. I was no math whiz, but that wasn't a ton of mileage for a serial killer. From the number of bodies the FBI found in Kansas, our guy wasn't a once every five years kind of killer.

"That doesn't add up," I said.

Fats and the cops stopped hopping over stacks of files on the floor and waited expectantly.

"No, it doesn't. I should've thought of this. It's what you pay me for," said Spidermonkey.

"I've loaded you up and this is a small detail."

"There are no small details."

Like no small time crimes.

"He has another vehicle," I said. "We just have to find it."

"Easier said than done. I already went through his registrations, taxes, and tickets. No other cars. Period."

Patton waved at me. "A girlfriend's car?"

I nodded. "Did he have a girlfriend? A wife?"

"He was an ex-con living in a single-wide trailer in the middle of nowhere Tennessee," said Spidermonkey.

"Women marry multiple murderers on death row," I said. "It's not beyond the realm."

Patton smiled at me, glad to be of help, and I smiled back.

"I'll double-check his email and cellphone, but I saw no sign of anyone in his life, other than work colleagues."

Ding. Ding. Ding.

"Work!" I said. "Did he have a company truck?"

"Company credit card," said Fats. "Look at that."

Stratton shook her head. "No way. Who in their right mind would give a convicted murderer a company credit card?"

Fats smiled. "Who said anything about 'give'?"

"Yes," I said. "That's excellent. Spidermonkey, can you get in the businesses he worked for?"

"Yes, yes, I'm on it. He worked for six different outfits since he got out of prison. I'll look at them all working backwards."

"Six companies? That's a lot."

Fats squatted in front of a stack of files casually dumped on the floor. "He was fired. Find out why."

"Fats says he was fired. We need to know why," I said.

"Agreed. There were no arrests or lawsuits. If he was caught stealing, they let him walk away," said Spidermonkey.

"Have Loretta call them and ask. She has a great phone voice and she's Southern. I bet somebody will spill the tea."

"Spill the what?" he asked.

"The tea," I said. "It's slang for gossip. Get with it, Grandpa."

"That hurts, Mercy. You know I'm barely in my seventies."

"Whatever, dude."

He laughed and said he'd give Loretta the companies to call. She'd be happy because the daughters-in-law were now discussing chemtrails and Loretta was looking more and more like she was ready to take a long walk off a short pier.

I pocketed Fats' phone and looked around. The company truck and credit card idea was exciting. That attic was not. For a second, I questioned if I really needed that police report. Was it really imperative? Could I possibly take a micro-nap and pick the caked blood out of my nose instead? The latter was getting to be an issue.

"Are we doing this or not?" Fats asked.

I sighed. "How many years are in here?"

"I've got a robbery in 1953." She fanned out the stack and checked the bottom file. "And an indecent exposure in 1944. On D-Day. What a dirtbag."

"1962 over here," said Patton. "It's a murder. We had another murder. Weird."

"Only outside of town," said Stratton. "Never inside the city limits or close to them."

"What are all those evidence boxes?" I asked, picking my way through the mess. "I thought you hadn't investigated any murders."

"I haven't, but Will had one in the nineties in another town. We handle things for the places that don't have a department of their own. Most of those are probably from accidents. Will takes drunk driving seriously. He treats them like they're regular homicides."

We went quiet and she said, "Yes, I get the irony. Move on."

Accidents.

"Accidents, like plane crashes?" I asked.

"Huh?" Stratton muttered from behind a cluttered shelving unit.

"Plane crashes. Would that be in here?"

She stuck her head out from behind the shelving. "We don't investigate plane crashes. That's the NTSB."

"But if you had evidence it would be here?" I asked.

"How random is that?" Patton asked. "We never had a plane crash."

"You did. In the eighties."

Stratton stepped out. "Is this the accident you were asking about before?"

"Yes. My great grandparents died in the accident," I said with an unexpected lump in my throat.

"I'm sorry to hear that, but the NTSB would've handled it. We'd have the initial report, maybe some findings, but that's it."

"Found it!" Patton turned around with a stack of two evidence boxes.

There it was. The accident date and my grandparents' names written in faded black marker on the evidence labels. My knees got weak. I'd asked, but I didn't think anything would be there. Jeff City should've taken it. The NTSB. Somebody.

"Don't look at that." Fats took the boxes from Patton and tucked them in a corner with the labels hidden. "It's Maggie right now. That can wait."

The cops gave me curious looks but went back to searching. I couldn't drag my mind away from those boxes. There could be something important in there among Agatha and Daniel's belongings. Possible clues as to what was bringing them to the Bleds in a rush. Did they have what The Klinefeld Group wanted? Why weren't their effects released to Nana and Pop Pop after the investigation was closed? Maybe they didn't know it was there or that they could get it. Maybe they didn't want to have it.

"Mercy," said Fats. "Focus."

"I...I didn't think there was any evidence," I said.

She set aside her files. "Do you want me to take a quick look?"

"Is there something you're looking for, in particular? A family heirloom?" Stratton asked.

"Something like that," I said. "Please look. I don't think I should right now."

Fats opened the boxes and went through them quickly.

"Well?" I said.

"Nothing useful. We've got clothing, wallet, purse, hat, a Rubik's Cube, and some makeup and glasses."

Don't cry. It didn't just happen. Don't be a wuss.

"Two boxes for that?" I squeaked out.

"The coats take up space," said Fats.

"No boxes? Artwork?"

Stratton frowned. "Artwork?"

"I don't know," I said. "Something special. Unique. Paperwork? Files?"

Fats shook her head. "No. This is just what they had on them. Personal effects."

She didn't say it, but I knew was Fats meant. I'd thought for a long time that what Agatha and Daniel were bringing was information, something they knew and that died with them, which was, of course, why The Klinefeld Group bothered to kill them. That knowledge was lost forever. The Bleds didn't know what Stella Bled Lawrence sent back to the States or where it was, if it even existed anymore.

"Are you alright?" Stratton asked.

"Yes. There's a mystery about why the plane went down and why they were flying in the first place," I said.

"Your father hasn't solved it?"

He hasn't tried.

"No. I guess some things are unknowable."

"Not Maggie's murderer's name," said Fats. "Get to work. When 44 opens up, the FBI is going to kick us to the curb. We don't have a lot of time."

"I thought you wanted to give it to the FBI," I said.

"That was then." Fats pointed at her stitches. "This is now."

Stratton checked her watch. "An hour until teams arrive at the Turkey Shoot. Let's get cracking."

Cracking was right, but it was mostly my back.

My mother always says that nothing good comes easy. In this case, nothing bad does either. It took us twenty-five minutes of back-breaking file rummaging to find the file on Kenneth Young alone and another fifteen minutes to find Maggie's.

Patton found Maggie's evidence box straight away, but we didn't open it until we got the file. Nobody was in a hurry to see inside her death, which was how that box felt. Maybe all evidence boxes feel that way. I don't know, but after that day I had no interest in finding out.

"Who wants to do the honors?" Stratton asked when we were down in an interview room, also known as the city council's meeting room.

Suck it up, buttercup.

"I'll do it." I lifted the lid off the plain cardboard box, not knowing what to expect from evidence in 1965. First off, nothing was in plastic evidence bags. I took out a plain black wool coat that had leaves, twigs, and dirt stuck to the fuzzy fabric but no label. Underneath were Maggie's clothes and they looked almost exactly like what Aunt Miriam wore. Very little had changed in the way of nun fashion. I didn't find her veil, but everything else was there, her blouse, under-wear, bra, skirt, stockings, garter belt, sweater, and a pair of chunky black pumps and a matching handbag. Maggie's rosary and a pair of plain gold stud earrings were tucked in a corner with some torn paper bags. The bags had some faded handwriting with the time and date. First, "unknown thirty-year-old female nun" was written on them and then crossed out and replaced with Maggie's name.

"Is that blood?" Patton asked.

It was blood. A lot of blood. I laid out Maggie's clothes the way Miss Elizabeth had done without the creepy breathing, of course. Dried blood covered the front of Maggie's blouse and it had soaked through to her bra. There were smatters of blood on the dove grey sweater but not a lot. The coat appeared to be blood-free, but it prob-ably wasn't.

I picked up a pump and turned it over. Fairly new with just a modest amount of wear on the bottom, but the toes of both shoes were gouged and scraped. The knees of her stockings were shredded and there were long runs going up to the waist and down to the toes. I was so afraid to look at her panties, but they appeared to be intact and had no visible fluids.

"Anything in the purse?" Patton asked.

I opened the handbag that was so like one of Aunt Miriam's it was freaking me out. Inside was a date book, compact, a nude lipstick, a mini hymnal, address book, and Maggie's wallet that had a church identification card, a plastic picture holder with pictures of The Girls, her family, and other nuns, including Aunt Miriam, and a coin purse. The coin purse was empty, but I did find a nickel at the bottom of her bag that the killer must've missed.

I skimmed the address book. It was well-used with names,

addresses, and numbers filling nearly every page, but no name stood out, and Stott certainly wasn't in there.

"Check out the datebook," said Stratton.

Fats and I bent over that little book, searching through the months before Maggie's death. The only thing we found was the day before she died Maggie had an afternoon appointment with June Pierce. That was a new name. On the day of her death Millicent was scratched out and replaced with Dr. Desarno and Bishop Fowler at ten. That was the only appointment, but she had written sideways across the page, "Call SSS&L."

"That's a lot of initials," said Patton.

"It's probably a business," said Fats. "A law firm or an accountant would make sense with the money situation."

"You can call your research guru. I bet he'll find it."

I pulled out Fats' phone. "We can google it. I don't want to call when it might be easy."

Stratton put her hand on my arm. "It is easy."

"It is?"

She swallowed. "I thought you were wrong and Will was right."

"What about?" I asked. "He knew about SSS&L?"

"No. He said there was nothing here. I thought I'd let you in and we'd find nothing."

"Spill it, woman," said Fats. "I'm losing my patience with you people."

"It's the St. Sebastian Savings and Loan," said Stratton.

Son of a bitch!

I grabbed Maggie's address book and went through it, carefully this time. I only got to "C". Bianca Crider SSS&L and a number.

"Do you know any Criders?" I asked.

"There are some in town." Patton shrugged. "Bianca's a weird name. No Biancas. Are you going to call your guy?"

"No. I want him on Stott. Where's the bank?"

"The riverfront branch is four blocks away. The other one is by the Walmart," said Stratton. "I can't believe the nun was going to call here on the day she died."

"I can," I said. "It was always coming back to St. Seb. I just couldn't get why."

"We still don't have why." Fats cracked her knuckles. "Is the bank open?"

"It's always open," said Stratton. "They don't close for weather."

"Give me fifteen minutes." Fats turned on her heels and went for the door with Stratton running after in a panic.

"You can't go over there punching people," she said.

"Who said anything about punching?" Fats asked. "It generally doesn't get that far."

Patton wrinkled her nose. "Who are you?"

"Pink the Impaler," I said.

"Huh?"

"Pro wrestler."

Patton was simultaneously impressed and horrified. What she didn't do was ask more questions about Fats Licata the knuckle cracker.

"Hold on. I'll go with you. Let's take a look at the police report," I said.

"Fifty bucks says you find Bianca Crider's name on the interview list," said Fats.

Stratton and Fats shook on it while Patton eyed them. The young cop didn't say anything, but I had the distinct impression she thought Fats was right. It just wouldn't be good to show up her boss.

I, myself, didn't have much hope for Maggie's file once I saw how thin it was. Dad occasionally brought home his murder books, as they were known, and I'd seen the ones Chuck worked on. They were the binders from hell. Timelines, interviews, forensics, every nitnoid scrap of anything that pertained to that particular murder. Dad didn't pin pictures of corpses up on the wall and there certainly weren't any 3D skeletons being projected out of nowhere. It was all in the murder book. I caught Dad weighing one once. Fifteen pounds.

Maggie didn't have a book and her file was less than an inch. But it had been bigger. I could tell by the way the bend was folded. Much bigger. Somebody had sanitized the file. I found the initial report, interviews from people who didn't see anything, part of the interviews with Desmond and Mary Shipley. Bianca Crider wasn't in there, but nobody considered that a win. We didn't have anything on the body being abused or what Des thought. There was a kind of index noting what was supposed to be in there. Whoever removed the evidence didn't think to change that. We were supposed to have thirty-two crime scene photos and the negatives. He left us seven and they weren't of the body. We had trees and the tire marks though. Maybe tires weren't thought to be important. I had a hand drawn map of the area that showed the position of the body in relation to the tire marks, road, and rocks. Tank was right on the money with his guesses. And on the pictures it had little notes. "Brush sawed down." "Truck unloaded."

Chief Lucas had started out doing his job, but something had changed it.

I went through the pictures and skimmed a few pointless inter-views. When I turned the last page, I gasped. There it was. The autopsy report. I never in a million years expected to find it.

"Why in the hell?" Fats asked.

"Well, you said the chief was a drunk," said Stratton. "Maybe he missed it."

I flipped back to the index. "No, he didn't miss it. The report came in after Father Dominic jumped off the bridge and was put in by this guy. Initials J.T."

"Sound familiar?" Fats asked the cops.

It didn't, of course, but who put the autopsy in didn't really matter. That it was there and forgotten was important. Dr. Jean Albert August did the autopsy and he was thorough. The cause of death was strangu-lation as Sister Frances had told me, but that wasn't the end of it. The doctor thought Maggie had been struck from behind by a narrow blunt object, possibly a crowbar, and then strangled. She had a signifi-cant skull fracture and bleeding in the brain and was unlikely to have been conscious when she was strangled. The material used in the stran-gulation was wide and smooth. No fibers were found on her neck and the doctor concluded a tie might've been used.

It was awful and it was going to get worse. The doctor found traces of two different kinds of oil, hay, and fertilizer on her coat and in her hair. Livor mortis showed she'd been lying face down in one position for approximately three hours and then she was flipped over. That's when it got rough. Usually there was one rough outline of a body and the doctor would note injuries to the victim on it. This doctor, being who he was, did six different pages of the normal sketch.

The first one had the head injury and strangulation. The second had a set of stab wounds. The third her throat cut and wounds to the chest and stomach. The fourth I can't even talk about. The fifth a broken arm and leg. The sixth the back was sliced open after the kidneys were stabbed.

Patton clapped her hand over her mouth and walked out. I didn't blame her. I was a nurse and it was hard to look at. Fats didn't blink, but her face grew harder. When I got to the fifth page, she held out her hand and I gave her her phone. She pressed a button and said, "I need Calpurnia now." Then she left and I was glad of it. Whatever she and the mob boss were going to discuss was no business of mine.

Only Stratton stayed. She didn't look away. She read with me. It was good to have company. I needed to hear someone breathing and feeling it the way I was.

"So that's the abuse," said Stratton after we'd read the coroner's conclusions.

"He practiced on her," I said. "Over several days and Desmond Shipley knew it."

Patton crept into the doorway. "I'm sorry. I just couldn't. She was a nun and..."

Stratton went over and put a motherly arm around her deputy. "I know. I know. We're going to do right by her now."

Patton wiped her eyes and said, "I'm not totally useless. I called the bank to save us a trip and I found out who Bianca Crider was."

Fats walked in behind them, her face smooth and untroubled. *That* troubled me. What in the world had Calpurnia said?

"Who is she?" I asked Patton. "Can we interview her?"

"She's dead now. Lung cancer like twenty years ago. But back then, she was in trust management."

Fats and I smiled. A trust, of course.

"What was she? A vice-president?" I asked.

"A secretary actually, but I think you'll like this. Sadie over there told me that Bianca Crider was really wealthy."

"A secretary?" Stratton asked.

"That's what I said," said Patton. "My sister's a secretary and she's not exactly rolling in it."

"How do you know she was wealthy?" Fats asked.

"Well, there's these big pavilions over on the fairgrounds," said Patton.

"The Crider Pavilions!" Stratton said.

"Sadie said Bianca Crider donated the money for them and she left a bunch of money to the Parks department and the ASPCA."

Fats mouth twisted. "I wonder how she got that."

"Nobody knows," said Patton.

I closed the autopsy report and picked up Maggie's date book.

Bianca Crider, what did you do?

CHAPTER TWENTY-NINE

I finished photocopying Maggie's sad little file and handed Stratton back the original.

"I hope I did the right thing," she said. "This is against every regulation we have."

"As far as I'm concerned," I said, "you took a second look and broke the case."

Stratton slapped the file on top of Maggie's evidence box and looked out at the snow crusted up on the window of the St. Seb police interview room. "Nobody's going to buy that."

"People believe what they're told." Fats walked in and tossed me her phone. "I think you want to hear this."

It was Spidermonkey and he'd done a deep dive into the companies Stott worked for. Loretta sweet-talked the secretaries and got all the tea from the last two companies. Fats nailed it. Stott had used and abused the company credit cards and trucks he used on both jobs. He charged a ridiculous amount of gas and put on hundreds of miles that he couldn't account for. The last company fired him two months before he moved back to St. Seb and they were pissed. Like the other companies they decided taking a broke ex-con to court wasn't worth it and they didn't want him arrested because they looked like idiots for hiring him in the first place. They chalked it up to a lesson learned, but they called every electrician in the state and had Stott blackballed. He couldn't get a job wiring a light switch and Loretta thought it went beyond just Tennessee. A couple of Kentucky companies called J and R Electrics to see what was up after he applied to them. They didn't hire him either and that's when Stott up and moved to St. Seb where he never applied for a job but did start rolling in that trust dough.

"So that solves why he moved back," I said. "He had something on someone and needed to use it."

Spidermonkey was quiet, not even typing.

"Hello?" I asked.

"I'm here, but I'm going to give you to Loretta."

Loretta took the phone and said, "He's upset."

"I got that. Is it the autopsy? Maybe I shouldn't have sent it."

"No. It's that the credit cards from the companies showed some interesting activity," she said.

"Like what? Something other than the gas?"

"It's where he bought it."

"Have we got a trail to the Kansas site?" I asked.

"We do and to Florida, Mississippi, and New England."

Stott was a busy boy.

"Did he find cases connected to the areas he visited?"

"He didn't look. We'll leave that to the FBI," said Loretta.

I looked at Fats and she touched her stomach, tenderly. She did it without thinking and it was the first time I'd seen her do it. The pregnant thing. The mommy thing.

"Was it a kid?" I asked.

Loretta got a little choked up. "He got gas in St. Seb, Mercy. Every time he went to Kansas, he made a detour and went there. You were right. He didn't come back for Maggie."

I knew it before she said it. I probably always knew.

"The first time was in August 1999," she said.

"And he drove in from Kentucky," I said.

"Yes."

"Bertram Stott killed Janet Lee Fine."

"We think so," said Loretta. "A white panel van was seen in the area before she disappeared. That's what he was driving. He filled up one town over three hours before. That night he was in St. Seb."

"During the fair."

"Yes."

I couldn't say anything. For a second, I was back there, digging in the dirt with images and sounds of the fair all around me.

"Are you okay? Finding that little girl must've been terrible," said Loretta.

"It's all terrible," I said. "But maybe it will help the parents."

"I hope so. You'll hand this all over to those obnoxious rookies now?"

"I have one more thing," I said.

"What's that?"

"Can you find out who June Pierce is?"

"Oh, I'm sorry. He already did. June Pierce was the asylum secretary at one point," said Loretta.

Spidermonkey got back on the phone and although his voice was strained he told me that June Pierce retired from her job in 1955. In 1965, when Maggie presumably met with her, she was living in a retirement home having had a series of strokes.

"She must've known something about the money," I said.

"I think she gave Maggie St. Sebastian Savings and Loan," said Spidermonkey. "Then Maggie called Bianca Crider."

"And she called Maggie's murderer," I said.

"I'll be through the bank's firewall in a couple of hours. We'll have the accounts," said Spidermonkey. "Just sit tight. 44 is almost clear. I don't want you risking yourself."

"I have my Mauser."

"I'm not sure that's enough."

"Me, either."

Spidermonkey cleared his throat. "Mercy?"

"Uh-huh?"

"This could all have been prevented. That poor little girl. The people in Kansas. All of it back then in 1965."

"I know."

We hung up and I asked Stratton, "I don't suppose you can go arrest Stott?"

"On info from a hacker? No."

Patton slammed down her coffee mug, sloshing cold coffee all over the table. "This is fucked. We've got a serial killer hanging out in Shady Glen and we can't do anything? My mother told me to get out of this weird ghost-infested town, but did I go? No, I didn't. She should've made me go. Kicked my butt out like the Shipleys did Carrie."

"She came back," I said.

"Oh, yeah. How long was she gone?"

"About six or seven months," said Fats.

"Why that amount of time?" asked Patton.

"We're not sure. Stott went back to Tennessee by January, so we assume it had to do with the other guy. The Shipleys were pretty scared."

"I don't blame them," said Patton. "I'm afraid of him and I wasn't even born."

"They didn't know who it was though," I said. "I don't think they would've kept quiet about it, if they had."

"It depends on who it was," said Stratton thoughtfully. "You saw the file. Even if they had a good idea they weren't going to get anywhere. He was well-protected."

Fats nodded. "I want to know how they ruled out Stott."

"That's the key," I said. "Is the school open yet?" I asked.

"Not quite," said Stratton. "That tournament's a crazy idea. The weather and now the grenades. I think I should shut it down."

"Can you?" I asked. "I wouldn't want to risk it."

"I can try, but I'm not chief and this town's stubborn."

"We need to see that yearbook," said Fats. "The grenade thrower took it for a reason."

"You think the nun's murderer's in the yearbook?" Patton asked. "Why?"

"Stott's in there," I said.

"Really? You didn't tell me that."

Stratton nodded. "That's how Mercy knew he'd been in town at the time of the murder."

"What year was he?" Patton asked.

"A senior."

The deputy got thoughtful. "When I was a senior, my friends were mostly seniors, but my best friend was a junior."

"We're hoping to find a picture of him with other people. It wasn't listed. He only had one photo that we know of."

Patton picked up her coffee mug and took a sip. She made a face and asked, "When exactly did Carrie get to come back?"

"August," said Fats.

August. August. August. What happens in August?

Patton and I looked at each other. "College!"

We got the slowest police escort in history. Ten miles an hour through the streets of the snow-clogged St. Sebastian. People thought we were some kind of sad three-car parade, two cop cars and Fats' truck. They came out and watched with their cups of hot chocolate and concerned expressions. Some waved. Some flipped me off. I get it. The word was out. Local boy Tank Tancredi was in the hospital and Chief Will Gates had been yelling about it being my fault. Bruce, the fire chief, had tried to contain him, but it didn't work as it often doesn't with drunks, who are fueled by fear and guilt.

Stratton had done her best to shut down the tournament, but she couldn't overcome her boss. Will called the principal and told her that it was all under control. He even claimed to have a suspect. Will didn't have a suspect. He barely had a coherent thought, but the principal bought it. Probably because she needed it to be true. A lot of planning and money went into the tournament. The school sorely needed to recoup that money and make some with all the damage from over-flowing toilets and the rest of the odd occurrences. I questioned the wisdom of having the tournament there at all, even if there wasn't a storm and a bomber on the loose. They had fire alarms that went off for no reason and doors that locked on their own. That couldn't be good for a crowd and what if our grenade thrower showed up armed to the teeth? What then?

Stratton had managed to pull every available cop within fifty miles. The high school would be crawling with uniforms and they were bringing metal detectors. She was moderately confident that it would be fine. Chuck wasn't. Dad wasn't. The FBI wasn't. Even Calpurnia Fibonacci said it was crazy, but the more outsiders said no, the more the community said yes.

Never mind that we had a bus jackknifed on the bridge and another one in front of us that had the entire team trying to push it out of a snowdrift. Common sense had gone bye-bye.

Fats slammed her hands against the steering wheel. "Go around them! Jesus!"

"Where are we going to go?" I asked. The road was mostly blocked and the sidewalks narrow.

Fats pointed to the left.

"That's somebody's yard. There's a swing set back there."

"It's twelve degrees. Nobody's on it."

"They'll be pissed," I said. "Look they've almost got the bus moving."

That was an exaggeration, but anything to keep us out of that yard.

"We're trying to connect a serial killer to a nun murderer. I think they'll forgive us."

"I should've looked through Carrie's yearbook when we had it," I said. "This would be moot."

"Stop beating yourself up. That's my job." She slammed her hands again. "Go, you little weak ass fuckers. That's it. I'm pushing that bus out."

I grabbed her arm. "Stratton said no. They won't like it."

"You think I'm worried about embarrassing a bunch of high school boys?"

"I am. She is."

"Why?"

She had me there. "I don't know."

"I'll give them two minutes and that's it. We're done coddling those spindly *athletes*."

"Fine."

"Fine."

We watched the clock and ignored Fats' phone. The men in our lives were pinging us at thirty second intervals to make sure we didn't go to the high school. As if. They knew us. Even Tiny was in on the act and he knew Fats could take a bullet and keep going. Literally. That had happened.

"Maybe Spidermonkey will call," I said.

"Maybe." She gripped the steering wheel and bared her teeth.

"What?"

"I want to do it. I want to go."

"Because of Calpurnia?" I asked.

"She's pretty hot about this. It'll look good for me," said Fats.

The clock clicked another minute down and I crossed my fingers for the spindly basketball boys.

"Since when do you look bad?"

She forced her hands to relax and one went to her stomach.

"Wait. You think Calpurnia will dump you because you're pregnant?" I asked.

Her hand snapped back to the wheel. "Not dumped. Put out to pasture, like Sal the Slayer Behar."

The Slayer? Yikes.

"What happened to him?"

Stabbed. Prison. Beat up Lorenzo the meatball nephew.

Fats sighed. "His wife got MS and he had to take care of her and the twins."

Bad but in a different way.

"He sounds like a good husband and father," I said.

"He is, but he used to be a badass. Now he's processing loans at a used car lot. Sal never gets the call when it's time to take care of business."

"Oh, I guess that's bad."

"It's bad. There's a lot of money in the call, respect, face time. I've got to stay in there with Calpurnia. Show her I can be counted on with a baby on board."

"I don't think I want to know what the call entails," I said.

She grinned wickedly. "You definitely don't."

"Just another reason I should've looked through that yearbook with a fine-toothed comb."

"Looked through it with a comb? A comb? You need to read some quality fiction and stop watching reality TV," said Fats.

"Shut up."

"You shut up about that damn yearbook." She slammed her hands on the wheel and said, "That's it. Here we go."

"No!"

"Yes!"

With a yank of the wheel, we were off-roading through yards. Horns were honking. Fists were shaken. Stratton tried to follow, siren blaring but got stuck in the first yard on some poor kid's sandbox.

"Do I have skills or what?" Fats asked with grim glee.

"Or what! You're crazy. Do you want to get arrested?"

"I don't mind. It's been a while."

"Well, I do! Get back on the road."

She drove up on a concrete patio, took out a planter box, and went down into a frozen creek. "I was made for off-roading. Why do you think I have an SUV?"

"Because you fit in it."

"That, too."

"Get back on a road!"

"Calm down." She gave me the side eye. "If you didn't want to go hard, why'd you bring me?"

"I didn't bring you. I never bring anyone. You people just show up."

She put it in gear and hit the gas. "Maybe you should've gone through that yearbook."

"Hey! You were there. You didn't think of the college thing either," I said, lurching to the right and grabbing Moe before she hit her noggin on the door handle.

"Why would I?"

"It's August. That's when everybody goes to college. Everyone in that room should've thought of it."

"I didn't," said Fats.

"What?" I asked.

"Go to college."

"You didn't go to college? You read Proust on purpose. Your explanation of String theory lost me two sentences in."

"You weren't paying attention." Fats took a sharp right and we climbed over a five-foot gravel pile. "You could get it."

"I was trying. Seriously. How did you *not* go to college?"

Fats drove us through another backyard and we went onto a road. An actual road. I was so happy.

"I was going, but I went to Hamburg instead," she said.

I straightened Moe's jacket and said, "What was in Hamburg?"

Fats smiled and it made me feel like I needed a shower.

"Christoph."

"Never mind," I said. "So where were you going to college?"

"He had the most amazing ass. Top shelf. An unbelievable butt."

Maybe not so smart.

"You gave up college for a butt?"

"And there was a great trainer who was working with Christoph. He wanted me for World's."

"Was it worth it?" I asked.

She shrugged. "He had a great ass."

"Enough of the ass. I'm having flashbacks to when you met my cousin."

"Great ass. Sad penis."

"Ew. Too much information."

We cleared the city limits and I spotted the sign for the high school. Thank God.

"Have you seen one?" Fats asked.

"A penis?"

"A micro."

"Again. Ew."

"Christoph took a lot of steroids. The effect was sort of mesmerizing. By the end it was like a pink jellybean."

"Oh, my God, stop talking," I said.

"This might be useful to you," she said.

"How?"

"You're a nurse," said Fats. "You might come across one and need to identify the cause."

We pulled into the high school parking lot that was already half full, mostly with squad cars and buses, but Stratton was right. Adverse conditions were nothing to basketball fans.

Fats parked next to an enormous snow pile in front of the school. It was so high you could barely see the first story.

"I have a picture," said Fats.

"No, thanks."

"It's truly astonishing."

"I believe you," I said.

She popped out a toothpick. "I wonder if medical textbooks would be interested. Good for training."

"I think we're good. It's like porn. You can't define it, but you know a steroid penis when you see it."

"Your loss." She put on the emergency brake. "Do we have a plan?"

"Find the yearbook," I said.

"That's it?"

"What else do you want?"

Fats took Moe and got out to dig in the back. "A Plan B in case the nun killer doesn't, ya know, look like an obvious maniac."

I put on my poofball hat and followed Fats across the lawn up to my shins in snow. "He doesn't look like a maniac. He went to college."

"Ted Bundy went to college," she said.

"Not helpful."

"We need a plan."

"I don't do plans. We'll look for a group shot and see if we can find him."

Moe growled and Fats said, "Oh, yeah, that's fool proof."

"Okay. Fine. We'll get the names of every dude in his class and eliminate them one by one," I said. "There can't be that many."

"Spidermonkey will get into those bank accounts before we manage that." Fats walked up to Deputy Mosbach, who was on the doors with a hand wand, and gave the startled cop her dog.

"What...I...uh...have to—" he stuttered.

"Check us for weaponry?" Fats asked as she yanked off her hat and quickly redid her French braid. "You don't want to do that."

"I don't?"

I hadn't thought of that. Fats had lost her Python, but she'd restocked from the back of her truck. Fats had enough weaponry and equipment to pull off an operation for the CIA . I had my Mauser, but that was just cute compared to her three automatics and the switch-blade in her left boot.

"No." She eyed herself in the reflection of the door's glass.

"How'd it go with Stott?" I asked.

Mosbach had a hard time focusing on me. "Uh...huh?"

"Stott. What'd he say when you interviewed him?"

"I didn't. He said I was a Triscuit and he was waiting for a Dorito," he said.

Fats took out her braid again and made it into two, identical and perfect. "He means you."

"Me?" Mosbach asked.

"Mercy."

"How do you get that?" I asked.

"Every guy I know calls you a tasty snack. Before the plane inci-dent, anyway," she said. "And you're connected with Kansas and Blankenship. Stott has to know that. Those psychos keep in touch."

"Awesome," I said. "Mosbach, did you mention Maggie's medal to Stott?"

Mosbach flushed. "I forgot. Sorry. He freaked me out."

"Did you find out if he left Shady Glen during the bombing?"

"That guy couldn't leave the bathroom on his own. He looks like shit. One of the nurses said he's got lung cancer and he refused treatment."

Cancer and congestive heart failure. Stott wouldn't last long.

"They're pretty free with info on a patient," I said.

"Dude, they hate him. The only people who will deal with that creep are the teen volunteers because they don't know any better and think they're tough," said Mosbach.

"They're letting kids talk to him?" Fats cracked her knuckles. "Any-body like that gets near my kid, it won't be pretty."

"It's during the school day. The parents don't know crap. Besides, he can't do anything," said Mosbach. "I'm telling you the guy has one foot in the grave."

Fats evaluated her reflection one more time after pulling out some locks to artfully conceal her stitches. "How do I look?"

He glanced at me and I smiled. "The stitches are hardly noticeable. Isn't that right, Mosbach?"

"Oh, yeah," he said. "You look great. Pretty...incredible. You could be an Incredible. Mrs. Incredible. But you're not old. You're young and not a man."

I took Moe from him. "You should stop talking and open the door for us."

He opened the door and just like that we were in a high school locked and loaded. Successful, but it made me think about home-schooling any future rugrats I might have.

The lobby was jammed with confused basketball players, coaches, and staff.

"We will have the gym doors open in a minute," called out a man over the crowd. "Please be patient."

Fats leaned over to me. "I bet they won't."

"Toilets are gonna blow any second," I said.

I was wrong on that. It wasn't toilets. It was the lights. All power went out and it took ten long seconds for the emergency lights to kick in.

"You said this was all taken care of!" a woman yelled.

"It's just a glitch!"

"Some glitch! We should've moved it to Owensville!"

"No, no! It's fine."

It was not fine, but Fats pushed her way through the crowd with one hand and me in the other. I now know what it's like to be a puppy being dragged around by the scruff of the neck.

When the regular lights came back on they were dimmed and flickering, giving the school an Overlook Hotel vibe. I had Stanley Kubrick to thank for a lot of nightmares and it was hard to make myself walk down the hall. Happily, I didn't have to. Fats had me by the good arm and she wasn't letting go.

A man yelled, "It's open!"

A cheer went up and Fats' grip tightened. "Idiots."

"Stratton tried," I said.

The sound of shattering glass echoed down the hall and a woman yelled, "I'm fine. I'm fine."

"This is not good," said Fats.

"No one is going to get hurt. No one has ever gotten hurt here."

"Because Maggie wouldn't hurt anyone?"

"She wouldn't," I said.

"What if it's not Maggie?" Fats asked as we stopped at the office door.

It's Maggie. It's Maggie. It better be Maggie.

"Don't do that," I said.

"Just stating the obvious."

"Well, don't." I tried the door and it was locked. "Ah, crap. I left my picks in my bag at Miss Elizabeth's."

Fats rolled her eyes and the lights went out and, along with the screams in the lobby, there was a loud click in the door.

"See," I said, opening the door. "It's Maggie."

"Let's hope. This town is questionable."

"Whatever." I shook off Fats' hand and went behind a tall reception desk. Lots of files and shelves of binders, but no yearbooks. The lights came back up, this time extra bright and we had to shield our eyes.

We stumbled through to a conference room and then a storeroom with no luck.

"Where else would they keep them?" I asked.

"Principal's office?"

"Maybe."

I checked the well-used emergency preparedness map that was on the secretary's desk, not a good sign for a school I wouldn't think, and found the principal's office was down another hall to the left.

We went out into the hall, which was now normally lit, and teenagers in band uniforms crowded us, trying to get organized.

"Why are there so many tubas?" Fats yelled.

"Maybe it's like a drum line but with tubas!"

"That's not a thing!"

It must be a thing because there were twenty tubas in that hall and they were all warming up. The clamor was amazing. When we cleared the tubas, my ears were ringing.

"Holy crap," I said.

"My kid is not doing band," said Fats.

"Tiny was a tuba player."

"No."

"Yes."

"Tell me you're joking. I might agree to drum line, but that's it," she said as she assessed the principal's door and then gave it a swift kick. It popped open and the glass didn't even shatter.

"It wasn't locked," I said.

Fats reached up to the shoulder holster on her left. "Correct. Stay here."

I didn't stay there. I never stay there. I don't know why people order me to do things, unless they want me to do the opposite. That was a distinct possibility, but not in Fats' case. When she eased inside the office, she tried to stiff arm me, but sometimes being short comes in handy. I ducked down, pulled my Mauser, and got in ahead of my oversized bodyguard.

She gritted her teeth behind me as we advanced through an outer secretary's office and then into the principal's office. Also unlocked with the door open. I didn't know if that was normal, but I didn't feel good about it. I eased the door wide with my foot. The room was quite nice with floor-to-ceiling bookshelves that had a college professor vibe and a big desk with a blotter, a bible, stacks of paperwork, and a bunch of nun photos. The heavily-padded chair was off to the right, almost to the window. Other than that, nothing appeared to be out of place.

Fats held up her hand and silently went around the desk. "Clear."

"It seems like it should've been locked," I said.

"Agreed."

We started going through the bookcases on the wrong side of the office. I should've started where the chair was. Duh. Only a person tall as Fats could've reached the shelf where the yearbooks were, in order, starting in 1920.

I stood on the chair, staring at an empty slot. "It's gone. He got here first."

"I never should've waited behind Stratton," said Fats.

"It could've been gone for weeks. We don't know."

"We know he's a moron. Another yearbook's going to turn up."

I climbed off the chair and picked up Moe off the desk. "It's very short-sighted. He's really just reacting or overreacting, I guess. There's no plan. If anything, blowing up the Sentinel gets more attention not less on Maggie's case."

"He's an idiot."

"Or young, like Stratton said," I said. "Who's more impulsive than a teenager?"

Fats chewed on her toothpick. "My Aunt Marie. Every tattoo a mistake."

"Stay with me. The first fires were definitely kids with links to the high school and that bar fight when they couldn't get served. The ones ten years ago are the same style with the dumpsters and the Sentinel being hit in the middle of the night. Tank's house, that was electrical. Stott was an electrician."

"We already know this isn't him. He's tucked up at Shady Glen, safe and sound, the bastard."

"And what did Mosbach say?" I asked. "The only people who would deal with Stott were the teen volunteers because they didn't know any better."

"Where's a kid going to get a grenade?" Fats asked.

"I can't believe you asked me that."

She knocked her head with the palm of her hand. "Must be the hormones."

"You're fine," I said. "Let's go."

"Where to? No Plan B."

I grinned at her. "We just got one."

"And what's that?"

"Attendance."

Moe started growling and Fats took him from me. "Shush. What about attendance?"

"Mosbach said the kids came during the school day," I said. "We need to know who's been signed out for that program. They must somehow be connected with Maggie's murder. Why else would they bomb us?"

Moe struggled and barked, but Fats wouldn't let her go.

We started into the secretary's office and she said, "Attendance as a clue. That's a new one."

I stopped her at the door. "Attendance."

"Yes. Attendance. Let's move. I'm craving a cheeseburger and I don't eat anything that's described as a cheese product, so we've got to find a good place."

"Listen," I said. "That's how Des and Mary knew who didn't kill Maggie. They checked the attendance. If Stott was in school, he couldn't have killed her."

Fats pointed a gun finger at me. "Old files in the basement."

"Old files in the basement."

We turned around, the outer office door opened and something long flew across the room. It crashed through the window and the next thing I knew I was eating tile.

CHAPTER THIRTY

Cinderblock construction is the bomb and I mean that in a good way. The explosion outside the high school did almost no damage. It took out some upper windows, but that's it. The grenade broke through the window, flew over the enormous snow pile that was up against the building, hit the sidewalk, bounced off the snow pile on the other side of the sidewalk, and exploded. The sidewalk was toast, but the snow piles absorbed most of the blast.

It was shit luck for the bomber, but I was grateful he had crappy aim. I'd have been more grateful if I could breathe.

"Get off."

Fats rolled off me and jumped to her feet, Glock out. "That was a potato masher."

"What?" I touched my face. Blood. "I think you broke my nose again."

"Stay here," she said and ran into the secretary's office with Moe at her heels.

I did not stay there—see previous comments—I ran after her, slipping on the paperwork that was still fluttering to the floor. "He heard us!" I yelled. "He's going to the basement."

"I know!" Fats ran into the hall and it was pure pandemonium. Half the people were duck and covering. The other half was so terrified they were trampling the duck and cover ones. Everyone was screaming.

"Gun!"

That didn't take long.

"Drop the Glock!" I yelled.

"The hell I will!"

Wrong answer. That hallway was full of heroes and I'm not saying that facetiously. Fats got hit with tubas, flutes, and one trombone. One band nerd did a flying leap at her head and clamped on. She went spinning off and a girl wrestled the Glock out of her hand.

I grabbed another kid who was pressed against the lockers, arms splayed and eyes wide. "Where are the stairs?"

He extended a shaking hand and pointed at an exit sign.

"They're attacking the wrong person. Help her." I pushed him at the beleaguered Fats and ran for the exit.

"Go, Moe!" Fats yelled behind me.

I was down one flight of stairs before I realized I had a pocket dog on my heels.

"What the hell?" I expected her to try to stop me, but she just went along, snarling. And when we reached the bottom, she sat on her tiny butt, making a throaty growl.

"I totally get why Fats kept you," I said, pulling out my Mauser and checking the safety. Off. Definitely off.

There was one door and it had a sign above it that claimed there was a pool. That seemed unlikely, but I could smell the chlorine. The door had a little window with reinforced glass, but I was too short to see through it, so I just opened it instead.

Water flowed over my feet as I walked into the hall. It was empty and flooded with about three inches of water. I shed my stupid pink coat and soft cast. My arm hurt like hell but it was useable.

Moe and I crept into the hall. So many doors. We passed the girl's locker room. The boy's. Utilities. Music storage. Sports storage. Furniture storage. Janitor storage. So much storage.

Moe splashed ahead and stopped in front of another door, growling. File room.

Breathe. He probably doesn't have another grenade. Probably.

I reached for the doorknob and the lights went out. A door opened. Splashing. A shot fired and, for a second, I thought it was me, firing in panic, but it wasn't. My barrel was cold. The emergency lights flickered and someone ran at me in the dim red gloom. He shoved me into the water. My face went under and I fought back up, throwing an elbow. I connected. A scream confirmed it, but I dropped the Mauser. Moe was barking. A wave of water hit us and we all went over.

I couldn't get my feet under me. Something kept hitting them and taking me down. Then the lights came on. I looked up and a desk chair came hurdling through the air and I mean through the air all the way down the hall. Fifty feet. Someone screamed and the doors all opened. Chairs, music stands, and mop buckets came flying out. A violin case narrowly missed my head. I was afraid to move. It was like a tornado in that hall, but it didn't touch me. Behind me, Moe made an ungodly scream. She was caught in a door. I dove for her and yanked her out, tucking her to my chest.

A man yelled, "Run!"

I spun around and ducked a flying life preserver. Down the hall under an exit sign was a man in a nice suit gesturing to me to hurry. I started to go, but an old-fashioned desk, the kind that had the desk and chair attached, flew past me and shattered on the wall, pelting me with metal and wood.

"Run! You have to run! Please!" the man yelled at me.

"No!" yelled a voice behind me.

I looked back. A boy was standing there in a bloody band uniform. He was hunched over in rage with a hunting rifle in his left hand and a yearbook in his right.

The girl's locker room door burst open and a wave of water came out. He staggered to the side, but raised the rifle. A music stand sideswiped him, cutting a ribbon of flesh from his cheek, but he didn't seem to notice.

"You want this yearbook?" he asked, dodging a chair and a mop. "You want it?"

Say no.

"Yes."

Dammit.

The boy aimed and the man yelled, "Don't do it!"

"It doesn't matter," I yelled. "We'll have the financials any second."

That made him hesitate and a football hit him in the chest knocking him back. I saw confusion mixed with the hate. Baseballs pinged off the walls. Tennis rackets and golf clubs. He was hit multiple times. The right equipment in the right place and he was done. He was so young. So deranged.

"There's a money trail!" I yelled. "We followed the money."

"I don't care about money," the boy yelled back with blood flowing out of his mouth. "It's in here. I know because you wanted it. Zoe told me."

Zoe? A girl. There's always a girl.

"She likes you. She told me," I said.

More confusion and the rifle lowered.

"Good, Robbie," said the man. "Drop it."

Fats burst in through the stairwell door behind him. She had her Glock drawn and ready. The boy spun around and raised the rifle, aiming at her chest.

"Shoot him!" the man yelled.

"Dad!"

Fats shot him.

💋

Everything dropped the second Fats fired. Every instrument. Every chair, mop, bucket, and desk. They hit the water as the boy did with a tremendous splashing. The boy was screaming. So was his father. I'd like to say I didn't make a peep, but the Peep peeped. A lot.

Fats holstered her Glock and looked at Moe in my arms. She was whining and had an odd bend to her.

"She's okay," I said. "I've got her."

Fats didn't respond. She stalked over to the screaming boy, ripped the rifle out of his hands, snapped it in half, and said, "Shut up. You hurt my dog. You're lucky I didn't blow your head off."

The boy wailed in response, clutching at a bloody spot on his shoulder. "Dad! Dad! Get the book! You have to get it!"

None of us moved. His father's handsome face held an odd blank expression. If he was thinking anything at all, it didn't show.

The boy kept wailing and I should've gone to put pressure on the bleeding, but I didn't. I didn't want to. Not my best nursing moment, but I don't regret it. He wasn't going to bleed out. The wound was a clean through and through, nowhere near a major vessel. If he was suffering, good.

Moe, on the other hand, was not good. Her whining got worse and, as I started to examine her, the door to the stairs opened, and an unknown nun ran in with Clarence on her heels. They splashed through the water, carrying bats. Aunt Miriam wasn't the only one who could look badass in a veil. No, I don't mean Clarence. Her face was resolute, but she was shaking so hard she could've given herself a concussion. The other nun was a whole different story with her black hair, pronounced jaw, and practiced batter's stance that should've made the sensible run away. No question. Of course, not a single person in that hall was sensible.

"I heard a shot. What happened?" yelled the nun. "Where'd all this water come from?"

Fats turned around with her Glock in her hand again. The nun went straight at her, not one ounce of hesitation. But this was Fats Licata we're talking about. The nun swung and Fats caught the bat just before it connected. She ripped it out of the nun's hands and tossed it away.

"I'm not your problem, Sister," said Fats calmly.

"She's really not, Sister Emily," said Clarence, dropping her own bat in relief.

Sister Emily glanced back and then nodded.

"Sister! Sister!" yelled the boy. "She shot me. She did it."

The nuns ran for him, yelling for someone to call an ambulance. Sister Emily pressed her hand to the wound and yelled, "Robert Junior, my goodness, what are you waiting for? Come help your son!"

Robert Junior didn't move, but his expression did change. If anything, he looked like he wanted to leave, not come to his kid's aid.

"Robert!"

He took a step and the second he did, all the objects that had been flying around rose up out of the water, swirled around, and began putting themselves away.

"Holy smokes!" The nun didn't let go of the boy's shoulder as buckets went past her, a desk reassembled itself to go back into furniture storage, and golf clubs went back in their bag. Clarence ducked as the life preserver flew over her head and musical instruments whizzed past, returning to their cases.

We watched in amazement as mops went into buckets, furniture, lacrosse sticks, everything put itself away and the water drained. It happened so quickly it looked like fast forward on a movie.

When it was done, the hallway was completely dry and clear, except for one thing. The yearbook. It lay between me and the boy. We all watched as its cover flipped open and the pages—now dry—turned, like someone was looking for something. Then it stopped and no one moved as the smell of honeysuckle filled the hallway, sweet and overpowering.

Maggie.

I crawled over to the yearbook with my bad arm tucked around Moe and looked at the page, holding my breath. It was the same page I'd seen before. Senior pictures. Stott's page. This was 1965 and there weren't any baby pics or parent love letters, just a name and a list of accomplishments for each of the six pictures on the page. In Stott's case, there was only a name. He joined nothing and accomplished nothing. There had to be something new that I hadn't seen before, but there just wasn't.

"What is it?" Fats asked.

"I don't know," I said. "It's the same. Six seniors. Black and white photos."

"Nothing on his picture? What's he wearing?" Fats came over and gingerly took Moe, who cried out, bringing tears to her eyes.

"Just a suit. It looks like the exact same suit as the...oh, my God," I said.

"Young lady, please," hissed Sister Emily.

"Mercy?" Fats asked.

There was one other guy on the page and four girls, all with grand accomplishments, but the boy stood out. I knew that name. I should've seen it before with its list of clubs, sports, and offices that were as long as his photo.

I looked back at the man, Robert Junior, who hadn't budged from the doorway. "Are you Robert Snider's son?"

He took a deep breath and said, "Yes, I am."

"Dad," wailed the boy. "Don't tell her."

"What, son? What shouldn't I say?"

The boy clammed up and his father walked over hesitantly like he couldn't quite get his balance, and said, "Answer me? How did you know?"

The boy started crying. "You'll never be president now."

"President?" Robert Snider Junior was truly astonished. "You did this because you thought I was going to be president?"

"Everyone said so."

Robert Junior took over for the Sister, pressing his hand against his son's bloody shoulder. "Someone please call an ambulance."

"Robbie, you threw the bomb into my office?" Sister Emily was just as astonished as the father. "But why?"

Robert Junior looked at me. "If you call an ambulance, I'll tell you everything."

I didn't get a chance to respond. Stratton and Mosbach burst through the door with Patton just behind them with guns drawn. They looked at our small bedraggled group and were more than confused.

Stratton lowered her weapon, checked Robbie's wound, and called for EMTs before asking, "Why are you wet?"

"It's a long story," I said.

"We're not moving until the ambulance gets here," she said. "Somebody tell me what happened."

So I told her, complete with flooding and flying musical instruments.

"You expect me to believe that?" Stratton asked me.

"It's true," said Clarence. "I would swear before God that it is."

Sister Emily silently nodded in agreement and went to open the door for the EMTs who were making quite a racket coming down the stairs. Once they were in, Robert Stratton III was strapped to a gurney and read his rights before being hauled up the stairs wailing to his father to say nothing.

His father didn't go with him. He leaned on a wall looking down at the pool of water forming beneath his feet.

"She needs a vet," said Fats with Moe nestled in her arm.

Patton, whose father was a vet, took over with Moe, checking her and deciding she needed emergency care. Stratton decided not to arrest Fats for shooting Robbie and let her go to the vet with Patton. Mosbach went up to announce that the bomber was caught and the tournament could go on as planned. As if there was any doubt that it would. St. Sebastian was nothing if not single minded.

"Are you going to arrest me?" Robert Junior asked.

"What for?" Sister Emily asked. "You tried to stop him."

He looked at me and I wasn't sure what to say. It was wrong, years and years of wrong, but was it criminal? That I wasn't sure about.

Mosbach came back down with an evidence bag and a box of tissues and said, "The FBI are almost here and one named Gansa said to tell you that your boyfriend is with them and he is pissed."

"Swell."

Mosbach opened the evidence bag and I dropped the yearbook in. "Your son knew about Bertram Stott and your father? Did you tell him?"

Robert Junior raised his head. "God, no. Sorry, Sister Em."

"That's alright," she said, looking almost demure in her bewilderment. "I don't understand about this yearbook situation. 1965? Why that year? How did Robbie know it was important?"

I took the tissues and started mopping up my face. "He said Zoe told him. I think he must mean Carrie's granddaughter Zoe. She said a bunch of high school students were at her house for the snow day and they were all excited about me being here, Stott, and the murder."

Robert Junior nodded. "He and Zoe have been friends forever." He hung his head and his voice got tight and throaty. "I didn't know he knew. I tried so hard to keep it from him, from everyone, but I should've known the minute Stott came back, it was over."

"This is about Sister Margaret?" asked Sister Em. "But that was so long ago."

A flame started inside me and I clenched my one working fist. "You think it went away just because you and the church decided to forget her?"

The nun's face flushed. "I didn't forget her. I pray for her soul every day."

"Well, it's not enough," I spat at her and turned to look at Robert Junior. "You knew what happened to Sister Maggie and you knew what happened after, didn't you?" Blood was spraying from my mouth and nose, but I didn't care. "People died because you didn't say anything. Tank's in the hospital because you had to keep your family secret."

Robert Junior's mouth trembled, but he didn't speak. The secrets started before he was born. He inherited the horror, but he didn't have to go along. He didn't have to keep it going.

"I don't understand," said Sister Em. "Obviously, Robert Junior wasn't here when she was murdered."

"His father was," I said. "Isn't that what we'll find in the file room? Bertram Stott was in school on the day Maggie was murdered. Your father wasn't."

Sister Em scoffed. "Don't be ridiculous. Robert Snider was a Snider. His family is a fine upstanding family. He wouldn't have killed anyone. He was practically a child."

"A high school senior is hardly a child," I said, "but he was just as scared as Robbie, wasn't he?"

"Scared of what?" She looked at Robert Junior and he raised his eyes to meet hers, guilt written all over him. Then he slid down the wall, all the strength gone out of his legs. "I can't believe it's finally over."

Stratton clicked her walkie and asked the voice on the other end for an ETA on the FBI. They were almost there and she surprised me by telling her deputies and the fire department to hold them back for a few. "I want to hear this and not second hand or on the news."

Robert Junior swallowed and he did as promised, he told me everything. Me, not Stratton or the nuns or Mosbach. It seemed important that he talk to me. Maybe because I was covered in blood from his son's attack or because I was an outsider, I don't know, but Robert

Junior confessed to his family's crimes and I swear he lost twenty pounds in the process.

Irene was right. The Snider family crimes went all the way back to Decatur. Daniel Snider did rob that bank and used the money to buy up properties during the Great Depression. It's easy when you have stolen money and zero compassion. Daniel used his so-called windfall to good advantage, but he had a family of spenders and layabouts. The properties had to be sold one by one since they always exceeded their income. By the late fifties, the Snider's were down to a farm and the land Maggie's body was found on. They couldn't find a buyer, so Davis Snider, Robert Junior's grandfather, had to find an alternative income, other than, you know, working for it.

His wife, Helen, was very active in church affairs and she was invited to join the asylum's council in 1950, but she always used her maiden name in business matters, Helen Smith, which was why we didn't connect her.

Robert Junior didn't know how it happened or why, but his grandfather Davis started serving on the council instead and he was the one who decided to syphon money into the trust fund at St. Sebastian Savings and Loan.

"How did you find out?" I asked. "Did your dad actually tell you his father stole money from the asylum?"

Robert Junior took a deep breath and shook his head. "No. I don't think they ever would've told me anything, but my father got killed and I got curious."

"Curious?" Stratton asked.

The Snider family was a close one and hunting together was something they always did, but in the fall of 1999, something changed. Robert Junior came home from law school for the annual turkey hunt, but everyone was surprised that he showed up, since he hadn't been specifically invited, and they weren't happy about it. His father was strung out on painkillers. His mother was hysterical and his grandparents silent and dark. Most importantly, nobody else his age was there. Siblings, cousins, no one else showed. The next morning when they would normally have gone out for the hunt, Robert Junior was told in no uncertain terms that he was to go back to school. His grandfather put him in his car and watched him drive away from his rocker on the porch.

Since everyone was acting so odd, Robert Junior didn't go. He drove down the block and waited to see what would happen.

He watched his mother drive away crying and a few minutes later the rest of the family, his grandmother and uncles, drove by with his father in their trucks. Everyone but his grandfather, who never hunted because he'd lost a leg in the war. The rough terrain was impossible for him.

Robert Junior didn't know what was going on, but he did suspect his parents were finally getting a divorce. His father had been a mess for years and his mother was miserable.

He didn't want to leave, but, since no one wanted him there, he did go back to school. Not long after he got to his apartment, his grandfather called to say his father had been shot accidentally and he was dead. Robert Junior drove back to St. Seb and was ordered to hunt down his mother who had gone to a bar, where she'd drunk herself into a stupor. Her son had to scrape her off the floor, literally.

It was Joan Snider, his mother, who let it slip while she was drunk out of her mind. The family had killed Robert because he had to be punished. Robert Junior searched his father's belongings when no one was watching and he found a nun's veil and letters quietly threatening to expose the Snider family's crimes. He confronted his grandparents and Helen admitted to shooting her own son and dared her grandson to turn her in. She told him that Robert had murdered a nun because she found out that his father had been stealing from the church. She didn't say orphans or the mentally ill, but Robert Junior figured that out on his own.

"But why kill him then?" Stratton asked. "It'd been a long time."

"Because he helped Stott bury Janet Lee Fine's body," I said.

Robert Junior nodded. "But I didn't know that then. All they would say was that my father was a murderer and they found out. It was a kindness to kill him and not put him in jail."

"When did you find out about Janet Lee Fine?" I asked.

"Stott showed up at my office out of the blue. I didn't know who he was. Nobody said there was someone else involved in the murder. My mother never spoke to me about it again and she died a few years later. Overdose. My grandparents were gone and when I asked my uncles about it once, they threatened to take me hunting."

An involuntary shiver went down my back. What a family.

"Why did you believe him?" Stratton asked.

"I didn't at first, but he had evidence." Robert Junior swallowed hard. "Pictures of the body. Of my father moving the body."

"Janet Lee Fine's body?" Stratton asked.

"No, I mean, yes. He showed me pictures of the nun first. He said he wanted money, enough to live on the rest of his life. I didn't have that and even if I did, my wife handles our finances. She was going to notice thousands going missing. But then he threatened her and my kids. He told me about the little girl. He said, 'If she can go missing, so can your boy.' That's when he showed me the other pictures. It seemed like they were real, but he didn't give me a name. I didn't know who she was."

"Your father was in the pictures?" Sister Em asked in a choked voice.

Robert Junior wiped his eyes. "He was."

"What was in the pictures?" I asked.

He described a white panel van with the back doors open, his father reaching in toward a small figure, partially nude. There was a pink bicycle next to the body. His father looked drunk, which he often was, and he had a bruised face.

"So you sold the land and gave him the money?" Sister Em said.

"I did. I had to. He was serious. He would hurt my wife and my kids. I sold the land and told my wife that I put it in trust for the kids."

"You never thought about going to the cops?" I asked. "You could've had Stott arrested. You had evidence."

He wiped his eyes again. "No, I didn't. I'd burned the veil and letters. I didn't want anyone to know what my dad did. Sure he was an asshole and a loser, but a nun killer, how could I ever have a life with that hanging over my head?"

"What about her family?" Sister Em asked.

"They thought that priest did it. It was solved." He paused and then said, "Sometimes I thought I dreamt it all up. That it was all a nightmare. Grandma didn't kill Dad. Dad didn't kill a nun. That little girl. None of it happened."

Sister Em took his hand. "It was easier that way."

"Nothing was easy. I'm just as much an asshole as my old man. I drink. I'm a nasty bastard to my only son and he's trying to blow people up to protect me. I don't deserve protection. Someone *should* take me hunting."

"How did he find out?" Stratton asked.

Robert Junior rubbed his eyes. "I don't know. I didn't tell him. My wife doesn't even know. There's nothing in our house to find."

"Where'd he get the grenades?"

"That's easy. My grandpa brought them back from WWII. My uncle had them out at his cabin. It was always the family joke that someday we'd throw them at our enemies."

"Hilarious," said Stratton.

"I didn't think it would happen," he said, "and they're so old. I thought they must go bad at some point."

"I guess that's it." Stratton clicked her walkie. "They here?"

The voice answered that the FBI and a very pissed off St. Louis police detective were in the principal's office.

"Tell 'em we're on our way." Stratton took Robert Junior's arm. "I think I should arrest you, but I'm not sure what for."

"Hold on," I said.

"What?"

"Where did your grandfather serve in WWII? The Pacific with Chief Woody Lucas and Barney Scheer?"

Robert Junior's eyes widened. "How did you know?"

"They covered up for your father or, at least, looked the other way."

"I always wondered how no one ever found out, but that makes sense," he said.

"Does it?" I asked.

"Those two were in my grandfather's brother's platoon during the war. He didn't come back."

"So they were close? Woody, Barney, and your grandfather, I mean?"

He shrugged. "I have no idea."

"Any pictures of them together? Woody and Desmond Shipley were tight until Maggie's murder. There are all kinds of pictures of them together."

"I don't remember any, but I wasn't looking. My grandfather never talked about it, except to yell about the Japanese every once in a while. He thought buying a Japanese car was the act of a traitor."

I pulled out Fats' phone, but it was waterlogged. Spidermonkey would have to wait. "Robert, how did you get down here?" I asked.

"Through that door there's an emergency exit," he said, pointing down the hall. "What are you going to do?"

"I'm going to see a man about a murder."

"What about the pissed off boyfriend?" Stratton asked.

"Let me worry about him," I said. "One last thing, does the name Kenneth Young mean anything to you?"

"Who?" he asked.

"That's what I thought." I turned to Clarence. "How did you get here?"

"I took an Uber," she said. "Irene taught me how. My kids will be so impressed."

Robert Junior frowned. "Have you been cloistered?"

"In a way." Clarence smiled and gave him a hug. "I will pray for you and your son."

That brought fresh tears to his eyes. "Thank you, Sister. I need all the help I can get."

"Where to next?" Clarence asked. "Sister Frances is very impressed with your progress."

"I'm going to give a serial killer what he wants," I said.

Stratton got stiff. "You're going to see Stott? That's not a good idea."

I smiled. "Not good ideas are my favorite kind."

CHAPTER THIRTY-ONE

We didn't take an Uber. Deputy Mosbach snuck us out the back exit and drove us in his squad car after a quick stop at Fats' truck for supplies. Getting out was easier than it should've been. I was a soaking wet and bloody marshmallow Peep, tromping through knee-high snow with a nun and a cop, but nobody looked twice.

To be fair, Robbie was being loaded into an ambulance, wailing for his father, and Robert Junior walked out before us. He apologized to everyone in sight. I don't know if it was simply the spirit of St. Sebastian or the fact that nobody but Robbie got hurt, but forgiveness was in the air. Whether the promises for prayer and help would materialize after they found out the rest was an open question, but I was betting they would. Robert Junior hadn't done the right thing. He hid what should never have been hidden, but it wasn't hard for me to put myself in his place. I was the age he was when he found out what his family had done. A murderer father in turn murdered by his grandmother and a couple of uncles who would cheerfully do the same to him. What would I have done? I wish I could say I knew for certain that I'd do the right thing, but I'd be lying. And once you start keeping secrets, more secrets come your way and they never die. I wished Robert

Junior had done the right thing in the fall of 1999 and taken so much pain away from Maggie's family, Millicent and Myrtle, not to mention Aunt Miriam, but he didn't and it was up to them to forgive if they could.

"Do you see your boyfriend?" Mosbach asked as he put me in the back of his squad car.

I squinted at the crowd and the steps up to the front doors of the high school. Gordon and Gansa were there, trying and failing not to look like they just won the lottery. A bunch of other agents were working on the impact area outside the principal's office and still more were arguing with what I assumed were basketball coaches. They tried to put up crime scene tape and the coaches kept tearing it down and yelling the way only irate coaches can. The show aka the tournament would go on.

"He's probably in the basement looking for me," I said. "Better get while the getting is good."

"Do you really want to see Stott?" Clarence asked as she tucked an emergency warming blanket around me. "I think you should go to the hospital."

"I should, but I won't."

Mosbach drove slowly out of the parking lot weaving between buses, cars, and FBI vans with no lights on. I thought that looked pretty suspicious, but we got away clean and were driving back into town through increasing snow.

We drove down Fifth Street and slid to a halt at an intersection with a cop directing traffic.

"Mercy?" Clarence whispered.

"Yeah?"

"Do you see that?"

"Definitely."

Mosbach smiled at me in the rearview. "It happens."

"Should we be scared?" Clarence said, wringing her hands.

The deputy patted her on the shoulder. "No, Sister. He's just helping out."

The shadowy figure dressed in a cop's uniform that looked to be from the 1930s waved us through the intersection. I took a breath and then leaned over to peer out at him. It was the weirdest thing. He was there, well-defined and semi-solid, but I could also see through him as we drove past. The officer glanced down at me and touched the tip of his phantom hat and then went back to waving the traffic through.

"Who is he?" squeaked Clarence.

"Thomas B. Thompson," said Mosbach. "He was killed in a collision during a thunderstorm in 1936 and he's been directing traffic when there's bad weather or an accident ever since."

It took me a second to find my voice. Being seen and acknowledged by a ghost is unsettling to the extreme. If I'd had something in my stomach, I would've thrown it up. "How is he not all over TV?"

"You mean like *Ghost Hunters* and crap like that?" Mosbach asked.

"Yeah."

"What makes you think ghosts are stupid?"

"Um...I never thought about ghost intelligence one way or another," I said.

He looked at me in the rearview again. "Really? Haven't you met Miss Elizabeth? I thought Lefty said you had."

"Oh, well, I guess I have."

"Isn't there a brain at work?"

Miss Elizabeth had a brain. I wasn't crazy about it, but she had one.

"You're saying that ghosts...decide who's going to see them and when," I said. "Irene said that about Miss Elizabeth, but I thought maybe she was unique."

"She's unique but not in that way," he said. "If Thompson didn't want you to see him, you wouldn't. Personally, I think those paranormal hunter people insult them. Like you can just sit in a house with a camera and a ghost will wander by like a mindless moron. Give me a break."

"Aren't they...scary?" Clarence asked.

"Some aren't great, but what of it? Live people aren't always so hot either," said Mosbach. "Speaking of live assholes, here we are."

The deputy pulled into the parking lot of the Shady Glen Retirement Home and parked beside a hearse that had backed up to a ramp.

"I hope he's dead," said Clarence suddenly and then she crossed herself and began praying for forgiveness.

"Clarence, is it really wrong to wish for the death of a serial killer?" I asked.

"Yes. Punishment is not for me to say. It's God's will and I shouldn't wish for something like that. I should find it in my heart to forgive."

We got out of the squad car as the snow became mixed with ice. Mosbach hurried us up the ramp through a back door and we stomped off an unbelievable amount of snow and ice. My teeth were chattering so hard they hurt.

An LPN at the desk jerked her head up from a chart and her jaw dropped. "Dallas, what on Earth are you doing here? Wasn't there a bomb threat at the new high school?"

"It's all under control. An arrest's already been made," he said.

A nurse named Stephanie came out to greet us and stopped short. "Oh, my...goodness. Were you going to the hospital? She looks—"

"Bad?" I asked with what I hoped passed for a smile. My nose had swollen to epic proportions and my entire face had a throbbing ache that went through it at ten second intervals.

"Well, yes," she said. "Were you caught in the explosion? Why are you wet? Sister, you're wet, too. You'll get hypothermia."

Stephanie kicked it into high gear and got us into an empty room. I was out of my Peep wear and into fresh scrubs that were—you guessed it—pink in five minutes. Only Clarence's feet and stockings were wet, so she got a pair of support hose and slippers.

I needed help with my incredibly disgusting swollen face and talked Clarence into leaving for the gory part. She wanted to stay, but pointing out the amount of crusty blood I had got her moving. Stephanie wasn't happy, but she did as I asked. It was pretty easy and I was having coffee in under five minutes.

"You really have to go to the hospital," said Stephanie. "We can't do anything about your pain. Nobody can prescribe."

"I want to see Bertram Stott before the FBI gets here," I said.

A shiver went through her and she wrapped her arms around her waist. You'd have thought she was soaked to the skin. "He won't talk to anyone. Didn't Dallas tell you?"

"He'll see me," I said.

"Because you're famous?"

I could tell the idea bothered her. Some people are impressed by fame, any kind of fame, and others are repulsed. She was in the latter category.

"No," I said. "He asked for me."

Stephanie turned to Mosbach and he nodded. "He wouldn't say why."

"I know a friend of his," I said.

That repulsed everyone.

"By friend, do you mean someone like him?" she asked. "A murderer?"

"Yes."

"Who?"

"Kent Blankenship." I told them as little as possible about my fan, the mass murderer, and Stephanie shrugged. "I don't see why that would help."

"There's more to it, but we're on a time crunch here."

She agreed to take me to his room, but I could tell she didn't want to go anywhere near him. Shady Glen had admitted Stott in a fit of compassion, saying that he'd served his time. Yada. Yada. Yada. But they'd been regretting it ever since. People were afraid of him on instinct, even those who didn't know who he was. Stephanie said he had a thing about him, but she couldn't describe or explain it. There were no other residents on his hall. Nobody would agree to live near him. The staff went in three at a time and had to be paid double to do it. I'd known a lot of scary dudes, but this was freaking me out. Stott sounded worse than Blankenship and that was hard to imagine.

Stephanie stopped at Stott's door with her face flushed. "Are you really going in there?" She looked at the three of us.

"Just me," I said.

"I can do it." Clarence looked quite brave when she said it, but she didn't know what "do it" meant.

"No. He's going to tell me things that you won't be able to forget. I wouldn't do that to you and Aunt Miriam would never forgive me if I did."

She bit her lip and nodded.

Mosbach put his hand on his revolver. "I'm definitely going in. You can't do it alone. He's crazy and violent."

"That's nothing new for me," I said.

"Someone has to go in with you," said Stephanie.

"He won't talk unless I'm alone. They like me alone. It makes them feel powerful."

"You really think he'll talk to you?" asked Mosbach.

"I do."

"Why?"

"His is a small world and I'm good company."

Stephanie shook her head. "I don't know what that means."

"But he does and that's the point." I reached to push the door open, but she cut me off and knocked. There wasn't an answer.

"He never answers," she whispered. "I think he hopes we'll think he's dead, so we'll come in alone."

Creepy.

"He's going to get his wish," I said.

Stephanie knocked a second time and pushed the door open a mere three inches. "Mr. Stott, you have a visitor."

No answer.

"Mr. Stott?"

I eased her out of the way. "Never mind. I don't have all day."

"But...are you sure?" she asked.

"No, but it usually works out for me." I pushed open the door and walked in, letting the door silently close behind me.

Stott's room was a cheery yellow with marble-patterned tile on the floor. To my right was a bathroom and past that I could see the foot of a hospital bed with one rail up. It smelled like Vicks VapoRub, a smell that I always found comforting but never would again. The faint odor of unwashed man accompanied the VapoRub, not strong but like an undercurrent ready to overwhelm you at any moment.

I walked to the edge of the bathroom wall and looked at the bed. It was empty and I had a moment of panic, thinking he was in the bathroom and would come out behind me, but I quickly spotted a figure slumped in the corner. Stott sat in a plain institutional chair with a pillow behind his back and blanket on his lap. He was smaller than I'd expected, probably five six or seven, at most. His gnarled, liver-spotted hands had a TV remote and something else that he'd quickly concealed when I walked in.

My eyes went up to his face and my stomach went instantly queasy. The old man was smiling at me in a way that was completely predatory and so sexual I could see why no one wanted to be in the room alone with him. I certainly didn't. The incongruity of that smile in a face that was much older than his seventy-one years was bad enough, but the eyes got me. He had Blankenship's crocodile stare. There was a reptile looking at me and he was trying to figure out how to get me closer.

"Our friend told me it would be you," he said in a honeyed voice that belonged to a much younger and less frightening man.

"Friend's putting it strong," I said. "Do you actually know Blankenship?"

His eyes roamed over me, looking to see if I'd concealed a phone or a wire. The scrubs were certainly loose enough, but my hands were empty.

"Are you going to answer me or should I scoot?" I asked. "I could be at the hospital getting some painkillers right now."

"How much pain are you in?" he asked, licking his bluish-grey lips.

"Plenty."

His breathing increased, only a little, but I could see it. Pain excited him. "What happened to your pretty face?"

"Two explosions and slammed into a floor."

"The arm?"

"Rebroken."

"That must be excruciating."

"It's not great," I said.

"Let me see the arm," he said.

I held my arm out to show off the swelling, the purplish tinge that was rapidly spreading. I didn't move any closer. "Back to Blankenship."

A flicker of disappointment went through his cold eyes and was quickly replaced by nothing, which was definitely worse. "I've never met him personally, but we're old friends. What took you so long? He claims you're a smart one. I like the smart ones."

"He didn't tell me you existed," I said.

Stott eyed my body again and I swear I could feel it like fingertips tracing over my skin.

"I'm not wearing a wire," I said.

"Come closer and prove it," he said.

"Nope. Not gonna happen."

"Then you may as well leave."

I rolled my eyes and yanked my scrub top up, exposing my naked breasts to him. A girl's got to do what a girl's got to do.

The essence of predator got more intense and he said, "It could be on your lower half."

I dropped my scrub bottoms and did a quick spin. I'd taken the precaution of losing my panties and I was glad I did. Stott was satisfied. More than satisfied, so it was worth it.

I put my palms up. "So?"

"You're fatter than I imagined."

"And you're grosser," I said. "Let's do this. What do you want to tell me?"

Stott reached up and tugged at the oxygen line under his nose. "He sent you to my garden. Is it still beautiful? Did you enjoy the view?"

"I didn't actually go to Kansas myself."

"What a shame. My family does like their work to be acknowledged," he said.

"Don't worry. The FBI's acknowledging the hell out of your family and they gave me a little gift."

The smile got wider. "Come over here."

I sighed and rolled my eyes. "How in the world did you ever get close enough to kill anyone?"

"You don't like this?" he asked and his face transformed into someone else entirely. Now, instead of looking at an obvious predator, I was seeing a harmless old man with sweet, watery blue eyes and trembling hands.

"Is that how you sucked Robbie in?" I asked.

He chuckled. It sounded like a rock on a cheese grater. "It's easy when they're sad or stupid. That boy is both."

"How long did it take?"

"Only a few weeks. He was so lonely and desperate for a father. Robert Junior wasn't the best parent."

"And you were? Everyone hates you."

He held up a finger with hideously swollen joints. "I get what I want."

"Why bother? You couldn't kill him. Look at the state of you," I said.

"But I could own him the way Blankenship owns you."

"That's debatable."

"It's not. I owned his father and his grandfather. Unhappiness runs in that family. It was too easy. I don't know why people think they're smart. They're not."

"Did you tell Robert Snider to kill Sister Maggie?" I asked.

He shook his head and the few hairs he had left waved around in the air like thin tentacles. "I didn't have to. I'd prepared him to act when the time came and it turned out better than I'd dared to hope."

Stott told me how he met Robert Snider. Because of their names, they were usually next to each other in every class. Stott knew a kindred spirit, as he called it, when he saw one. Robert had already been robbing houses and unlocked cars when he met him. Stott only had to introduce Robert to making Molotov cocktails and he was eager to throw them. Killing animals was more difficult, but by then Stott had him cornered. Robert had committed multiple felonies and Stott was willing to go to the police or so Robert believed.

Stott had been working his way up to kidnapping. He wanted Kathleen Coulter because she was beautiful and ignored him once in the hall at school. That was enough to incite murder, I guess. But before he could get his friend on board, Robert went home for lunch the day before Maggie's murder and overheard his parents discussing what to do if Sister Maggie reported them to the police. He understood that his parents had been stealing thousands of dollars from the church and his life was about to go under. His reaction was to go out and throw a cocktail into Liquor Mart.

Stott claimed that he had nothing to do with that and I believed him. Mainly because he didn't know how Davis Snider found out that his son had done it. He only knew that Robert wasn't at school and was waiting for him in the parking lot at lunch with Maggie's body in the back of his father's farm truck. Davis had planned to take Robert to St. Vincent's Mental Hospital for an evaluation and as a kind of punishment, he had made Robert drive it to St. Louis while Davis drove his nice, cushy Bel Air. They went to the asylum first. Davis left Robert in the hall while he tried to talk to Maggie, but she wouldn't speak to him. She left the office, brushing past Robert and saying something about meeting the bishop. When he looked in the office, he saw his father bent over with his head in his hands, crying, and knew he had to stop her from telling the bishop.

Robert told Stott that he beat Maggie down the stairs, got a tire iron out of the back of his father's truck and cracked her skull with it in the parking lot. But she didn't die like people did on TV, so he strangled her the way Stott had taught him.

Stott steepled his fingers and smiled that awful smile at me. "Robert was very weak. I admit I was surprised."

"Why?" I asked. "He was already a criminal before you showed up."

He made a face full of disdain. "Robert was small time. A little boy who wanted Daddy's attention. He needed me to be serious."

"Gross."

"I'm pleased you think so."

"Why are you telling me all this? Just because of Blankenship?"

He smiled again. "What are you going to do? Put me on trial? I'm practically dead already."

"They're still putting Nazis on trial, why not you?"

"The publicity won't be good. I've been running rings around them since I was fifteen."

"You started when you were fifteen?" I asked.

In truth, Stott had started with fires when he was twelve and progressed to robbery and assault at seventeen, which was why he ended up in St. Sebastian. His parents got him out of state because they found out that he assaulted a classmate. It was dark and she couldn't identify him so they sent him to his grandfather's brother, Otis Harmon. Otis was at the town meeting and he put it together that his grandnephew came to town and fires started, so he sent him back when the semester ended. Not nearly soon enough.

"Like I said, running rings around them," said Stott.

"Not anymore," I said.

"Sadly no," he said. "If you come closer, I might have another one in me."

"I'll pass."

"Pity." Then his eyes brightened. "How about you tell me something?"

I picked some of the crusty blood from under my nose and said, "Why not? I figure the FBI will be here any minute."

"Then I better hurry."

"That would be good."

"How did you connect my garden to me?" he asked for the first time genuinely interested.

"You left an Easter egg for us to find."

His eyes were blank. This time from confusion. "An Easter egg?"

"Sister Maggie's St. Brigid medal was found between two of your bodies."

"Ah. That's where it went. I hated to lose it." He tilted his chin down in a coquettish manner and batted his red-rimmed eyes at me.

"Barf," I said. "What happened to you?"

"Nothing happened to me," he said. "I happened to other people. Want to hear about it?"

I lifted one shoulder and sighed. "Fine. Knock yourself out." That's what I said, but I didn't want to hear it. His words would stain me forever, which I suppose was the point.

"You don't want to hear about my little family and our good times?" He transformed into a truculent child with a simpering voice and a bottom lip that poked out in a pout.

"Nailed it," I said. "I don't enjoy talking to Blankenship either, by the way. He bites."

"Ooh, do tell. Did he really bite you?"

I told him what happened during my last visit to Hunt Hospital for the Criminally Insane and he practically salivated. "Would you visit me there? I'm sure I'd be a model resident."

"I thought you were dying."

He smiled. "Eventually. Come closer. I want to show you something."

"Would it be the blade in your hand? I'll pass."

"You're no fun."

"Tell me about Kenneth Young," I said. "And maybe I'll go into the fishbowl with you strapped to a chair."

"Promise?"

"Why not? I'm considering visiting Harvey the Head Case. I hear he's interesting," I said.

"He's not as interesting as me." He started naming names, so many names and places. There's no way I could remember them all and he knew that by the way he rattled them off.

"You're diverse. I'll give you that," I said. "But you're not telling me what I want to know."

He batted his eyes again. "Do you want to know how it feels to come inside a corpse?"

"That's not exactly news I can use."

"You can't use any of this," he said. "It feels like pumping—"

"Kenneth Young."

"That's not interesting," he said with a pout.

"Try me."

"He's not mine."

I raised an eyebrow and Bertram Stott told me that Robert Snider followed the reporter out of town, ran him off the road, and while he was dazed drowned him in a creek. Then he called Stott in Tennessee in a complete panic. Stott came and "used the body" before burying it on the grounds of one of the Augusta wineries. Stott drove Young's VW until it got out on the news that a man who'd murdered several women had been driving a 1968 beige Beetle.

"Ted Bundy?" I asked.

He scowled. "Amateur. They thought he was so smart. If he was smart, he wouldn't have been caught. You haven't caught most of my family."

"You've been caught," I pointed out. "Here I am."

"But I won't go to prison. It's just your word against mine."

"You'll be arrested at the very least."

"I knew when I came back here I'd probably be found out."

"Why'd you do it then?" I asked.

"I had to. I couldn't get work anymore and appearing like other people was getting harder. I didn't expect that nun to kick up a fuss at the building site and put that skinny hippy on my trail, but he was easy to put off."

"Tank Tancredi?"

"Yes. Easily distracted that one."

"You call that easy. You burned down his business, his house, and killed his dogs."

"Yes, I killed them," he said with a most horrible smile. "And not in the fire either."

He told me what he did to Tank's dogs. I don't want to say it was worse than what he did to Maggie, Kenneth, or all the others, but in those moments it was. Dogs and kids. Dad always said they were the hardest. As usual, he wasn't wrong. I only hoped Tank and his family would never find out.

"It's so nice to share," he said. "It takes me back."

My skin felt tight on my body, like I couldn't quite fit into it anymore, and I began to wonder what was taking Chuck and the FBI so long. I wanted them to come and stop this horror, but they didn't and I had to keep going.

"Tell me more about the others," I said. "You have other sites, not just Kansas."

"You're not just a pretty face."

"Not right now."

He smiled and told me. He had sites in Rhode Island, Florida, and Kentucky. He told me about Janet Lee Fine and what he did. I decided to lie on the spot and swore to God that her parents would never hear what happened from me. If they asked me, I'd lie to their faces, and I wouldn't be sorry.

To make it worse, that little girl wasn't the only one. Stott's tastes varied and if he had a M.O., I couldn't find it, unless you count insatiable. The woman in Tennessee was his one mistake. He'd gotten so good so young, he'd become careless. He was never careless again.

"What about Dr. Desarno?" I asked. "Was that you or Robert?"

"That again?" he asked. "It's not nearly as interesting as that family in Newport. They still believe the father did it and ran off."

"Dr. Desarno."

He sighed and adjusted his oxygen level. "Yes, that was me. Robert wasn't up to it. He was delicate. I was surprised he didn't blow his head off earlier."

"He didn't blow his head off," I said.

"No? I assumed the hunting accident was a story to tell the kids."

"His mother shot him, on purpose."

"Helen was a tough nut. I liked her and that tells you everything you need to know about her mothering," he said.

A knock on the door startled me and Mosbach said, "I think they're heading this way. You better wrap it up."

"But I'm not done with you," said Stott.

"Bummer," I said. "One more question."

"If you promise to visit while I'm briefly in jail."

"I told you I would."

Liar, liar, pants on fire.

He frowned.

"I'll visit just like Blankenship," I said.

"Quality time with me isn't like Blankenship. You know he's only a garden variety psychotic."

"Whatever," I said. "Did you kill Father Dominic?"

He licked his lips slowly and admitted he did it at Robert's request. Chief Lucas had told people that Bishop Fowler thought Father Dominic was having an affair with Sister Maggie. Dominic seemed an obvious scapegoat and Robert was scared. His father noticed that he left the asylum and didn't come back. Robert made up an excuse, but Davis was suspicious. Despite their own criminal history, Robert feared that killing a nun wasn't going to be okay. So Stott called up the young priest and told him he had information about Maggie's murder to lure him to the bridge.

"He was a grown man. You were just a kid," I said. "How'd you do it?"

"We walked up on the bridge, I hit him in the head with a hammer, and threw him over."

"No one saw? How'd you manage it?"

"I was lucky."

"Just lucky?"

He smiled that smile again. "I've always been lucky." Then he transformed into a helpless old man again. It was so creepy I shivered and he totally enjoyed it.

"There were witnesses," I said.

"Were there?" he asked innocently. "A young man who happened to be taking a walk and a couple coming out of a bar, perhaps?"

"You were a witness?" I was truly astonished by the audacity of it. "How?"

"I told you that it's easy when they're stupid. It's even easier when they're drunk."

After Stott threw Dominic off the bridge, he went to a bar overlooking the river and waited for a couple to come out. He started yelling about a man falling off the bridge and when he got done with the drunk duo, they were convinced they'd seen it themselves. Stott was pretty proud of that and I had to admit it, he had skills.

"So that's why the three *witnesses* didn't see the second person on the bridge," I said.

He smirked, picked something out of his yellowed teeth, and ate it.

"Who was the fourth witness? The one that did see you."

That question wiped the smirk away and he said, "I couldn't find out. The newspaper didn't name them."

"What would you have done if they had?"

"Guess." The smirk came back.

"I'm going to tell the FBI everything you told me," I said.

"No, you won't. Not everything. You won't tell him how I climbed on top of—"

"Almost everything."

"They won't be able to convict me on hearsay and that's all you've got."

"Robert Junior confessed. He's with the cops right now," I said.

"His kid will talk."

If Stott had an inkling of worry, he didn't show it. Maybe he couldn't feel fear. "And say what? He saw some pictures? Where are the pictures?"

"We have the businesses that you worked for. You used their credit cards and vehicles to move bodies."

"I like to take road trips."

"The businesses can press charges for theft," I said.

"Statute of limitations." Stott turned back into the horrid predator he was and he looked like he wanted to bite me. He probably did and that wasn't the end of his desires. "Miss Watts, I don't make mistakes. You won't find a strand of DNA to connect me to any of what I've told you."

"They'll throw everything they have at you."

"Even if they plant evidence, get witnesses to lie, it won't matter," he said with ultimate confidence. "Trials like the one you're talking about take at least a year. How long do you think I'm going to last?"

I smiled at him. "I'm willing to give it a shot."

"The worst that will happen is that I'll spend some pleasurable time at Hunt while they try to pick me apart." He leaned forward. "I won't come apart, Miss Watts."

"I believe you," I said and turned to go.

"Miss Watts."

I looked back and he tossed me something. I caught it, which probably wasn't a good idea, but it was the switchblade that he'd been concealing in his lap.

"I'd like you to have my favorite tool, since you alone know how many times I've used it and how much pleasure it gave me," he said. "Put it in your panty drawer. Every time you get dressed you'll think of me."

"I'll put it in an evidence bag," I said.

His face distorted further. It hurt me to think that for so many that was the last face they saw. "You won't find anything on it."

"We'll see."

"Yes, we will."

I went out and nearly ran Mosbach over.

"Are you okay?" He was panting and sweat ran from his temples and stained his collar. "You were in there forever."

"I'm fine." *Totally horrified, but fine.* "He confessed to everything or at least a lot of things."

"That won't be enough, but we can get a warrant for his room." Mosbach said something else but my legs started to buckle.

Clarence grabbed me. "You have to get to the hospital."

"I need some air." I walked as fast as I could without running, since running wasn't an option in my braless state.

Unfortunately, they chased after me. Stephanie said she'd get a wheelchair. Mosbach was on his walkie, asking where the hell the FBI was. Clarence was tearfully praying. I turned a couple of corners and said, "Please, just give me a minute. I need a minute."

They stopped at the nurse's station and I followed the signs toward the exit alone. When I turned a corner, two men came walking toward me. I probably wouldn't have noticed them at all, since I was so upset, but they were wearing what I guess you'd call leisure suits. They were straight out of the seventies, one wearing avocado and the other sickly beige. Both had fuzzy mustaches and feathered hair. They were so weird I questioned whether I was seeing actual live humans. It was St. Seb after all.

When we crossed paths, they glanced at me and did a chin thrust, signaling that they knew me, but I didn't recognize them. I nodded and turned the last turn to go to Mosbach's cruiser, but standing at the exit was Chuck Watts, casually leaning on the handrail and looking at his phone.

"What the hell are you doing here?" I asked.

He looked up and he clenched his jaw for a second when he saw my face. "I'm waiting for you. Did you get it?"

"You're just standing there? I was talking to a serious psycho."

Chuck came to me and put his hands on my shoulders. "Tommy told me to let you do what you do, so I did. Now did you get it?"

"What?" I asked.

"Proof. Evidence," he said. "I assume you didn't go in there for kicks."

"That's why you didn't try to stop me? You thought I might get something on Stott?"

"Mercy, my love, I've been trying to stop you and it just pisses you off. I thought I'd help for once and see how it works out. Did you get something on Stott?"

I reached up and painfully pulled away a good portion of the bloody bandages over the splint on my face.

"Wow...that's really bad," said Chuck as blood droplets started hitting the floor. "Maybe you should think about stopping that."

"Nope." I peeled a little black disk attached to a wire and tiny battery pack off my nose and cheek.

"Holy shit. You recorded him."

"I did."

Chuck looked down at me, his blue eyes getting all moist and red. "I've never loved you more."

"I'm not sure how to take that," I said.

"I want to kiss you so bad."

"Please don't. My face is on fire."

"Hospital?"

"Hell, yeah."

CHAPTER THIRTY-TWO

Bertram Stott was dead and he didn't go easy. I went to the hospital, got enough X-rays to make me glow in the dark, while two men went into Stott's room and severed his vocal cords. Then they made small, strategic cuts in his neck that spoke of their expertise, and Stott choked on his own blood slowly. Very slowly. I was still in the ER when Stott's body was brought in. My doc guessed it took around fifteen minutes for him to die. Fifteen minutes is a long time, but not long enough in my opinion. Stott couldn't suffer enough for me and I said so, which wasn't the best idea. Luckily, the tiny body cam and voice recorder I wore worked. Fats always had the best equipment, thankfully, or I might have been suspected of killing Stott.

The recording was clear and captured everything, but Gansa and Gordan crabbed that I didn't always point my nose directly at Stott. It was a conversation. Give me a break! The FBI is never satisfied, not with me anyway. I was up half the night giving my statement over and over again. I fell asleep halfway through the fourth time and Gansa's boss shook me awake. Chuck threw a fit and got me out of there, but not before they stuck a couple of rough sketches in front of my face. I wasn't the only one who saw those two weirdos at the nursing home. Three nurses, including Stephanie, saw them. She said that they looked like they stepped out of a 1975 Sears catalog. Mosbach and Clarence saw them, but were so transfixed by the clothes and hair, they couldn't give the remotest description of the men's features. Mosbach thought they were white, but he couldn't swear to it. I was no better. I could pick the suits out of a lineup, but not a face or even a build or height. They were taller than me. That's not hard and Clarence thought they were wearing lifts. They left no prints and were so good that when the nursing trio went in to check on Stott a half hour after I left, they thought he was asleep. No blood and they'd superglued the incisions closed. Somebody heard something fall a couple hours later and that's when they found Stott's body on the floor.

The seventies guys were back in the current decade and long gone. They wouldn't be found and while the cops and FBI were putting on a good show, nobody gave a crap. Doc said Stott had two months to live on the outside. He wasn't going to trial. I got asked repeatedly who I thought might've murdered Bertram Stott. I played dumb, which is easy to do when your face is covered in bandages and the guy asking is looking at your breasts when he asks. And I didn't know who killed him, but I damn well knew who ordered it. My vocal cords may as well have been cut 'cause I was never ever going to say it.

When Fats came into the ER, I said, "Stott's dead."

She nodded, gave me a look, and that was it. Calpurnia Fibonacci let me investigate and she delivered the sentence. Justice and it was quick.

Two days later, I was curled up next to Irene and Lefty's wood stove and there was a party going on. If you haven't seen law enforcement celebrate, let's just say, everything's Irish and the stories never stop. And Tommy Watts was the biggest storyteller of them all.

Dad was in his element with the FBI agents, firefighters, locals hanging on his every word. I'd traded my recording of Stott and his switchblade for a statement at the press conference that the bureau had misjudged my father, they apologized, and welcomed him back into the fold where he always should have been. Mom was so happy she did the ugly cry and I got credited for assisting the FBI in their investigation into the death of Sister Maggie. Nobody had said I was a brainless dingbat so far and they wouldn't if they wanted me to talk to Blankenship or any other psycho in the future.

It was all worth it just to see my parents smiling. Mom was out in public, not hiding or covering her mouth. The droop was still there, but even that seemed better. My dad was back with a vengeance and was already scheduled to teach a seminar on work/life balance while tracking murderers. One breakdown and he was an expert. Mom was in the kitchen making five kinds of bread pudding with Aaron and Grandma Janine in hopes that it would soak up some of the alcohol. Grandad was talking bachelor parties with Tiny and Fats.

When Tiny heard his beloved had suffered an injury on the news, he hightailed it down to St. Seb with The Girls in tow. My cousin, the big sweetheart, walked into Miss Elizabeth's, took one look at the stitches on Fats' face and dropped to one knee.

"Mary Elizabeth Licata, you are the woman I dreamed of and never believed existed, will you marry me?"

Fats tried to hold it but broke down in tears and dropped to her knees to kiss his face off. They had to get a room. I wish I could unsee that.

Later, when they emerged, she cornered me. "How did you do it?"

"I didn't do it," I said. "I've been a little busy, if you haven't noticed."

"You didn't tell him about the baby?"

"No, of course not."

Fats frowned, wrinkling her stitches. "Then why did he do it?"

"Oh, for God's sake. He loves you madly."

She got all shifty-eyed. "Ya think?"

"It's not because he knows and he had to. He saw those stitches, thought about losing you, and did what he's been wanting to do since he met you."

"It was love at first sight," she said.

"I know I was there."

"Do you remember when we were in your truck and he said—"

I held up my hand. "Do not take me back. I've never heard anything so clean and dirty at the same time."

She had a good laugh and then asked, "When should I tell him? I can hardly wait."

"Wait," I said. "Let him enjoy this moment fully. Then he can enjoy that one the same way."

"For someone so uptight you can make sense every once in a while."

"Thanks and I'm not uptight," I said. "You've seen me on the DBD covers."

"Those are just pictures, not who you really are," said Fats.

It was my turn to get teary-eyed. "Thanks."

"I wish I could do something about your face."

"Haven't got any spackle?"

"Not the kind that covers black eyes from hell," she said. "You're going to have to live with it."

And I was living with it, but I didn't mind so much. The bruises would go away. Doctor said the nose would be fine, but my arm was back in a cast. When I looked over at Grandad with his back covered in burns from Vietnam or Mom with her stroke issues, I just felt lucky. It could be worse and it was worse for a lot of the other people, including Millicent. She sat next to me, looking pale and weak. She should never have come down to St. Seb in that weather, but she insisted. She wanted to see me. She wanted to hear it from me.

As promised, I didn't tell her everything, but a reporter managed to get a shot through a window at a table in the police station and got a clean photo of the series of autopsy sketches from Maggie's file. It was all over the news and Stratton was forced to make a statement. The news had hit The Girls hard and Millicent had cried herself to sleep. She was so weak the next morning I wasn't sure she could walk, but she surprised me by coming down for the party. She sat next to me and petted Moe, who was curled up on my lap. The pocket dog had some cracked ribs and some stitches, but she'd be fine, especially with the special pâté Aaron had made her.

"Mercy?" Millicent said softly.

I leaned over to hear her better over the toasts to justice and booming laughter. "Are you okay?"

"I am. Myrtle told me this morning that she hired you to...to find out what happened to dear Maggie. She's very torn up about it. She assumed the man was dead. She didn't think you would get hurt."

I took her hand and squeezed. "He is dead. She wasn't wrong."

"But it was so much bigger and the church...I never imagined even with the way the bishop behaved after it happened that he..."

"Bishop Fowler was a thief and now the world knows it."

That was an understatement. Details on Maggie's murder came out fast, thanks to Gordon and Gansa enjoying their time in the limelight. The church had a new scandal to reckon with and it had gotten so much press attention that Pope Francis had made a statement about it. That appeased the press and it didn't take long for them to focus on Chief Woody Lucas, his lack of investigation, and why. The alcoholism and loyalty might've helped him believe that distraught Father Dominic did it, instead of a college-bound boy of prominent family, but long-term guilt and a little blackmail persuaded him to end his own investigation. *The New York Times* wasted no time in digging up the history and it was horrid to say the least.

Chief Lucas and the St. Sebastian Sentinel editor, Barney Scheer, were in Joseph Snider's platoon in the Pacific. Joseph, injured, somehow ended up in a Japanese tunnel where he was captured and I'm told there was cannibalism. I didn't read the article. I had nightmares enough.

It didn't get much worse than cannibalism and Davis Snider held his brother's horrific death over the heads of the police chief and the newspaperman. There was a question as to whether Joseph was abandoned by his platoon to save themselves and that was enough to get Lucas and Scheer to look the other way when Maggie was murdered. Robert Junior's uncles confirmed his version of events and said they didn't know Robert had killed Maggie until years later when he confessed to them while drunk. According to them, their parents, Davis and Helen, had a hard time believing Robert did it, even after the confession. They'd only been trying to protect Robert from the taint of being mentioned in relation to a murder at the time and that Chief Lucas and Barney Scheer didn't want to believe that the clean-cut Robert was a murderer any more than they did.

By the time Kenneth Young was kidnapped, Chief Lucas was dead, but we could safely assume that Barney Scheer told Davis or Robert what his intern was up to. No one else but Desmond Shipley knew. Whether Barney meant for Kenneth to be killed will probably never be known. Former Chief Melanie Gates said she knew nothing about it at the time, but that her father had warned her to never cross the Sniders and she made sure she didn't. Melanie took a lie detector test about Kenneth Young's murder and passed with flying colors.

Every news outlet in the country and a good number abroad were leading with how a serial killer could've been stopped if the horrors of WWII hadn't interfered. They weren't wrong, but a lot of people could've stopped Bertram Stott. If someone had stepped up, the network of killers he founded would never have happened. One murder became dozens, maybe hundreds. A small time crime Chief Lucas called it. Maybe one murder did seem small to a man who lived through Iwo Jima and Sugar Loaf Hill. But that one crime became big and it didn't have to be that way.

"I hope you'll be okay, dear," said Millicent. "You shouldn't have been asked to look into it."

"I hope you'll be okay," I said.

"It will get better now that we know the truth."

Will it?

The door opened and Clarence walked in. She wasn't alone.

"Or it could get worse," I said.

Millicent kissed my cheek so lightly it was like a butterfly kiss. "It can't get worse. I refuse to let it."

"Aunt Miriam's here."

It might've been my imagination, but Millicent seemed to go a shade paler. "She does love you."

"Are you sure about that?" I asked.

Aunt Miriam shot me the stink eye and Millicent hesitated. "I'm sure."

"She asked me to leave it alone and I didn't."

"You did the right thing. Don't let anyone tell you different. Look at how proud Tommy is."

"He's talking about himself, Millicent."

She smiled. "And you. You're in there."

"You are the nicest person I know."

"I doubt that, but I'm going to go say hello to Miriam." Millicent tried to stand, but Tiny and Fats had to rush over to help her up and take her to Aunt Miriam.

Myrtle and I exchanged a glance across the room past the cheerful firefighters, cops, neighbors, and FBI agents. No one else felt the way we felt. She asked me and I did what was asked. The two of us did that together and now Millicent looked like the pain of it would pull her under.

Millicent spoke to Aunt Miriam briefly before Fats picked her up and carried her from the room. She needed to go back to bed. I wasn't entirely sure she didn't need to go to the hospital, but she'd already rejected the idea.

Aunt Miriam stood next to the door with her purse that no doubt had a brick in it and her cane. Clarence tried to soothe her, but she kept giving me the hairy eyeball until I hoisted myself to my feet and came through the crowd to take my medicine.

"Alright. Go ahead," I said.

"Mercy," said Clarence, nervously. "Guess what I just found out."

With effort, I refocused. "What's that?"

"The St. Sebastian Catholic High School is going to be renamed the Sister Margaret Mullanphy Catholic High School and they're going to build a memorial garden for her. Isn't that wonderful?"

"It really is," I said. "I think she'll like that."

"Do you think the toilets will stop overflowing now and all the other stuff?" asked Clarence.

"The toilets will be over, but the comforting won't stop," I said. "She'll always be with them. This is St. Sebastian."

"I think that's a good thing." Clarence's eyes sparkled. "I was on the news. Can you believe that? Me."

"I totally believe it."

"My principal called me and she said she was impressed. Parents are calling and asking to have their kiddos in my class next year. Nobody's going to say I don't know anything about the real world anymore."

"You rock, Sister," I said.

Clarence beamed at me and Aunt Miriam pursed her thin lips.

"Now to the bad news," I said. "Let me have it."

Chuck rushed over and got between me and that cane. He's a good man, but it wasn't necessary. "Everything alright?"

"Probably not."

"Mercy did good," said Chuck. "You have to know that."

Aunt Miriam made a throaty growl that made both Clarence and Chuck take a step back. For someone so old and tiny, she was pretty freaking scary. But not to Moe. The pocket dog growled right back and I considered trying to steal her from Fats. You gotta love a dog that doesn't give a crap.

"How about you get me another hot chocolate?" I asked Chuck.

"Are you sure?"

I was and I sent Clarence to Myrtle, since she looked like she might need a gentle hand to sit her down.

Clarence hugged me before going. "We did good. I'm so proud."

It doesn't feel good, but it is good.

"We did."

Clarence and Chuck left me with my elderly, angry aunt and I got myself ready for war or, at least, a minor skirmish.

"Okay," I said with a good amount of belligerence. "You're pissed. You know what? Don't care. A serial killer is dead and victims' families are going to get the answers that they've been waiting decades for. So, as Grandad says, put that in your pipe and smoke it."

"You went against the family," she said in a low hiss that made the hair stand up on the back of my neck.

"I did not," I said. "The Girls are my family and you know it."

"I know no such thing."

"Whatever. Can I ask you a question?"

"No."

"I'll tell Clarence," I threatened.

Aunt Miriam's wispy brows shot up. "Clarence loves me. I'm her mentor."

"She helped me, Aunt Miriam. She's here because she thought this should happen. Sister Frances sent her and she wanted to do it."

Her lower lip trembled. "I don't know about that."

"I do," I said. "Why didn't you save me the trouble and identify Sister Maggie's medal? You knew it was hers."

Chuck brought us mugs of hot chocolate, took one look at our faces, and said, "I'll just be waiting over there."

"Tell me," I said.

"You don't deserve anything from me," she said.

"Look at my arm and face and say that again."

She flicked a brief glance at me and looked away to Myrtle, who was in a quiet conversation with Clarence. "I didn't want to know."

"What? Who really did it?"

"I knew who did it."

"Father Dominic? Seriously?" I asked.

Aunt Miriam forced her watery blue eyes to look at me. "I knew what no one else did. Maggie told me a couple of days before she disappeared that she'd decided not to abandon her vows. She wasn't going to run off and marry Dominic."

"So?"

"She was scared, very worried about what he would do when she told him," she said.

I almost couldn't respond. "Maggie thought Dominic might kill her?"

"No. Pay attention, Mercy."

"I am."

"She thought he might hurt himself. She was very scared about that and I thought with the way he acted that he must've hurt her instead and was wracked with guilt."

"But what's that got to do with identifying the medal?" I asked.

"I didn't know where her medal went. We never found Dominic's body. Someone could've gotten it out of the river or maybe he gave it to someone. Maybe she lost it. I didn't know. The way he was after Maggie was found..."

"Did you think he might not be dead?"

"No. Of course not." She raised her voice and the whole room turned and looked. "You still aren't paying attention."

I bent over to her. "I am listening. I'm trying to understand."

A tear rolled down her cheek. "I knew that she was going to tell him no. I knew, only me, and I wanted to tell Mother Superior about it, but Maggie asked me not to and I didn't. I felt in my heart I should, but I didn't, and she died. Then he died. I could've prevented it. I had a feeling something wasn't right. She was so worried and upset. She wasn't sleeping. Something was coming and I ignored it."

"You had a feeling, like Dad gets," I said astonished.

"And you get." She glared at me. "Except you wouldn't have ignored it."

"Er...maybe."

She snorted.

"Okay. Probably not."

"I let my friend and mentor die because I didn't follow my instinct. Seeing that medal brought it all back. The way she looked when she told me her decision. Dominic's uncontrolled grief. I just couldn't and I didn't think it would do any good. How could that terrible place in Kansas have anything to do with Maggie? It didn't seem possible. Dominic did it. I was sure and bringing all this up again would just hurt Millicent and Myrtle. They would have to know that I had let Maggie down. Did you see Millicent? She's heartsick. The thought of what that man did to Maggie—"

"Don't think about it," I said. "Don't give him the satisfaction wherever he is."

"Burning in hell," said Aunt Miriam with complete conviction.

"Exactly. Let him burn."

"And what about you?"

"Me?" I asked.

"They said on the news that the other one told you all the things he did. You heard it all."

"It is what it is." I risked gently touching her arm and whispered, "How are you feeling?"

"Very well, thank you," she said primly.

"So I may have—"

"Told Sister Clarence and Sister Frances about my predicament? Yes, I know and I do not forgive you."

"They understand."

"Frances says that she will attend my next appointment thanks to you."

"She can help," I said.

She brushed my hand off her arm. "You'll be the one to help."

"Huh?"

"I hear you will be running the fish fries during Lent," she said.

Oh, no! Oh, no!

"Well, actually I won our bet," I said. "So no fish fries."

"Is Frances coming to my appointments?" Aunt Miriam asked.

"Er...yes?"

"I'm glad we understand each other." The stink eye was sizzling and I took a step back. "And, Mercy, you will come to the special mass tonight."

"I guess," I said.

"Wrong answer," she said.

"Okay."

Aunt Miriam left it at that, for the moment, but I had no illusions about my having a choice. I would be at mass, and if I had to guess, there'd be a lot of masses in my future.

She headed into the party that had switched to telling ghost stories and, unless I misunderstood, there was a vampire living at the bowling alley and witches a couple of towns over. Vampires and bowling alleys do not go together in any book I'd read, so I chalked it up to the tequila shots and whiskey ice cream.

I wasn't feeling very raucous so I sucked down my hot chocolate and gave the mug to Aaron for a refill before I went out into the hall to have a breather, but Patton came dashing down the stairs and nearly bowled me over.

"Holy crap!" she exclaimed. "I'm sorry."

"It's fine. Everything okay?"

"Oh, yeah. I left the boxes on your bed," she said. "I hope that's alright."

I drew a blank. "Boxes?"

"Oh. Um...Chief Stratton decided to release the evidence from your great grandparents' crash to you. I thought you knew."

"Somebody said something," I said. "So it's Chief Stratton now?"

"Yeah, Will resigned and she took the reins. It's about time."

"How'd that happen?"

"He saw himself on the news and it was so bad. He's going to rehab. We're crossing our fingers."

"Here's hoping," I said.

"How's your uncle? Did the surgery go okay?"

I smiled, remembering the relief I felt at hearing Uncle Morty bawl me out over recovery time and not coming to the hospital through a blizzard and closed highways. He was doing fine but his family had finally gotten there. His mother insisted on sleeping in his room and you'd think she was poking him in the eyeball with a red hot fork.

"Good. But he can't fly for a while," I said.

"Bummer," she said with a big grin.

A big burst of laughter erupted behind me and Patton headed in. Aaron had promised her a heavenly hot chocolate with spiced rum. She went toward bliss and I went up the stairs. Those boxes were calling to me. It was time. Ready or not.

I was afraid of what I'd find in the Lilac Room. Irene moved me there when Chuck turned up and it was one of those rooms that ghost-seeking guests sought out. Nothing had happened so far, but it couldn't last. Miss Elizabeth thought I was interesting and she wasn't likely to forget.

"Can you give me one small break?" I asked with my hand on the doorknob.

"No," said the voice in my head.

"Ah, come on."

Miss Elizabeth laughed and I opened the door. There on the foot of the bed were the evidence boxes, open with the contents arranged as if Agatha and Daniel would come in at any minute and get dressed.

"You kind of suck, you know that?" I asked.

"Yes."

"Mercy?" Chuck came up beside me with a worried look on his handsome face. "Who are you talking to?"

"Me," Miss Elizabeth said.

I glanced at him to see if he heard that, but he didn't. Creepy was my department apparently. "Nobody. Myself. I might be losing it."

"You are not losing it."

"Thanks."

"You already lost it a long time ago."

"You skunk!"

Chuck wrestled me into submission—I didn't try very hard—and carried me to the bed where he dumped me unceremoniously on the bed next to the evidence. I reached for the police report folder, but he stopped me.

"We need to talk," he said. "That can wait."

I bit my lip.

"It's not bad."

"Is it about moving?"

"Yes."

Then it's bad.

"Can't that please wait? I know you have plans and listings and more plans, but I just—"

"Mercy, you promised," Chuck said, standing in the Superman pose next to the bed. It totally suited him, but I was not in the mood for a power stance.

"Fine. I'll just tell you then," I said.

His eyelids went to half-mast and he watched me carefully. "Tell me what?"

Suck it up, buttercup.

"I'm not moving. I don't want to and I'm not going to."

"Hold on now."

"You hold on. I am not moving out to some house in the sticks away from my family. Uncle Morty's in the hospital and Millicent looks like a stiff wind could blow her away. My mother needs me and my father is...him so I'm not doing it."

"Will you listen to me?"

"You listen to me. I love you but no. I don't care where you found a perfect place or if it has outdoor space where you can grow kumquats. I can't leave them." Tears were rolling down my cheeks, soaking my bandages, but I didn't care. I couldn't look worse or feel worse than I already did.

"I did find the perfect place," he said.

We're going to break up over this. It's happening. Fats is getting married and we're breaking up.

"No," I said totally heartsick, but I had to go with my gut.

"You'll like it."

"I won't." I looked up at the one I loved, expecting fury and seeing a hint of a smile instead. "Aren't you mad? Aren't we going to break up?"

"Break up?" Chuck laughed and kissed my forehead. "You're not getting rid of me that easily."

"But you want to move. You want space and to grow kumquats."

"For the record, I don't want to grow kumquats. I don't even know what a kumquat is," he said. "But we are moving."

"You aren't listening," I said.

"To Hawthorne Avenue."

Crap on a cracker.

"We are not moving in with my parents. Are you crazy? Did you take my painkillers?"

"I did not take your painkillers and I'm eighty percent not crazy." Chuck grinned and my heart melted for a second.

"Eighty percent?" I asked.

"Hey, that's pretty good. Have you met your father?"

"Good point. So…"

He sat on the bed and gave me a wad of tissues. "I'm not going to make you leave your family. I should've been paying attention before. You don't belong anywhere else and they do need you. I see that."

"We're still not living with my parents," I said.

"Correct. We're moving into one of the apartments above the stables," he said.

"Huh?"

"There are apartments above the stables at the Bled Mansion. You know that."

I blew my nose as much as I could. "I forgot about that, but we can't just tell The Girls that we're moving in."

"It's all settled," he said. "The Girls are thrilled. They promised to let me tell you."

"I don't know about this. That stupid Brooks sued to get control of The Girls estate because he thought I had too much influence. What's he going to say about this?" I asked.

"Brooks is a pinhead. While you were having *your* head examined, I called Lawton and the cousins. The Bleds are on board. They've been nervous since Lester got killed. Having a cop on the property suits them fine."

I leaned back woozy. I don't know if it was relief, painkillers, or Aaron's spiked hot chocolate. "You're serious?"

"It has two bedrooms and it's three times the size of your apartment," he said. "Are you in?"

I kissed him carefully so as not to get my soggy nose bandages on him. "You sure you want to take this mess on?"

"I'm all in." He kissed me back, not at all worried about my moisture. "Now answer the question."

"I'm in."

Chuck leaned back on the headboard and kicked off his shoes. "That's settled. What's next?"

"Does there have to be something next?" I asked.

"It's us."

"True."

There was a little metallic pop and Chuck sat bolt upright. "Did that purse..."

"Open on its own?" I asked. "Yes, yes it did."

He shrugged. "That happens, right? I mean, it's an old purse."

"Well."

The purse snapped closed.

Chuck looked at me, his eyes wide. "I think we should move now. Like right now."

"I think we should open that purse," I said.

"You first."

"What a big scaredy-cat."

"Guilty as charged."

I crawled over the bed, scattering a bunch of plastic evidence bags, and pulled the purse into my lap.

Chuck got off the bed and crossed his arms. "Were those bags open when you found the box?"

"I think so. Fats didn't tear anything open when she looked through them," I said.

"Somebody's already been through it," he said.

"Well, killing Agatha and Daniel wouldn't be enough to make sure The Bleds didn't get any leads on what they had. My family should've gotten this stuff way back then."

Chuck came over and rubbed my back. "Sometimes family can't bear to pick up their loved ones effects."

I tossed an evidence bag away. "This is all pointless. The Klinefeld Group was here first and there obviously wasn't anything to be found or they wouldn't have come back again and again."

The purse popped open and shut again and Chuck jolted away. "That's not right."

"Like so many other things," I said, reaching for the clasp.

"You're just going to open that?"

I shrugged. "How bad can it be?"

"I saw floating eyeballs last night," he said.

"It happens." I snapped open Agatha's purse, laying out the contents on the bed. There was nothing unusual, just the stuff you'd expect to find in an older lady's purse. Antacid pills, a compact, a couple lipsticks, tissues, checkbook, and a fat wallet.

"That's it?" asked Chuck visibly disappointed.

It couldn't be. Miss Elizabeth knew her stuff and I thought she kind of liked me. I leafed through the checkbook and took everything out of the wallet. Nothing stood out. Then I turned the purse upside down. There was a little thunk.

Chuck took a breath and said, "Did you hear that?"

"I heard it." I flipped the purse back over several times. Thunk. Thunk. Thunk.

"Check the lining."

I felt around the silk lining of my great grandmother's purse and found a slit on one of the sides. My hand fit in and tucked behind the side pocket was a slim packet. I pulled it out and we held our breath. It was a small manila envelope that was stuffed full and sealed.

"Should I open it?" I asked.

"Are you kidding?" Chuck asked. "You do it or I will."

I forced my fingernails under the flap and it popped open easily. I dumped the contents on the bed and it took me a moment to process what I was seeing there. On top were two transatlantic steamer tickets from late November 1938.

"Do you think those are *the* tickets?" Chuck asked.

"They have to be," I said.

Underneath the tickets, I found a letter from Florence Bled thanking Amelie and Paul for helping Stella and Nicky. There was some talk of reimbursement for expenses and a job for Paul at a very nice salary. At the end, casually, like it hardly mattered at all was a postscript. "Please send along the item we discussed. This address is the most appropriate."

"That's our house," I said. "They sent it to our house."

Chuck didn't move or reach for the rest. He let me do it, but I almost couldn't. It was too much to hope that the answer was there in front of me.

"Go ahead. See what that paper says."

I picked up a tri-folded sheaf of papers, but at first I wasn't sure what I was seeing. One sheet looked like an accounting ledger. It had elegant old-fashioned handwriting that was so faded I could barely make it out.

"It looks like a manifest," I said. "The date's right. Same ship. Here's their names."

Under Amelie and Paul's names was a list of items that went on board, trunks, suitcases and one other thing.

I looked at Chuck. "A wooden crate already packed."

"It doesn't say what's in it?"

"No, just the size. It's pretty big. It has to be artwork."

Chuck put his arm around me. "You always thought it would be art."

"The Klinefeld Group was looking for a box. This is a pretty damn big box."

"What's that last thing?"

I unfolded the other paper. It was delicate, fragile like airmail paper, but it wasn't a letter. It was a receipt. A shipping receipt.

"I can't believe it," I said.

"That can't be right," said Chuck.

"It has to be."

The receipt said that an antique liquor cabinet had been packed up in New Orleans in January 1939 and shipped to Josiah Bled in St. Louis. There was only one liquor cabinet that I knew of, the one in our butler's pantry. The cabinet was tucked into the built-ins like it was intended to be there with delicate wooden hands and vines that reached out of the other cabinets and held it fast. I thought the liquor cabinet was original to the house, but it wasn't. It couldn't be. And that cabinet wasn't unknown. Josiah's quirk of installing an 1800's marquetry liquor cabinet into his house had been featured in magazines and newspapers. Josiah hadn't hidden it. The cabinet was in a coffee table book produced in the eighties called *Bled Family Architecture*. Mom had that book. It was on *our* coffee table.

"I don't understand," said Chuck. "Is there something special about it?"

"There must be." I gathered up the contents of my great grandmother's packet and slid off the bed.

Chuck jumped up. "Where are we going?"

"You stay here. I'll be back."

I turned to go and he grabbed my arm, holding tight, grounding me. "Promise you're not leaving this house."

"Promise." I went up on my tiptoes and kissed him, not worrying about my nose. "We're moving in together. Think about what to pack."

He grinned at me, glowing with the charm that always sucked me right in. "Everything."

"No beer signs."

"Especially the beer signs."

I darted out the door and tossed over my shoulder, "We'll discuss it later."

"No, we won't," he called after me.

I laughed as I hurried down the hall. Stupid beer signs. So not happening. Who needs a giant Schlitz sign? We're Bled people, for crying out loud.

I stopped in front of a room with "Miss Elizabeth" on the door and crossed my fingers. I had it on good authority that her room was the one you didn't want to be in if you scared easily, or at all really, but The Girls took it and claimed they hadn't heard a peep. Maybe two widows were just Miss Elizabeth's speed.

"Come in," Millicent called out in response to my knock and I walked in to find my godmothers sitting in a pair of rockers by the bay window that was missing a few panes and had been boarded over. Their faces were calm and dry, but I knew they'd been crying. I could feel it.

"I have news," I said.

Millicent's face lit up as much as it could. "You're moving in. We're so pleased to have you close."

I hurried over and sat at their feet on an embroidered stool. "Yes, but it's not that."

"What is it, dear?" Myrtle asked with a warning in her voice.

"It's good news." I held up the receipt. "Stella shipped Josiah's liquor cabinet back from Europe. That's what it was."

The Girls' faces truly lit up.

"How extraordinary!"

"Marvelous. You must tell your mother immediately."

"We'll examine it."

"You know how Uncle Josiah loved secret compartments."

"We'll find out what The Klinefeld Group wants."

"We're going to know."

I hugged them both and showed them their mother's letter. They touched their weathered fingers to her handwriting and to her signature especially.

"She knew," said Millicent and some tightness left her thin shoulders.

"Of course, she did. Mother knew all Stella's secrets," said Myrtle, "and I imagine she had quite a few. We didn't know about Bickford until a few days ago. Imagine what else we can learn."

Millicent nodded and leaned forward to touch my hand. "Perhaps uncovering more about her will help us connect some descendants to pieces from her collection. We could return more to the rightful owners."

"Can I use your phone, Millicent?" I asked. "Mine's done for."

"Of course," she said. "What are you up to?"

"We haven't called Dr. Wallingford for his friend's list of the Bickford House *Kindertransport* children yet, have we?"

Millicent tilted her chin down and a thrill of excitement went through her. "We haven't."

"We should," said Myrtle.

"Right now?" I asked.

"This minute."

So we called with a new plan, discoveries and Stella ahead, and past pains firmly behind, just where we wanted them.

The End

PREVIEW

Bottle Blonde (Mercy Watts Mysteries Book Eleven)

T he law of unintended consequences says that you make a choice and something unexpected happens. Makes sense, unless you're me. In Mercy Watts' world, some dude I don't know makes a whack-ass choice, and I end up in a basement hunting turtles for six hours. That's right. Turtles. 'Cause it's me and I live in St. Louis. Grandparents keep turtles in their basements. I swear to God, it's a thing.

Turtles happened because exactly one week ago, I was mid-way through the annual Bled baking day, which is actually three days long, but let's not quibble. Decades ago, my godmothers, Myrtle and Millicent Bled, started baking for friends and family at Christmas time and it's gotten a bit out of hand. We now bake for staff at the Children's Hospital and all the families stuck there over the holidays. I'm sorry to say that's a lot of kids and we can't hire anyone to help. It has to be friends and family so on the first weekend in December I was trying to figure out how to roll gingerbread effectively with one arm in a cast. Like so many things, it didn't work out for me.

My gingerbread was wafer thin on one side and super fat on the other. It seemed like I was pushing down with equal force, but, clearly, I wasn't. I sighed and looked up at Stella Bled Lawrence's portrait. She watched my failure with pale blue eyes over the stacks of Christmas tins that reached up to her nose. The breakfast room was what my mother called the staging area because we did all the packing and labeling in there. The enormous kitchen was where all the action happened, but not that year, not for me. I got exiled with a lump of dough, wax paper, and a rolling pin, because I was in the way and pretty much useless. I thought I'd prove them wrong, but thirty minutes later the opposite was true.

I'd first broken my arm while doing a favor for family friend Big Steve and rebroken it three weeks ago during another favor for Myrtle. I'd looked into the death of The Girls' childhood friend Sister Maggie with some pretty unexpected results, including breaking my nose, uncovering the origin of the serial killer network with ties to the Kansas graveyard, and, last but not least, the answer to the question of what Stella had sent back from Europe on the eve of WWII. People had died because of that secret, my great grandparents, just for starters, and it was in Great Grandma Agatha's purse, hidden away in the St. Sebastian police station attic, that we found it. Stella had shipped back the liquor cabinet that had been tucked away in my parents' butler's pantry and right under our noses the whole time.

Three weeks had gone by and we still hadn't gotten in that cabinet and not for lack of trying. Getting into my parent's house when it was empty was more of a challenge than you'd think. My mother knew everything I was doing, but my father, the great and difficult detective, didn't.

After serious problems with the FBI and the media, Dad was trying to rebuild his business and the way he'd chosen to do it was a problem for us. My grandad came out of retirement as did Avery Sampson and Leo Frame to help him. The geezers had a system and it included our kitchen table, just about twenty-four hours a day. My mom had to sneak out of bed at three in the morning to search the cabinet because that was the only time nobody was looking and even then Dad turned up, asking what she was doing.

Mom didn't find anything, no secret compartments, nothing, but it was the dead of night and her eyesight wasn't great after her stroke so she may have missed something. Bled baking day was our last shot for the next week at getting in that cabinet and searching it completely. My dad was off tracking a rapist in Hannibal, and Avery and Leo were in Memphis chasing down leads in a missing persons case. My grandad was the only conceivable problem. He was home recovering from a broken ankle. He'd slipped off a curb and broken it in three places, revealing that he had osteoporosis, but he wasn't buying the diagnosis. In Grandad's opinion, osteoporosis was a woman's issue akin to menopause, not that he uttered the word menopause. He'd rather break the other ankle than refer directly to anything that had something to do with a woman's nether regions.

Because he didn't believe his doctor or me, Grandma J had to take away his car keys, relegating him to the couch with orders to eat and sleep while she helped us bake. He wasn't happy and threatened to walk over to my parents' house so he could get at work files. I wouldn't put it past him. Did I mention that Grandad was a workaholic? The man could not not work. If he wasn't hobbling out to an Uber, he was probably taking apart the plumbing looking for hairballs or oiling hinges that didn't squeak or attempting to break into his office to go through old files, looking to unearth clues in unsolved murders from his father's and grandfather's time as policemen. He coveted those ancient cases and collected more whenever he had the chance like some kind of ghoul. Occasionally, he tried to rope me into finding out what happened to Maude in 1921, but I always managed to slip the net, which is why I was trying to make gingerbread. Grandma J said I should hang out with Grandad since we were both broken. Nope. Not falling for that. I'd rather roll gingerbread badly for seventy-two hours than be picking the lock on Grandad's office and looking into Maude's mysterious end. If I'd known turtles were coming, I'd have chosen differently.

Instead of balling up my dough for another attempt, I texted Chuck, "Are you in yet?"

"Almost," he wrote back.

"What's taking so long?"

"Carlson had a breakdown. Delayed. Be in in a minute."

That damn Carlson. He was always having a breakdown and it wasn't about work either. Carlson was the squad-designated wreck. On his third divorce and in a custody battle that made Brexit look like a tiff, that idiot got some woman he met at the DMV pregnant and then to cope, he started gambling. The squad put him on a desk and then leave, but he kept coming to work, trying to explain that he was really okay and could do the job while snotting all over the place.

Yesterday, my parents' house was empty, too, but Chuck and his partner, Sidney, had to lure Carlson out of the station with the promise of chili dogs and ended up sitting at a bar for four hours, listening to how all these women shouldn't hate him, because Chuck was afraid he might hurt himself, and we missed our first chance to get in the liquor cabinet. If he ruined our second chance, I'd start hoping one of those women would take him out and protect the rest of womankind from the plague that was Daniel Carlson.

"In?" I texted.

"No." Chuck was irritated with me, but I couldn't help it. We were so close. Whatever had The Klinefeld Group coming after us since WWII was in that cabinet and I was on the edge of insanity with the waiting.

I slammed my rolling pin onto the dough and bent over, putting my casted hand's fingers on the wood and trying to inch it forward evenly. I should've just said yes to the doc when she said I could take the cast off a couple of days ago. The rebreak wasn't bad and had healed well. She assumed I couldn't wait to get it off and she wasn't wrong, but something held me back. I didn't want that cast off. There was this weird attachment, a need for the cast that I couldn't explain, and I said no. The doc shrugged and said to come back in a week. I wasn't at all sure I'd want it off in a week, but I said I would. I told Chuck and everyone else that I had to keep it on. Nobody doubted me except Fats Licata, my sometimes bodyguard and newly-minted best friend. Fats raised an eyebrow, but quickly got distracted by morning sickness.

She was in the second trimester now, but her nausea wasn't letting up. If anything, she was getting worse. I could hear her in the kitchen, where she'd gotten the honor of rolling the cinnamon rolls with her two good hands, making noises like a drowning yak. The Girls were trying to get her to take a break, but Fats Licata didn't take breaks.

What she lacked in delicacy, she more than made up for with size and determination.

"I can do it," she said. "I just have to breathe."

"You don't have to do it," said my mom. "You're pregnant. Relax. Put your feet up."

"I can't do that," said Fats.

She was right. She couldn't. I'd never seen Fats relax. That wasn't a thing for her. We went to a movie last week and she did squats while we were in line and bicep curls during the movie, when she wasn't in the bathroom throwing up, which was at least half the time.

"Please, Fats," said Clarence, the little nun who'd gone to St. Sebastian with us and had turned out to be a good friend to a woman who didn't have female friends before us. We were an odd trio, I'm not gonna lie.

"Make way!" yelled Aunt Miriam and I only had a second to step aside before Fats came barreling through the breakfast room with wild eyes and both hands clamped over her mouth.

I heard her run to the nearest bathroom and prayed she made it. Sometimes she didn't. It was that bad.

My mom walked in and leaned on the table. "Can't you talk to her?"

"About what?"

"This isn't normal."

"Correct," I said.

"What did the obstetrician say?" Mom asked.

"That it should be getting better."

"It's not."

"Nope."

Mom glared at me and wiped her frosting-covered hands on her apron. "You have to talk to her."

"And say what?" I asked.

"Isn't there medication?"

"She won't take it. She's afraid the baby will be affected and grow a nipple on her forehead or something."

"That's not going to happen," said Mom.

"When I said that, she said, 'That's what they said about Thalidomide.'"

"What does Fats know about Thalidomide?"

"Everything. She's been researching."

"Oh, Lord."

"Exactly."

The sound of retching echoed through the Bled Mansion for a second time and Clarence came in wringing her hands. "Is she okay?"

"I'm going with no," I said.

"Can't you do something?"

"I got her to drink ginger tea."

Clarence bit her lip and then said, "I don't think it's working."

"It works," I said. "But not enough."

"You should go in there," said Mom.

"Why me? I haven't had a baby."

"You're a nurse."

"I was a nurse. Now I'm a licensed PI, whose father doesn't trust her to do more than background checks."

Mom came over and hugged me fiercely. In a strange way I think she was mourning the loss of my nursing career, but I don't think she was ever that into it. She just didn't want me to follow in my father's footsteps, that much she knew, but I had to earn a living. With all the events of the last few months, I was persona non grata in the nursing world, not because I sucked, but because I was a disaster waiting to happen and everyone in St. Louis knew it. Nobody wanted to hire me, at least not until I could be normal for a while and not get a clinic rammed with a tractor or something else equally ridiculous. So in a moment of weakness I agreed, after a tremendous amount of badgering from my dad, to take the PI license test. Now I was employed by my dad and, in his words, working my way up. It didn't matter how many cases I'd cracked for him in my so-called spare time or how many murders I'd solved, I got to start at the bottom as a glorified file clerk. I was bored out of my mind, making less money than I did as a student nurse, and just about ready to pay the Columbia clinic to take me back.

Clarence came over and hugged me, too. "You'll be a nurse again."

"I don't know," I snuffled, getting all weepy.

"You will," said Mom. "Or I'll make your father give you something good."

That did it. I was an adult and my mom had to help me get a decent job. I started crying for real and that's when Aunt Miriam came in and smacked my legs with her cane. "I never heard so much cater-wauling about good news."

"Good news? What's the good news? Fats can't stop barfing. We have less than forty-eight hours to fill these tins and we're not even close. I can't get a real job and..."

She gave me the stink eye. "And what?"

I was going to say we can't get inside the liquor cabinet, but Aunt Miriam was in the dark and she had to stay that way or else. "Nothing. I just feel rotten and useless."

"You are useless."

"Aunt Miriam!" exclaimed Mom.

"I mean with baking, but I have a job for you." Aunt Miriam glared at me and whatever the job was I wouldn't like it.

"Oh, yeah?" I asked. "Is it clean out the gutters or unclog a toilet?"

"Don't be ridiculous. You can't even roll dough."

"Then what?"

Aunt Miriam pulled a large bottle out of her apron pocket. "You can make yourself useful by getting some more vanilla."

"We're out?" I asked. "That's a lot of vanilla."

"We have some," said Mom.

"Aaron says it has to be his cognac vanilla."

With that, my weirdo partner, Aaron, trotted into the breakfast room wearing a pink hairnet and a frilly apron that once belonged to The Girls' mother. He was pulling on my hoodie, which is to say Chuck's hoodie, and it hung halfway to his knees.

Mom stepped in front of him. "Oh, no. Back you go."

Aaron stopped, looked to the left, and said, "Vanilla," before attempting to bypass my mother.

"We'll get it. You are not leaving us with that crazy Baumkuchen."

Aaron look confused, but that was nothing new. The only thing I was confused about was why we were making Baumkuchen. It's a

German cake that's baked in layers and takes four hours. Like we didn't have enough things with delicate timing.

Mom turned him around and Aunt Miriam stripped off the hoodie before handing it to me.

"Go and hurry."

"My dough will get dry." The gingerbread was kicking my butt. It could not be allowed.

"That ship has sailed, Mercy," said Mom.

"Fine," I said, but before I could zip up, Fats staggered into the room. She was pale, sweaty, and her usually perfect hair had come loose from its slicked back ponytail, sticking out around her face like wilting petals on a flower. If it hadn't been for her tremendous size and the hot pink leopard spandex she was wearing I might not have recognized her.

"I'll go," she wheezed.

"Not happening," said Mom.

"You can go to bed," said Aunt Miriam, primly tucking a few ginger hairs back into her veil.

"We have work...to do." Fats tried to lean casually against the door-frame, but instead sort of toppled into it and the wood made a worrisome snapping noise.

I went over to check her temperature and heart rate. Not great but not sick, in the regular sense anyway. "You have nothing to do but drink tea and rest," I said.

"No, I've got to get ahead of it," said Fats.

"Ahead of what?"

"The sick. I need some exercise."

"The last thing you need is exercise."

She straightened up and, for a second, looked normal, minus the sweaty. "I'll go and you roll the crap out of that gingerbread."

It's you and me, gingerbread. Let's do this thing.

"Hey!" My cousins, the Troublesome Trio, stuck their red heads in the door to the kitchen.

"Are we taking a break?" asked Sorcha aka Weepy, although she didn't weep much anymore since becoming engaged.

"No," said Mom. "Don't get any ideas."

"I'm not getting any ideas. I love this."

Jilly looked like she thought she was crazy, but my cousins were thrilled to be included in something Bled for the first time and weren't complaining...much.

"What about lunch?" asked Bridget. "Rodney says he has some crab that he wants to use up before it goes bad. Crab cakes?"

Crap on a cracker.

Before I could squash that, Fats made a horking noise and ran for the bathroom again.

"What did I say?" asked Bridget.

"Crab," we said in chorus.

"I thought it was coffee that made her sick."

Aunt Miriam shooed my cousins back into the kitchen saying, "It was. Now it's crab."

"Does that mean I can have a latte?" asked Sorcha.

I didn't catch the answer since Aaron tried to dart past me and I had to grab him by the apron. "You have to do the Baumkuchen."

A timer, one of about twenty-eight we had going, went off and I turned him around. "I'll get it."

"Sto-Vo-Kor," he said.

"I know."

"Six months."

"Of course," I said, not really knowing what he was referring to, but I figured the meaning would become apparent. Or not. Whatever.

Mom pushed him back into the kitchen toward the enormous La Cornue stove with its multiple ovens all fired up. "And take Pick with you. He hasn't been out for hours."

"Anything else?" I asked sarcastically.

"Hurry. We've got the next batch of sugar cookies to do."

I saluted my mother, wrapped my crusty gingerbread dough in the wax paper, and headed for the library. Pickpocket, Chuck's giant poodle, was curled up on a cushion next to the fireplace. He desperately needed a haircut, so it really just looked like someone dropped a pile of black curls in the dog bed. I couldn't make out so much as a foot.

"Time for walk," I said, picking up his leash.

Nothing.

"Walk."

Pick didn't move. I didn't even get a wag and he loved walks. To be fair it was flipping freezing out and he was a poodle with poodle-type sensibilities.

"Come on," I said. "I gotta put on your booties."

Taking Pick out for a walk was a whole thing. Booties and a red-checked jacket. He was adorable, but it was a pain.

The poodle opened one dark eye and then firmly closed it before putting a paw over his face.

"Fine, but don't come crying to me if you have to pee five minutes after I get back," I said.

Nothing.

I tossed his leash on the settee and went to the receiving room to try and suit up in my puffer coat, hat, and scarf. It was freezing, but I wasn't convinced the five-minute walk over to Aaron's bakery was worth the effort to get my jacket over my cast, so I forgot the coat and stuck with the hat and two scarves.

I went out the back of the Bled Mansion, leaving the incredible smells of fifteen different kinds of pastries behind and dashed through the rose garden to the stables that would soon be my home. Chuck and I had decided to move into the apartment above the stables, but, true to form, The Girls had insisted on renovating it for us. The sound of sawing and hammering echoed down the street as I passed though the stables and went into the alley, slipping on the ice but catching myself in the nick of time.

My phone buzzed and it was Chuck. Finally.

"I'm in," he said.

"Nobody's there?" I asked.

"Who would be here?"

"No idea, but I never count my dad out."

I heard a door close and a zipper unzip. "Yeah, you never know with Tommy. I was half-expecting him to be at the table with your Grandad."

"You and me both," I said.

"I'm going to make a coffee. I'm freaking freezing."

I rolled my eyes. "Will you just search the cabinet?"

"Maybe I should make sure nobody's here."

"Nobody's there."

"You just asked me if somebody was here," said Chuck.

"I was paranoid."

"Well, now I'm paranoid." He paused. "Wait."

My stomach twisted. "What?"

"I heard something."

"It's probably the Siamese." I turned the corner toward Sto-Vo-Kor. "You can take them."

"I...don't think it's the Siamese unless they gained a hundred pounds," said Chuck.

"Get out."

"Let me see who—"

A voice behind me called out, "Mercy!"

I turned and a man rushed at me. I put my hands out to fend him off, but I slipped when I stepped back, falling on my back. I knocked my head on the concrete and the wind rushed out of my lungs with an oomph. He was on me, shoving a wet rag over my face. I was screaming and clawing at him, but he was bigger than me and had the advantage. My vision narrowed and he started dragging me by my hoodie, keeping the rag over my face. Then he had me in a chokehold and I was lifted, thrown into something. The rag came off my face for a second. A trunk. He shoved me down and pressed the rag back over my face. I must've blacked out for a second because the next thing I knew, he'd flipped me over and was grabbing at my arms.

"Son of a bitch," he said as he twisted my casted arm behind my back and tried to force my hands together, muttering obscenities and attempting to tie me up. I screamed with everything I had, he let go, and I looked over my shoulder to see with blurred vision a man in a parka with the hood up looming over me.

"Fuck it!" He slammed the trunk.

I don't know what happened or how long it was happening. I remember sort of rerealizing where I was, so I must've passed out. The car was moving. Fast. Highway speed.

This was one of those times when being Tommy Watts' daughter comes in handy. Dad was always worried about me getting kidnapped when I was little. He dealt with some pretty bad guys during his police career and some of them got out of prison. Dad lived in fear that I'd be taken in retribution, so he trained both Mom and me in self-defense. It didn't work out in the alley, but his training included how to get out of a car. I still had my glass-breaking tool in my purse at the mansion, not that it would've helped me in a trunk. Luckily, trunks were big in Dad's training and I did not appreciate it at all. What eight-year-old wants to spend Saturday afternoon being tossed in various detectives' trunks to see if she can escape under different variables? I got timed and graded. Dad didn't reward. Living was my reward, he said. But Mom was all about the reward. I got so much ice cream for those trunks, so I learned it. I can learn anything if Ben and Jerry's is on the line.

So without any thought at all, I started searching the trunk and used Dad's annoying breathing techniques to calm myself. The trunk was empty. No tools or rubbish of any kind, but it was dirty and smelled of trash and tools. Not new, not a rental, but maybe it would have a trunk release anyway. They'd been required forever.

I looked for the glow-in-the-dark lever but didn't see one. Then I felt around where the release would normally be, but, when I found the spot, the lever had been clipped off.

Stay calm. Dad taught you what to do.

I felt to the edge of the trunk liner and tried to pull it down so I could maybe get ahold of the wire. I couldn't do it. The cast rendered my hand useless and I couldn't do it with only one. I wasn't strong enough.

Taillight it is.

"Alright then. It's a good thing I've got boots on," I said to myself.

I angled myself with my feet toward the right tail lamp and started kicking. The plastic cracked. Encouraged, I kicked with both feet at the same time. Something snapped and I had daylight. I turned myself and began prying at the plastic covering. I yanked out the light apparatus and peered out to the road whizzing away under the car. It was a highway and a busy one at that. There was a truck directly behind us and another vehicle in the left lane that we were passing. I stuck my hand out of the taillight and instantly horns started honking. I waved frantically and wished I knew sign language or something. All I could've done was given a thumbs-up or an okay sign and that was hardly helpful.

The car started swerving, jerking in and out of lanes. Then slowing and speeding up wildly. The other drivers must've been trying to stop him. I loved them for it but prayed they didn't cause a crash. I didn't know what the survival rate was for crashing in a trunk and I didn't want to find out.

It seemed like forever before I heard sirens and the guy behind the wheel was panicking. I was rolling around in that trunk like a number ball on bingo night. Then there was an abrupt swerve, an acceleration, and we were going up. An exit ramp. More sirens from every direction and then he touched the brakes before flooring it. There was a bump followed by a weird thwacking and slappy sound. Strip spikes. They'd punctured his tires, but that changed nothing. He kept speeding to who knows where, toward who knows what, as the tires peeled away.

Who is this idiot?

A sudden thump and then the sound of metal grinding filled the trunk. I covered my ears as best I could. We were on the rims and I could smell the burning metal.

Oh, come on, dude. It's over.

Apparently, the guy in the driver's seat didn't agree because we yanked to the right and were going over rough ground. I was bumping up and down so fast. Now I know how popcorn feels.

What was the point? Driving through a field was not an effective escape route. I knew it was a field because I'd accidentally driven into a cornfield in high school when we were out at a party and everyone was yelling directions in a panic because we were going to miss curfew. I took a turn too fast and drove into the bumpy furrows. It stopped me, but it didn't stop this guy. We were going slower and slower, but we were still going. It seemed like miles and miles of bumps.

And then he stopped. I was actually surprised when he did. It'd gotten to the point where I'd started to think it would last forever. I know, I know, that's crazy. Hey, I was locked in a trunk. Don't judge me.

The sirens surrounded us and people were yelling. Then gunfire. Three shots and then nothing. I could hear people yelling but couldn't make out what they were saying. I hoped to God a cop wasn't hit, but I didn't really think that was a possibility. It was probably fifteen armed-to-the-teeth cops against one moron. I liked our odds.

I laid there patiently for a while until it seemed the reason for the chase had been forgotten. Namely, me.

Is somebody going to open this damn trunk?

I started yelling and yelling, working myself into a fury. I could've been bleeding out. Choking to death on my own vomit.

Over my caterwauling, I heard a click and the trunk popped, flooding my prison with blinding light. I blinked up at a large figure looming over me. Was it possible the cops had not won the day and this was the moron getting ready to axe me to death? I didn't think my heart rate could go higher, but it did. It really did.

"Calm down," he said. "We've got you."

I shielded my eyes. "Calm down? Are you serious? I'm kidnapped here."

"You're alive, aren't you?"

"So I have to be calm unless I'm dead? Is that what we're saying?"

He chuckled and reached for me. "You're alright. Come on."

I slapped his hands away. "Get off me, ya dickhead." I climbed out of the trunk on my own and I'd like to say I was elegant about it. But no, I wasn't. I flipped over the end of the car and lay splayed out on dried corn stalks. There was some small satisfaction of being right on that count. Very small. There were at least five cameras on me. I'd gotten so I could feel the lenses. Bastards.

"Do you want help?" the cop asked.

"EMTs on their way," said a woman and then she was at my side, kneeling on the crunchy stalks and quickly assessing my condition.

She clicked her walkie and said, "Mid-twenties white female. Head injury. Possible broken nose."

I felt my face and it was bloody. Dammit. She said some other stuff, but I was thinking about my poor nose. How many times can you break a nose before it gives up and decides to look like meatloaf? I know the head injury should've been my first concern. But I *had* a head injury, thinking straight wasn't my thing just then and I'm vain. There I said it.

"Check it out." The other cop held up a rag and sniffed it, making a face. "Jesus, what the hell is this?"

"Bag it, Derek," she said.

"Yes, ma'am."

Then there were other cops talking about the suspect who was dead. A guy squatted by my head. "Mercy Watts. First major crime in three years and it's you."

He said it like it was my fault and I wanted to say, "Drop dead," but I was getting more and more dizzy. It came out like a croak.

"Ah, shit," he yelled. "Where's that ambulance? We can't have Tommy Watts' daughter dying on us."

Die?

I croaked again.

"She's not going to die," said the female cop. "She's tough. She's been here before."

To be fair, it was my first straight-up kidnapping. Even thinking that isn't a good sign. When you say "first" it means you expect it to happen again and I pretty much did.

"Alright. Alright. Let's not get worked up," he said. "You survived to wreck shit another day."

I hate you.

"Jesus, Dustin," she said. "She's the victim."

He stood up and walked away. She put her hand on my forehead and said, "The ambulance is arriving. You're fine. You're going to be fine."

I managed to croak out, "I hate him."

"Yeah, I know. He's not usually like that. I'm Sam, by the way. Samantha Samuelson."

I held up my good hand. "Mercy Watts. I think I'm going to throw up."

Sam turned my head for me and I threw up just as the EMTs

turned up in an amazing display of professional and unprofessional behavior. They assessed me, got me on a gurney and IVed, all the while discussing how I'd managed to get myself in this fix. I was kinda out of it, but I'm pretty sure one looked inside my hoodie and whistled.

They rolled me over to the back of the ambulance and I got a glimpse of a clump of cops standing around a body lying in the field, toes up. It was the oddest sensation. He was trying to kill me, I assumed, and he ended up dead. How did this happen? Dustin thought it was my fault. Was it? My head injury must've been bad because it seemed reasonable. I made that dude kidnap me.

"Alright," said one of the EMTs. "You're going up and in. It's okay."

They slid me in, strapped the gurney down, and away we went with siren wailing, bumping slowly over some soon-to-be irate farmer's field. Three weeks. It'd been three weeks since something crazy happened to me. Not a record, but still.

The EMTs chattered back and forth and, in a stunning move, got out their cellphones.

"Dude, Justin isn't going to believe this. She is Marilyn Monroe."

"It's totally whack."

"We are so gonna trend."

"Number one, baby."

They wouldn't.

They would. Two EMTs in the back of an ambulance took selfies with me, a head injury with nausea and blurred vision, and started posting to Instagram.

This cannot get any worse.

One EMT held up his phone to the other one and said, "Hey, that weird stuff on her face really shows up. I didn't even use a filter."

Crap on a cracker.

Read the rest in
Bottle Blonde (Mercy Watts Mysteries Book Eleven

A.W. HARTOIN'S NEWSLETTER

To be the first to hear all about the A.W. Hartoin news and new releases click the link or scan the QR code to join the mailing list. Only sales, news, and new releases. No spam. Spam is evil.

Newsletter sign-up

ABOUT THE AUTHOR

USA Today bestselling author A.W. Hartoin grew up in rural Missouri, but her grandmother lived in the Central West End area of St. Louis. The CWE fascinated her with it's enormous houses, every one unique. She was sure there was a story behind each ornate door. Going to Grandma's house was a treat and an adventure. As the only grandchild around for many years, A.W. spent her visits exploring the many rooms with their many secrets. That's how Mercy Watts and the fairies of Whipplethorn came to be.

As an adult, A.W. Hartoin decided she needed a whole lot more life experience if she was going to write good characters so she joined the Air Force. It was the best education she could've hoped for. She met her husband and traveled the world, living in Alaska, Italy, and Germany before settling in Colorado for nearly eleven years. Now A.W. has returned to Germany and lives in picturesque Waldenbuch with her family and two spoiled cats, who absolutely believe they should be allowed to escape and roam the village freely.

Made in United States
North Haven, CT
29 May 2023

37136586R00311